NAMES CAN NEVER HURT ME

WADE KELLY

Published by
DREAMSPINNER PRESS

5032 Capital Circle SW, Suite 2, PMB# 279, Tallahassee, FL 32305-7886 USA
http://www.dreamspinnerpress.com/

This is a work of fiction. Names, characters, places, and incidents either are the product of author imagination or are used fictitiously, and any resemblance to actual persons, living or dead, business establishments, events, or locales is entirely coincidental.

Names Can Never Hurt Me
© 2015 Wade Kelly.

Cover Art
© 2015 Christy Caughie.
Cover content is for illustrative purposes only and any person depicted on the cover is a model.

ISBN: 978-1-63476-196-3
Digital ISBN: 978-1-63476-197-0
Library of Congress Control Number: 2015931048
Second Edition February 2015
First Edition published by Dreamspinner Press, August 2014

Printed in the United States of America
♾
This paper meets the requirements of
ANSI/NISO Z39.48-1992 (Permanence of Paper).

Readers love *The Cost of Loving*
by WADE KELLY

"A lot of novels tackle difficult subjects. Some are brave enough to take on one or two. In *The Cost of Loving*, Wade Kelly is ballsy enough to battle beaucoup painful topics and leave you smiling after all the crying is finished. Any writer who can pack homophobia, self-injuring, drug addiction, depression, dysfunctional parenting, "religion" (the quotes are mine, not hers), guilt and grief (I am probably forgetting some) into one emotionally moving yet satisfying-on-a-gut-level novel has huge cajones and the keyboard to back it up with. Vigorously, firmly recommended."

—The Novel Approach

"I was wrapped up and carried along by this very skilled author and I discovered, along with Matt, that sometimes the joy is in the journey."

—Hearts on Fire

"I'm a huge fan of love stories that are rooted in reality. Characters that have depth and overcome enormous odds to be together and be happy. Kelly delivers all these attributes and many more within the pages of this book. Her writing is intense and gripping."

—MM Good Book Reviews

"The story is quite long, detailed, informative, and heart-breaking, but there are also moments of joy, happiness, and forgiveness. I recommend this story to fans of the first story, of course, and to others who want to read a book about serious subjects which will make you think, feel, and react. Thanks, Wade, for continuing Matt and Darian's story."

—Rainbow Book Reviews

By WADE KELLY

My Roommate's a Jock? Well, Crap!
Names Can Never Hurt Me

UNCONDITIONAL LOVE SERIES
When Love is Not Enough
The Cost of Loving

Published by DREAMSPINNER PRESS
http://www.dreamspinnerpress.com

I would like to dedicate this book to my father. R.I.P. 12/1/11. Visiting Knoebels Amusement Park recently reminded me of how much I miss you. As Carly Simon says, "Nobody does it better, it makes me feel sad for the rest."

Also, a special thank you to Tina for beta reading this novel and telling me she would "never want my name on something she knew would be poorly received." Thank you for helping me retain my reputation.

And to my best friend Tanya for always listening to me ramble on about my stories and characters; you are a patient woman!

Plus, to Jeff Adams who said, "This is an absolutely wonderful book. It's soooo romantic and packs a good message too." Thank you for your kind words my dear friend. Both you and Will have a special place in my heart.

—Wade Kelly, August 2014

Prologue: *Last Year*

IT WAS last year's party at Mary-Louise's house that got me thinking all the wrong thoughts. She threw a kegger on Saint Patrick's Day and I guess I should have known better than to tempt fate by overindulging and letting my eyes wander. I would have been better off numbing my brain and sticking to what everyone else did and what everyone else thought, but I'm *me* so of course I couldn't conform. Except fantasizing about Corey Parrish, more precisely his luscious mouth, was *not* what everyone else did! At least not the people I knew. The guys I hung around with normally ignored him, while the girls flocked to his side for advice on outfits or hair. Whatever. I didn't care about any of that. But I also shouldn't have cared—or wondered—so much about the flavor of his lipgloss. Damn!

So, like I said, it was last year and I was multitasking: drinking green beer and thinking at the same time. At the beginning of the night nothing mattered except the booze and contemplating which girl might take me home. I scanned the packed living room of Mary-Louise's house and couldn't help but chuckle. It's always the same. No matter how many "frat" parties I went to, the girls stood around giggling while the guys got slammed.

"Says the guy who's out of Budweiser." I tipped back my plastic cup and swallowed the last drop of beer as I mumbled about the irony before meandering through the house to the keg in the crowded kitchen.

Mary-Louise was a pastor's kid determined to sow some wild oats. She was nice enough to throw parties practically every weekend, but not nice enough to spread her legs for me—yet. That was fine, I didn't care. Someone else would. At least she hadn't slapped me for trying to get her into bed with me four times. I'd met her at the local community college when we were freshmen. In the following four years, while I took classes on and off at the same local school, Mary-Louise did two years there, transferred to a four-year college, and graduated with a bachelor's in business. By now—were I a dedicated, forward-thinking student like my friend—I'd have a degree too. Instead, I had loads of casual acquaintances who liked to throw parties, and lots of time to get drunk instead of having figured out my future.

I just didn't know what I wanted to do.

Life after high school pretty much sucked. I wasn't expecting that. I'd been popular back then, and I guessed I still was, but life's more difficult now. I had bills to pay, and I didn't know what career path to choose. Luckily, I still lived with my folks, and they didn't ask for rent. They'd made a deal with me, that as long as I paid my car insurance and maintained a three point four GPA (when I was actually taking classes that was,) I was free to stay at home. But how many years would they tolerate a slacker son? I didn't know. And really, the list of "I didn't know" was longer than the list of shit I was sure of. It was depressing if I thought about it.

So I didn't think—I drank!

I filled my cup with beer and watched the crowd chant as one guy stuck his head under the keg nozzle and another guy opened it full blast. "Idiots," I mused. Not that I was all that different; I realized I was an idiot.

"Hey, Nick."

I turned toward that oh-so-familiar voice behind me. "Hey, Dawn," I said with a slight lift of my chin. "What's up?"

Dawn, my ex-girlfriend, grinned and looked at her perky little friend before answering. Her long brown curls bounced around her face and reminded me of the time I'd watched her go down on me and all I could see was that lovely hair spread like a blanket over my pelvis. *That* had been sexy as hell. "Well," Dawn said, "Chrissy and I were wondering if you'd take on a little dare?"

I leaned on the doorframe next to me. I was curious enough to listen because they were a precocious pair. I took a swig of my newly filled cup. "Oh yeah? What kind of dare?" Not that it mattered. If I did them a favor, maybe they'd be willing to do me a little favor later— possibly together, naked, and with whipped cream. Besides, I liked a challenge every now and again; it kept life interesting.

They giggled and—yes—I rolled my eyes. Girls.

I surmised it was Chrissy's turn to talk for the two of them because she smiled and got a devilish look in her eyes. "You see Nick, Dawn and I dared Corey Parrish to kiss a straight guy. He said he would if we could find someone up to the task who was sober enough to remember it happened, yet cute enough not to be desperate." Chrissy blushed deeply and ducked her face against Dawn's shoulder. She acted embarrassed, but I didn't buy it for a second. She was a hussy if ever I'd known one. She held Dawn's hand and nibbled her bare shoulder playfully, but I knew for a fact they both liked dick.

Corey? My stomach quivered. I'd just been thinking about Corey.

Corey Parrish was hot as fucking fuck, and the thought of his mouth did things to me I was trying to not dwell on. Something in the way he talked made me picture kissing him and biting his lower lip until it bled. *Shit.* To make matters worse, Corey was openly gay. Did I really need to get mixed up in Dawn's and Chrissy's little dare with a gay guy?

I took a swig of my beer and casually tucked my fingers into the front pocket of my jeans. If I remained calm, they'd never know I was about to puke. (From nervousness, not excessive drinking.) "What's in this for Corey? Don't you think it's a cruel joke allowing him to kiss *me* and get nothing in return?"

"He wants my brother's cell number. I said I'd give it to him if he did something for me," Dawn replied.

Blackmail? Yeah, that was Dawn's MO. Still, I played dumb. "How is me kissing Corey something for you?" I swallowed more of my beer.

Dawn smiled wickedly. "I think it's hot."

"Hot?" I lifted one eyebrow.

Chrissy agreed, "Oh yeah! Two guys kissing is so hot."

Two guys kissing is hot? Fuck yeah! I totally agreed. Only last week I'd been browsing online, clicking different shared-links on Facebook, when before I knew it I was pulling one off over a picture of two guys kissing, extending their tongues into each other's mouths. It was a black and white photograph; one guy had facial hair and the other didn't. As I'd stared at it, I began fantasizing about Corey right there in my bedroom. That was a first for me, thinking about another guy like that. I'd wanted to kiss Corey from the first time I saw him at Mary-Louise's New Year's Eve party, but jerking off over it hadn't happened until last week. It had shocked the shit out of me mostly because, as I said before, Corey's gay. I'm not. I dated girls all the time. I had sex with girls all the time. Just because I was attracted to Corey didn't make me gay. *Bisexual* maybe, but certainly not gay.

Suddenly, my mouth was answering, "So, all I gotta do is kiss him?" *Shit, I'd just agreed to it!* That'd teach me to daydream in the middle of a conversation.

Dawn's eyes went wide. "You'll do it?" she exclaimed with delight.

Suddenly, I had to talk myself down off a ledge. *Calm down, Nick, it's only a kiss.* "Yeah, it's just a kiss, right? No big." I tried passing off nervous exhilaration as nonchalance.

"Seriously? You are so cool, Nick!" Chrissy squealed. "I knew you wouldn't care. You're so open-minded."

And apparently they bought it. If only I remained this calm as I kissed him.

I grinned. "Yeah, anything to make the two of you happy and horny." I licked my lips and lifted my eyebrows twice. They didn't need to know I was into it because Corey was their pawn, not me.

I followed them into the other room to where Corey lounged on the couch chitchatting with some girl I didn't know. Corey talked to every girl, and although I tended to be overly verbose, I wasn't surprised there were a few ladies I hadn't seen before. Mary-Louise invited everyone to her parties, and I was in no way jealous of Corey's congeniality or charm. I had plenty of my own.

He was wearing a tight green T-shirt with a V-neck, which allowed his chest hair to curl over the edge of the fabric. The word "alluring" came to mind like one of those dialogue tags in a cartoon, and I questioned my agreement to do this. I'd have to be extra careful kissing him, because if I fingered the hairs on his chest like I was itching to do, these girls might start rumors. I didn't need "gay" rumors squelching my frequent, no-strings-attached sex life. No way, José!

"So Corey, we found someone," Chrissy announced proudly, bouncing on the balls of her feet. Chrissy tended to have more energy than a seven-year-old after a two-pound bag of Skittles. She always bounced.

Corey looked up and smiled. *Fuck me.* My stomach fluttered. "Wow," he replied. "I'll say you did!" He licked his top teeth with the tip of his tongue and batted his eyes, showing off his green-glitter eye makeup, which did not ease my apprehension over kissing him. He was fucking adorable, and I knew it.

Corey asked flirtatiously, "I recognize you. Nick, right? I saw you at the New Year's Eve party making out with Laney. Why do you want to kiss me?"

Knowing he'd noticed me back on New Year's did not help my trepidation. Plus—*want? He thinks I* want *to kiss him?* "I thought it was a game," I interjected, making sure I kept my voice low and casual. "They want to play with you, and you want Andrew's number."

Corey's pleased expression disappeared, but I wasn't going to change my orientation to coax it back. "True," he relented. "Okay, it's a game, but you're conceding to it. Why? What do you get?"

Now was the test. Could I portray arrogance and not overdo it to the point of absurdity? I hoped so; I surely had experience. I slid my palm over the T-shirt clinging to my muscular chest (oh yeah, I was cut,) and replied, "I get to add another name to the list of those who want me."

"God knows *I* want you," Chrissy said from the side. *Perfect timing.*

I tilted my head in her direction and grinned. "Thanks babe." I winked for emphasis. "You'll get your turn."

"Oh, someone is sure of himself." Corey shooed the girl next to him away and patted the cushion. "Come here, honey. Let me see what you got."

"Here, hold this." I handed my beer to Dawn and sat next to Corey. The prospect of kissing this guy shot sparks of tingling desire through me, but I had to play it cool. No way was I getting hard and giving the girls the wrong impression. This was a game. I wasn't gay.

I questioned Chrissy with a look. "Am I kissing him or is he kissing me?"

Before she could answer, Corey took hold of my chin and turned my head to face him. He planted his lips firmly on mine and lingered before pulling back with a sigh. "Nice. You willing to take it further?"

Corey asked, teasing my lips with a swift flick of his tongue. His pale blue eyes were firebrands.

Helplessly, I nodded and leaned in. All my nervous energy from before transformed into a surge of adrenaline. I had to have more of that mouth.

The girls squealed in delight, but I ignored them as Corey's hot mouth connected with mine again. Corey curled his fingers into my neck and pulled me closer. He parted his lips, and I slipped my tongue inside his mouth, taking control of the kiss and causing Corey to moan. This was so fucking good. As our tongues clashed, I felt a deep need to fuck like I'd never felt before.

This was way different than kissing girls, I thought. It was seriously intense, for one thing, and for another, when I kissed girls, I often felt it in my toes, but I had never felt like my groin was catching fire. Not that that meant I would react the same with *any* guy I kissed, but Corey surely did a number on my dick.

I turned him on the sofa and leaned in, pushing him against the back of the couch. He whimpered and moved his hand down my neck and onto my chest. His warm palm rested over my pectoral muscle, and it made me want to flex for him, but I didn't. As soon as I thought about it, he pinched my nipple and those tingles I felt all over my skin intensified. My body was humming in ways I hadn't expected, and I conjured up thoughts of *doing things* I didn't expect. Instinctively, I moved my leg over Corey's knee and angled my hips a smidgeon. *Oh God, I need friction.* I gripped his shoulder with one hand as I held the side of his neck with the other, but man-oh-man did I want to touch myself or rub against his leg a little. Anything.

Corey felt unbelievably good against me.

As if it was the most natural thing in the world, I slid my fingers into the short hair behind Corey's ear and that was when someone commented, "Jeez, you were right. Nick'll fuck anything." The sound of an unfamiliar female voice behind me uttering such a toxic comment squelched my unexpected hunger, but I controlled my resentment. It was far better to ignore the comment and pretend it hadn't happened than cause a scene and draw unwanted attention to the fact that I was hard as hell and seconds from dry-humping Corey's leg. If I was cool about it, maybe Corey and I could slip off somewhere.

I slowed my pace, kissing him gently, and pulled back as if nothing were amiss. The heady look in Corey's eyes stroked my ego, so I winked at him before facing the gathering throng of horny women.

Three eager girls sat side-by-side on the coffee table in front of the couch: Dawn, Chrissy, and a red-haired girl I didn't know. A few more stood behind them. It seemed a lot of girls liked watching two guys kiss. *Hmm.* "Well? Hot enough for you?" I asked, knowing exactly what they'd say.

"Oh yeah," Dawn moaned, placing her hand on Chrissy's thigh, caressing her skin and running her fingers up the inside of Chrissy's leg.

Chrissy cooed quietly and spread her legs. "Yes... hot." She swallowed hard and closed her eyes. Her reaction kind of made me think of reaching up her dress, but Dawn beat me to it. Dawn's hand disappeared under the fabric as she kissed her friend—her *girl*friend— and felt her up.

Hypocrite, I sneered, chastising whichever girl thought it fine to judge me by saying I'd "fuck anything" while Dawn sat there, insult free. She was doing the exact same thing! I knew personally just how she liked to fuck, and how often, because she'd been my first way back in high school.

My attention was drawn back to Corey when he sighed. He was still recovering from my kiss. I shook my head and scoffed, "Women! I'm outta here."

I had to leave. Watching the two of them kiss after I'd just made out with Corey made my need to come stronger than ever. I dashed upstairs to find the bathroom. No sooner had I locked the door and unzipped my jeans when I heard a quiet knock. "Shit!" I hissed. "It's occupied," I called.

"Nick?" Corey whispered.

I did up my zipper and opened the door a few inches. "Corey, now's not the time to—"

Corey pushed his way inside the bathroom. He closed the door behind him and said, "I'm sorry, but I wanted to catch you before you finished."

"Corey, I—"

"Save it," Corey insisted, holding up a hand. "There's a garage out back. Meet me behind it in fifteen minutes, and I'll take care of your little... problem." He made his insinuation clear by boldly palming my erection. "Unless you think allowing me to suck you off is a little *too* open-minded."

I couldn't answer. In fact, if he touched me a second longer, I was going to come in my pants. Having someone else rub my dick felt so amazing. Sure, girls did it, but rarely without my insistence. Corey, however, seemed to know what I needed without prompting. All I could do was close my eyes and groan.

Corey took his hand away and snickered. "Meet you out back." And he was gone.

I regrouped and contemplated his proposal. He said he'd suck me off. *Would Corey want me to reciprocate?* I'd never sucked a dick before. Corey was the first boy I'd ever kissed. Or ever wanted to kiss. Did it matter? Would people think I was gay? Did *that* matter? It was just sex, right? I wasn't dating Corey. I wasn't getting emotional about it. It was just sex. Two guys getting off. No big deal.

I once heard a saying that overanalyzation leads to paralyzation. I don't even know if those are real words. Needless to say, I left the bathroom in a hurry.

Finding Corey behind the garage wasn't a problem. I slipped out of the house without too much hassle. I got stopped a couple times, but by now, most people at the party were drunk, and they weren't paying attention to where others were going and whom they were with. I walked out the front door and headed around the side of the house after pretending to puke on the lawn, the classic excuse to leave a party.

Corey grabbed me as soon as I drew near and pushed me up against the side of the building. His kiss was urgent and his hands greedy. He was a little rough, and I liked it. It was nice not having to take charge for once. It felt liberating. Corey kissed me for a minute or two before sinking to his knees. A warm rush surged through my extremities as I looked down at him; his eyes glinted in the faint light. Corey unzipped my jeans and freed my rigid cock. *Oh fuck, that's hot!*

Corey's tongue made me shiver. Corey's hands made me weak. But it was the suction of Corey's throat that made me tremble like never before. I rested my hand on Corey's head and gently encouraged his bobbing motion. I even felt daring enough to thrust my hips forward and force myself down Corey's throat. And Corey didn't mind! Girls hated to be forced to take more of me in. Not that I'm porn-star material, but I'm not small by any means. Being with a guy was a refreshing change of pace. Corey sucked wildly and it didn't take me long to feel close.

"Corey," I whispered, leaning my head back on the brick wall. His wet friction was unlike anything I'd ever felt. "Corey," I whispered again more urgently. "I'm gonna... come." I tugged on Corey's hair, but he didn't let up. Seconds later, I emptied into his throat and Corey didn't pull back. He kept licking and swallowing until I was finished, and only then did he get off his knees and kiss me.

The taste was strong, salty... *different*.

Corey tasted like... *me*, and to my surprise I liked it.

Tentatively, I reached between us and touched Corey. I felt the same hardness in his pants I'd recently had in mine. I knew what Corey wanted, what he needed, but suddenly there were voices close by, and I shoved Corey away and did up my zipper before anyone had a chance to see what was going on.

"Let's go back inside," Corey suggested.

I thought about it. "Nah, I think I'm going home. My parents told me not to be out too late."

"Okay. Can I give you my number? Maybe we can hook up sometime?"

"Yeah, sure."

We exchanged phone numbers, and I said good-bye without another glance.

AT HOME, before I found sleep, I thought about his kiss and our actions by the garage. Corey was really sexy, and the things we'd done tonight had felt so fucking good, but what would people think? Was it worth a good lay to be labeled "gay"? I didn't really care about Corey, even if he was adorable. It was about sex. And if it was just sex, then going out with *girls* and hooking up with *girls* was much less complicated.

I grabbed my phone and texted Chrissy: *Hey. Go to the movies with me next Friday?*

A few minutes later she texted back: *Of course!!!*

I grinned in the quiet of my room and placed my phone on the nightstand. Chrissy was hot and easy. I knew I'd end up fucking her Friday night.

Nah, I'm not gay.

Chapter 1: *Now*

I BROKE up with Chrissy through a text. I knew it was insensitive, but it was the third time in fourteen months we'd split, and I wasn't up for the obligatory "date" just to give her the boot. That would have been pointless. Chrissy knew we weren't made for one another; we'd only ever had sex. Not that I was complaining about that, but pretending to be a couple was plain stupid. Besides, during those few times we had been apart, I'd been out with four other girls as well as hooking up with Corey, and I'd seen Chrissy out with several other guys. I knew she'd be fine with it.

Her text response: *K.*

It was shorter than I expected. Way shorter. Some part of me had hoped for something along the lines of "Oh, really? Are you sure? I'm gonna miss your huge dick. Please don't break up with me, you big stud." But that was just wishful thinking on my part. It was my fantasy, not reality. In reality, Chrissy gave me a one-letter reply: *K.*

I pocketed my phone and headed down the steps. My hard-working mother, meticulous and self-sacrificing, was in the kitchen washing dishes much like she'd done every morning of my existence. I yawned and wandered over to the cabinet and took out a glass.

"It's about time, sleepyhead," my mom said. She was normally talkative and full of energy in the morning. I, on the contrary, was not.

I looked her way and smiled groggily. "Good morning." Two words were all I could muster.

She dried her hands and walked up behind me. I felt her head on my back and her arms encircle my middle. This was the way she hugged me every morning if I was pouring juice or standing by the toaster. On rare occasions, I would turn around and hug her properly like a normal son, but mostly she hugged me from behind. She wasn't bothered by the method as long as "the hug" was had first thing. I kind of liked the affection, even if I wasn't a kid anymore. She released me and commented, "Morning was about three hours ago, Nicky, now it's afternoon."

"What?" A jolt of panic prompted me to stop pouring my juice and whirl around to find the clock. A quarter of ten. My terror defused, I grumbled, "No it's not. I still have fifteen minutes to get to work. *That* signifies it's still morning."

She patted my back and resumed washing the dishes. Of course, she couldn't allow the silence to linger long. Mom had a hard time doing that. "For a person who got up at four thirty," she explained, "to get your father off to work, who has done three loads of laundry and ironed six shirts and four pair of pants, it's the afternoon. One of these days you'll realize how cushy your life is, mister. It must be nice having an extra-long weekend ahead of you. Will the family see your face, or will you sleep through it all?"

I swallowed a mouthful of juice and set the glass down. "Mom, I know I live like a king. That's why I'll never leave." I joked. Truly, I did know how good I had it. It was the one thing I had going on that I didn't want to change. "And yes you'll see me this weekend. You asked me to take off Monday, so I put in for it weeks ago. And it's not my fault my normal Saturday off this month falls on the same weekend." I chuckled and continued, "The boss was actually a little peeved about that. It was funny."

My mother didn't see the humor. "But you were off yesterday. Working three days a week must be nice." She dried a dish and put it away, la-dee-da. She often ribbed me about the comfort I enjoyed, except it was never done maliciously. I secretly thought she was jealous.

I instinctively defended myself. "Hey, Sunday we're closed because the owner is a Christian. Don't mock his religion, Mom. The schedule has been like this since I started. Why are you busting my chops about it now?" I wasn't sure where the conversation was leading, and I wasn't overly enthused about asking, but when she remained silent, I asked, "Mom, what are you getting at?"

She shrugged apathetically, which bothered me because she rarely hesitated to share her opinion. If she was holding back now, it was probably because she knew I wouldn't like what she had to say.

"Mom?" I pressed.

She finally explained, "You sleep all day. You go to work, barely. I mean, I know you work almost forty hours a week now, and I'm glad, but we hardly ever see you." Then she sighed. Sighing was never a good sign. "When you come home, you go out with that girl." Her emphasis on the word "girl" made the conversation gel.

"Chrissy and I broke up," I told her. It was a knee-jerk reaction. The comment popped out on its own. She didn't deserve agonizing over Chrissy and me if we weren't a couple.

Her chin lifted and her shoulders relaxed. "Oh... well, I'm sorry about that, but I'm sort of glad. She wasn't really... right for you."

I knew my mom. What she was saying without saying it was that Chrissy was a tramp. I knew that. When she came over all we did was make out in my room before dinner, then she'd make small talk with my family while groping me under the table. She was even hornier than Dawn, come to think of it. It wasn't that Chrissy didn't know how to respect my parents; she was simply tactless.

"You don't have to worry, Mom. I'm not seeing her anymore." I sincerely hoped not. I had meant it the other times we'd broken up, but somehow that itch just kept showing up and Chrissy knew how to scratch it.

"Oh, good." Mom was pleased. I enjoyed hearing the perkiness return to her voice. "Chrissy took up a lot of your time," she said. "Whatever happened to your friend Corey? He hasn't been around in ages."

Of course she liked Corey. He was super social. Plus, he knew decorum. Around the parents, Corey put on a straight face even if he dressed outrageously. He didn't flirt, he didn't grope me, and he certainly didn't kiss me in front of them. We looked like buds. And Corey really *was* my friend. We talked... sometimes. Most of our long conversations were at the dinner table when my mom invited him to stay. It was those evenings with my family that I learned about his sister's drug problem and about him growing up on a farm in Carroll County. Over dinner, I learned about his family and upbringing and things he wanted to accomplish in life. But when we were out, it was all fucking and grunting and very few words besides "harder," "deeper," and "don't stop."

Oddly, I felt a pang of longing. Hearing his name out of the blue reminded me I missed him. The few times we'd hooked up in the past year had been sensational, but they never lasted. Corey wasn't looking for a boyfriend. He was up front with that stipulation, and I was fine with it since I was straight most of the time. Besides, I had Chrissy to fall back on.

"Um, Corey moved to DC," I explained. I grabbed a pot out of the cabinet and put some water on for ramen noodles—my staple of life.

"Oh," she responded sadly. "I'm sorry, dear. He seemed like such a nice boy. You don't have too many guy friends over. I guess I was glad to see you had at least *one*. And he was such a good-looking boy, too."

Good-looking? What did that have to do with anything? I ignored that particular comment. "I have friends, Mom. Paul at work is pretty cool." I tried to be upbeat about not having male friends, but really, that fact nagged me all the time. I basically didn't talk with anyone outside work.

"Well, maybe you could invite Paul to dinner sometime."

She was all cheery and optimistic, and I hated squelching her bliss. "Mom, guys don't have dinner with their buddies' families. It's just not done. I'm not in high school."

"Well, all I'm saying is *if* you ever decide to bring over a buddy to watch sports with your dad or something, he will be welcome to stay for dinner."

"Watch sports?" I arched an eyebrow. Something fishy was going on in Denmark, and I was starting to figure it out. "You just want me in the living room so you can watch what I'm doing."

"No...," she tried to say but relented. "Okay, yes. I didn't like you and Chrissy up in your room doing who knows what with the door closed. It's just not a good example for your little sister. At least with Corey, I knew you weren't having sex on the bed I'd just made."

I nearly choked. "Mom!" I coughed a few times expelling juice from my lungs.

"Sorry for being so blunt, but that girl wasn't quiet. I heard you a few times when I came home with groceries."

The thought of my mom hearing me have sex was just gross, but I was relieved she had fixated on Chrissy. My shock, and near-death experience from choking, was from her slight inference to me having sex with Corey on my bed. Because that *had* happened. "Mom," I tried explaining again when my hacking-up-a-lung attack subsided, "I'm sorry. I didn't mean for you to hear that. It won't happen again." And I meant it.

"Good," she replied. "I think we need to implement the 'no friends in the room' rule anyway. Jennifer's talking about boys on the phone with her friends. If she brings one over, I can't let her take him to her room."

"Jenn's dating?" That was a shock. It made me feel old for some reason.

"Not yet, but soon. She *is* going to be sixteen. We should be happy she hasn't pressed the issue sooner."

"I guess. Wow, Jenn dating. Weird."

"I know," Mom agreed. "Anyway, have a good day at work, dear. If you'll excuse me, I have to get ready for Zumba." She kissed my cheek and left the room.

"Bye, Mom. See you after my shift," I called after her, still standing at the stove stirring my noodles.

After adding the flavor packet, I drained the juice, poured the noodles in a bowl and sat down to eat. I had five minutes until I had to be at work.

My phone buzzed. It was a text from Mary-Louise. *Hey, I'm throwing a party this weekend. It might be one of the last few. My schedule changed, and I'll have less time for fun. I guess I have to be a grown-up now.*

I grinned. She had moved to Arlington, Virginia after she graduated. Not that Arlington was all that far away—less than two hours south wasn't bad—but I hadn't seen her in months. Some of the regular crowd had driven down a few times, but it hadn't interested me. It was a lot of money in gas just to drink and get laid. I could do that right here. But then again, she was my friend.

I texted: *Nah, I'll pass. I work a lot too.*

It wasn't a lie. Since I had gotten the job at Papa's Pizzeria, I worked full-time, and that included most weekends. It was the first full-time job I'd held for longer than two months. My mom had even told me she was proud of me when I hit the ninety-day mark and had gotten a raise. So far, it had been seven months of employment for the Nickster! Oh, yeah! I was so stoked.

Mary-Louise texted back: *We will miss you! :^(How are things with Chrissy? Still seeing her?*

No. Broke up this morning.

Sorry. :^(She wasn't right for you anyway.

I know. I think I knew that the other couple times we broke up too, but being with her was easier than being alone. IDK. I paused a second. Some thoughts had swirled around my foggy brain on occasion, and this seemed like as good a time as any to ask. *Can I ask you a question?* I pressed send. I had to know. We'd been friends for years, and she was the only one of our usual crowd I hadn't slept with. I needed to know why. Because now that Chrissy was history, maybe M-L would be interested in a little *tête-à-tête.*

Shoot, she shot back.

I've known you for years. Why is it we never hooked up?

Mary-Louise took a long time responding, unusually long. So much time that I had finished my noodles, thrown on a work shirt, and was in my car before I received a reply. She wrote: *I really thought you knew, especially since you were close friends with Corey. I'm a lesbian, Nick. I was dating Shawna my senior year. I'm sorry if that freaks you out. I hope not. You've always been so nonjudgmental.*

"Shawna?" I questioned out loud as I pulled into the parking lot at work. I was baffled. I had fooled around with Shawna a couple of times and never known she was a lesbian. *Fuck me!*

Before getting out of the car, I texted a response: *No, I didn't know. And yes, it's fine. It doesn't bother me if you're gay. At least it explains why you never went out with me when everyone else was taking a turn. I hope you're happy.*

I am, thanks. What about you and Corey? Anything ever happen with him?

Corey. Why does it keep coming back to him? I texted: *He moved to DC, and I haven't seen him since New Year's. But I think he's fine.*

Too bad. You two made a cute couple.

"We weren't a couple," I complained out loud as if she could hear me. Now she was just agitating me. *I'm not gay, M-L!* I tended to shorten her name in text to initials. Mary-Louise was just too long. And even when we spoke, I sometimes shortened it, and she didn't mind.

Oh! No, of course not. I'm sorry. I just thought you and Corey had a thing going. I'm sorry if I was wrong. Please don't be mad.

No, I'm not. Just frustrated. I do miss Corey, but it's not 'cause I'm gay for him.

Okay. I believe you. Listen, I gotta go. But I hope you find someone better for you than Chrissy. She's so trashy. You deserve more!

Like Dawn?

Oh God, no!

LOL

Bye, Nick.

Laterz M-L!

I locked my car and walked into work feeling glum. Why had M-L thought I was gay? Did I look gay? I thought not! *Breaking up with Chrissy was a good thing. But missing Corey...* I shook away the feelings bubbling up concerning him. Denial was best.

Chapter 2: *Marcy*

WORK. I like it, but I hate it. When I'm bummed about whatever, I just don't want to be here. Day in and day out, it's the same old thing. Maybe that's the reason this was my first long-term job? I get bored too fast and need to move on.

I'd worked for Sprint for two months and got an employee discount for an android. That was neat. I'd never had a smartphone before, so the job had paid off. But I hadn't cared much about selling phones. I'd also worked for a mortgage company for six weeks, but I wasn't the salesman type. I closed one deal and made nine hundred bucks, but it was too much work. Then I worked for Safeway in the deli department, but I didn't like the manager's constant bitching. After that I worked as a bank teller, and although counting other people's money was super cool, the job had too many requirements. The bank had wanted me to learn about selling IRAs and home loans and shit; it wasn't for me.

So now I was here: Papa's Pizzeria. I made pizza for a living, and sometimes sandwiches, but the point was, it's all food. One of the cashiers, Marcy—she's pretty—was teaching me how to ring people up on the cash register. Broadening my skills, as it were. The boss moved me from one job to another so often I wasn't bored yet, and I liked the manager most of the time. Result: I'd kept the same job long enough for my mom to be proud. *Go me!*

When Mom had said that, it made me smile. I didn't think she'd ever said that before. My dad had a few times when I'd gotten good grades in school, but my mother has always been hard to read. We may historically talk easily, but the talks didn't usually go deep. I'd wondered what she thought of me. Now at least I knew she was proud, so I was holding onto this job as long as I could. I might even get another raise.

After the morning's reminiscence of Corey, the last thing I needed was twenty questions from Marcy. She was nice, but she's also extremely talkative, nosey, and pushy, not to mention out to get me into bed. Oh, the life I lead.

Being God's gift to women as I was, it's never created an issue unless it involved someone I worked with. I learned that on my first job—not the Sprint store, but the one at Dairy Queen. I had gotten caught in the back seat of a girl's car during break with my tongue down her throat and my hand down her pants. She happened to be the owner's daughter, and I was fired on the spot. After that, it became a personal rule: no dating in the workplace. Now, if I left the job or got fired, all women who worked for the previous employer were fair game. I wasn't completely stupid.

Marcy, though, was becoming a problem. So far, I'd been able to fend off her advances because I was "technically" dating Chrissy. I tended to be a one-woman guy, and I could stick to my guns around Marcy. Chrissy was it, so she'd have to deal.

But now….

Oh, God. What will Marcy say about our breakup? Worse, what will she do?

It's not like I wasn't attracted to her. I was. In fact, her long black curls and stunning green eyes were exactly my vision of perfection, but she worked with me. I couldn't date her. Girls rarely stuck around after being with me. Why, I didn't know. I kind of liked Marcy, and I wanted to keep her in my life for more than six months. If we fucked, I'd lose what little we had growing between us. I didn't have friends whom I hadn't slept with except for M-L, so Marcy and I had to remain platonic.

As soon as I put a lid on the chicken noodle soup I'd finished scooping for a customer's order, I saw Marcy bouncing my way and cringed. We were friends. I had to tell her about Chrissy before she found out from someone else, but I feared her reaction. It was funny how her bouncing reminded me of Chrissy.

"Oh my God, oh my God, oh my God!" she exclaimed, hopping over to me like a brunette bunny, bristling with the energy level that only teenagers on NOS Energy Drink could attain. *Yup, just like Chrissy.*

I wasn't in the mood for whatever had revved her up. I had too much on my mind already, and I needed quiet. "What is it, Marcy?" I asked halfheartedly.

She leaned in extra close and whispered, "That guy at the counter is staring at you."

I shifted my gaze to the customer at the counter and then back to Marcy. "No, he's staring at the menu board."

"No, I swear, he walked through the door and did a huge double take in your direction. He thinks you're hot." She lifted her eyebrows and smirked.

"Everybody thinks I'm hot," I corrected. Internally, I was thinking, *But he's a guy!* I turned away in a huff, picking up the tools of my trade—a griddle scraper and a sandwich spatula—and proceeded to take out my surge of aggression on the steak I was cooking. The metal-on-metal sound hurt my ears, but I didn't care. I was angry at her insinuation. When I spoke, I made sure my voice was low enough that the scruffy-looking dude at the counter couldn't hear me. "Marcy, how many times do I have to tell you, I'm not gay." *Why, of all days, does she have to bring it up—again?* I tossed some onions and green peppers on the grill and squirted some oil on them.

Marcy walked away and took that guy's order. I finished one sub and threw some burgers on the grill for the next order as Marcy waltzed back over. She hung the ticket up on the metal strip above my head and crossed her arms. *She isn't leaving if I know that look.*

"Oh come on. Aren't you at least a teensy-weensy bit interested? After all, you *did* say you dated a guy last year."

Why did I ever have to mention Corey to her? I'll never learn! I stopped midchop and glared. I was mad, and she might as well get the full blast through my look if I couldn't shout at her at work.

"No, I didn't," I replied sternly. "I said we hung out a few times. A few! Hanging out with a guy doesn't equate to dating. Okay? And hanging out doesn't make me gay." Although sex might, but I was in denial about that.

I didn't understand what the big deal was, and why Marcy, as well as other girls I'd met, got so hyped-up over guys hanging out together? And God forbid I mention I'd kissed Corey. Marcy might end up squealing like Dawn had last year at M-L's house when I kissed him for the first time. I'd done it. It was done. And I hadn't thought of going out with Corey for almost five months until my mom brought it up this morning.

No matter how much I wanted to get past it, something inside would not let it go. I grumbled more as I cooked. "If hanging out made guys gay, then all guys would be gay. We hang out, it's what we do!"

She wasn't put off by my assertiveness. "Then maybe you're *bi*?" she proposed.

I exhaled loud enough to be heard at the counter. "Oh, for fuck's sake. I told you I'm not. I date girls. Several. Just because Chrissy and I aren't on the best of terms doesn't negate that." I turned my attention back to preparing the cheese steak sub for my ticket while Marcy watched. Why was she watching? Surely she had better things to do than wait for this order and stare at me.

"Nick, come on, it's no big deal. Gay is the new straight," she said cheerily.

I almost missed the roll as I transferred the meat from the grill. "What? No, it's not! And what the hell does that even mean?"

My melodramatic coworker placed her hands on her hips. "You don't have to get all snippy about it. I was just saying…."

I gawked. "Saying what? I don't even understand what you mean." I tucked in the meat and turned, sub in my hands, to the workstation behind me so I could wrap it up to go. As I rolled it in wax paper and aluminum foil, Marcy prattled on.

"I mean being gay is no big deal anymore. You know? Like it used to be a big scandalous act that got kids beat up and stuff, but now it's more like… like the cool thing to be. Like if you're gay, you're in."

I handed her the wrapped sub and an order of fries and tilted my head. "You have no idea what you're talking about."

"Sure I do!" she said as she bagged the order and called for number twenty-three through the microphone. After Marcy handed the order to the customer, she turned back to me. Of course she turned back to me. I was the new guy at work, and she had some deep, sadistic need to figure me out. Today, she was convinced I was gay. *Joy.*

"No, you don't," I insisted, standing my ground. I might not know loads about being gay, but I knew she didn't either. "I'm not sure what planet you live on, but around here, gay isn't 'cool.' It's more like a disease others hope not to catch."

"Oh, come on, Nick. It's not that bad."

"Yes, yes it is! Remember when that chicken place up the road had all its patrons rallying to show their support *against* same-sex marriage? This town is full of right-wing extremists who'd like nothing more than to kick every last gay person out!" I was exaggerating, but I needed to for Marcy's sake.

Her eyes lit up instantly, and she snapped her fingers. "So you admit you're gay."

"No."

"But you're not against it."

I threw my hands out. "No. I'm for letting people live their own lives. Gay or straight. I happen to be straight. Very straight. Like an arrow."

"You know what they say about people who protest too much." Marcy wagged an accusatory finger at me.

"Stop, okay? Just stop. I hate when you do that. It's like beating a dead animal with a stick. It doesn't get you anywhere." I was so done talking about it. I started wiping down my work area as a way of distracting myself. I wished I'd stayed home in my nice warm bed and never woken up to a day with Mom asking about Corey, M-L telling me she was a lesbian, and Marcy playing matchmaker with me and a male customer who *might* have been looking in my direction. I was sooo done. *When does my shift end?*

Marcy shrugged. "I guess not. You're gorgeous whether you're gay or straight, and I still want to go out with you. I can't blame Scruffy Dude for stealing a glimpse of your squeezable ass."

Oh my God. Shoot me now! She'd used the very same adjectives I'd used to describe him, and it irritated me even more. Why did we have to think alike?

I looked up and saw her expression. It was all "teasing and flirty" and reminded me of Dawn a few years back. Marcy wasn't the type I'd consider a "floozy," so every time she tried flirting, I couldn't hide my smirk. I knew the corners of my mouth would not remain firm for long.

It was curving. Up it went. Traitor. I couldn't help it. I was smiling, and my anger waned. She did have a way of making me laugh with all her winking and sexual innuendo and comments about my great body.

I *was* pretty damn sexy.

Marcy was very innocent compared to Chrissy, and way more modest than Dawn. I thought she was appealing for the different qualities she possessed, not for the ways she tried to be similar. But she was young; I supposed there was still time for her to develop the skills necessary to fill Dawn's Prada leather wedge sandals.

I guess I lamented the time she'd become one of those girls so deeply that I allowed her too much space to argue about something she clearly knew nothing about: homosexuality. I should have shut her down days, even weeks, ago. She was often talking out of her ass and had no clue. But could I say something? I wasn't gay either.

I chose to ignore her smack about my "squeezable ass," and about her insinuation that I was gay, and question her nicknaming the customers. That was neutral ground. Why would she do that anyway? "So you've dubbed him 'Scruffy Dude'?" I asked. "What's next, are you going to create a nickname for everyone who comes in?" That guy *was* sort of scruffy. Even twenty feet away from the counter, I noticed he needed a shave, but to point that out (out loud) seemed rude.

"Yes," she answered promptly. "I already have a name for all the regulars who dine in."

"What? No way." I found that mildly amusing. I put my chicken cheese steak on the roll and handed it to Marcy. "Here, this is Scruffy Dude's sub."

Marcy's eyes glinted when she heard me use her term. We got along well for the most part. She took the sub and put it on a tray. "If you don't believe me, then come up here after you're done with that tuna sandwich, and I'll point the customers out one at a time."

"Okay, deal." I made a point not to look at the counter when the scruffy guy picked up his tray. I kept my eyes glued to the sandwich—thank you very much. It was a very nice sandwich. Cut evenly with the lettuce tucked under the bread. I made the best-looking food around.

I saw movement peripherally and knew Scruffy Dude was gone. I relaxed my shoulders and took my beautiful tuna sandwich to the counter. I called the number over the microphone and handed the tray to the customer. When he walked away, I spotted Marcy texting over by the ice cream machine.

"Marcy! What are you doing?" I hissed as I walked over to her. True, no one in the restaurant was paying attention, but this was still a workplace. I was a rule follower for the most part. "You know you could get into trouble. The boss said no texting."

"We should date."

"What?" How and why she kept jumping back to the subject was tiresome. "No. I'm dating Chrissy!" Or… I had been until this morning.

"If you're as straight as you say you are, then we should go out. You know Chrissy wouldn't mind. I just got a text from Deena that said she saw Chrissy kissing Terrell Burke. That means she's cheating on you. You should dump her and date me. I'd be loyal. I promise." Marcy accentuated her point by crossing her fingers over her heart and holding up three fingers. I was pretty sure that was the Boy Scout sign and salute, but I didn't need to drag her off on some tangent about being a scout. I had too many conversations going on with Marcy at one time to add another. My brain could only handle so much.

I replied, "I told you, I don't date people I work with. And besides, I know about Terrell. He didn't know she was seeing me at the same time. Chrissy and I already talked about it." I should have told Marcy the truth. Truth, always truth. My mom had told me that. "Besides, we broke up this morning."

Her eyes lit up instantly. "You did? Why didn't you say something?"

"Because I didn't want to think about it. We've been on and off for a long time, and it's draining. Can't we just drop the subject?"

She frowned. "I'm sorry it's been hard." She reached out and rubbed my arm. She was nice that way. "You know Chrissy wasn't good for you, right?" She sounded sincere, and that made me feel good. Then she had to ruin it by adding "But still, we should go out" with a perky change of expression. Why did she have to be so persistent? "I could make you forget about that cheater." Now she was pouting and sticking out her lip. *God, I can't handle it!*

"I already told you why; we work together."

She bit her lip and squinched up her eyes. Oh no, contemplative Marcy.

"Is it my boobs? It's my boobs, isn't it? They're too small. I know guys like big boobs. Mine are a C-cup. That's too small for you, isn't it? You look like a double-D kind of guy to me."

I think I was more annoyed at her prattle about her boobs than her talk about homosexuality. Or even about Scruffy Dude looking at me. I didn't fucking care about her boobs. I had never understood the fascination over breasts anyway. I liked nipples, but all that extra flesh just flopped around. "They're fine, Marcy." I was getting a headache.

"Oh, really?" she peeped, pleased as punch, stepping closer and leaning her C-cup boobs my way. "Then we should go out."

"No. Stop. Just... stop." I returned to my station, wiping the cutting board and straightening the boxes of wax paper as I went. I had to look busy, or she'd never leave me alone.

As I'd thought she would, she followed me. "You're giving me a headache, Marcy. Can you just... go away?" Honesty is the best policy. Again, a lesson from Mom. Marcy didn't look happy, but she didn't say anything either.

Luckily, a customer fake coughed to get Marcy's attention. The conversation was dropped. And it stayed that way for several more hours. Thank God!

I WENT home with a migraine. Too much thinking. That was why girls drove me crazy. How could they think up so many different things to talk about in the same conversation? It was exhausting. One subject at a time, please.

I didn't eat dinner; I went straight to my room. Mom gave me a questioning look, but left me alone. She seemed to understand my need for silence. Today had been draining. I took out my phone and opened the pictures folder. *Corey.* I sighed. Why was I so attached to him? He wasn't that special. He didn't fawn all over me, and he didn't compliment me about my body constantly like Marcy did. Corey was somewhat detached, actually. We'd mostly fucked, so why was I missing his company so much?

I turned my phone off and went to sleep, confused.

Chapter 3: *Boredom*

I HEARD a knock at my door and my mom asking me if I was still alive. *Alive?* Yes, barely. "Yeah, Mom. What time is it?" I don't know why I asked, but I did every time. I had a cell phone within reach. I could have easily looked at it.

"Twelve thirty," she answered through the door. It wasn't locked, but she respected my privacy enough not to open it. "Listen, your father had to work this morning and wondered if you'd mind splitting some wood. He mentioned the need to split it before autumn so it has all summer to dry out, and I told him you had today off."

I groaned. Having the day off—a Saturday off— did not include splitting wood for my dad, let alone before three in the afternoon. Logically I knew I had to do it before it got dark, but I wanted to remain in bed as long as possible. Surely Dad could wait a little longer. "Oh Mom, why did you do that? And why'd you wake me up so early?" I moaned, pulling the blankets over my head.

She knocked again. "Can I come in?"

"Yes," I grumbled.

The door opened, and she gasped. She'd discovered the mess on my floor. "Nicholas Emerson Jones, I cannot believe what I'm seeing! Are these the clean clothes I folded yesterday?"

I grunted. It was my noncommittal response. If I said yes, I would indeed confirm that I was in deep doo-doo for tossing them on the floor in my attempt to find my SpongeBob shirt. That was my favorite shirt to sleep in because it was the last thing my Nana had given me before she died two years ago. And if I said no, I was flat-out lying and she would yell even louder. She did not tolerate lying.

"Nicholas!" she scolded.

I lifted my head, the blanket still clinging to my back. Leaning on one arm, looking at her apologetically, I said, "I'm sorry, Mom. I'll pick them all up soon."

"You'll do it right now, mister!" she demanded, one hand on her hip and wagging a finger at me. "After all my hard work. Do you think I *like* doing your laundry? Do you think I have nothing better to do than clean up after you?"

I sat up. "Mom, I don't. I'll clean up, I promise."

"Now!"

"Okay!" It was hard not yelling back, though I knew it didn't help the situation.

"Well?" she insisted with a look.

"Mom, I'm not getting out of bed with you standing there. I don't have any pants on." Yes, I was irritated and I wasn't hiding it. What I hid was the stiffy under the sheet.

"Fine." She turned and slammed the door behind her. I heard her voice come from farther down the hall. "If it's not clean, you don't eat!"

She was gone.

Phew! I pushed the covers away and looked down. My wood was sticking through the front of my boxers. "Exactly why I didn't get out of bed."

Before my mom had so violently rapped on my door, I'd been dreaming about Corey. His ass was in my hands, and I was pounding my way through his back. Sex with him had been so much more satisfying than with Dawn, Chrissy, Margret, Leslie, Elaine, Karen, Tina, Beth, Laney, or…. *Damn, I've done a lot of girls!*

But Corey….

I reached down and stroked. I was so freaking hard, and that dream had been so vivid. I missed the way it felt to press my prick inside him and thrust. Sex with Corey was the best I'd ever had. Even Dawn's marathon sex wasn't as good. Her pussy had always been so wet and loose. Corey's ass was tight, and I'd controlled how much lubrication felt necessary.

Speaking of… I walked over to my dresser drawer and took some out. I lubed up my palm and stroked harder. *Oh yeah, that's the ticket.* I closed my eyes. Sliding my thumb over the slit, I pictured Corey's hole squeezing me as I sank in. After only a couple minutes, I was shooting onto the carpet.

I looked down. "And all over my clean shirts," I snarked, bending down and taking inventory of which ones had gotten spunked and which ones were safe to put back in my drawer. If I'd only been careful when I'd looked for SpongeBob, I could have avoided dirtying my shirts before I'd worn them. *Idiot.*

THE UNEVENTFUL weekend flew by as it normally did. I split wood for my dad and slept the rest of the time. My mom only blasted me for the clothes on the floor, so once they were cleaned up, she calmed down.

I didn't do anything else. I guess I could have, but sleep seemed so appealing.

My dad invited a friend over to watch the Orioles play the Blue Jays, and they had fun arguing with the umpires on the television and talking stats and ranks. They had been buddies for a long time, and I was glad to know my dad had at least one good male friend.

Hmm, kind of reminiscent of what Mom said to me.

The similarities got me thinking, and I wondered if the guy was single. And what did he do when he wasn't hanging with my dad? What did single people do? What did I do? Sleep. Oh gosh, I was that single guy who had nothing to do but sleep, eat, and masturbate. True, I shouldn't sink into depression over my singlehood yet; I'd only been on my own for a few days. Maybe if I flew solo for a week or two, I'd have reason to beat my head against the wall, but not yet.

"Maybe my mom's right," I mumbled. I took out my phone. I was lying on my bed, staring up at the ceiling, contemplating all the deep, theoretical questions of life, when it dawned on me I should call Paul. I'd told my mom he was my friend. I could prove that to myself by asking him over. As far as I knew, he was another one of us single fellas. I dialed his number.

"Hello?"

"Hey. It's me. Nick."

"Hey, Nick. How'd you get this number?" Paul asked suspiciously.

"Um, you gave it to me. You said to call you if I needed a ride. Remember? My car was in the shop two months ago and—"

"Oh yeah! Gotcha."

"Does it bother you that I have your cell number? I could delete it." It bothered me to think it bothered him. I mean, why give it out if you minded people calling? Right?

"No, dude, it's fine. You're cool. I don't share it much because I've been harassed in the past. But I don't get the impression you'd be on that list."

"No. Not unless you piss me off, and then I'd probably crank call your ass pretending to be the villain from *I Know What You Did Last Summer*. I'd breathe heavily in the phone and leave dead mice on your car, and—"

"Dude, you're sick and twisted. What's on your mind?"

I was glad he'd joked about it instead of calling me out on using a movie reference almost older than I was. I should have said *The Collection* or something, but I'm not that swift. "I wanted to know if you'd like to come by sometime and watch an O's game with me and my dad. My mom thinks I have no friends." I found direct and to the point was the best way to communicate, but adding humor was more fun.

"Sure. That'd be fine. I like baseball. But I didn't realize *you* liked it."

"It's okay. I played in high school. I'm fast and I could hit. I played varsity." It was a little known fact, but one that should not have been a surprise. I was good at most anything I tried.

"Really?" Paul sounded surprised.

"Yeah. I played baseball and soccer. How do you think I stay in such awesome shape? I work out a lot." Although not much lately. I was depressed over being single.

"I don't know. I guess I never thought about it. But if you're interested, I play softball with a bunch of guys on an adult league. We're always looking for new players."

Huh. Paul just invited me to hang out with him on an extended basis. *Interesting.* Maybe I did have a friend, and my mom was going to fawn all over him. Paul wasn't as nice as Corey, but he was talkative and hugged a lot. My mom would love it! I answered him, "Yeah, cool. Sounds fun. Although I'm not sure when I can fit it into my schedule."

"That's okay. You could be on the standby list in case someone gets sick and we need a player. No pressure. But if you're looking to hang out, we have all sorts of options."

Neato. "I'll keep that in mind."

"Which game do you want to watch?" Paul asked. "They play the Tigers next weekend, and the Devil Rays the weekend after that."

"I don't know. I'll think about it and get back to you." I'd called him, but I guess I wasn't ready for Paul to jump at the opportunity. I wasn't used to that degree of spontaneity. I tried dialing it back. "They play for months, right? I'm sure we'll find a game or two to watch together. Maybe we can even go to a game in Baltimore."

"That'd be fun. Listen, I gotta go. See you tomorrow?"

"Okay, Paul. Laterz." I hung up. I *did* have a friend! Holy crap. I had friends I didn't know were friends. Maybe I had more? I exhaled and turned over and got comfy on the mattress. After expending all that energy talking on the phone, I needed more sleep. I closed my eyes.

Before I knew it, I'd be back at work Monday afternoon. Life always seemed to roll like that for me, like an endless wave of monotony. Monotony, yes, but packed with chocolate-filled cupcakes. I fell asleep grinning.

"NICK! THAT guy's out front again. The one who was watching you last week."

Marcy's urgent rasp yanked my attention from counting dough balls to the one fucking subject I was reluctant to talk about: that guy. The scruffy looking dude who was in the pizza shop last Wednesday, who Marcy had deduced was staring at me. I certainly hadn't noticed any staring going on. Marcy was being ridiculous. Guys didn't stare at other guys. Except for Corey, but I was trying not to think about him.

I pulled my head out of the pizza fridge located under the pizza station and bonked it on the side of the cabinet. "Ouch," I grumbled, rubbing the side of my head. I stood up and looked out into the dining room in time to see Scruffy Dude walking up to the counter to order. A warm rush of fear rolled down my extremities. Why? What was the big deal? So what if some guy came in last week and was here again today? Regulars returned all the time. It was essential in the restaurant business to have repeat customers.

"Stupid Marcy and her cockamamie ideas," I griped, turning around. I didn't normally talk to myself, but there was no one around to notice or care.

Marcy was taking the dude's order. She leaned against the counter, writing up the ticket before ringing him up on the cash register. Then she strolled in my direction with a stupid grin on her face. "Figures he wanted pizza," she said, hanging the ticket above my workstation. "If you'd been on grill today I bet he would have gotten a sandwich."

I flipped her off and she stuck out her tongue. Sometimes she reminded me of my sister. Sisters were annoying. "Whatever." I rolled my eyes.

As she went back to the cashier area, I dared to glance to where the guy stood filling his cup by the soda machine. Just before he turned with his full cup, he made eye contact with me. *Shit!* I quickly turned away.

"Is he really looking at me?" It was hard to tell since Marcy was more or less in the same line of vision as me. I was diagonal to the soda machine in the dining room, and Marcy happened to be smack-dab in between us. In fact, every time he'd been in here she'd been either next to me or somewhere close-by. It was very possible the guy she'd *thought* was looking at me was really looking at her, and since she wasn't interested, she'd imagined the guy had the hots for me. "Stupid girl." I rolled my eyes and dismissed her assumption.

Marcy was pretty. Of course he'd been checking her out these last couple times. *Yeah, way more logical.*

Only… it felt oddly comforting that he *might* have been looking at me. I hadn't had sex in over a week and I felt the need tugging hard. I'd never felt that for another guy before Corey came along. All the secret feelings I'd had toward Corey surfacing after weeks of dormancy had me inexplicably frustrated. I hadn't called him, although I'd wanted to. And Chrissy certainly hadn't called, though I was glad she hadn't. I'd been a mixed-up mess of emotions lately. So yeah, I suddenly had difficulty ignoring the idea that Scruffy Dude might have been looking at me. I was just as desirable as Marcy.

I glanced at the order: a small cheese pizza with green peppers, mushrooms, and onions. Easy enough. So, Scruffy Dude liked veggies. Personally I preferred loads of meat on my pizza, but I tolerated vegetables now and again. I liked green peppers.

I took a small dough ball off the rack and started flattening it. *So he ordered a pizza? This is a pizza shop.* As my fingers worked the edges of the dough, my mind went blank. I liked blank. Thinking of nothing while working made life easier.

But fuck if my mind could stay empty for more than a few minutes.

I sprinkled cheese on his pizza and pondered Marcy's speculation. *Was he looking at me? And even if he was, did it matter?* I was 90 percent certain the guy had been staring at Marcy. She was really pretty, and she *did* have nice boobs. I liked her soft black curls and her sparkling green eyes, but I wasn't telling her that, or she'd bug me to go out with her again. She was also funny and perky and had a way of brightening my day. *That is, when she isn't annoying the shit out of me!*

So what if there was a 10 percent chance Scruffy Dude liked me. Who cared? Not me.

TWENTY MINUTES later I was in the dining room sweeping the floor. Some kid had dropped his tray and fries flew to all corners of the room, not to mention all the bits of trash customers had left under several tables. The boss didn't like a messy dining room, so he sent me out to tidy things up. I didn't mind. It was all a part of the job. But what I didn't think about when I'd volunteered to sweep was that Scruffy Dude was still finishing his food in the corner booth. And as I swept, I found it hard keeping my eyes on the floor.

First glance: he was overweight. His sweatpants were tattered, and they hugged his thighs.

Second glance: his Nike sneakers were very old. They had a hole in the toe and what appeared to be paint splattered on the black canvas. His long-sleeved, black T-shirt was faded, but I could make out the name Led Zeppelin across the back. I wasn't a Zeppelin fan. In fact I wasn't much into music, but I knew the band because my parents sometimes played old rock music and sang together in the car. They thought I was asleep or engrossed in my iPod when they did it, but I noticed how much they liked crooning together. Sometimes I was even jealous. They had each other, and I was… well… alone by choice. Right?

I made sure I looked busy as I checked him out. Marcy had dubbed him "scruffy" because he seriously needed a shave. It would've been okay if he'd had a beard or some sort of style to his facial hair, but it just appeared unkempt. Not to mention the unibrow he had going on and the acne that covered his face. And his hair was pulled back into a messy looking ponytail, which looked as though he never brushed it. Dude was seriously "scruffy" in every sense of the word.

So what if this guy had checked me out? It didn't matter. I had girls checking me out left and right. It was an everyday occurrence I'd grown accustomed to. Surely it was no big thing to have a guy's attention too? Except... it was, even the prospective attention from a guy who wasn't all that appealing to look at. I hadn't thought about it since the last time I saw Corey. Some part of me missed the way Corey looked at me. The hunger in *his* eyes was more powerful than any of the girls I'd dated. And the intensity of his kisses was something I couldn't easily forget no matter how much time passed.

Probably why my dreams about him are so intense.

But I'm not gay, and I'm not about to have people spreading rumors.

Just as I dumped a dustpan full of fries into the trash can, my phone buzzed in my pocket. I looked up, checking behind the counter quickly to make sure the boss wasn't watching before I fished it out. It was a text from Elaine.

I heard about you and Chrissy. Sorry. I have time to kill. You free after work?

"Everybody wants some," I muttered. As if on cue, I heard Van Halen on my mental radio. "Next time I drive somewhere with my folks I *am* listening to my iPod," I said to myself. I texted back: *Yup. 8ish okay?*

:) Thank you! Elaine responded.

"You're thanking *me*?" I chuckled, pocketing the phone. See? I got sex without even trying. *So what if this guy wants me? Everybody does.*

I let out a deep sigh of satisfaction and strutted my stuff down the hallway, holding my broom like a scepter. Being a sexual god was such a difficult job, but somebody had to do it.

Chapter 4: *Scruffy Dude*

I LIKED it when nothing was going on in my head, but sometimes… sometimes I pondered my life. Weeks dragged on into months, into years, and nothing really changed. I was bored. Did everyone feel like this?

I flipped a burger and heard the overhead radio morph between stations. It was all static and sound bites, which suggested either something was seriously wrong with the radio or someone in the back was searching for a different station. Normally the boss preferred listening to prerecorded "dinner" music or Christian contemporary, but he was out this afternoon. Change could be good. But when the static landed on pop music, I cringed. One Direction. Now this was torture!

I threw my head back. "Seriously?" I complained in vain, knowing no one was in earshot.

The bell rang, indicating the front door had been opened, but I didn't bother looking up. Customers weren't my thing. I wrapped the cheeseburger sub I'd finished making and heard Marcy bellow from the back.

"Can you get the counter for me, Nick?"

She's the one messing with the radio. I begrudgingly huffed, "Sure." She was always getting me to do parts of her job when the owner wasn't around.

I set a tuna sub on the counter and placed the cheeseburger sub under the heat lamp, grabbed a pen, and walked toward the customer at the counter. As soon as I looked up, my eyes locked with Scruffy Dude's. A nervous tingle flowed through my chest and arms. *Shit!* I picked up an order ticket and placed it in front of me. My fucking throat was dry, so I tried clearing it. "C-can I help you?"

The guy's eyes darted over the menu board above my head. He licked his lips and stammered. "U-umm, I-I want a… t-turkey sub with… mayonnaise and lettuce. No, make that a sandwich on wheat toast."

I wrote the order casually, purposely *not* looking up in any particular way to draw attention to the fact that I *was,* or *was not,* looking at Scruffy Dude. Still, it was hard not to notice *some* details about the guy. I could check him out briefly. I just wasn't about to memorize anything about him. He was just some guy.

He was sweaty and greasy, which was kind of gross. Either he was on lunch break from a job requiring loads of manual labor, or he'd slacked off in the personal hygiene department. God, I hoped for the former. His hair was black, but it was tucked inside a backward baseball cap so I wasn't sure if it was in a ponytail again. Only wisps stuck out from the sides. Maybe he had green eyes behind his glasses, but I wasn't going to risk another glance. If Marcy was right, I didn't need to encourage any attraction. Corey had been my first and *last* guy.

Scruffy Dude added, "Also, french fries and a Dr Pepper."

"Gravy on the fries?" I asked impulsively. The customer didn't answer right away, and I hoped he hadn't gotten the wrong impression. I'd asked because I thought this guy looked like a gravy fan. It had nothing to do with being pudgy or frequenting a sub shop. Thin people liked gravy too. I sure did.

"Sure." His voice was deep and soft. But his one word reply made me think either he didn't like talking to people or he didn't like talking to *me.*

Without making eye contact, I took his money after ringing him up and headed over to the grill area to fix his food. I hung up the ticket before I strolled to the sink to wash my hands. Marcy bounded over as soon as I pulled out the loaf of wheat bread to start his order.

"So, he's back again, is he? Third time in a week. What'd he get?"

I shook my head in disgust. "You're relentless."

"Of course I am! So what'd he get?"

"Turkey sandwich." I popped the bread into the toaster.

"Because you're on grill today. Just like last time you were on pizza and that's what he ordered." She seemed so sure of herself. I hated that.

"I've only seen him in here a couple times, it doesn't prove anything."

Marcy wasn't bothered. "Maybe, but I bet he'll come in more now that you've spoken to him."

I scrunched up my face. "And *when* did I talk to him?"

"Just now."

"I took his order. That's hardly considered talking."

"Whatever," she said with a shrug, walking over to the fryer. "Are these his fries?" She shook the basket, watching the little white fries floating in the grease.

"Yeah. Can you *not* mess with them? Just go back to the counter and do your job for once." I shooed her away with a flicking motion of my hand. She was always poking things.

"Testy. Testy. No need to grumble at me. I can do my job."

"Go!"

She jumped, but finally went away. She wiped off food trays as I finished assembling the sandwich. I dumped the cooked fries in the bin and shook the saltshaker over them, scooped a portion into a little red-and-white checked carton boat, and then coated them in gravy, half-tempted to snag one for myself, but I'd *so* get in trouble if I did. Marcy was on the phone taking a carryout order by the time everything was done, so I placed his food on a tray, set it on the counter, and called Scruffy Dude's ticket number into the microphone. "Four sixty-two."

The guy had shed his cap, but I didn't think it helped his appearance any. His hair was slicked back into a tight ponytail like before, the length of which was indiscernible due to tangled curls, and it was equally as greasy as his face. Plus, he needed a shave. *Why am I so fixated on that?* I didn't want to make eye contact, so I didn't. He took his tray, and I turned away from the counter. He was just some guy. He didn't matter.

As I shook off my thoughts and zoned in on nothingness, the bell at the front door sounded again and Tara Jackson walked in. *My fucking brain never gets a rest!* Tara was blonde, thin, and stacked. Any guy would kill to go out with her, including me. Her parents had money, and she was reputed to treat her boyfriends well. I'd seen her at a few parties at M-L's, but we had never really talked. Today was the day.

"I got it, Marcy." I held up my hand as Marcy took two steps Tara's way. "I'm out of orders anyway."

"Oh, okay." Marcy didn't seem too bothered, but I could tell by her voice I'd get an earful of questions later.

Tara smiled and pointed at me as she stepped up to the counter. "I recognize you. You're Corey's friend, right? Nick...something?"

I couldn't help the sound bite that played in my head when I responded in a deep sultry voice, "Jones. Nick Jones." It sounded a lot like a young Sean Connery from the old James Bond movies. Yeah, I could be a spy. I'd make an awesome spy. Plus, Bond always ended up in bed with his costars. My brain was having a conversation with itself, as it often did while I held a different conversation with someone else. I said to Tara, "And yeah, I know Corey. He invited me to some of the parties, but we weren't there together every time."

"I remember you. You were on the couch that time at Meghan's house making out with Laney."

"Oh, yeah, right!" I tried to sound like I remembered, but I seriously didn't. Did I have to? I went to loads of parties and kissed lots of girls, especially Laney. I remembered Meghan's house. And I remembered a keg. But I also remembered waking up on the front lawn. Nothing else from that night registered, so I'd have to go with it. If Tara said I'd been kissing Laney, then it must be true. "I remember," I answered easily. I could fake it.

"She said you were an amazing kisser."

My ego was stroked. "Did she? Well, tell her I said thanks." I brought the ticket up and leaned in to write. I gave her a dazzling smile and winked. "What'll you have?"

"Can I get a slice of pizza?" she asked with a smirk. "You don't remember any of that, do you?"

She had me. *Damn!* I shook my head. "No. I don't. I passed out. Anything to drink?"

She laughed. "Yeah, you and every other guy there. Don't sweat it. I'll have a Sprite."

"What gave me away?" I put the pen down and rang her up. "Three eighty-five."

"Intuition. Plus, you were very drunk."

I chuckled. "True."

Tara smiled seductively and batted her eyes. I knew that look. She wanted me. "We should hang out sometime."

I was used to girls acting like that. "Yeah, okay."

"Like, what are you up to Friday night?" She grinned at me. Jeez, could she be more obvious?

"Are you asking me out?" I glanced at Scruffy Dude. Why? I had no fucking clue.

"Yes."

"Yeah, okay. I can do Friday, but I work grill 'til eight."

Tara smiled. "That's okay. Nothing fun is going on before then anyway." She placed her change into her posh-looking purse. Coach?

"Okay. Let me just grab you a slice. It'll only be a minute." Tara turned toward the soda machine and walked away.

"You're going out with *her*?" Marcy gawked.

"Yes." I didn't think I had to answer to Marcy, but I wasn't going to ignore her either. We *did* have to work together.

"What, is she better looking than me?"

"I'm not even going to answer that."

"Nick."

"Look," I pleaded in exasperation, "I'm not here seeking your approval, Marcy."

"Approval for what?" I jumped when Paul walked up behind me. I liked the guy, but shit he was quiet. "What are we talking about?"

I sighed. Why did I always have to clarify everything to everyone? Why couldn't I find friends who appreciated silence and personal space? "Approval to go out with whomever I wish," I explained.

"Nick has a date with Tara Jackson," Marcy blurted, hands on her hips. I was starting to think it was her permanent pose.

Paul's eyes lit up. Of course they would. "All right!" He high-fived me. "She's smokin'! And"—he leaned in—"she's easy." Paul nudged my arm and waggled his eyebrows.

I rolled my eyes because statistically, his response was 99.9 percent expected. "Yeah, exactly why I'm going out with her." I grabbed the slice of pizza and walked to the counter.

Tara came to get her food and handed me a slip of paper. "Here's my number. See you Friday." She winked and took her tray.

I stared at her number. *She's easy.* Every girl's easy. As I pocketed the number, I looked up in time to see Scruffy Dude emptying his tray into the trash. He looked at me briefly before walking out. Deliberately? I wasn't sure. I turned and found Marcy standing right behind me. I jumped. "What are you...?"

"I'm sorry," she offered. "I don't mean to give you a hard time. I'm just jealous. You know I like you." She touched my arm. "I'm finding it hard being your friend when I want more."

"Marcy, I like you too. But you can't act like this and be my friend. I talk to you more than anybody else. Can't that be enough?"

She looked disappointed. "Yeah, I guess so."

I squeezed her upper arm. "So... we're good?"

"Yeah, we're good."

"Work on Paul," I suggested. "I think he's single."

She shrugged and said, "Yeah, maybe. He is cute."

"And I hear he can clog. Not many good cloggers around."

Marcy chuckled, and I knew we were okay. She simply needed to get her mind off me and onto someone who'd reciprocate her feelings. I'd seen Paul checking out her ass a few times. If she showed interest, he'd be all over that action.

I grabbed some pots from the dish area to swap out my station, glancing at the front door as I went about my daily routine. Scruffy Dude was gone. *I guess he was looking at Marcy after all.* Disappointment made its presence known, but I dismissed the notion with a shake of my head, which was exploding from overuse. *I'm being ridiculous.*

"ARE YOU picking Tara up?" Marcy had more questions than a loan application.

"Yeah, after I leave here. First I need to make this turkey sandwich for an eight o'clock takeout order." I grabbed the wheat bread as I pointed to the ticket hanging over the grill.

"Oh," Marcy replied. She snagged a french fry from the bin and popped it into her mouth. I hate when she does that. If I did it, I got in trouble, but Marcy—nooo.

I wrapped the sandwich and taped it shut before handing it to her with the ticket. "Here, bag this order for RC. I'm done." I undid my apron strings.

"Who's RC?" she asked.

"Um...." I indicated the name written right on the ticket and raised my eyebrows. She could be dense.

She looked embarrassed. "Oops."

I could only shake my head. I went to the back of the restaurant to punch out on the time clock, and as I strolled down the hallway, which led to the dining room and then out the front door, I heard someone say, "Carryout order for RC." As I rounded the corner, the customer came into view. It was Scruffy Dude. *His name's RC? Or are those his initials?*

"That's your name!" Marcy exclaimed, looking pleased as punch. Again, we think alike. "We just call you...." She hesitated, making eye contact with me before finishing her sentence. "Dude."

"Dude?" he asked Marcy.

Marcy answered with her normal exuberance. "Yeah, you know, when you come in sometimes, it's like, 'Oh, Dude's here again.'"

I tried slinking past them, all the while listening in and hoping to heaven she wouldn't mention my name.

"Who is 'we'?" RC asked.

"Me and Nick. That'll be six twenty-four," she chirped. "Wow, this is the third time you've been in this week. Four, if you count last Wednesday. You must *really* like the food."

I cringed. *Why'd she have to say my name?* Not to mention emphasizing his frequent visits. I felt bad for him.

RC handed her the money and asked, "Nick?"

Marcy was smiling so wide, I thought her face would crack. "Yeah, you know, that guy." She pointed at me as I crept by. I'd make a terrible burglar, by the way. It was my fault for lingering so I could eavesdrop. I very well could have jetted by without being seen, but something in me wanted to know what he'd say.

I stopped midstride and gave a guilty grin as RC turned and spotted me. "Uh, hi." I tentatively waved a hand.

"I know you've seen him." Marcy said. "Nick's here all the time."

"Uh, yeah, I've seen him. He took my order on Wednesday." He lowered his eyes and the baseball cap he wore shaded his face. I think Marcy's chatter made him uncomfortable.

"So, your name's RC? Is that like a nickname or are those your initials?" Marcy asked, giving a little more interest to Scruffy Dude than I thought appropriate. Poor guy. *What's her deal?*

"Both, actually." RC looked from me back to Marcy as if unsure whom to speak to. He also seemed rather shy being the center of Marcy's attention and that made me think maybe the guy really *did* like her. RC gripped his carryout order and blurted, "I gotta go."

"Okay," Marcy said, smiling still. "Nice to meet you, RC." She was way too pleased for comfort. I knew she'd only be worse the next time RC came in.

"Nice to meet you too." RC's eyes swept from Marcy to me and then dropped to the floor as he lumbered out.

As soon as the front door closed, I got on her. "Marcy! Seriously? Can you be any more invasive?"

"Invasive? What do you mean? I just asked about his name, no big deal."

I crossed my arms on top the countertop and leaned in so the customers in the dining room couldn't hear me. "No big deal? Didn't you see how embarrassed he was? He totally has a crush on you and you acted as if he's just another guy."

"Me?" she questioned with a hard glare. "I did not, and no he doesn't. RC likes *you*."

I was sick of fighting her. "Whatever. I have a date. Laterz."

I was getting laid tonight and nothing was going to stop it.

Chapter 5: *The 5 Senses*

TYPICALLY, I liked to taste things. I was fascinated with flavors of all sorts. I enjoyed anything from strong black coffee to fresh kale out of the garden. I liked bitter, sweet, sour, spicy, tangy—you name it! What I didn't like was *bland*. Water was the only thing I drank that shouldn't taste like anything. Water-flavored water was perfect as is. Oddly, "flavored" water was the only thing I didn't go for.

This helped when my mom cooked dinner because I'd normally eat anything she put in front of me. I craved ethnic foods of all sorts. I didn't have a favorite. I'd eat German food, Chinese, Italian, Mexican, Indian, Thai… heck, anything as long as it was full of flavor.

So it should have been easy to understand why taste was my favorite of the five senses when it came to sex. Wait… did I just say that? Touch was a sense too. Yeah, touch was probably my favorite sense with regard to sex, but taste was a close second. There was something about tasting the person I was with that gave me such a thrill. I got lost in it.

I studied the tortilla chip I held between my fingers. Salty chips were not what I had in mind. I wanted to taste something else on my tongue. *I'm bored.*

I leaned over and whispered into Tara's ear. "This fucking movie is practically half over, and we haven't done anything." I wanted to taste her, but she wasn't budging. So not fair.

She shushed me. Then, when Christian Bale stopped talking, she whispered back, "Be patient. I'm pretty sure my mom said they were going to my aunt's house for dessert or something."

Tara's parents were home, again, and we sat in the living room pretending to watch a movie together while they were in the kitchen. Her parents had been home last night too, so my expectations of first-date-sex got squelched. Irksome! Now we were watching a movie. At least *I* was faking it; I'm pretty certain she was actually paying attention. I reached over Tara's shoulder and leaned closer. Her eyes were glued to the television screen, and she didn't seem to notice my breath on her neck. I touched her thigh. She ate another kernel of popcorn.

Her dad walked in, and I jerked my hand away.

"So Tara, your mother and I will be gone for a little while. I trust you'll be fine if we leave the twins here with you?"

She hit pause on the TV remote. "Yeah. Of course," she answered enthusiastically. "Are they going to play in their room or join us out here?"

Oh God, I hope not.

"No," her father said. "I think your mom said they had a long day with Grandma so they both fell asleep fairly early. You kids remember they're in the house, though, and try to refrain from anything inappropriate." Her dad's gaze shifted to me. "Nick, I trust you'll be respectful of my daughter."

"Of course, sir."

Tara got off the couch and hugged her parents as they readied to leave. Then she made sure the car pulled out of the driveway. She scurried to the back bedroom and checked on her siblings before returning to the couch. I thought she was going to tell me all was clear to get down and dirty, but instead she turned the movie back on. Seriously?

I had other things on my mind. I slid my hand down her inner thigh and slowly edged my fingers back up. Who knew how long her parents would be gone, and we'd already wasted a good portion of our "alone time" doing nothing. *Who does that?*

I risked being slapped, moving my hand north while kissing her neck. Women normally responded to the neck kiss. Extra sensitive I guess. Mine was. The denim covering her crotch was warm and damp, and the thought of tasting her made me harder. I rubbed her more aggressively, and she made a noise. A good noise or a bad one? I tried again as I licked her ear. She made another sound. Ah, a good one. She tilted her head back, moaning softly.

"Oh, yes," Tara hummed.

I think Christian Bale was forgotten as I sucked on her earlobe. She spread her legs, and I took that cue, slipping off the couch and settling between her knees. Tara helped me slide her jeans and underwear off, and as she moved to a more comfortable position, I ducked my head between her thighs. I liked her sour taste.

Sex for me was more than a one-dimensional experience. I enjoyed using all my senses, especially taste. I liked listening to the different sounds I could coax from her throat. I marveled over the texture and suppleness of her skin compared to Corey's. I inhaled her scent deeply, enjoying it, but often thinking she wore too much perfume. And as far as taste, I'd noticed over the years each girl tasted different, and it made me wonder if guys tasted different too? I'd only ever tasted Corey. Corey's flavor was spicy and musky. Tara's was bland compared to his, and I hated *bland. Corey's juice.... Mmm.*

"Hey, why'd you stop?" Tara asked, gasping for breath.

I blinked and shook away my inner monologue. Oddly, I hadn't noticed I'd stopped giving head. "Sorry, brain freeze." Quickly, I got back to business, and she instantly forgot. She dropped her head back onto the cushions and moaned loudly.

"Oh, yes! Fuck, yes! Oh Nick, oh God! Right there!"

Yeah, so fucking easy.

After she came, I climbed up her body and kissed her deeply.

She shoved me back, instantly wiping her mouth and making a face that could have killed me. "What the hell?" she yelled, wiping her tongue on her shirtsleeve. "Why would you do that? That's disgusting!"

"What?" I asked innocently. "I thought it'd be hot."

"Hot?" she asked, but it didn't quite sound like a question with her inflection. "You thought that licking me *down there*, and then sticking your tongue down my throat was *hot*? Yuck! Where would you get that revolting idea? Eww." She jumped off the couch and ran to the bathroom, exclaiming, "Now I need to gargle with mouthwash!"

I sat on the couch and waited for her to return. I didn't know why she'd gotten so angry. It was sexy, wasn't it? Sex was messy and sticky and tasted sour. What was her deal? I adjusted myself and looked around the room. *Fuck, I'm hard.* I rubbed myself briefly. I didn't want to keep going or I'd come, and that was Tara's job. I fought the urge to whistle because if Tara thought I was bored she might get angrier. I didn't understand why she was being such a bitch about it. I'd just made her come, she should be happy. What was her problem?

Tara returned and sat at the other end of the couch. She ignored me completely and switched the movie back on.

What? I gawked at her. She ignored me. Surely she knew I was painfully hard after what I'd just done? "Um, Tara... help a guy out here?" I motioned toward my groin and pleaded with my eyes.

She looked from my face to my pelvic area and back up. "After what you just did, I don't think so."

"But Tara! Come on. It wasn't that bad. It's *your* body, what's the big deal?"

"Eww. I can't believe you'd ask me that."

I wasn't sure where this attitude came from but it was really annoying. "Tara, please, I'm so hard for you, it's painful."

"So? The bathroom's right there. It's your body, go take care of it."

My jaw dropped as Tara turned her attention back to the television. It was obvious I wasn't getting any, so I got off the couch, bewildered by her insensitivity. I found the bathroom and closed the door. Doing the hand jive alone was not my idea of fun, and Tara's mood swing had given me a headache, an ongoing occurrence of late. Still, it didn't take too much stroking to get things done.

I looked down. There was cum on my hand. I stared at it and felt its stickiness as I rubbed my fingers together. Corey's looked like this: milky, kind of thick. His didn't taste so bad. *I wonder....*

I brought my hand to my mouth and licked. The taste was different than Tara or Corey, but not bad. I remembered when Corey had gone down on me and then kissed me after. It had been hot. And the memory stirred up a desire to taste myself in Corey's mouth again.

What's Tara's deal? I took another lick and then sucked the rest off my fingers. I didn't find the taste offensive at all. I rather liked it. I did up the front of my pants and washed my hands. Just then I heard voices in the other room.

"Hi, sweetie. What happened to the boy you had over?" her mother asked.

"Nick's still here. He had to pee," Tara answered.

Pee! I scoffed. *I don't frickin' have to pee.* I dried my hands and stepped out of the bathroom. "Hello, Mr. and Mrs. Jackson." I greeted them politely. "That was a quick trip."

"Hello, Nick." Mrs. Jackson gave me a gentle hug. She was nice. Reminded me of my mom in some ways. "Yes, well, my sister's dog suddenly had diarrhea on the living room carpet, so we were forced to call it a night."

"Eww, Mom, that's so gross!" Tara squealed.

Her mom ignored her and kept on talking. *Yup, just like my mom.* "Besides, Tara never seems to bring boys over when we have the chance to talk. I'd like to get to know you."

I tucked my fingers into my front pocket. "I'm sorry. I think I'm out of time anyway. My parents don't like me out late." I didn't exactly have a curfew, but I knew my dad liked me home early. He said my mom slept more soundly knowing I was safe. "Plus, I have to work tomorrow." *Oh wait, tomorrow is Sunday. I hope they don't call me out on that one.*

"Oh, you still live at home?" She sounded interested, but she'd missed my slipup.

"Yeah. My parents need help around the house sometimes, and it makes it easier if I'm there."

"Oh, are they elderly?" she asked.

"No, they just like my help with stuff." I didn't want to explain my cushy situation with my folks, or the fact that I didn't want to move out. Ever. Avoiding the conversation was best. "So, Tara, I'm gonna head." I motioned toward the door.

"Okay," she said, hopping up. She walked over and gave me a stiff hug. *Gee, thanks, Tara.*

Her parents also said good night and left the room.

I moved to kiss her, but she turned her face away so my lips landed on her cheek. "Good night." I walked to the door and Tara placed her hand on my shoulder so I turned. "What?"

"Just so you know, I'm not against"—she paused and looked down—"Popsicles." She winked, and I chuckled. "You just threw me off with the whole licking-me-kissing-me thing. I'm sorry."

"It's okay. I won't do it again."

"Thanks. I just think it's gross."

"Yeah, you spelled that out loud and clear."

Tara leaned in and kissed me on the lips. "Next time, we'll do it right."

I grinned. "Okay. Next time." At least there would be a *next time*.

Chapter 6: *Apologies*

ANOTHER DAY another dollar!

A well-known phrase which kept circling around my mind as I scraped the soggy toppings from inside the refrigerator. How pieces of pepperoni and green peppers had made their way underneath the trays and into the refrigeration unit, I could only guess. *Perhaps it's gremlins?* I certainly didn't make that much of a mess when I cooked. When I made pizzas, very little fell to the side of the crust as I piled on the cheese. I was an *artiste*. We artistes didn't waste good material or good pizza toppings. Someone else must have jostled the containers around as they'd rushed to make a pie, not me!

"Here you go, Niko." Julie stuck the ticket under the clip above my station. She had the habit of rhyming my name in different forms. I never minded. She was a quirky girl who rhymed most things, so extending her habit to include my name seemed normal. "Sorry. I know it's a drag having to make a pizza while you're cleaning." She shrugged and walked away. Julie was nice, and not as chatty as Marcy.

Speaking of…. Marcy sidled up to me, and I greeted her. "Hey, Marcy."

"Hey. I saw Scruff—RC, in the dining room when I came in. What'd he order? Pizza?" She looked at the ticket in front of me. "I knew it!"

"Don't look so thrilled," I said. "Your ego doesn't need more stroking." Marcy looked way too delighted as she tugged on my sleeve. "What?" I asked, agitated as always while working the dough on the table.

"He's watching you again."

I followed her line of sight and caught RC looking our way just before he sat down with his drink. "Marcy, I hate to say this, but you're a freak. He's not looking at me; he's looking at you. You're standing right next to me and because you're obsessed with *my* sexuality, you're projecting his interest onto me. Stop it. Okay? Just stop it. I'm not gay, I'm not bi. I'm dating Tara. Speaking of which, she's supposed to text to let me know when she's free, and then we are going out again."

Marcy's face sagged along with her entire body. "Oh. Sorry. I don't mean to be a pain."

She trudged to the counter, and I felt bad. She might be annoying, but I didn't want to hurt her feelings. She simply pushed the gay thing too far. I made RC's veggie pizza and watched Marcy. She was sulking. It was stupid for me to feel guilty for calling her out on her own foolishness, but on the other hand, she wasn't doing any harm. Maybe I'd been too cold to say it like I had? Maybe I should apologize?

I popped RC's pizza in one side of the conveyer-belt oven, and then took the next pizza that came out the other end and slid it onto a silver tray. "Order up," I called to the cashiers on duty after cutting it and pushing it under the heat lamp.

It was Wednesday. Normally I was on grill on Wednesdays, but the boss liked to mix things up. He'd figured out I was more efficient when I moved around, so he switched up the schedule often. Whatever. I didn't care. A couple more pizzas came out, and I cut them before Julie sent them out. After a few minutes, RC's little pizza was done. I cut it evenly and set it under the lamp. "Order up."

Julie walked over and placed it on a tray. She called RC's number and looked over at Marcy. "Hey, what's up, buttercup? Why the frowny face?"

Marcy folded her arms over her chest and leaned back against the counter. "Nick's being a jerk," she huffed. "He thinks some fat guy likes me. I know he's only saying that to get me off his case about dating Tara instead of me."

I fucking could not believe my ears. She did not just say that! And to make matters worse, RC happened to walk up to get his pizza at the exact same time. He hesitated picking up the tray and looked at her. The look on RC's face made my stomach turn over. Poor guy.

Marcy must have felt his presence behind her, because she turned in his direction. "Oh, I didn't mean you."

"Marcy!" I hissed from the other side of the heat lamps. I looked at RC, hoping to convey some regret for having such an insensitive friend, but RC wasn't engaging me. He lifted the tray and walked away without saying a word. He retrieved his cup from the table he'd been sitting at, and moved to the far corner of the dining room. I rushed around the pizza-station table and got right in Marcy's face. "I can't believe you just said that! How fucking rude can you be?"

"Well... you... he... I don't know!" She threw her hands in the air and stormed to the back.

"What's her dealio?" Julie asked innocently. Her unusual way of talking normally made me grin, but I wasn't in the mood.

"I don't know." I shook my head. I looked through the shop to where Marcy stood in back, talking to the boss. He was a good one to talk to; she'd be fine. Then I looked out into the dining room. Scruf—RC—was facing the window instead of the counter as he normally did. "I need to stop calling him that," I mumbled to myself.

"Will you watch my station for me, Julie? I'll be right back." I knew nothing was coming out of the oven in the next few minutes, so she should be fine.

"Sure thing, ding-a-ling," Julie peeped.

I grinned and shook my head. "You're a trip."

She walked over to the pizza counter and poked around the toppings as if it made her look busy. Silly girl. She was an odd one, but sweet as peach pie.

I took a deep breath and straightened my apron. I needed to apologize for Marcy's words, if she wasn't going to do it herself. My mom always told me, "If you don't have anything nice to say, then don't say anything at all." I felt it was only fair to apologize, but I'd never done that kind of thing before. And I admit I was a little scared. Pulse racing, nerves unraveling, I walked over to RC thinking, *This is the right thing to do.*

RC didn't acknowledge my presence as I stood beside his table. When I cleared my throat, he finally glanced up. He didn't look happy. He went right back to eating without saying a word. Shit! Failure. I wasn't sure what to do. "Um, can I sit?" I asked tentatively.

He responded sarcastically. "I don't know, can you?"

I was slightly shocked. Sarcasm, really? He didn't know me. What if I'd been the kind of guy who got all in his face about it? Huh? But I wasn't. I stood there like a dufus. *What should I do now?* Was this guy really so angered by what Marcy had said that he was cross with me too? Or did he think I was the one who'd called him fat? Should I sit? Or stand here and wait? Then I started questioning why I'd walked out here to apologize to begin with.

RC broke my awkward pause by demanding, "You gonna sit? Or stand there all day?"

I sat quickly, embarrassed that I looked guilty as charged. "I'm sorry," I blurted. "That's all I wanted to say. I'm sorry. Marcy shouldn't have called you fat. I'm not sure why she did except she's mad at me for going out with Tara and sometimes words just spew from her lips without her thinking about it. But, for the record, *I* didn't say you were fat. She did. I'd never call you fat to your face like that." My stupid mouth kept moving, and suddenly I was saying things I knew I shouldn't have said.

RC's brown eyes looked directly into mine. It was unnerving really. And odd. I could have sworn they were green the other day, but I'd only had that one glimpse. "So you're saying you *think* I'm fat, but you won't say it to my face?" The edge in his voice was sharp.

"No. Oh, heck no!" I scrabbled to explain. "I try not to judge people by their looks, really. People do it to me all the time. It gets annoying."

"Yeah, I bet." RC didn't sound convinced.

"No, they do!" I purposely tried to sound like Chrissy by using my high-pitched girly voice. *"Oh that Nick, he's such a stud with his long, muscled legs and strong back. I bet he'd fuck anything!"* Quickly realizing I'd cursed, and remembering how much the boss told us not to, I apologized. "Oh, sorry. Didn't mean to cuss."

RC lifted his eyebrow, forcing the opposite one down. The look was even more dramatic than I could accomplish, and I was pretty good with facial expressions. "I don't give a fuck if you cuss." He was so terse. I wondered what his voice sounded like when he was happy.

I held up my hand and explained the rule around here. "I'm not really apologizing to you. The boss doesn't like it. Although I was rude, I'm just saying I shouldn't cuss at work."

"Team player?"

"Yeah, I guess. I like following rules." I admitted it, but it sounded lame coming out of my mouth. Made me look like a pussy.

RC nodded and took another bite of his food. Maybe he didn't care?

I felt like the moment was over, and I should return to work. Sitting here watching him eat was weird. I stood up. My fingers lingered on the table surface as I searched for one last word. "I guess I should get back. Again, I'm sorry. I hope you don't hold it against her. Marcy is really nice once you get to know her."

RC's voice stopped me from walking away. "Is it true?"

My brain was like... *whaat?* I had to step back and ask, "Is *what* true?"

"That you'll fuck anything?"

Okay, now I was really embarrassed. What should I say to that? It's not like he should have even asked the question, right? He was the rude one now. But I was the one who'd thrown the comment out there in the first place. Shit. It wasn't like I knew the guy, so it shouldn't have mattered either way, but I also saw RC every week when he came into the restaurant. Should I tell him personal details, or be vague? *Truth, always truth.* "Um, I...." I started slowly, looking at the floor, searching for a sentence. Nope, nothing there, only some crumbs I'd missed with the broom. "I guess it's true." Never had I felt so ashamed. "I've been with a *lot* of girls."

"Sucks to be you."

The way RC said it, I wasn't sure if it was praise or sarcasm. I decided not to ask. "I'm gonna head...," I said, motioning toward the counter.

RC nodded. "But hey, Nick," he said as I stepped away. "Thanks for apologizing. No one's ever done that."

I turned. "Called you fat?" I questioned. His countenance fell even further, if that was possible, and I regretted my mouth again.

"No... apologized for it."

The look on his face made me feel even worse. No one should live through that. Before walking away, as I had tried to do three times now, I lifted my hand and squeezed RC's shoulder. It was a strong shoulder, solid and muscular, not what I'd expected.

He didn't say anything.

I went back to work, and the monotony of my life seemed less depressing. No one had ever called *me* fat or ridiculed my looks except to say they envied them. But still, there had been times I wished I didn't look this way. If I weren't so good-looking, I wouldn't be the center of attention all the time. Girls might leave me alone.

Okay, that was just stupid talking. I banged my head on the wall and went back to forming a pizza. I wasn't fooling anyone. I liked the way I looked. RC, in contrast....

I wondered what he'd look like if he lost a couple—fifty—pounds? And if he got rid of the acne? And if his hair wasn't a royal mess all the time? And if he slipped on a dress shirt and pleated slacks? He could be handsome. He sure had nice lips peeking out from under the overhanging facial hair. I sighed. None of it mattered. He'd probably never speak to me again.

"I HEARD what you did the other day. That was nice," Paul commented as he put on his apron.

I was in the back by the timesheets, jotting down next week's schedule, when he clocked in. "Oh yeah? What'd I do?" I honestly had no clue so there was little point pretending. I didn't pretend with Paul.

"The way you apologized to that customer." He smiled warmly at me and patted my shoulder. "You know, the one who looks like Joey Fatone."

"Joey who?"

"You know, one of the guys from that '90s boy band *NSYNC. I swear that guy looks just like him except with longer hair. Anyway, that was really caring of you to apologize for Marcy. She doesn't always think before she speaks." He winked.

I liked Paul, but sometimes I felt like he was flirting with me. And I wasn't sure I'd mind if he did. Good thing we worked together because I had a difficult enough time with Marcy. Shit, these two *had* to get together or I was going to get caught in the middle, and I rarely did threesomes. "Thanks," I replied. He nodded and turned away. Maybe my instincts were wrong. He didn't look interested now. In fact, as soon as I answered, he went back to working his station. *Hmm.* I scratched my head. Perhaps I didn't know anything about anything? One minute Paul looked flirtatious, then the next, detached. But Corey was like that too, only with sex in the middle somewhere. I didn't know what to think; guys were as much a mystery to me as girls.

"Because I have no friends," I lamented. Well, I was determined to make one. I followed Paul to where he was filling the pizza sauce bin. "Hey, Paul."

"Yeah?" He looked at me, but without the warmth. He set the can down, focusing strict attention my way. I felt special.

"Um, are you free sometime?" I knew I came off stupid.

"Yeah. You free to watch some baseball now? Tara out of town or something?"

"I'm trying to broaden my circles."

He laughed. "Like on Google plus?"

"Nah. I'm not online much. I meant circle of friends. I tend to hang out with the same people all the time. Tara is part of that group. Maybe I need a break. I thought if you were free sometime, we could watch a game. Or something." Why on Earth did I sound nervous? I wasn't nervous. I was a cool cucumber full of confidence. I cleared my throat.

"Sure. But I'm busy tonight."

"That's fine. I meant in general. My dad loves to watch any and all sports. And my mom is always riding me about having friends over. She thinks I have none."

"I remember you said that. It's probably because you spend all your time with Tara. And Chrissy before that, and Laney and Becca before them." He must have seen the shock in my eyes. He smirked. "Don't sweat it, Nick. I pay attention to the conversation around here, and you'd be surprised how little Marcy keeps to herself. Besides, I think I know a lot of the gang you run with."

"There're not a gang," I said, jumping to their defense.

"Chill. It's cool. I know you have a close-knit group. I only meant I know most of them; I went to high school with some. I was invited to a couple parties at Mary-Louise's house."

"You shoulda come." Drinking with Paul would have made the same old scene way better.

"Nah. Not my thing. Terrell drinks too much. Dawn is very handsy. And Mary-Louise isn't on my radar seeing how she's gay. So… not really much to look for in a party. But if you want to hang, just the two of us, or with a small group of guys, I'm into it. Your mom makes a killer lasagna."

"How'd you know that?"

"She made one for Bill when his wife had the baby. Remember? But five other people had the same idea, so he ended up with six lasagnas. He gave me one. I'm fairly certain he said your mom made it."

"Oh."

"You have my number. Text me. I'm free most of the time."

"Okay. Well, how about Monday?"

Paul tapped his chin with a finger. "Hmm," he mused. "They play the Angels. Okay. I'm in."

PAUL CAME over Monday, and we had a great time. I think. There was a moment when I wondered if he was enjoying himself because he looked at me all suspicious-like, and I hadn't done anything except pass him the bowl of chips. He gave me this intense stare, but it only lasted a couple seconds. Then someone hit a grounder to short for a double play and he cheered at the screen with my dad. Come to think of it, my mom was acting weird too.

I followed Paul out and walked him to his car. "That was great. Thanks for coming over," I said.

"I had fun." Paul was fishing in his pocket for his keys, standing by his car door, and eyeing me with that same suspicious expression he'd had when I passed him the chips earlier.

I had to ask, "What's up? Why are you looking at me like that?"

Paul unlocked his door and opened it. "Like what?" he asked.

"I don't know. You have this look. Do I make you uncomfortable?"

"No." He looked down and paused. Maybe he was thinking about it? Then he looked up and sighed. "Your mom makes me uncomfortable."

"She does? Why?"

"I don't know. I can't explain it. She kept watching me. And when I went into the kitchen for more beer, she asked how long I've known you and if I was going come over again sometime."

"That doesn't sound so bad."

"No. It's not. Not by itself. But every time I glanced away from the TV, I caught her staring at me. It creeped me out."

"I don't know why she was doing that. But… I guess… I never have anyone over. Maybe she's in shock?"

"Or maybe she thinks I'm your date."

I blanched. I couldn't see my face, but I felt cold all of a sudden. *Date?* That was completely embarrassing. "What?" I shrieked. I cleared my throat and repeated the question in a more manly tone. "What?"

Paul grinned and shook his head. My shock and surprise had made him relax. Good. Glad he was all relaxed while my mom was pinning him as my boyfriend. "Don't sweat it, Nick. Moms are weird. She said something like 'Nick's a good-looking guy, isn't he?' and I casually agreed and left the kitchen with my beer. It's no big deal."

"You agreed?"

"Well, yeah. I'm not going to lie to your mother."

"Lie! Please. Lie to her. Now she's going to think I'm gay." My heart was pounding in my chest. I didn't know what to do. Did I go in and confront her? Did I tell her to stay out of my love life? Did I explain to her Paul was only a friend?

Paul must have sensed my panic, or read it on my gaping expression, because he walked up and placed his hand on my shoulder. "Dude, chill. It's fine. I think your mom's cool for looking out for you and being so open-minded. The more we hang out, the more she'll see we're just friends. Don't sweat it." He removed his comforting hand and got into his Cavalier. "I'll see you Wednesday."

He left. And I was in the driveway wondering if my mom had been watching out the window this whole time. *Great.*

Chapter 7: *Tara*

I PICKED Tara up at her house and drove to Olive Garden. Tuesday was my normal day off, although I worked Tuesdays if I was off the Saturday before, or if someone asked off and they needed me, or if the boss forgot. It didn't matter. Most of the time I was off on Tuesdays and this particular one, I took Tara out to dinner. She liked to eat. I liked to eat. It was a happy coincidence. The cuisine at OG was different than Papa's Pizzeria, and we could attempt a conversation without interruption from her family or my coworkers. Don't get me wrong, I liked family, but there was a time and place for them to encroach on a date or hang back. I wanted some quiet. Her mom had asked to get to know me, and she got her chance. I'd talked plenty the last couple times I went over there. Now I was ready for some silence.

We were seated in a rather secluded spot, which I appreciated. I glanced at the menu, thinking about all the yummy dishes I could choose from, when a squeal behind me ruined my previous satisfaction of restaurant choice. Tara immediately leapt from her seat and hugged Elaine. Shit!

"Oh my God!" Tara declared. "It's so great to see you! It's been so long. Where have you been? What have you been doing?" Tara was so freaking happy, you'd think she was more excited to see Elaine than be with me.

"Doing?" Elaine asked. Then I felt her hand on my shoulder. "Hey, Nick. Nice to see you again."

Wow. She was playing innocent with Tara, but I read between those lines. Way to remind me subtly of three weeks ago. *I hope she doesn't mention it to Tara. That would be so rude.* "Hey, Elaine."

She winked at me, but luckily asked about our drink order instead of bragging about blowing me in the movie theater. Dawn would have done both. We ordered, and I excused myself to the bathroom. As I washed my hands, I stared in the mirror.

"Is this really my life? Everywhere I go I run into girls I've slept with. Maybe I need a change, but how? And a change to what? I've been hanging with the same people so long, I don't know how to stop." I pouted at my reflection. "Or if I even want to."

I sighed and left the bathroom.

Tara had her drink when I returned.

"Where's my Coke?" I asked.

"Oh, it's coming. Elaine said they had to switch the tanks or something."

"Oh." No sooner did she say that then Elaine sat the glass in front of me. I looked up. "Thanks."

"No problem. So, Tara, has Nick taken you to the movies lately? He just loves the movie theater."

Tara, innocent of Elaine's implication, replied, "No. But it's funny you should say that. Just the other day, Dawn asked me the same thing. She said Nick had taken her every week." She eyed me. "Why haven't you taken *me* every week?"

"Tara, we've been dating less than two weeks. I'll take you to the movies. What do you want to see?"

"Oh, it doesn't matter," Elaine interjected. "You won't see any of it anyway."

"Do you mind?" I asked.

She shrugged but didn't continue harassing me. She took our order and left us alone. Finally.

"I want to see *The Internship*," Tara said. "And I want you to take me on Friday after work. Saturday we're going to go to my aunt's house and help her rip up the carpet her dog ruined. Remember, when he crapped everywhere?"

"Yeah, got it. We don't need to talk about the dog. This is a restaurant. And besides, can't your aunt get the carpet cleaned instead? Replacing it seems excessive."

"I asked that same question, but Mom said he's done it more than once and she's done cleaning it. They're replacing it and putting up a gate so the dog can't go in that room. Anyway, I volunteered you to help."

"I work Saturday."

"Not until five, I checked. So you're free all day to rip out carpet."

"You could have asked me first. What if I had plans?"

"Plans without me? I don't think so. Your work is sporadic enough; I can't keep track of your schedule. Maybe you need to find a different job? One with banker's hours. PNC has banker's hours...."

Because it's a bank, I thought.

"... and it's great. We would get to go shopping all the time and do lunch. Wouldn't it be fun to shop whenever we wanted and have lunch together every day? I think so. You should write down your schedule every week so I can plan ahead. That way I don't have to call your boss and ask."

"You called my boss?" I was astounded.

"Well, yeah. How else am I supposed to plan when you can help my aunt?"

"I don't know. Talk to me about it, maybe?"

"I am talking to you. I'm talking to you now. You're not going to let my aunt down, are you? My dad thought you were a responsible guy. I can't tell him you're bailing."

"No. That's fine. I'll help."

When did this happen? Suddenly my life was hers. My schedule was hers. My precious sleep-in Saturday mornings had become hers. I slouched and picked at my calamari appetizer. Elaine reappeared at her side and the two of them were chitchatting away. I was there, but not there. I wasn't included in the conversation. My part was done. I'd brought her here. I was going to pay for dinner. And then what? Back to her place? I didn't know, nor did I care.

"I GOTTA go to work." I shoved Tara's nude body, and she grunted. At least she was alive. "Tara, I said I have to go to work." When she slapped my face as she rolled over, I gave up. I sat up and searched for my clothes. I really didn't enjoy the thought of wearing the same clothes two days in a row, but then again, I hadn't expected to sleep over. It just sort of happened. Her parents were somewhere and she'd thought having sex all night was the way to celebrate. I should have been happy, right?

I guess I was.

I didn't like sleeping with girls because it only brought to mind all the things I didn't want to think about, like being held in the middle of the night instead of always having to be the one doing the holding. I waffled between considering it a nonmasculine trait and something everybody needed. Corey had held me once—for about thirty seconds—and then was off doing whatever it was he did after we had sex. He never stuck around long. So far, no one I'd dated, boy or girl, got the fact that I needed some tenderness too. I always had to cater to their needs. What about *my* needs?

Dawn had been the most exciting to sleep with. She'd wake up horny and want to go a round before work. I'd liked that. Morning sex was great. And Dawn liked it rough. I liked when she took control and rode me like a bull in a rodeo. Tara wasn't like that. But I have to say even Dawn couldn't go the distance I had in mind. When I say "rough," my rough was always too rough, if you know what I mean. I shoved her up against a wall once and she about flipped out on my ass for giving her a goose egg on the back of her skull. It had been an accident! Still, nothing ever felt right, no matter whom I fucked. Dating merely filled time. Even Corey, with all his passion and fervor, hadn't quite footed the bill for whatever inside of me was searching for that something in someone else. I didn't even know what I was looking for.

My mom texted as soon as I got into my car. *Where are you? You didn't come home.*

I texted back: *I'm sorry. I stayed at Tara's. I forgot to tell you.*

As long as you're alive and not in a ditch somewhere.

I shook my head and grinned. *No ditches. I'm heading to work. I'll be home by 8:30.*

K. Luv U.

Love you too :)

I was grateful my mom at least cared enough to wonder where I was, but that she gave me enough space *not* to come home and go ballistic on me. I *was* twenty-three, after all.

I WENT to work feeling glum. Always glum. You'd think that would change since I kind of liked working at the pizza place. And because I'd come three times last night. I liked having a constant cash flow. I liked the people I worked with for the most part. What was wrong with me? Why was I never happy? Was it the job? Or was it the girl? Maybe I'd thought it would be different with Tara? Perhaps I was *hoping* it would be. Or was I kidding myself? Every relationship seemed dull.

I punched the time clock and got to work. An hour and a half flew by and before I knew it, we were in the middle of a busy lunch. Another few hours, and it hadn't let up.

"What is it with today?" I asked the owner, manager, and all-around nice guy, Bill, as he came over to inspect the progress of a particular order.

"Not sure, Nick. I heard there was a big real estate meeting in town. RE/MAX Realty or something, so maybe that's where all the business is from. But there's a huge pizza order that needs to get working in forty-five minutes, so you're going to have to take your break soon. Paul's the only one on pizza today, so he'll need all the help we can give him to get it out on time."

"But I'm not that hungry yet."

"Sorry. I can't have you going later because of the other orders we have called in for tonight. You get a break soon, or not at all. As soon as Marcy punches in, I want you on break."

I sighed, but agreed. "All right."

The boss walked away and Renee, another one of the cashiers, called from the counter. "Hey, Nick, can you help me out? Marcy's not back yet."

I took my last ticket down and shuffled to the counter. I looked up and a nervous flutter went through my stomach when I saw it was RC. *Oh, man.* I hadn't seen him since last week when Marcy had made that rude comment about his weight. Would RC say something? Should *I* say something? I didn't know why it mattered so much, but it did. I didn't want RC mad at me when I hadn't said anything. It was Marcy, not me. I didn't like people mad at me.

"Hi," I said. "How can I help you?" I secretly thanked the universe that my voice didn't crack, because suddenly my throat had dried up like it did when the dentist put that little suction thingy on the side when I got my teeth drilled. I tried clearing it a few times, and RC gave me this weird look. *Can I be any more idiotic?*

I picked up a blank ticket and a pencil. As soon as I brought them both to the raised part of the counter to take his order, the pencil hit the edge and unexpectedly flipped from my grasp. I wasn't an overly clumsy person, so when the pencil went flying at RC, I didn't react and grab for it. Instead I watched, embarrassed, as it sailed through the air, hit him in the chest, and fell to the floor.

RC widened his eyes, looked down at the object, and then raised an eyebrow at me. Just like the other day, he didn't have his glasses on—he must have been wearing contact lenses—but I noticed his eyes were indeed brown, not green. What a shame. After he retrieved my pencil, RC handed it back and said, "You don't have to throw things at me to get my attention."

I wasn't sure how to respond to that. "U-uh," I stammered. "I...." I was totally thrown. I was expecting snide, not sarcastic. Even anger or silence would have logically entered the flow, not witty comebacks that could contain a double meaning.

"Dude, I'm messing with you," he said, almost grinning.

I cleared my throat a final time and started again. "Sorry, what can I get for you?"

RC ordered a turkey sandwich on wheat, which seemed to be his favorite. *Not* that I was paying attention or anything, but I did have a habit of remembering what regulars ordered. He'd been in here enough. I remembered his choices.

When I took his money and left to make his food, I felt oddly unsettled.

It was like, if I were walking to my car at night and the streetlight was out and I felt eyes on me.... No, wait, that was creepy. RC didn't make me feel creepy. Um, more like, when M-L and I had last spoken and I wanted the conversation to go on longer, but it didn't. I knew I had lots to say, but I didn't want to open up like that and expose the things that went through my mind. I tended to be sort of private like that. I didn't share. When RC walked away, I'd felt that same sort of nagging sensation telling me I wanted to say more. Or that *he* did. Or something.

Why did I dwell on thoughts like these? I would drive myself insane.

Luckily, I didn't have long to ponder. Right after I took out RC's bread, a large group walked through the door. They looked like lawyers. Probably weren't, just because we didn't get too many lawyers in our little pizza shop. They ordered lots of food, and I was rolling in sub orders. LOL. "Rolling." Get it? I was making subs with sub rolls. Yeah, never mind. Sometimes having a conversation with myself just emphasized the fact that very few people got my sense of humor.

Ten minutes went by, and my boss was taking the spatula from my grasp. "Sorry, Nick, you need to get on break now, or I don't see it happening."

"But Bill, it's busy. How is this all going to get done? Can't I just skip lunch today?" It seemed like a good suggestion to me. No big deal. I could eat when I got off at seven thirty.

He smiled. "Although the offer is tempting, and sacrificial of you, I can't. You know I have rules. It's code to get a thirty-minute break when you work eight hours. Law is law. What if the Labor Department strolls in later today and finds I'm not giving my employees the breaks they are entitled to?"

"I didn't know they inspected small businesses."

"They might. You never know. I like to play things safe. That's why we have rules. It's best to go by them. You get half an hour, Nick. Enjoy it."

"Okay." I couldn't argue. Bill was the boss, the owner, the head honcho. He was always making sure we had our breaks, but he also made sure we didn't get lazy when we were on the clock. Work was work, and break was break. At least I knew what to expect from him, and it was comforting.

I slapped together a chicken salad sandwich and dumped some beef gravy on an order of fries. Working at a restaurant had its perks. I never had to worry about eating.

I took my tray and surveyed the dining room before walking through the little swingy-door that separated the work area from the dining room. It looked full. *I better head to the back and sit at the boss's desk to eat.* I traveled around the cashiers and the pizza station and passed the sink and the busboy, only to find the back of the building sealed off by stacks of cardboard boxes filled with pizza sauce, fresh green peppers, onions, and several boxes of tomatoes. Sysco; they were here unloading the week's delivery. That meant sometime after the lunch rush and before dinner, I had to help put all the supplies away. *Joy.*

Since I was effectively cut off from using the back, I had to find somewhere to sit in the dining room. Marcy left her seat, but before I could make it to her vacated table, a customer claimed it. The shop was *that* busy. Crap! I scanned the tables and booths as I made another sweep through the aisles. Then RC's eyes caught mine.

He was at a booth. He was alone at a table built for four. I stopped midstride and contemplated what I was about to do. I was going to ask someone who potentially hated me to allow me to sit with him for lunch. Did I have the balls?

I pulled my shoulders back. *Yeah, I have balls of steel, baby!*

Before I even asked, RC moved his tray from what would have been my side of the table. I hesitated before taking a seat because I wanted to know I wasn't intruding without permission. RC rolled his eyes at me and shook his head. "Sit down, Nick."

I sat. I don't know why my name sounded different coming from him, but it did. It felt—comfortable. Way different than the vibes I'd gotten off him after the Marcy incident. "Thanks."

Before I could eat, I had to rearrange my food. I didn't know why, but my drink always had to be on the left side and my fries on the right. I took a bite of my sandwich and glanced up. RC was reading something in the newspaper. It looked like politics stuff about healthcare reform. I didn't know much about that, so I definitely didn't want to have a conversation about it. And what if we disagreed? I didn't need one more thing for him to hate me for. I liked people to like me. I remained quiet so he could read.

"You're a brave guy, sitting with the fat dude. I could get this wrapped to go if it makes you feel better."

A wave of guilt flashed through my chest as I looked up. "RC, I'm so sorry." I impulsively apologized. "I don't know why Marcy said that, but *I* never once called you fat. I swear."

RC's eyes softened, and he smirked at me. "I'm just messing with you, Nick."

I stared at him a second. He was "messing" with me? He'd said that twice now. Why? It made me a little angry. "Does it amuse you to jab at my guilt? I feel really bad for what she said, but I already told you I'm sorry. What else do you want me to say?" His constant presence in the restaurant would become problematic if he was going to throw this in my face every time I saw him.

His smirk faded. "Nick, it's not about guilt. I'm messing with you because I find it amusing how easily you get flustered. But I'll stop since you think I'm trying to bust your ass over that girl's comment. I'm not really bothered by it."

"Really? Because it sounds like you are to me."

"I'm used to comments like hers. It's not the first time someone's called me fat, and it won't be the last."

"But you aren't fat," I contested. "Maybe overweight, but I'd never consider a few extra pounds fat. Chubby, at best, but not fat. Fat is like, another sixty pounds, and rolls around your waist." I meant what I said. Realistically, everyone gained weight. I'd really hate it if I gained a few pounds and someone I knew called me fat. It's rude.

He grinned again. "Thanks, Nick. I appreciate your honesty." He took a sip of his soda. "I know I'm heavy. I've been overweight since I was a hundred pounds in the fourth grade. It's taken years to care, but I've finally managed to lose some weight: eighty-one pounds."

My jaw dropped. He really *had been* fat at one point. "Shit!" Of course, I couldn't leave my obvious astonishment hanging in the air like the MetLife blimp; that was also rude. *Oh my God, now I mentally compared him to a blimp. Way to go, Nick.* I cleared my throat. "I mean, um, wow, that's incredible!"

He shrugged. "I'd like to lose another thirty or so, but it's not easy." RC's cheeks flushed, and I could tell he was embarrassed talking about it.

"I guess not."

RC took another sip of his drink, and I went back to eating my fries.

Several more bites of sandwich and half my fries later, and we still hadn't said another word to each other. It was weird. I thought it would be uncomfortable, but in some ways it wasn't. I was trying to think of what to talk about other than his weight, but nothing interesting came to mind. I kind of enjoyed being able to sit with someone and not have to talk. Sometimes I just wanted to eat my lunch. Maybe RC liked the same reprieve?

LUNCH BREAK went by faster than usual, as if my thirty minutes had been reduced to ten. I regretted it, not because of the work I had to do as much as the company I was about to leave. It was a strange sensation. "I guess I have to go back to work." I explained as I stood, picking up my tray.

"Yup."

I nodded. "So, I guess I'll see you next week?"

The corner of his mouth lifted, and RC nodded. "Later, Nick."

"Laterz." I turned away and felt that same buzz at the sound of my name as when I'd sat down at the beginning of lunch.

I think I just made a friend.

Chapter 8: *Mistakes*

ON SATURDAY, I helped Tara's aunt as promised. It was grueling. Anyone who has ever ripped carpet out knows it is *heavy*. I'm talking lugging-a-dead-elephant heavy. And it still stank of dog crap. I almost puked several times. If there is one thing that makes my stomach churn, it's the smell of dog crap. Tara was appreciative, but I didn't care.

LUNCH ON Wednesday was quiet. I sat with RC again, but this time by invitation. "Sharing a table with me today? Or are you going to sit three tables over and pretend you don't know me?" Those were his exact words. This time I knew he was messing with me, and I told him to shut up, which made him smirk. I sat with him. It was quiet, and I needed that. Thinking about Tara's overly controlling grasp on my life gave me a headache, so I wasn't up to talking.

In fact, I was off this coming Saturday, and I didn't even tell her. And to my astonishment, she hadn't asked my boss. I planned on sleeping in and picking her up at five as if I'd worked all day. I wouldn't actually lie, because so far she hadn't questioned me, but I knew I'd end up feeling guilty about it. Guilty, but not enough to tell her I was scheduled off.

I PACED the grill area with nervous anticipation. It was late Wednesday afternoon, and RC hadn't shown up. *Is he coming?* He'd been in for lunch the past five Wednesdays—not that I was counting—plus a couple other times, but that didn't mean he was going to continue to eat lunch here. Or that it would be every Wednesday. We had eaten together twice, and I'd enjoyed his company so far. Really enjoyed it. *Maybe he doesn't like mine, and he was too polite to say it last week?* We hadn't said more than five words to each other. Maybe I'd been *too* quiet?

I paused long enough to flip a burger before continuing to pace up and down the narrow aisle. I stopped when I heard the bell on the front door. It was RC. I grinned as his eyes caught mine. His slight nod and the tiny smirk that curved his mouth made the pinball machine inside my gut power down. I turned back to the grill and completed the sandwich I was making. Fried onions, a slice of American cheese, and all I had to do was move the patty to the roll I had prepared, which was waiting on its little paper plate. Two pickles on the side.

I finished the order and called the customer's number, but RC was still standing at the counter. Renee was on the phone taking a large order. No worries; I had no problem helping RC as long as I didn't throw another pencil at him. I casually strolled up with a pen in hand. "Hey. How can I help you today?" I asked, silently thanking the heavens he was here late because I hadn't gone on break yet.

"I'll take the special."

I nodded. RC didn't appear nervous, but he wasn't telling me what he wanted. "Um, what kind of sandwich?"

RC looked at me. He wasn't grinning, but there was certainly some sort of gleam in his eye. I hoped he wasn't going to challenge me to a staring contest because I was no good at those. "Surprise me," he said. That wasn't the answer I expected and my words got lost. Before I could protest, he reached in his pocket and pulled out his money. "Here. It should ring up to be seven twenty-three." He handed me exact change. "Call me when it's ready."

I was stunned, but also amused. He may not say much, but he was direct and clever. I liked that. It was as though he selected the words instead of shooting his mouth off. I appreciated that as well. He'd made my job easy with correct change, and after I put the money in the register, I washed my hands and walked over to the grill.

RC made his way to his favorite corner booth and sat down.

I faced the grill. *What should I make?* He'd said to surprise him. What did he like? Turkey sandwiches. I went to the grill refrigerator and pulled out the turkey. I took out two slices of wheat bread and popped them in the toaster. Fries! My thoughts were churning. RC liked french fries with gravy. I set a basket of frozen fries into the hot grease and retrieved the bread from the toaster after it popped up. I don't know why I felt so buzzed, but it was like an adrenaline rush. I was even humming while I smeared a thin layer of mayo on the toast. I added lettuce, fresh green pepper—I remembered he liked green pepper—tomato, and a dash of oregano. I cut it diagonally, and ta-da! The perfect turkey sandwich.

I grabbed a tray from the stack and rested it on the front counter while I waited for the fries to finish. Renee walked over to hand me the order she'd been writing down. "Sorry, Nick," she said. "It's a long one. Eight different subs, three soups, side orders, and everything." Renee was cool, but I liked working with Julie more because she had a great sense of humor. Renee was all business.

"It's okay. I'll take care of it. I'm just gonna walk this out to RC." I poured gravy on his fries and placed them next to the sandwich on the tray.

"You don't have to. I can just call his number," she explained as I opened the swingy-door to the dining room and kept on walking. Then she got attitudish. "Or not."

"I got it," I stressed. I snagged a Dr Pepper on my way by the soda machine and strolled up to RC. "Here you go." I set the tray in front of him. "I hope you like it."

RC inspected it by lifting a corner of the bread. When he glanced up at me he seemed—dare I say it—emotional. It was not an expression I expected. "Thanks, Nick. It looks great." He gave me a smile, but the shine in his eyes wasn't exactly happy, it was more... *sappy.* If he wasn't straight, I'd wonder about the way he looked at me.

I might have said something if I hadn't been distracted by an order I knew I had to fix. Instead, I said, "I have to take care of a big order. If you're still here when I'm done, maybe I can share your table again while I'm on break?"

"Yeah."

The door tinkled. I turned and saw Tara enter, all smiles and excitement. "Nick!" she exclaimed, rushing over and hugging me before I could stop her.

"Tara...." I struggled to untangle myself from her grasp, but she kissed me anyway. "Tara, I'm working." I stepped back.

She glared momentarily and then huffed, "Whatever. I got off early so I thought I'd stop by and have lunch. Did you eat yet?"

"Um, no. But I have this huge order. I don't know how long it'll take." I walked back over to the grill, and she followed me until I went through the swingy-door. I looked over the ticket and started slapping portions of steak onto the metal surface. Some onions and a little squirt of oil; I had it all going on. I was a master at lunch rush. Eight subs? No big deal. I'd have it done in eight minutes.

"Is it going to take a while?" Tara asked, still standing by the swingy-door.

I glanced out to RC. He was eating quietly. "Um, yeah, maybe." I put two orders of onion rings into the fryer basket and walked over to Tara. "Sorry. I don't think today's a good day." I wanted a peaceful lunch. Not a chit-chatty lunch. Tara was all chitchat.

"Okay. Maybe next time?"

She was smiling, and I knew she wasn't upset by my total lack of enthusiasm for a spontaneous lunch date. I just didn't want to. "Of course. Next time. Only, text me first."

"Okay. Are we still on for Saturday night?"

Saturday night? Oh yeah, she'd told me her parents were helping with a church dinner or something. I've never known busier parents. They were never home. I felt guilty about banging their daughter while they were being all spiritual, but they were *her* parents. Getting laid was getting laid. Did I need to analyze it? "Yeah, sure," I said. I continued working and heard Tara clear her throat. I looked over. "What?"

"Aren't you going to kiss me good-bye?"

Oops. I glanced into the dining room before kissing my girlfriend. Why did I feel weird displaying public affection? It was normal for couples to kiss.

"I'm going to glance at your schedule so I know when to plan stuff. Be right back."

Before I could stop her, she skipped down the hall.

I wanted to put my head down and cry. If I'd found a minicamera in my car recording my every move, I would not be surprised. When she returned, she wasn't happy. "What?" I asked. Because how bad could it be? She had my balls in her fist most of the time.

"You were off last Saturday!" she yelled.

"So?" I knew why, but I played dumb anyway. I'd made her mad? Oops.

"So?" she shrieked. "You were off and didn't tell me! We could have spent the entire day together. I can't believe you did that. Don't you like spending time with me? Don't I make you happy? I make you come all the time, doesn't that count for anything?"

"Tara!" I cringed, jumped, and searched for listening ears. Not that it would take much for people in China to hear; she was very loud. Luckily, no customers seemed to have heard. And Renee, thank goodness, had gone to the back for something.

"Don't 'Tara' me. Next time you have off, we spend it together, or you're not getting any."

"Okay. I'm sorry." I stepped over to the swingy-door and kissed her cheek. I'd said I was sorry, but a little whisper in the back of my mind told me I wasn't really. I'd liked sleeping all day last Saturday. I wasn't sorry at all. Even if it meant she'd cut me off from sex. So? There were other girls.

As soon as she left, I felt as though a mammoth weight had been lifted.

Weird.

And my grill order didn't take long; I had it done in minutes. As soon as all the food was wrapped and bagged, I made my food for break. By my calculations, RC still had some time to sit with me. I hurried out and sat across from him without asking.

"So, you sit. Just like that?" RC asked.

It made me question whether or not I had the right to be so bold. Maybe I didn't. "I'm sorry," I said as I quickly stood up. I reached for my tray and noticed the smirk on RC's face. "You're messing with me again, aren't you?"

He snickered. "Yup. You're so easy."

I didn't say anything, but it occurred to me that was the second time he'd used what could be a double entendre. *Easy? Me? I suppose I am, but how would he know that?* I chose to ignore the comment for now. "So, you're okay with me sitting here?"

"Third time's a charm. Yeah, Nick. Sit. I've got about twenty minutes before I have to go."

Again, his lips were straining at a smile. It was in the way his cheeks lifted. I could tell he was internally laughing at me because of my dorky way of people pleasing. I couldn't help it. I didn't like to do something wrong and having anyone mad at me.

"If you're sure." I sat and arranged my food.

"Yeah. Tomorrow's my birthday, so"—he gestured across the table—"this is nice."

"Oh, really? That's cool. My sister's birthday was yesterday. How old are you?" I have a propensity toward impulsivity. He wasn't a girl, so asking his age shouldn't have offended him, but he appeared perturbed.

"Twenty-seven."

His bland tone told me he wasn't happy about it, so I made a joke. "Twenty-seven on the twenty-seventh! Ha, ha, that's funny."

My attempt to lighten the mood worked. He grinned at me and rolled his eyes. "You goofball."

That made me feel good. RC was twenty-seven, four years older than me. Not bad.

"Your girlfriend's hot."

I looked at him. "Thanks." The change of subject back to Tara must have meant he didn't want to talk about his age or he was trying to make small talk. Either way, I didn't mind. We rarely talked at lunch, so it was nice to hear him try. Plus, he had a nice voice.

He said, "Too bad you blew her off to eat lunch with me."

I stopped abruptly, my mouth hanging open, inches from biting my sandwich. I set it back down. "You heard that?" I couldn't believe it.

"Nick, sound travels through this dining room as if it was an amphitheater. If there aren't any customers, then, yeah, I hear everything."

"Did you hear about Saturday?"

"Yup. Blew her off so you could sleep?"

"How did you know?" I was astounded. It was as if he could see into my head.

"That's what I'd have done. A girl like that, who talks as much as she does and controls your every move, would tend to be exhausting. I'd need a day to sleep. Or a week even."

I nodded in agreement and took a bite of my sandwich. He seemed to be in tune with my exact train of thought. Although, him listening in to our conversation was a tad unsettling. And he'd made it sound like he could hear me talking all the time. What kinds of things had he heard? Marcy and I talked about lots of stuff. Had he eavesdropped on her talk about me dating Corey?

Crap. I didn't want to think about that. I would end up overanalyzing everything I had said in the past six weeks. Instead I picked up a gravy-drenched fry. Maybe he hadn't heard any of our discussions. I hoped. I put the focus back on Tara. "Was I obvious?" I asked. "You know, about not wanting to eat lunch with her?"

RC shook his head. "No. Not really. I think I was the only one who could figure it out, because you had *just* mentioned eating with me. You're good. Plus, she's pissed over missing your day off. Lunch is the last thing she'll obsess over. Most likely, she'll put out on Saturday."

His reference to our date made me uncomfortable, but only because I wasn't looking forward to seeing her as much I should have. Yes, I would get laid, but I almost didn't care. "Yeah, you're probably right." Slowly, my nerves settled. RC read the newspaper like he normally did, and I ate.

Silence. It was bliss.

We were having lunch together for the third time. I barely knew him. Last week we hadn't said one word to each other, and I'd loved it. But now... I didn't know. I enjoyed the silence, but I also wanted to know more about him. *Shouldn't I ask him something?* For example, where did he work or did *he* have a girlfriend? I was almost done with my food; what if I ran out of fries and had to punch back in? What, then? I'd have to wait another week to ask him something about himself.

"Spit it out," RC said matter-of-factly.

"Spit what out? My food?" I was stumped as to why he'd tell me to spit out my half-chewed fry.

"No, Nick, your questions. You keep glancing at me and then looking away. I can tell something's on your mind. You're either on the verge of peeing yourself, or you have a zillion questions perched on the tip of your tongue. So ask."

RC had a certain way of speaking that was both stern and direct, but with enough softness that I knew he wasn't bothered. I didn't know *how* I knew he wasn't bothered, but I did. Maybe it was how he kept nervously glancing at me in the same way I was nervously glancing at him. I saw that same tip-of-his-tongue edginess, but I guess I wasn't forward enough to point it out. I *could* be bold—I had the balls—but with RC, so far, I'd felt reticent. I didn't want to screw up the budding friendship before it was secure.

He'd told me to talk, so I did. I said, "Your skin's clearing up."

He shrugged. His shoulders dipped down away from his neck, and it made me think he liked that I'd noticed. "That's not a question," he said as he sipped his soda through the straw.

"No, it's not. But I was wondering what changed."

"Job."

"You got a new job? Where?"

"Same place, different position."

"Oh?" I lifted my eyebrows. I was hoping he'd catch the hint I wanted to hear more, because so far, one to three words at a time was not my idea of the conversation I was itching to have. Not too chitchatty, but enough to get to know the guy. Luckily, my expression seemed to work.

RC explained, "I work in a clothing factory. I used to press fabric with a machine that looked like a gigantic iron. It was very hot, and I sweated profusely all day long. My face broke out in March, and I haven't been able to get the acne under control since."

"You have acne?" I couldn't believe I'd said it, and by the look on his face, RC didn't either. He glared.

"Annywaay," RC huffed at me. "I went to the doctor and he gave me some cream. It didn't work. I tried all kinds of cleansers and shit, but nothing cleared it up. I even had to stop shaving because razor burn, on top of the acne, made my skin painful and horribly red. After months, one of the nurses asked me what I did for a living. When I told her I was around hot presses all day, she suggested the acne had to do with sweat and oil buildup. She recommended a facial cleanser from Arbonne." He suddenly pointed at me. "And don't you make fun of that!"

I held up both hands and shook my head.

RC continued. "So I asked for a transfer to something less sweaty. Last week I was moved to the Alteration Department."

"Cool. So you do alterations on stuff?" I was trying to sound excited about his new job, but I had no idea what it was he did.

"No. Basically, I collect the mail from the dock. I bring suits that come back for alterations to my department. I inventory them. I go to the office and pull the paperwork. I deliver them to the appropriate departments for the alterations. Then I do everything in reverse and collect suits at the end of the day and box them up to mail. It's not that exciting, but I do move around all day. It's a ton of walking, so I'm hoping it will help me lose more weight. The downside is that I used to be alone most of the time, just me and the pressing machine. I didn't have anyone to answer to. I took long breaks, but as long as my work was done, no one cared. Now? Not so sure I can keep it up. The work is more demanding, time-wise."

Worry wiggled in my stomach. "So, you won't be able to have lunch with me once a week?"

RC smiled. I liked the way his brown eyes softened when he looked at me. "Nice to know you'd care. But yeah, I'm not sure. It's difficult to get away for an hour. I have to drive here, order, wait for the food, and then drive back. Eventually someone will notice I'm not taking thirty-minute lunch breaks like everyone else."

A light bulb went on. "What if *I* make you lunch at the same time every day? I surprised you today and you liked it. I could do that every week. It would save you time. I could just make your food when I make mine and have it ready for you." It seemed like a great suggestion to me.

RC smiled again. I liked his smile. Sure, his unruly, patchy facial hair was getting on my nerves because it practically grew into his mouth; but when he smiled, his eyes lit up like a little kid who'd gotten a puppy for his birthday. "You'd do that?" he asked.

"Sure. We're friends, right? I like eating lunch with you. You're not demanding I stop the world to pay homage. You're not giving me shit for sleeping in on Saturday mornings. I don't feel pressured to talk every time we're together, and you aren't trying to get me into bed like all the girls I work with."

RC chuckled. "You have a really tough life, don't you Nick?"

"You have no idea."

"And it doesn't bother you?"

"What doesn't?"

"Being on demand for sex? Like a man-whore." I guess that cleared up whether or not he'd heard Tara's comment about cutting me off. *He heard her.*

The word "whore" slammed against my pride, though. The way he said it took my thoughts away until I was only left with that one word: whore. Was I a... *whore*? A slut? Was I really on demand for sex? I fucked the girl I dated. And I only dated one girl at a time. I only had sex with my girlfriends, not random girls. No, I wasn't a slut. "Why would you say that?" I asked, because it hurt my feelings.

He shrugged. "I don't know. You said you had lots of girlfriends and you fucked practically anyone. Seems kind of slutty to me. And you said girls are out to get you into bed. Isn't that what happens when the guys are the ones after one particular girl? She's the slut because she's easy. Well, you're apparently easy. Hence—whore."

I swallowed hard. I'd never thought of myself like that before. I *was* pretty easy. I didn't think I'd ever turned someone down except Marcy, and that was only because we worked together. If she didn't work here, I'd have fucked her. Suddenly I didn't feel like eating. I was a little nauseated with myself. I was a man-whore. That's what RC had called me, and it was true. Here I'd been thinking all along that I was God's gift to women. I was sexy, and therefore, they all wanted me. But maybe I was wrong? Maybe they wanted me because I was *easy*?

My brain stopped after two seconds of contemplation. No, I was a hot stud. I was cut. I could make a girl come so hard she'd shake for ten minutes. They wanted me because I was God's gift to women. I sat back and smiled at RC.

"Slutty or not, everybody wants some, because I'm *that* damn good!" I flashed him a self-assured smile and reached for my cup. I sipped the last of my drink until there were only dribbles left among the ice, and I slurped some more.

RC chuckled. "Are you always this arrogant and vain?"

"Yup," I replied.

He laughed. It was a hearty, deep laugh, and I liked it.

"So, why do you wear long-sleeved shirts all the time? It's June."

RC lost his smile. Why he was so serious, I wasn't sure. "I don't like people seeing my arms."

"Are they messed up? Like a serious, deforming burn or something?" I asked, concerned about what the reason might be.

"No," he said. "It's to hide my tattoos. Besides the fact some employers dislike tattoos, I don't like people staring."

"But I thought the idea of having a tattoo was to get people to look. I think they're pretty cool. Ya know?" Because now I was interested to know what he was hiding. "I'd like to see them."

"My tattoos are personal. I don't like people looking at me. People are always pointing out something they don't like, and I'm tired of it. I liked my job with the presses, because I basically saw no one. Now, I'm surrounded by people all day, and I hate it."

"Why?" I asked, because I truly wanted to know.

He raised his voice a little, and it came out harsher than I'd ever heard before. "Because people are shit, Nick, and they treat other people with judgment and ridicule without the slightest thought given to another human being's feelings!"

RC abruptly rose and grabbed his tray. He practically stormed over to the trash can and dumped his trash. He was out the door before my brain could catch up to the fact he'd just walked out on me for no apparent reason. Then it clicked, and I jumped up to follow.

I rushed, yelling, "Wait!" I made it to RC as he was opening the door of his Ford Ranger. "RC. Stop!"

He turned. "Go back inside, Nick. Go back to your happy little sex-every-day life. Go back to your girlfriend and your perfect world of vanity where everyone wants you. I'm happy for you. Planet Nick sounds like a great place to live."

He shoved me away and shut the door. Before I could protest, he'd turned the engine over and pulled out of the parking spot. Just like that, he was gone.

"What?" Bewildered, I watched his truck go down the road until it disappeared.

Chapter 9: *Pretty People*

I PICKED my shirt off the floor and pulled it on over my head. Tara was still cooing in her contentment, so I made use of my time and got dressed. I knew my mom wouldn't be out forever, and I was *not* about to get caught having sex in my room. Or worse, have Mom *hear* me again.

"Tara, come on. You have to get up," I said. I looked in the mirror and fingered my hair. I wanted it to look perfect enough to seem like I hadn't had sex, but not so perfect Mom would think I was covering for the fact I'd just had sex. My hair looked awesome most of the time anyway. It had just enough wave to keep it from being flat, but not so much it ever stuck out. I had perfect hair; others probably envied me.

I smoothed the sides one more time and turned back to Tara. "Tara!"

"Okay, okay. You don't have to yell. Just because you couldn't get it up doesn't mean you have to get snippy with me for enjoying *my*self."

Tara tossed back the covers, and I turned away for some bizarre reason. I didn't know why. I mean yes, I was a little weirded out that I couldn't get hard this time—a first for me—but I wasn't mad at Tara. There was this inexplicable, subconscious response in my gut that told me I shouldn't look. I've seen her naked loads of times, but why I couldn't bring myself to look at her now made me worry about myself more than if I'd just named a random nonreason. She had a wart on her toe—anything. But no, I was the guy who had a very beautiful woman in his bed and couldn't get it up. I was the guy who stood stock-still in my room after getting her off, as if I was eleven all over again, scared shitless I'd get caught looking at my dad's porn. I had this baffling surge of fear that told me I didn't want to be here.

"Are you okay?" Tara asked.

She startled me because I'd thought she was looking on the floor for her bra. Instead, she was fully dressed and standing by my side. "Um, yeah, fine. Why?"

"I've never seen you so jumpy. Are you sure you want me to meet your mom? We can do it another day. It's gotta be embarrassing not being able to… you know."

She was rubbing my back, which I thought was really nice, but her rude comment about my inability to perform ruined it for me. "Yeah, okay. I think you're right. Maybe I won't be so nervous if we wait. Mom didn't like Chrissy much. She's going to be harder on you."

It was easier to talk about Chrissy and meeting my folks later on. Everything else going on in my head was a swampy mire of a muddled mess, and I couldn't wade through it. I needed something easy to take away the confusion. This was the one time I longed to go to work. Or sleep. Fuck.

Tara opened my bedroom door, and I followed her out, rubbing my face. She laughed, reminding me of the comment I'd made one second before. "Well, I think I'm way better looking than her. And I'm better at talking to parents. Chrissy's mom is never around, and her stepdad drinks all the time. I don't think she's had good examples to relate to."

What Tara said made me sad for Chrissy. "Yeah, maybe not."

We left the house, and Tara suggested a movie—shocker! But it was fine. As we sat in the theater, I had my arm around her shoulders. She watched, and I contemplated my behavior. I wasn't sure what had gotten into me, but I'd felt strange since Wednesday.

Wednesday. *How odd.*

RC! He had to be why. I just didn't understand why he'd left like that. What had I said? I sighed and squeezed Tara's shoulders, and she leaned closer. It was nice, I guess, snuggling in the seats, but if I was honest, I didn't want to be at the movies. My mind was *not* on Tara. I hadn't been thinking about her the entire evening, which could have been why sex was so disappointing for me.

I don't think I even remember the movie we watched.

Later, we played minigolf, which made me realize it was the first time in a month of dating we'd done something fun together, out of doors. We were on the fifteenth hole when she asked, "Are you going to Dawn's party?"

She mentioned Dawn, and I missed my putt. Shit! "Uh, I don't know," I shrugged. I took my shot and sank it. "Why do you ask it like that? Wouldn't we go together?"

"I guess. I know you dated her."

"And I know you're friends with her. So?" I asked. "What's the big deal?"

Tara lined up her ball and tapped it. "We are friends, but I don't want you to feel uncomfortable."

I grinned at her. "Tara, we're fine. Dawn and I have always been fine. If you want to go to the party, we can. When is it?"

"Next Saturday night. Do you work?"

I tapped my ball as I thought about my schedule. *I'm off one Saturday a month unless I ask ahead or switch with someone. And I am* not *going to mention the Saturday I had off and risk her wrath.* I replied, "I'm pretty sure I have to work, but I think it's eleven to eight. We could go after."

She smiled so brightly an onlooker would have thought I'd given her the moon. She hopped up and down, clapping her hands. "Yay! I'm so glad you don't mind. A lot of the old gang will be there. Like Mary-Louise's parties, only with marijuana."

"Seriously? Who's got the drug connection?"

"Terrell knows a guy," Tara said it like it was no big deal, but it was.

"Tara, what if we get caught?" I didn't trust Terrell, and it had nothing to do with him screwing my ex-girlfriend.

"We won't. Believe me." She putted and sank a hole in one. Then she screamed, "Woohoo! Did you see that?"

"Yeah. Good shot." I tried to seem enthused, but I wasn't. I kept looping what she'd said in my head. Like I needed one more thing to think about. "The old gang." I hadn't seen them for months. Who would be there? M-L and Shawna? More specifically, would Corey show?

I WATCHED everyone. It's what I did. I was like the "creeper" in some horror flick trying to pick out my next victim. *How macabre,* I thought. I wasn't that sadistic. I only observed. I found watching people more amusing than getting butt-stupid drunk. I drank beer, but it was more social than for any other purpose. On occasion I'd end up passed out on someone's lawn or living room floor, but it was less and less frequent as the years progressed.

Tonight, though, I wouldn't have minded getting drunk. My mind had not shut down all week. I was fucking tired of thinking. Last Saturday, I'd been thinking about the possibility of seeing Corey and gotten all fluttery. But as the week progressed, my mind looped reruns of the last time I'd seen RC, and thoughts of Corey drifted out an open window. RC hadn't shown up on Wednesday. Ten days had gone by since he'd stormed out, and I didn't know if I'd ever see him again. Would he be in next week? It made me miserable to think he wouldn't be.

I'd spaced out a million times this week thinking about what he'd said and what I'd said, and what I could have done differently. Nothing made sense. There really was no logical reason why he would have bolted like he had. RC had just up and disappeared out of my life, and I was left going through the motions of enjoying myself at a pointless party with a bunch of people I knew in the biblical sense, yet didn't know at all. I hated my life.

I felt a presence behind me, but before I turned, M-L said, "Hey." She nudged me with her elbow as she sidled up next to me.

"Hey back," I replied, giving her a one-armed hug, careful not to spill my beer. "I didn't know you'd be here." One small glimmer of happiness in the mass of depression.

"Neither did I. It was a last minute decision, or I would have texted you. I was at my mom's, helping her after her surgery, and Chrissy told Shawna she should come," she said and sighed. I could tell she wasn't thrilled.

"How's your mom?"

"She's fine. It was laparoscopic gallbladder surgery. No big deal. But it was nice to see she felt so much better having me there."

"So things are good between you?"

"Yeah. She likes Shawna a lot, so that helps. It's a strain with my dad. He's not too happy. We're still shaky, him being a pastor and all. One day at a time."

I'd missed the fact that M-L was gay for a long time, but she'd come out to her parents as soon as she and Shawna were officially dating. "So, Chrissy's here too, eh?" I leaned against the doorframe and scanned the crowd. There must have been a hundred people crammed in Dawn's parents' house.

M-L smirked at me. "Is this your version of hell? All your ex-girlfriends in the same room?"

I gave her a thin smile. I knew she was only trying to be funny. "Shut up. No. I don't really care. They all know each other anyway. The weirdest part is looking around the room and realizing I've slept with 90 percent of the women here."

"And I think I slept with the other ten."

I looked at her in shock.

M-L winked. "Just kidding. I'm not promiscuous. I can only imagine how weird it feels for you. I guess the only one missing is Corey."

My cheeks got warm at the sound of his name. I looked away, focusing instead on a group of partygoers in the living room. Everything came back to him, didn't it?

I heard her continue, though I was trying to say without speaking that I wished she'd drop the subject. I wasn't in the mood. "Is that what you're doing here? Are you taking inventory of the guests, hoping to spot Corey in the crowd?"

"No!" I blurted defensively. I furrowed my brow. Why did she keep bringing him into the conversation? I wasn't sure I was ready to talk about all the strange feelings he stirred up in me.

M-L didn't shrink away from my angry glare. She gave me the hairy eyeball right back. It was a look my aunt used to use when she asked me about sneaking brownies before breakfast, and I answered "no," but had the remnants of evidence smeared up my cheek. M-L's look said, "Are you sure that's your answer, because I know you're lying."

I hung my head but stuck to my guns, only with less conviction. "No, I wasn't looking for Corey. Really."

"Then what's eating you? You're not acting like your swaggering self."

I didn't know what to say. I wasn't feeling like myself, but there were too many people around to talk about it in the house. I shook my head and drank some of my beer. I guess the silence was too much for M-L, because she looped her arm around mine.

"Come on," she said. "Let's go outside and sit on the back porch." She tugged and I followed.

I was somewhat concerned to leave without saying anything to Tara, but then I glimpsed her sitting in another room with Dawn, Chrissy, Terrell, John, and Steve as M-L and I walked down the hall. Tara would be fine. She probably wouldn't even notice I'd gone.

Outside, the stars were bright. The air was warm, and I smelled the rose bushes that were planted beside the deck. It wasn't quiet, because the music could still be heard, but it was more private. We sat on the bottom step of the stairs that led from the deck to the yard, and I finally relaxed. I needed this. M-L was very thoughtful.

She was quieter than usual. It was as if she knew I needed to think before I spoke. The problem was how messed up my thoughts were. I couldn't organize them to make sense.

"Have you ever made someone angry, but you didn't know what you did?" I said, finally.

"Yes, I think so. It's hard to please everyone all the time."

"I know. But… it's like… this time, I really don't know what I did."

"Tara doesn't seem angry."

I looked M-L in the eyes and shook my head gently. "No, it's not Tara." I looked back to the yard, trying to make out the shapes of things in the dark. One silhouette looked like a bicycle and another shape was a birdbath.

"Then who's got you in a tizzy for making him or her upset?"

"A friend." I paused and added, "I think."

"You *think* he's a friend? Or you think you made him mad?"

"I didn't say it was a *he*."

"No, you didn't. But I've never seen you unsure over a woman. You're normally very confident. Although… I guess if you were in love, it would mess with your brain enough to—"

I interjected, "I'm not in love."

"Okay. Not love. But worried about hurting someone. Who?"

I sighed, "This guy at work." I had to get my feelings off my chest. I trusted M-L. If anyone would *not* make fun of me for caring, it would be her. "He's a customer. I thought we were friends, but last week he got angry and stormed out of the restaurant." I huffed again, my chest rising and falling fast as I blew the air out of my lungs. This was harder to talk about than I'd thought. "He didn't come in this week. He's normally there every Wednesday. We eat lunch together. Then he didn't show, and I don't know what to do."

"Did you call him? If it's only been a week, maybe he's ill."

I shook my head. "I don't have his number." Ill? I guess he could have been. "Maybe he is, but it's oddly coincidental he'd be sick when last week he got mad at me."

"What did you say?"

"That's just it. I don't know. I've been going over the conversation in my head for days. We were talking about Tara, he said she was hot, then the next thing I know, he's yelling at me about people being shit and bolting out the door. We were having a conversation, and he left in the middle of it. On top of that, he called me a slut. I'm the one who should have been angry."

"Why'd he call you a slut?" she asked, and then she snickered.

I glared at M-L, who was trying to hide a smirk behind her hand. "It's not funny!" I snapped.

She tried to contain herself, unsuccessfully. "No, it's not. You aren't slutty at all." She burst out laughing, and I jumped off the step. She followed me into the yard. "Nick, I'm sorry. I didn't mean to make fun of you."

"Yes, you did!"

"All right, I did. But I didn't mean to hurt your feelings. Really. Come on. Sit back down with me. We haven't talked like this in a long time. I want to know more about this guy. Please?"

I took a deep breath and exhaled. Reluctantly, I returned to the step with her.

After a few minutes, she broached the subject again with more tact. "So, this guy, he called you a slut?"

"An easy slut," I corrected her. "Actually, I think his exact words were man-whore."

"Ouch. But you didn't get angry about it? He did?"

"Not exactly. It wasn't about that. I asked about his tattoos, and he got crappy with me."

"Oh? What were they of?"

I shrugged. "I don't know. He wears long-sleeved shirts all the time. They're covered up."

"In the summer?"

"That's what I said! But RC explained he doesn't like people staring at him, and I guess tattoos do garner a certain amount of attention from people."

"RC?"

"That's his name. Or a nickname. That part's not clear."

"Hmm. Sounds like he got upset over something you aren't privy to."

"What do you mean?"

"You pushed a button, Nick. Sometimes irrational anger comes out when a person's button is pushed. If you aren't aware of it, then you sit around dumbfounded." She reached over and cupped my cheek. "Hence, this sad look upon your beautiful face."

I grinned despite my irritation and said, "Shut up. I'm not a girl."

"No, but you're beautiful all the same."

"If you weren't into girls, would you sleep with me?"

"No."

Her answer came way too quickly for comfort. I was offended. "Why?"

"Because I value intimacy. Sex isn't intimate by itself. It's just sex—sloppy, carnal, fleeting. I want more."

"More?"

She smiled. "More. Conversation, breakfast in the morning, and snuggles at night. I want to hold hands through a park and swing on the playground. I want more."

I'd never thought about it like that before. "'More' sounds nice." I took a deep breath. The faint sound of crickets could be heard if I concentrated on blocking out the music from inside. Crickets. The sound soothed me. "Last week, when Tara mentioned the party, I admit I was hoping to see Corey."

"But...?"

Normally I would finish my thought when I looked at her, especially after she seemed to know I had more to say on the matter. Except I couldn't, not right away. This part was more difficult. My eyes darted from her left eye to the right and back again. My only comfort was knowing she wouldn't judge me. "I was thinking about Corey until Wednesday. Up until then, I was wondering if he would be here and if he'd want to hook up again, and if he'd missed me like I've missed him. Then, after RC didn't show, I couldn't think about Corey anymore. I wanted to know why RC wasn't there. What RC was thinking when he sped off in his truck. Why was he so mad? I thought we were friends. I can't stand the idea that I'll never see him again. Things were going so well. And then it all stopped, and I feel... helpless."

"You really like him, huh?"

I nodded.

"Is he cute?"

I snorted through my nose. "No."

She looked surprised by my reaction. "Wow! Way to cut the guy down."

I knew I needed to clarify or she'd think I was really horrible. "I mean, I wouldn't categorize him as 'cute,' exactly. He's more... rugged."

"Rugged like a mountain man?"

"No, just, rugged. Overweight, unkempt, kind of gross."

"That's not helping."

"I'm sorry. I know I sound awful. RC's just... well... I don't know. He's kind of burly, but he has potential, put it that way. When I first met him, he had horrible acne because he had this job that made him sweat and stuff, so his skin got nasty looking in the past few months, but it's clearing up now. Plus, he couldn't shave, so his beard is all squirrely, and he has a unibrow. I hate those."

"Me too."

"But it's not his looks that matter right now. I don't care about that. I want to know why he's mad at me."

"Such the peacekeeper."

"No, that's not it. Not this time. I know you know I can't stand people being mad at me—I get that—but this is different. It's *RC*. I was just starting to feel comfortable with him. Like, we could sit there through thirty minutes of lunch and not talk, and it was okay. And he could walk in during a busy lunch, nod in my direction, and that was all the communication we needed. I didn't feel obligated to drop everything and hug him like I do Tara. She gets mad if I don't kiss her good-bye. I don't like that kind of pressure. I want comfortable. I want content. I want to be myself without trying to anticipate when the other person is about to have a shit-storm because I did or didn't brush my teeth after giving head."

"Who did that?"

"Tara."

"Oh."

"I'm just sick of everything. I hate my life."

M-L leaned her head on my shoulder and looped her arm around mine. We sat there awhile before talking again. It wasn't like the conversation was over, and we both knew it. It was more like we needed to breathe and think about stuff. I could hear people in the house, but in this moment, it felt like we were alone.

"So, RC, he makes you feel content?" she asked softly. I liked that she wasn't pushy.

"Yeah. But it's different, ya know? He's not like one of us."

"Us?"

"The crowd. Our gang."

"Oh, you mean the stuck-up, pretty people?" She said it like a lament.

"Yeah," I replied, feeling the dread over the truth of it sinking into my skin. We were a shallow group, and the reality of it hadn't hit me until now. "We're all snobs, aren't we? I mean, our crowd. We've been like this for years." It was my turn to lament. "I never saw it before. Every one of us is 'perfect' on the outside. We're all beautiful. Dawn, Chrissy, even Terrell. All the people inside that house could be models or Hollywood superstars. We're all vain. We party, we all sleep together so often it's one step away from an orgy, and we've talked smack about the same things since high school. Nothing changes."

"I think something has."

I glanced over at her and waited for her explanation.

"You and me."

I laughed, "You think I've changed?" It was an absurd thought.

M-L grinned back. "A little. I think you're on the verge of change. You're maturing. And I'm hoping when we leave here tonight, Shawna will feel the same stagnation I felt when I hugged Dawn tonight. College is over. It's time to move on. I think that's why Corey didn't show. He told me he loves his job and really likes living in DC."

"I'm glad."

"Is RC gay?"

I got inexplicably defensive. "I don't know. Why does it always have to come back to that? Corey and I were never together. I told you, I'm not gay!" Although hearing myself protest the point… again, made me wonder how long I could go before someone other than Marcy called me out on my bullshit.

She quickly lifted her head off my shoulder and apologized, "I'm sorry. My question wasn't about you. It was about your friend. Is *he* gay?"

"I don't know. How am I supposed to know? He doesn't *look* gay."

"And what does 'gay' look like?"

I paused. *What does it look like?* "Corey."

M-L started laughing hysterically. She laughed long enough I couldn't help joining in. "Oh, God. Corey, the poster child for gay pride days everywhere. Nick, honey, you can't use Corey as your plumb line."

My laughter slowly faded. "I guess not, but I don't know what *gay* means."

She hugged me. "You'll figure it out."

"I haven't been able to figure much out lately. I've been so confused. I can't stop thinking about RC. I wish I knew what was wrong."

"Then ask him."

"How?"

"Do you know where he lives?"

"No."

"Works?"

"Sort of. I know it's a clothing factory."

"Then google it. There can't be that many clothing factories within lunch distance of Papa's Pizzeria. Do you know what he drives?"

"Silver 2002 Ford Ranger XLT with a regular cab, bug guard, lift kit, and a dented rear bumper. It also has an Exo Terra sicker in the window, but I don't know what that is."

She gave me an odd look and said, "Okay, then find out where all the clothing factories are in and around Westminster and drive through each parking lot until you find it. Then follow him home, knock on his door, and ask what's up. You're not a backseat driver, Nick. Take the bull by the horns and ask him."

"You want me to stalk him?"

"Basically."

I thought about it. "Okay. I think I will. But not yet. I'm gonna give him another Wednesday to stop in for lunch. After that, I'll do it."

"Good! Then maybe, when you get your head straightened out over your sexuality, we can talk again."

I didn't know what to say about her comment. I wasn't confused over my sexuality, was I? I wanted to know what had happened to RC, that was it. I was interested in RC as a friend. A friend. Not a gay friend, and certainly not a fuck buddy like Corey. It wasn't about sex or my sexuality. *God, why can't people leave it alone?*

Chapter 10: *RC*

I OPENED my computer and searched "clothing factories" in the Westminster area. Two popped up. Suspecting that it was a very small number, I also searched the yellow pages online and it produced one hundred and thirty eight results, many of which were not helpful. I didn't think RC worked at Rue 21. I wrote down the ones Google Maps cited, and perused the other list for businesses that sounded more likely than Old Navy or Kohl's.

I sat in my car a full ten minutes before I started the engine. *Am I really going to do this?*

I was about to stalk him. I was literally going to drive around town and randomly search parking lots for his truck until I found it. *Do sane people do these types of things?* Oh God. I didn't know. But I was desperate. I had to know what I'd done to make him mad, leave, and not return. Part of me wished he was sick because then there'd be a rational explanation that had nothing to do with me and my big mouth.

Deep breath. I started the car and left my house. I had gotten out of work ten minutes early so I could go home and change. Plus, I had to shower the stink of grilled onions off my skin. RC said he normally got off work at five. That didn't give me much time. I had maybe an hour. If I pulled into a parking lot too long after five o'clock, chances were higher he would have already left. At the top of my list was English American Clothiers. It was logical to start with the closest to the pizza shop and work my way out. I turned into the parking lot and drove up the short hill to where I assumed the employees parked. I only saw one parking lot. It had to be correct. I looped around the first row, but as I turned the wheel to head down the next, I spotted his truck.

Oh my gosh, I am so fucking lucky!

But now what should I do? I could slowly circle the parking lot until he came out, but then someone might spot me and call the cops for loitering. I stopped and waited with my foot on the brake. Maybe I could park along the street and watch as the cars left? Or I could waltz into the building and pretend to be his brother and ask to speak to him for a second? "Or you could paint 'obsessive asshole' on your forehead in yellow and humiliate yourself in front of everyone he works with!" My brilliance astounded me sometimes, and I felt the need, on occasion, to congratulate myself audibly.

The need to obsess was short-lived as I caught sight of someone leaving the building. A woman in a suit jacket and dress slacks hopped into a Mercedes and pulled out of a space on the back edge of the lot. Yippy. I could slide my Civic into her spot and scan the crowd for RC. So that's what I did. Five fifteen rolled around, and RC came strolling out of the building. Well, not so much strolling as lumbering. His head was down and his shoulders slumped. He was wearing a baseball cap and the bill obscured his face. Same long-sleeved black T, same tight sweats, same ratty shoes. He climbed into his truck and left.

I pulled the hood of my sweatshirt up in case he looked into his rearview mirror—no need to have him spot me prematurely—and pulled into the stream of exiting employees' vehicles. At least they were a polite crowd and allowed me to leave. I was nervous enough thinking about his reaction to getting tailed. Would he yell? Would he slug me? Would he call the police? I allowed two more cars to pull in between us, but no more. I didn't want to lose him. The idea was to follow RC to his house and confront him there, not here in a parking lot full of his coworkers.

M-L had told me I was not a "backseat driver." I wasn't. I was assertive. I was. God, it sounded like I was trying to convince myself. I was assertive, but I also didn't enjoy chastisement of any sort. I'd never liked my mom yelling at me. I was all for getting things right the first time around. I hated being wrong. I wasn't a fan of trial and error. I wanted perfection without the trials and errors. For the most part, I'd been that model son. My mom never had to bug me to do homework and get good grades. I just did it. Then somewhere between high school and a year or two of college, something in me went all lazy-ass. I started slacking. It wasn't that I didn't want to do well; I was simply bored with it. Maybe I wasn't the college type?

Before long, I was following RC down Route 27, right onto Route 140, left onto Pennsylvania Avenue. Oh crap! He stopped. RC pulled into a parking spot along the street. Shit! I passed him, but I kept an eye on him in my mirror. Not the safest way to drive, by the way. Luckily, no one was behind me, so I stopped the car in the middle of the street and paid attention which building he went to. After he disappeared, I turned around and found a space relatively close to his truck and parked.

"But now what do I do?"

I sat in my car. I watched the building. It looked like it could be apartments, but I remembered Shawna telling me this part of town was were the drug dealers lived. Was RC a drug dealer? *No. Can't be.* I surveyed the area from the safety of my vehicle and noticed a group of sketchy characters, pants sagging way below their hips, exchange something. An envelope? A plastic bag? Shit! I looked away and slunk down in my seat. *I'm going to get shot, I know it.* Westminster was generally a safe town, but I didn't want to find out I'd run across a gang of criminals on my first outing as a stalker.

I waited. And waited. And my courage dwindled. The sky no longer held that hint of blue; it was sooty and ominous. I didn't recall a forecast full of rain clouds, but then again, I never paid attention to the weather. It was also 7:26 p.m. What was I doing here? Two hours drifted by and I hadn't ventured over to his building.

I took a deep breath and got out. I locked the car, not that it would stop a burglar if they wanted to steal it, and walked across the street to his building. I went to the entrance I'd seen him use and the stairs lead to two doors. Number twelve and number fourteen. Which one should I knock on? I rang the buzzer and waited. When the door opened, a gangly youth, maybe eighteen, wearing pants six sizes too large, stood there. I think he expected me to say something, but the shock I felt knowing it was the guy from earlier who might have made a drug transaction in front of me held my tongue.

I stammered, "Um, RC? I-I'm looking for RC."

The guy grunted and pointed to the other door before closing his promptly. Nice manners.

I buzzed RC's door, but stood with my back to it as kept my eyes on the other one. Something about knowing drug dealers lived there had my hackles up. I didn't feel right turning my back on that door. I pulled my hood up again and suddenly my sweatshirt felt like a security blanket, covering my exposed head and wrapping me in a warm shell. Nothing could touch me. I shoved my hands into my pockets.

The door opened and I turned. It was RC.

His facial expression transformed radically from confusion to shock to pinched annoyance before he curtly asked, "What are you doing here?"

My sarcasm spilled forth before I had time to consider I was in the wrong, since I was the one who'd done the stalking. I replied, "Gee, nice greeting. No 'hey, how ya doin',' or 'it's nice to see you'?"

Again, his face was awash with emotion. I saw it plain as day. He looked strained, as if holding back a storm, yet something in his eyes flashed fear. Fear? I guess I could instill fear in someone. I'm not the biggest guy in town, but I am built like an Olympic gymnast. I could probably do that ring thingy, hoisting myself up to flip and twirl, but it was the idea of wearing what looked like a manotard—slang for male leotard—that stopped me.

I halted my internal conversation in time to hear, "It's nice to see you. What are you doing here?" He didn't sound afraid, he only looked cautious. I guess I couldn't blame him.

I clenched my fist inside my pocket as a way of grounding myself. And then I said, "Where've you been? Two weeks and you don't stop by?" Oops. My voice came out all aggressive and shit. I didn't intend aggression.

RC's chest rose, and he pulled his shoulders back. He obviously wasn't going to go down without a fight. "Why do you care?" RC growled.

If he wanted a confrontation, I wasn't backing down. I was here for answers. Yes, he had every right to slam the door in my face, but until he did, I was holding my ground. "Because I thought we were friends," I spat, hitting him full force with the sentiment suddenly surging through my veins. "Or we had the potential to be friends until you left me high and dry in the parking lot after our first disagreement. *Which* I'm still bewildered as to what the fuck I said."

I may not be as intuitive as Mary-Louise, but I saw his face blanch right before his cheeks tightened, like he was gritting his teeth.

He was fighting his own emotional war. He hadn't expected me to call us friends. There was definitely something going on inside his head. He hesitated too long between sentences and his eyes wavered between fierce and frazzled. My presence must have been perplexing. He darted his eyes from my face to the door and then returned to me.

Through those now visibly gritted teeth, he hissed, "Let it go, Nick. I'm just some guy you barely know. You don't need me. You have loads of other friends to fill your time."

He tried shutting the door, but I wasn't easily dismissed. His assumption gutted me. *Loads of other friends?* Not hardly. And I was sure as shit not losing this one if that was the best argument he had. I shoved against the closing door, forcing it open. I stepped right up in his face and forced him to either back down and look away or ingest my words. He took a step backward, but held my gaze. "Shut the fuck up, man," I stressed. "I don't give a shit about any of my other friends. I'm here to find you."

"Why?" RC asked, confounded.

"Because...." I paused. This was the hard part. This was the edge of the blade that would emasculate me in his eyes or—as I hoped it would play out—win him over to the friendship side of the line. "Because... I like you, okay? With you, I'm just me, and I don't have to pretend. I don't feel pressured into being one thing or doing another in order to get laid. You're the first friend I've had who isn't out for sex. So shut up and let me in." Of course, the same argument could be used for Paul, but I wasn't fighting for Paul's friendship. To emphasize my point, I shoved RC back as I walked into his apartment like I owned it.

In about two seconds, I figured I'd get pounded senseless by a fist to my face or he'd give in. So I circled what appeared to be the living room. *He certainly doesn't own much in the way of furniture.*

"Gee, Nick, why don't you come in?" RC replied mockingly, and that was all the reassurance I needed to know I wasn't overstepping. His sarcasm rolled right off my back. His directness was a staple in our relationship. *He's glad I'm here.* RC shut the door and motioned toward the couch. "Have a seat?" His ill temper softened.

I glanced around, but there was only one place to sit. "Sure," I said, plopping onto the couch cushion. *Now what should I do?* RC was still standing next to the door. Planted there. I tried not to be obvious as I checked him out, but it was hard not to sneak a peek. There wasn't much else to look at. His walls were bare. He had a couch, a coffee table, and a TV.

"How did you get here?" RC asked, breaking the silence.

"I drove." I smirked at my quick wit.

RC, however, didn't seem to take it humorously. He lashed out loudly. "Are we going to do this all night? Your hard-ass attitude in return for mine?"

"I guess not." I relaxed and pinched the front of my hoodie, pulling it away from my body when I started to sweat. "I stalked you."

RC cocked his head sideways. "Excuse me?"

I shrugged. What else was there to do? It was the truth. "I stalked you," I reiterated. "I planned on casing the parking lots of all the clothing factories in town until I spotted your truck. Luckily I found the right one on the first try. I waited until I saw you come out, and then I followed you home." And if I'd been a serial killer, I'd case the joint for possible kill scenarios.

"How? I mean… I got off hours ago. What did you do in all that time?" he asked.

Although my confession convicted me as a creeper, RC wasn't bothered by it; he focused on the elapsed time instead. *Huh. Who'd have thunk? Dude really mustn't mind me being here.* I hung my head. This part made me look like a wuss. "I was… sitting in my car."

"Why?"

I shrugged again. For a guy who'd barreled into RC's place all guns-a-blazing, I knew I appeared idiotic. "I felt stupid," I explained. "I've never followed a guy home before. And you don't know me, not really. For all I knew, you were gonna think I was a self-obsessed freakazoid with a God complex who can't keep his dick in his pants. I flaunted my girlfriend in front of you, and I feel bad. I didn't mean to be all 'yeah, my girlfriend's so hot' at the restaurant. It just came out that way. She's always hangin' on me. I should have thought about your relational status and not rubbed it in. I'm sorry. And then when you yelled at me and sped off in your truck, I was worried I'd never get to see you again to apologize for whatever it was I said. I honestly don't know. So, if I said something wrong, I'm sorry."

RC didn't sound mad when he responded, "And you thought about all that while sitting in your car?" In fact, he sounded amused.

I nodded. "Yeah, a little. I also sat in my car because I was afraid you wouldn't open the door. It took a while for me to get the nerve up to ring the bell."

RC smiled. "You're an idiot." He chuckled softly, settling my nerves. "You want something to drink?"

I grinned. "Yes, please. It's hot as hell in here. You mind if I take off my hoodie?"

"Nah, go ahead. I keep it warm on purpose, so feel free to make yourself comfortable. I'll grab a couple bottles of water and be right back."

He walked out and I shed my sweatshirt, yanking it over my head. I was left with a plain white T, but unlike when out with Tara, fashion didn't matter. I was with my guy friend. We were hanging: no pressure, no judgments. I hadn't felt this free in a long time.

He didn't have much in his apartment, but I did spy a CD collection, so I walked over and sat on the floor in front of the rack in order to read the names of the bands on the cases. The first thing I noticed was they were all female singers. All of them. And only two I'd heard of. Second thing was how the CDs were alphabetized, and there had to be over two hundred. Incredible. He cleared his throat so I looked up. RC stood next to me holding out a bottle of water.

"I hope water is okay. I don't have anything else," he explained.

"Okay, thanks. Water's great." I took it from his hand and unscrewed the cap. "I'm dehydrated most of the time anyway. Working grill makes me sweat a lot." I took a swallow, which equated to half the bottle.

RC strolled over to his couch and sat, awkwardly silent. Possibly nervous. I didn't know what he was thinking, but the distance between us felt odd. I would have crouched next to me, if I were him, and talked about my collection. He took a position of safety, maybe? If anything, *I* should be the nervous one. This was his house, and I was the intruder, but I didn't feel anxious at all anymore. I took a swig of water and attempted a conversation. "I notice you don't have any male artists in your entire CD collection. Do you not like men?"

RC choked on his sip of water. He coughed noisily and leaned forward, probably trying to expel the water from his lungs. Bummer. But that's when the double entendre hit me! A cold chill rolled down one arm, but I knew I wasn't having a heart attack, so I ignored it.

"Oh, gosh. I mean, shit, I...." I scrambled to correct my unintended insinuation. However, it didn't slip easily off my tongue. Something about *this* apology seemed harder. How dumb could I be? "That came out all wrong. I'm sorry. I meant... you don't seem to be a fan of male singers. I didn't mean to suggest you're gay. I don't know why I said it like that."

RC cleared his throat and looked across the room at me. I felt stupid. I'd been all confidence and surety before, and now I wished I could crawl under the rug. But RC? He stared at me, but not in an "I'm going to kill you" sort of way. He looked fascinated for some reason. I didn't think anyone had ever looked at me as if I was fascinating unless the fascination was over how dimwitted I was. He hadn't known me long enough to think like that. Then he gave me a slight grin. The corner of his mouth lifted, and his eyes shone.

His expression melted into the one he'd had the first time we'd eaten lunch together. He was definitely amused by me. Knowing that made me feel less awkward. I grinned back. Suddenly I knew the rest of the evening was going to go well. The space between us wasn't "safe distance;" it was just air and four steps across the carpet.

RC put the cap on his water and set it down. "You're right. I don't really like male singers," he replied, standing up and joining me next to the CD collection. "I like the pitch of the female voice. I think women sing with more passion than men."

I pointed to the DVD stand and commented, "I find your CD selections an interesting juxtaposition to the action flicks you have stacked over there. *The Bourne Ultimatum, Die Hard, Face/Off, First Blood, Mad Max, Predator, Transformers, Where Eagles Dare.* Those are all tough and violent and full of male actors."

RC merely shrugged. I guess he didn't feel the need to explain his desire to watch men, yet listen to women, and I was okay with that. He liked what he liked. And we were fond of many of the same films.

I turned my attention back to the CDs. "I think I've only heard of two of these singers. I don't really listen to music."

"Seriously?" he said sharply. "I don't think I could get through the day without music." RC pointed to his collection. "Take Adele for example. Rich, soulful voice with a touch of sadness. I listen to her when I'm feeling down. Same with Evanescence. Tracy Chapman is bluesy and mellow. Mary Chapin Carpenter has a gritty voice I like a lot. Avril Lavigne is for the upbeat days because she's fun and perky. Alanis Morissette is for my cynical side. And Aretha Franklin is just plain classic."

As he spoke, I became extremely aware of how close his face was to mine. That's when I noticed the smell of his hair. It was clean and slightly damp, and best of all, not in a fucking ponytail! It was long and curly and tucked behind his ears. It looked soft and not greasy in the slightest. Gorgeous. "And Lady Gaga?" I pointed out the CD case.

"I like her style."

I grinned.

"Although I have to admit, I hadn't heard of her until I saw Johnny Weir skate to Poker Face. Then I looked her up and fell in love."

"And I thought you were going to tell me you liked the beat for workouts."

He nodded. "Yeah, there's that too."

I knew I'd just made a huge assumption, but no one had forearms like that by accident. And RC's biceps were like boulders. His extra weight must have all been in his gut, because his arms were tight. I had told M-L he was kind of gross, but I'd have to text her and recant. He wasn't gross at all. It was his sweaty job. Because his fresh-out-of-the-shower look was kind of hot. Not to mention his newly clear complexion and smooth cheeks. "Your skin looks nice. And you shaved." My voice came out soft and quiet, but I didn't even hear it until his eyes flicked over to me peripherally. *I am so losing my macho card tonight.*

He licked his lips and glanced at the floor. "Thanks," he said, still studying the CDs on his shelf. "A lot of people like Cher or Madonna. And although I like each of their music, neither one is my favorite singer." He purposely did not look at me. I think I was making him nervous all over again.

"Uh-huh." I heard him talking, but I was distracted by his beard. For the longest time I'd been bent out of shape over the squirrel nest he had growing on his face. Now it was gone and his skin was smooth. He had a neatly trimmed line of hair along his jaw from his sideburns to his chin where it connected with a goatee and short mustache. He looked really nice. "You know your thin beard and that long hair makes you look like a gangster. All you need is a Harley," I joked.

He smirked. I think he was trying hard *not* to look me in the eyes, although I'm not sure why. It's not like I was hitting on him; I was merely stating the facts.

He said, "I've thought about a hog, but I don't really want to spend the money on one."

I took that comment to mean I could continue with the compliments. "And I like your tattoo," I added, pointing at his exposed forearm. "It looks real."

His grin widened. "Yeah, his name is Tuck. He was my first snake."

"Was? Did he die?"

RC finally looked me in the eyes. *I like his eyes.* He shook his head. "No. He's four years old now. But he looks exactly like the tattoo on my arm." He turned his arm over and showed me where the multicolored brown snake tattoo wrapped around his arm and back again. I wanted to touch it.

"So, you have a snake? Cool. Can I see?"

"Um, I don't know." His eyes darted from me to his CDs and then back to me. Focusing seemed difficult, and I wondered if I had said something wrong again. He went on, "I don't like to disturb him after he eats. Maybe another day."

"Okay. Next time," I said, realizing in seconds he had inadvertently suggested I come over again. So I asked, "That means I'm welcome to come back?"

"I, uh, I guess. If you want to." He stood up and walked back over to the couch.

He was acting uncomfortable again. How did I keep doing that? What was I saying? Doing? I liked the Celtic cross on his upper arm, but I sensed it wouldn't be a good idea to ask him to lift his sleeve so I could see the whole thing. Maybe another time. I joined him on the couch. It was more of a love seat, so we sat fairly close to each other, which didn't help matters. Why the awkwardness?

"You hungry? I was going to make pasta, but I could order a pizza," he offered.

"No pizza, but pasta sounds great. Can I help?"

He slowly nodded. He couldn't look me in the eyes for more than a second. Was this too difficult? I didn't think I was hard to get to know. There wasn't much to me. He went into the kitchen and I followed, unbothered by his silence and inability to look at me.

"Can I get a pot out for you?" I asked.

"Um, sure," he said. "Under there." He pointed to the appropriate cabinet, and I bent down to retrieve the pot and then handed it to him.

He held it under the faucet and let it fill while I stood next to him.

"Can I grab the pasta?"

"Yeah," he said and pointed.

I opened a cabinet and found about a thousand cans of tuna. "Holy crap!"

He glanced over. "Oh, yeah," he said, "I eat a lot of tuna. Tuna out of the can, baked potatoes after I work out, and pasta about once a month. I'm trying to lose all the weight I can."

I knew it. His shoulder was too hard that time I touched it for him not to lift weights. "Then you probably shouldn't eat at Papa's Pizzeria."

"I shouldn't. But I got hung up eating lunch with my friend every week, so I made exceptions." He grinned, barely.

But his reference to our friendship brought out the biggest smile I had. He made me feel good. I liked the way he looked at me. As I waited, I glanced around. My eyes tended to wander when I had nothing else to do. His counter was clean. Everything was crumb-free and neatly aligned. And like the living room, there wasn't much in the way of furnishings. My mental inventory ended with the tattoo on the inside of his left forearm. "Is that the tattoo you were worried about me seeing?" I asked, sounding as casual as I could.

RC glanced at his arm, exposed because of his position at the sink. I heard him swallow. "Yeah," he whispered. He shut the water off and moved the pot to the burner on the stove, keeping his eyes averted.

"Pride flag?" I guessed, although I hadn't seen a flag like the one he had on his arm that wasn't associated with gay pride.

"Yeah," he muttered, studying the water in the pot as if tiny bubbles would instantly appear.

I had to ask. I had to have confirmation. "You gay?"

"Yeah," he responded. One-word answers flowed easily off his tongue, apparently.

"Huh," I grunted. I know it wasn't the best of responses, but I hadn't been prepared for that one. RC didn't *look* gay. I felt as though I'd stick my foot in my mouth if I gave any reaction that wasn't a compliment or something, so I basically said nothing about it. "Cool. You got sauce in a jar or are you making it from tomatoes? I ask because I noticed that bowl of tomatoes on the table and you look Italian. Making sauce from scratch is a pain in the ass, but I wouldn't want to assume you use jar sauce. I hear Italians are good cooks. Are you a good cook? My mom's a good cook. My friend Corey could be a pastry chef if he put his mind to it. I'm not a good cook myself. I know how to make hot dogs and ramen noodles, which I know sounds dumb considering I work in a restaurant."

Before he answered me about the sauce, I opened a cabinet and poked around until I found some. It was behind the tuna. I was babbling like an idiot. RC was bound to hit me over the head, but I couldn't stop. I rambled about his canned food selection and the type of sponges he stocked. I think I even heard myself say, "How many cans of anchovies does one guy need?" It was like I'd died and was standing outside myself watching me act like a fool. Was it because I knew about his sexuality? Why was that such a big deal?

"Nick, are you okay?" he asked.

I glanced at him and looked away. "What? Yeah, I'm fine."

There was a long pause, and then he asked, "Is this going to be an issue for you? You don't have to stay if it is. I understand."

"What? You being gay? No. Not at all. I've got plenty of gay friends. My friend Mary-Louise is a lesbian. She's probably my best friend if I had to name one. I'm okay with it. And my friend Corey's gay. I'm cool."

RC looked at me skeptically, but didn't press the issue. I think he was trying to figure out if I'd shrink away if he stepped any closer. I guess he'd just have to test it. I wasn't leaving. Then he pointed. "There's a small pot in there we can heat the sauce in. Do you want green peppers? I can sauté some."

I nodded. "Sounds good," I said.

He still looked strained and I wasn't sure why. I was the one who had to fit his gayness into our previously established friendship. He was gay. I was not. Unless he had issues with being around a straight guy? He went to the fridge and grabbed the green peppers, and that's when I noticed a piece of sub wrapping that read "turkey" under a magnet on his fridge. He had ripped it off the sandwich I'd given him almost, what, six weeks ago? I knew my handwriting. And I knew the smiley faces I made on the carryout orders. He'd kept it? Why?

"Hey, Nick, you mind grabbing the cutting board from inside the dishwasher?" he asked.

"Sure." I bent down and found what he'd asked for, but when I turned around, the scrap of paper on the fridge was gone. Had RC noticed his mistake and grabbed it, hoping I hadn't seen it? And why? Maybe he thought Marcy wrote it? But that would make no sense if he's gay. I was confused.

DINNER WENT great despite my inability to focus on more than his tattoo. He didn't talk a whole lot because I couldn't shut up. I told him I lived at home with my parents and I had a sixteen-year-old sister named Jennifer. I mentioned Mary-Louise, Dawn, Chrissy, and Corey. We cleared the table together and after dinner, we played Xbox. That was the best part. To his delight, and mine, we both like *Call of Duty*. And once we started shooting people, I forgot all about RC being gay.

He directed his character around the side of a broken down building and opened fire on the enemy. I laughed and shot someone on the other side. "Die, suckers, die!"

He commented, "I can't remember the last time I played with a real person. I normally play against people online, some from around the world, but never with someone sitting next to me on the couch. This is awesome."

"I think so too! My friend, Corey, doesn't like this game." I glanced at my phone and set the controller down. "I'm sorry, man, I gotta go. I gotta work tomorrow, and I don't function well on no sleep." I stood up and retrieved my sweatshirt from the floor. I slipped it over my head and held out my hand. "Thanks for dinner."

RC took my hand and shook it. "Thanks for stalking me."

"Thanks for not calling the cops or punching me for doing it."

He smiled and finally let go of my hand. He held it a little too long if you ask me. Was it a challenge to see if I'd freak if a gay guy held my hand? Or did he like my grip? Whatever. I went to the door, but paused in the open doorway. "Could I get a phone number? Maybe we could hang out sometime."

His eyes widened. "Okay. But, I, um… I don't have a cell phone. I only have a house number. You can reach me after six or leave a message." He grabbed a pen off a small table by the door and scribbled down the number.

I lifted my eyebrow. "What? You're kidding, right? Ninety-nine percent of the population have cell phones."

He looked as though I had held my hand up to my forehead with my fingers in an L-shape signifying loser. "I don't," he sighed. "Nobody calls me."

I chose to ignore that very pathetic admission. If he truly didn't have friends who called him, then that was going to end with me. "Well, then you need to get one. That way we can text. Easier and faster than calling. Seriously, think about it." I took a step out the door and added, "See you next Wednesday?"

He nodded. "Yeah."

After I got into my car, I had to pinch myself to make sure I wasn't dreaming. "Ouch! Nope, I'm awake."

I texted M-L: *I stalked RC and he didn't call the cops on me. We're friends. I feel great. Thanks for putting me up to that.*

She texted back: *No prob. Glad to help. Hope to meet him one day.*

"Meet him?" I mused. *I guess she would. If he's my friend, wouldn't I include him in the stuff I normally did?*

I drove home worried about the outcome if I did include RC by taking him to one of the near-orgy parties with the "pretty people" as M-L called them. Yeah, right. That would not go over well. I dismissed the ridiculous notion and drove home listening intently to the quiet purr of my engine.

Chapter 11: *Dates*

M-L WAS right. Stalking RC might have been a little iffy when I'd done it, but it totally paid off. Being there was awesome. He kept his guard up, even I could tell that, but overall, we bonded in a way I'd never done with anyone. We talked, we played Xbox, we even cooked dinner together. Jeez, I'd never done that. I barely cooked anything besides ramen noodles, and there I was in his kitchen, rambling on about tomato sauce. I was such a dork. Actually, a "dork" was a whale's penis. I was not that big. I glanced down and grabbed myself for good measure, and assessed. No, not whale sized, but not bad.

Ahem, I was distracted easily. Where was I?

RC. His being gay threw me. I admitted it. I hadn't expected that. But was I bothered? Not really. He was just a *different* gay than Corey.

M-L had asked me the other night what I thought gay looked like. Honesty I hadn't thought about it. Before Corey, none of that mattered. It was all about the women I fucked. But then Corey had entered my stable world, and since then I hadn't felt as secure. I didn't really know what I wanted anymore. "What does gay look like?" M-L had asked.

The heck if I knew. So, I googled it.

It turns out, if you googled pictures of "gay men" on the Internet, you got stuff ranging from celebrities like Elton John and Zachary Quinto to what Google termed "twinks" who seemed way too young for me to be looking at and not feel like a pervert, to guys who wore makeup and dresses, which I was *not* into, to guys kissing, guys posing, and to my surprise, pictures of guys who were large and hairy, yet sexy as *fuck*. Oh. My. God. I never knew about this before.

The pictures of hairy men were categorized as "bears." Wikipedia stated, "In gay culture, a bear is a large, hairy man who projects an image of rugged masculinity." RC would completely fit that profile. He might be quiet, but there was no doubt in my mind he was very masculine, strong, and able to take charge.

Maybe that's why I was so drawn to him.

I always felt like I had to be in charge. I had to be on my game everywhere I went and it was exhausting. Sometimes, I wanted to follow someone else's lead. I wanted to go where that person wanted to go, and do what that person wanted to do, and not have to think much about it. And I couldn't cite Tara. She wasn't *occasionally* drawn to take charge; she was controlling. With a little support, RC would fit that role. I wasn't sure how much confidence he had at the moment, because he did seem hesitant, but I thought it was because of what he'd said about "people being shit." If he'd been dicked around, then I couldn't blame him for being on guard around me. He didn't know me. Not really.

Still…. Surprising him like that was the best thing I had ever done. It was ballsy and exhilarating. I didn't know if he was going to let me in or punch my lights out.

And RC was gay.

Hmm, I was still pondering what that meant to me. And another thing I couldn't get out of my mind was his absolutely gorgeous hair. Holy shit, I wanted to touch it. It was long with looping curls like Dawn's, only RC's thin beard, which lined his jaw and framed his mouth with a neatly trimmed goatee, made him look really, really good. If he had a gold hoop in his ear and a puffy shirt, he could be a pirate. Ha, ha. I don't think he'd like that depiction. But yeah, he could easily pass for a pirate. Tats, long curly hair, brutish body. I'd had a thing for pirates since I was little and my dad let me watch *Sinbad of the Seven Seas* with him. It was a cheesy movie, but made me dream of sailing the ocean one day like Sinbad.

And if RC was the captain, I'd be on that boat in a flash! I could be his cabin boy.

My mental slideshow screeched to a halt. *Oh man, I need to stop thinking about him like this.* RC's my friend. That. Is. It.

AFTER MY visit, life returned to normal. RC didn't wait until Wednesday. He popped in Friday after work to get a sub to take home. I was working and we were slammed, but I got that surreptitious chin-lift of his and knew things were perfect between us. No words needed. I grinned his way, and he picked up his order and left.

Comfortable. I liked comfortable.

By the weekend I was out with Tara like always. I felt good. I had made a friend, a guy friend, I got laid regularly by my girlfriend, I worked, I played, and I considered that maybe, just maybe, my life wasn't sucky after all.

A COUPLE of days went by, and I was in my normal routine of work, sex, lunch with RC, work, sex… so boring. Tara texted me to say she was going on vacation with her family soon and asked if I wanted to go. Did I? I didn't know. I liked Tara, but was I in that place where I could spend a whole vacation with her and her family? I had to think about it.

Overloaded with "family vacation" thoughts, I sat in silence at lunch. We sat quietly several Wednesday afternoons, so RC didn't notice I was extra pensive that day. He asked, "What are you up to this weekend?"

I shook off the inner worries and said, "Um, I'm off. My parents are having family over. Cousins or something, I don't know. Mom wanted me to be social for a few hours. Later I have a date with Tara. Her parents are doing something, and she has the house all to herself."

"Doesn't that happen all the time? It seems the two of you are always at her house when her parents 'conveniently' step out for a few hours."

I wasn't bothered to answer. I could see why he'd think that. "Not really. It's only been a few times. We go out all over the place. Last week we had sex in my car at the park."

"Very romantic. Is that all you do together, have sex?"

"Yeah, I guess. We play minigolf sometimes. But, yeah, now that I think about it, we do have sex often. We've fucked in my car, at the park, her house, my house, and one time at a hotel when we pretended to have a room on the top floor. We rode the elevator a few times to case the joint and when it seemed like no one was around, I fucked her on the tenth floor up against the elevator doors. It was hot." I loved bragging.

"Seems very superficial to me," he commented before looking back at his newspaper.

RC didn't seem all that thrilled for me and I wondered why. Maybe it had to do with his single status? Oh well, I couldn't make everyone happy.

"Hey, Nick."

I looked up. "Oh hey, Beth."

She glided over to my side and touched my arm. "Let me know if things don't work out with Tara. Okay?"

"Um, sure."

"Okay. Bye." She blew me a kiss, got her carryout order, and left.

"Wow. Does that happen all the time?"

"I guess. I know a lot of people."

"You attract a lot of pretty girls."

I shrugged. And he looked irritated. Maybe if I moved the conversation back to his original question, he'd start talking again. "So, what are *you* up to this weekend?"

He drew in a deep breath and heaved a sigh. I couldn't tell if he was annoyed or didn't want to say. He folded his paper and shrugged. "I don't know. I was thinking of going to see *Iron Man 3* while it's still out. I'm a fan of Robert Downey Jr."

"Oh yeah? I wanted to see that. Gwyneth Paltrow is really sexy."

"Or *Man of Steel.*"

"No. Let's see *Iron Man 3.* I'm off at five on Friday; can we go together? It might give us something to talk about at lunch next week." I wasn't beneath inviting myself places. Most people liked my company.

RC stared at me. Then he smirked.

"What?" I asked. His smirking always meant he was thinking. And usually the thinking was some sort of joke at my expense.

"Nothing. Yeah, we can go Friday. You want me to pick you up after work, or do you want to meet there?"

I shrugged. "We can meet there, then you won't have to drive me back here to get my car."

"Okay. I gotta get back to work." He stood up and grabbed his tray. "I guess I'll see you then."

"Bye." I watched him leave and then cleaned up my trash before I headed back to the time clock to punch in.

This was cool. Something different.

Sex with Tara may have been monotonous, but a family vacation meant I'd have to "behave" almost all the time. I didn't know if I had it in me. When we were together, there wasn't a lot going on in the restraint department, ya know? What would I do with her for a week with her folks around? I didn't want to think any more about it. I pushed away my thoughts on Tara, because now I had a movie to look forward to.

The movies with RC sounded cool. Yeah. Cool. I had not done anything fun with anyone except Tara lately. Even Paul hadn't come by for a while. RC and I were friends, so we should be able to hang together and do stuff. And it could be new and different stuff. It didn't have to be parties like Dawn's. I could hang out with him and do anything I wanted. And this time, I might even get to watch the movie!

WHEN I showed up at the theater, RC was waiting for me. He snagged my arm as I moved to get in line. "I already bought your ticket," he said, holding it up. "Come on. Let's go find a seat."

He opened the door and allowed me to walk through first. Suddenly, this felt like a date, and my mouth went dry. I didn't want a "date." I wanted to hang with my buddy. I followed him across the lobby and up to the snack counter.

"You want anything?" he asked in a way that seemed innocent, but I would not let go of the word "date." I shook my head and looked away in case my trepidation was shining as bright as a neon sign. He bought popcorn and two bottles of water and handed me one.

"I was going to get you popcorn, but it was cheaper to get one big one. We can share."

Dread crept up my neck. What was I doing? I was on a date... with a guy. Shit! This was not my plan. I guess in some way I should have expected it; everyone wants a piece of me eventually, but RC?

Fuck. We sat, and I slouched against the seat waiting for the coming attractions to start. For weeks I'd been trying to forget the notion that RC liked me as Marcy insinuated. After going to his house, things between us were good, normal, some might say boring, but I liked the lack of tension. Marcy's intuition was wrong, and I had been convinced 100 percent RC and I were just friends. Well, 80 percent. Okay, 60 percent of my brain agreed we were friends and the other 40 was still debating whether or not Marcy was spot-on thinking RC was attracted to me. He was gay after all, and I was… me. Yet Marcy's silliness had faded into the background once we were actually friends and had lunch on a regular basis, but now… I didn't know. I guess his attraction to me was back on the table.

I wished I could just vomit out the bile churning in my stomach, but that would mean admitting to what I was debating. I liked denial, remember? *What the fuck do I do if RC comes on to me when the lights go down?* What if he wants to kiss in the movie theater? What if he gropes me? I had been to the movies hundreds of times and could probably count on one hand how many times I'd watched the movie. Girls always wanted to make out with me. Dawn and Elaine had even found the nerve to suck me off during the credits. Was RC just like them?

I was working myself into a knotted mess. When the lights dimmed, I finally got the nerve to ask what was going on. I had to know. Not knowing what he was thinking would make me crazier than ripping off the bandage and knowing for sure. I leaned toward RC and whispered, "RC, is this… is this a date?"

RC lifted an eyebrow and asked, "Do you want it to be?"

I got irritated. Why did he always look amused with me? And why did I get the impression he thought I was stupid? I grumbled at him, "No. Maybe. I don't know! You're the one who bought the tickets and held the door for me and bought the popcorn. That sounds like a date to me." I was shushed from somewhere behind us, and I ducked my head. The last thing I needed was to advertise that I was unwittingly on a date with my guy-friend. I whispered the rest harshly, "Plus, you're gay."

Even though I could hear the resentment in his tone, he replied calmly, "Nick, this isn't a date." He was sensitive to our surroundings and kept his voice to a whisper, but his jaw was tight and his eyes hard. "I paid because I got here first and there was a line. You can easily give me the money for the ticket, or you pay next time. And as far as the popcorn, you don't have to eat it. We're here to watch the movie, that's it. If my sexuality offends you, then move over there." He pointed to a row of seats down in front and went back to watching the previews. "I'm not catering to your insecurities. Besides, you invited yourself."

Oh shit. He's right. I did invite myself. I felt like a dick. Why had I thought this was a date? Because of what Marcy said weeks ago. She hadn't said anything for a while, so maybe that meant she hadn't sensed anything lately. Maybe all my anxiety was for nothing. RC's my friend, and we're just watching a movie together. Guys do that all the time, don't they?

I reached over and stuck my hand into the popcorn. "Give me some of that." I tossed a kernel in my mouth without an apology.

WHEN THE movie was over, and it was awesome by the way, we walked to our respective cars. I had spotted his truck when I pulled in, so I'd parked next to him. Now, my anxiety made things more complicated in light of my embarrassing assumption, I didn't know what to do. Should I follow him to his truck and give him a quick handshake? Or should I see if he stopped at my car on the way by?

The answer came when I hesitated by my bumper and he kept going. He called back, "Later, Nick."

He hopped in his truck and drove away.

I sat in my car feeling like an ass and thought about our conversation in the theater. This hadn't been a date. He didn't want to have sex with me. He didn't expect anything. I took the deepest cleansing breath I could and closed my eyes. *Why do I have to be so stupid?* Answer: "Because you're an ass, Nick!"

I SHOWED up at Tara's Saturday night and just as she said, her parents were out. She wasted no time getting me into bed. In some ways, she reminded me of Dawn. Dawn had been insatiable at least once a month. She'd said it had to do with her hormones, but I didn't care. Dawn fucked like mad, and I was happy. Tara seemed to be a girl along those lines, except so far it was more than once a month. We fucked first, and then she put on a movie and we sat on the couch.

I stared at the screen, but my brain wandered elsewhere. RC. What the hell had I been thinking last night? What's worse was the remnant of disappointment I'd woken up with this morning. I felt like something had been missing, and I was damn sure not going to voice it. I wouldn't voice it, but the thought still wouldn't leave me. RC had driven away and I was disappointed he didn't try to kiss me. He was gay, and I'm... *me*..., why hadn't he tried? Maybe he wasn't attracted to me? That would be a first.

Tara leaned against my arm. She seemed content. "Tara," I said.

"Hmm?"

"You find me attractive, right?"

"Uh-huh."

"Do you think other people do?"

"Mm-hmm."

"Like... do you think... guys would find me appealing too?"

"Yes, Nick. Now would you be quiet? I'm trying to watch this."

I leaned my head back and closed my eyes. She wasn't helping me at all. I went home after the movie was over and went straight to bed.

Chapter 12: *Mary-Louise*

I STAYED in bed most of the day on Sunday, but I couldn't shake my guilt. I called RC's house, but he didn't answer. Maybe he was out? I didn't leave a message. An hour later, after calling him three times and hanging up, I drove to Arlington.

M-L opened the door and invited me in, although I could tell she was surprised to see me.

I walked through her neatly organized apartment and thought how nice it would be to have her as a roommate. Her tastes were simple, yet classy. Earth tones and abstract paintings. I entered the living room and noticed Shawna on the couch watching television.

"Hey, Shawna," I greeted her.

"Nick. Wow, what are you doing here?" she asked.

I sighed. "I don't know. I'm... confused. I guess I don't understand people and Mary-Louise always seems to know what to say. I hope you don't mind." I didn't want to say I felt depressed. It sounded pathetic in my head to admit.

M-L walked past me and asked, "Do you want a drink, Nick?" She turned the light on in the kitchen and opened the refrigerator.

"Um, no, thanks."

"I have beer, water, Pepsi, and some red wine."

I shook my head.

M-L closed the refrigerator door after taking out a bottle of water. "I've never known you to turn down a beer. This must be serious."

I sat on the couch next to Shawna. "Shawna, can I ask you something?"

"Sure," she said. She picked up the remote and clicked off the TV. It was nice to have her full attention. I think she could sense I was in need of some advice. Often, when I talked with M-L for any reason,

Shawna slipped away and gave us some privacy. I guessed now that I'd come over unannounced, she didn't feel that same sense of secrecy. "Shoot," she said.

"When we made out those couple of times, were you attracted to me?"

Shawna choked slightly as if clearing her throat. She glanced at M-L, who had taken a seat in the recliner adjacent to us. M-L commented, "Way to dodge the small talk, Nick."

I shrugged. "I'm having a rough weekend. Plus, it's late. If I dick around with the conversation until it feels right to ask, then it may never happen. I've been living in denial for long enough."

"Oh?" M-L's voice went up. If she'd been a puppy, her ears would have lifted as well. "This doesn't have to do with or conversation last time, does it?"

"Yeah," I admitted with a sigh. I was looking at the floor as I spoke. I didn't want to face her.

"So, you and Corey worked things out?"

I snapped out of my self-reflection. "What? No. It's not about Corey." I huffed loudly. "Why does everyone assume it is all about Corey? Oh, my God! I like Corey, okay? And I miss him, but not everything in the world revolves around our on-again off-again relationship. Jeez."

"Okay. Okay. I'm sorry. Forget I mentioned his name," M-L said as she held up her hand like a white flag.

"So why are you here, Nick?" Shawna asked.

I looked at her. I didn't see judgment or frustration. She seemed interested, but it was a distant interest. Like Shawna knew I wouldn't leave until I talked about whatever was bothering me enough that I'd driven a couple hours on Sunday night to hash it out in person rather than over the phone. "Do you find me attractive?" I asked.

"I don't see how this is going to be of any help to you," M-L said, fingering her short hair.

"Why do you need to know?" Shawna asked.

"I guess… I guess because I'm not used to people turning me down. Or not being interested in me for sex."

"Nick," M-L said, "we talked about this before. It doesn't have anything to do with you. I'm into girls. Unless you have breasts and a vagina hiding under your tight muscle shirt and blue jeans, I'm pretty sure I'd have turned you down no matter what you look like."

"Shawna?" I pleaded for an answer.

"Nick, are you sure you want to know?"

"Yeah." I wasn't, but I needed to hear it.

"Okay. Here it is. When I made out with you, it was an experiment. I was afraid of what I felt for Mary-Louise, so I made a move on you in order to figure it out. I'm sorry. You were popular and all the girls seemed more than willing to have you all over them. I thought if I tried being straight with a guy like you, I'd know for sure."

She was making me sick with the truth. She'd used me. "And...."

"And? You know the 'and,' Nick. I like girls."

I hung my head. "So I'm *not* attractive."

"Nick, don't be stupid. Being attractive has nothing to do with it. You're a great-looking guy, but your looks won't make me straight. I thought you were a fine kisser. Does that help?"

I had to give Shawna some credit. She was trying. "Yeah, I guess."

M-L slipped into the conversation and asked, "So, what does this have to do with *our* recent conversation?"

"That guy, the one I told you about, RC—he's gay."

"Oh." Her voice went up a little. Was she surprised that I'd brought RC up again or was she surprised that I was talking about homosexuality?

"Yeah. He's got a pride flag tattooed on his forearm. That's why he flipped over me wanting to see his tattoos. He said, 'people are shit' and he doesn't like everyone staring at him. I don't know exactly what his deal is yet, but I bet he's been harassed."

"Poor guy," Shawna said.

"Yeah, and then I had to be a dick and say something inappropriate about it."

"You hassled him for his tats? Nick! You already said he's very self-conscious, and the way you described his looks didn't give me any reason to think he's confident at all about himself. Why would you harangue the guy about his tattoos?" M-L turned all accusatory on me. I didn't need her shit, but I had set myself up for it.

"I didn't! It wasn't about the tattoos. I'm fine with them. It was about being gay."

In unison they screeched, "What?"

M-L leveled her stern eyes my way and said, "Of all people, I never thought you'd be the one judging people over sexuality. What about Corey? Are you going to judge him next?" Her tone grew hotter as she spoke. "Are you going to spout off religious propaganda and tell him he's going to hell?"

"What? No." This conversation was getting ridiculous, and they were completely missing my point.

"Well, tell me, Nick, what about this guy made you switch sides and rail against his sexuality?"

"Nothing! I'm not attacking his sexuality. I just don't get why he's not attracted to me."

M-L opened her mouth, and then promptly closed it. She sat back and scrunched her eyes at me. "I thought you said you aren't gay?"

"I'm not."

"Then why do you care?"

"I don't know," I whined. "It just felt weird when we went out on Friday night, and I can't get it out of my head."

"What felt weird?" Shawna asked. She was at least asking without skepticism in her tone. She had always been a levelheaded, even-keeled person. No wild mood swings as I had witnessed in other women of our crowd.

In a nervous rush, I turned to her and explained, "Our date to the movies. He said it wasn't a date, but then he bought the ticket and held the door and offered to get me popcorn. I didn't know what to do. I got all jittery inside and kept thinking he was gonna go down on me in the theater like Dawn or Elaine. I didn't even watch the movie because I kept glancing at him, waiting for it to happen."

"Did it?" Shawna asked.

"No."

"Was it a date or not? I'm confused," M-L said.

"He said it wasn't."

"But he asked you to go to the movies?" Shawna asked.

"No. I invited myself along when he mentioned going to see *Iron Man 3*."

"If you invited yourself, then why would you think it was a date?"

"Because of the ticket and all," I explained, complete with agitated gesticulations. "And he's gay!"

"So?" said M-L.

Why couldn't she follow simple logic? "He's gay. Gaaaay. He's into guys. And I'm… well… a guy. He took me on a date to the movies."

"So?" Shawna was still waiting for an explanation, but I'd just given her one.

"So?" My voice was shrill, but I didn't care how ridiculous I sounded. "I want to know why RC didn't try anything. I'm hot!" I gestured to my body. "At least I thought I was. Most people want me. Most girls, plus Corey. I thought everybody'd be into me. But not him. We shared popcorn, and then he gets in his truck and leaves without trying to kiss me. I don't get it."

M-L gave me another confused look, perhaps beyond confusion, and shook her head. "Let me get this straight…. You went on a date that wasn't a date, with a man who's gay, and you assumed he'd make a pass at you, even though you tell everyone you're straight. You're frustrated because he didn't come on to you, and now you're doubting your sex appeal to the entire human race because you didn't end up having sex on your nondate with a gay guy whom you said was 'rugged like a mountain man' and 'wasn't the least bit cute'?"

I paused, considering her summary. "Exactly."

Shawna slapped her forehead, and M-L replied, "You are such an idiot, Nick."

"Why?"

"Not having sex when you go out with a friend doesn't automatically make you ugly. It makes your friend normal."

"But... but...," I stammered. "You weren't into me because you're a lesbian. He's not straight. He's into guys. So why wasn't he into me?"

"Nick, not everyone is attracted to the same physical traits. Just because I like girls, that doesn't mean I'm into every woman I walk by. I love Shawna. I told you, even if I was into guys I wouldn't date you, because I'm a monogamous person. You said RC ragged on you for being a slut. Maybe that's why? Maybe your friend RC has morals."

"You don't know what you're talking about."

Shawna touched my knee and said, "Nick, I mean this in the nicest possible way, Mary-Louise is right. You're an idiot."

"Why?" I questioned shrilly. "You haven't met him. He's single and overweight. His skin might have cleared up really well and he has great hair, but that doesn't mean he has room to be choosy. If I'm so hot, then he should have been all over me in that theater. He's gay. It's what they do!" I slumped back, crossed my arms, and grumbled, "Corey would have."

M-L rubbed her face and leaned on her elbow. "Oh good Lord, I'm getting a headache. You need to go home, Nick."

"What? Why? I drove all this way for your advice."

"My advice on what? How not to be a complete asshole? Nick! You've got to be the biggest dumbass I've ever met." M-L started yelling at me, and I felt trapped in a quagmire of indecision. I could bolt, but then I'd miss the possibility she'd say something smart. Or I could listen and risk my pride getting hacked to pieces by a feminist lesbian who was used to standing up for gay rights on a daily basis. I chose to take my lashes.

I sat and listened to her shout.

"I'm sorry I suggested that you're changing because it sounds to me like you're just as vain as you ever were. You're as stuck-up as Terrell and a nymphomaniac like Dawn. I've never met RC, but he sounds like a great guy to me if he thinks you're a slut and doesn't have sex on the first date just because you're hot. And don't roll your eyes, Nick. I might be a lesbian, but I still have eyes. I know a good-looking guy when I see one. I just don't normally want to have sex with them. Just like I know a good-looking woman when I see one, but I don't go around having sex with all of them either.

"And you know what? I'm glad you're not gay because you'd be an embarrassment to our entire culture if you were. I'm done." She stood up and headed to a hallway to the left of the living room. "Let yourself out, Nick."

I jumped up and followed her. "But…. Please don't go." I grabbed her arm and was relieved when she didn't turn and slap me. She *did* glare, though. "I just don't get why I have to define myself. Gay, not gay. I don't understand labels. Why can't I simply work out how I feel without a specific classification?"

M-L sighed sympathetically. "Labels and names are what we get, baby. Straight people are the only ones who get to walk around unfettered."

That didn't seem fair, but I could see how that was true. I sighed and then asked, "So… you *do* think I'm hot?"

M-L pulled out of my grasp. "Oh, for Pete's sake."

"No, M-L, please… I'm trying to understand. Are you telling me that just because RC's gay, that doesn't mean he's automatically attracted to me, even though I'm sex-on-legs?"

Shawna snorted from the couch.

M-L's mouth started to curve, but she paused before answering and controlled her reaction. "First let me say, you even having a male friend is a miracle. How anyone would put up with your vanity is beyond me. Second…. Yes, that is exactly what I'm saying. The rules of attraction differ from person to person. What is appealing to me isn't always what is appealing to you." She held up her hand, preemptively refusing my rebuttal. "And sexuality has nothing to do with it."

"So do you think he's still mad about me questioning him concerning the date that wasn't a date?" I had to ask, even though I felt awful admitting it to M-L.

"What do you mean, questioned him? Did you come on to *him* about it being a date?" She sounded shocked.

"Yeah. Kind of."

"Kind of? What exactly did you say?"

I didn't understand my mentality sometimes. Here I was in the hallway of her home, ten feet from the safety of the exit door, and yet I felt compelled to fill in all the gory details of our exchange. Her gaping mouth should have clued me in before she had the chance to voice her opinion.

"Oh my God, Nick. You're a fucking dick. How do you have any friends?"

"I don't know," I whined.

"Look. Just give him a few days to calm down. Assuming it was a date solely on the basis of his sexuality was a douche move. If he's still talking to you, I suggest *never* mentioning it again. Got it? That's like thinking I love pink because I'm a girl. Or assuming dolphins are fish because they swim in the ocean. If you consider RC a friend, then start by treating him like one without labels, and maybe one day you'll be able to safely assume things about him because you know him more completely. When the only fact you know is that he's gay, that only tells me who he's likely to sleep with, but it tells me nothing about him as a person. Friendship is about getting to know a person."

"I know he likes turkey sandwiches," I blurted.

She smiled. "Good."

"And he likes Adele and Tracy Chapman and all these female singers I've never heard of. And he likes snakes and Xbox. And he can cook pretty good."

She clapped my shoulder, and we walked over to join Shawna. "And he's a friend, you say?"

"Yeah. We have lunch together once a week. We don't normally talk too much, but I like that since I work with Marcy, and Tara can sometimes be demanding of my time on the weekends. I crave the mutual silence."

"Did you find out what his name is yet?"

I shook my head. "No, I haven't worked up the nerve to ask. It seems rude."

"But not rude to assume you're on a date because he's gay?"

I threw my head back and moaned loudly at the ceiling. "Oh, God, I get it. I'm an idiot."

"Yup," Shawna agreed.

"Hey, not to change the subject or anything, but Corey said he's going to be in Westminster this week. Maybe we could all have lunch at your pizza shop? Unless you want to drive down here?"

I lost my short burst of enthusiasm, and I couldn't even shrug a reply. "Whatever." I pulled myself off the couch and headed for the door. "I think I'm gonna go. Don't take this the wrong way, but remind me never to ask your advice again. It's too painful."

"But you love me," M-L called to me as I slipped from the apartment.

I huffed exasperatedly behind the wheel as I pulled out of the parking lot. "Lesbians."

Chapter 13: *Corey*

MONDAY NIGHT I got off work at five o'clock and drove home feeling empty. I couldn't figure out why I felt like that. I'd never felt so down. It wasn't about RC, it couldn't be; I was just going through a phase and soon it would disappear, and I'd be fine again.

I *did* feel guilty about what I had said to him, but I figured that would pass soon enough. If I ignored it, like M-L had suggested, maybe we could move on and he'd forget that I was so stupid. I'd wait until Wednesday to assess the situation; if he didn't show for our regularly scheduled lunch date, then maybe I needed to drive over to his house and apologize. It was easier to wait and see.

For once, Tara was busy with Laney, so I was free to do whatever I wanted. I parked and headed inside my house thinking of my mom's home cookin' and Xbox, but when I walked through the door, I smelled chocolate and heard giggling. *Corey.* I'd know the sound of his laughter anywhere. With mixed emotions, I rushed to the kitchen and found him and my mom standing by the stove, covered in flour, laughing.

"Hey," I said, giving an obligatory wave.

"Hi, honey. Look who popped in." Mom patted Corey's shoulder.

Corey tilted his head to the side, batted his eyes, and flicked his wrist out in a sort of pose. He was more flamboyant than I remembered. But then again, seven months living in DC on his own, loving life, could easily have changed him. I had to admit, he looked great! His dark blond hair was spiked in the front. He had on an orange, low-cut T-shirt and tight jeans. And his nails were painted to match. *Oh, God. If Mom didn't know he was gay before, he totally looks the part now!*

"Hey, darlin'," he greeted me with a smile. Corey walked over and kissed the air on either side of my face. "Long time, no see." Immediately, he crinkled his nose. "Oh honey, you smell like french fries and onions. Eww!"

"Sorry. I'll go take a shower. But I don't think the smell goes away." I looked at my mom, who was peeking in the oven. "Are you two okay until I get back?"

Mom said, "Yes, dear. We'll be fine. Corey got here an hour ago, so to pass the time we decided to make chocolate lava cake."

"It's to die for!" Corey said. "You just go and take your little shower, and I'll help your mom bake. Go." He shooed me away.

I walked up the steps thinking about the odd pair in the kitchen. Funny, I didn't remember his voice sounding so "lispy." He exaggerated syllables and drew out vowels; he could have been what they used to call a "valley girl" except I knew he was from Westminster, just like me. *Definitely more flamboyant than I remember.*

AFTER DINNER and dessert, which was yummy, Corey gave me that subtle look he had that said, "I want you." I excused us from the table and heard my mom call to me, "Keep the door open."

I popped my head back in the kitchen. "Seriously?"

She cocked a brow.

"Okay, okay," I conceded.

I left the door open.

"You want to play Xbox? I got Just Dance 4 for you. I thought you'd like it." I picked through the pile of games looking for it, and Corey walked up behind me.

"That's sweet, but it's not what I had in mind." His voice was so sultry, I couldn't help but shiver. His hands were on my hips, and I glanced at the open door. "I'll be quiet," he said, spinning me around.

I knew that look. It only took me a second to succumb to it. Corey's mouth was so sweet. I could taste the remnants of chocolate on his tongue mixed with his cherry lip gloss. I'd missed kissing him, but I didn't realize how much until his tongue touched mine. I grabbed him around the waist and pulled him into me. I felt his hands slide over my hips and continue down until they squeezed my ass.

Oh, yes! I'd missed Corey, and he knew it. Why would he show up today of all days? I had been so glum this weekend thinking about

RC, and wondering what the hell I wanted out of life, not to mention my monumentally stupid conversation with Mary-Louise. I didn't understand how things could get so confusing.

Being with Tara was easy, I guess, but it was the same old thing every weekend. I needed change, and right now, I needed Corey.

I guided him across the floor and over to my bed. I only let go of him long enough to quietly shut my bedroom door. I turned around, and he had already stripped off his jeans and posed with his ass in the air. I approved and commented, "Nice." I toed off my shoes and undid my belt and was out of my pants as quick as lightning, crawling onto the bed behind Corey, when a deep need to look into his eyes settled over me. Suddenly, I didn't want a quick fuck; I wanted a connection. Even if Corey wasn't the connecting kind, I still wanted to pretend.

"On your back," I said. "I want to face you."

"Anything for you, darlin'."

As he complied, I rolled the condom down my dick. I was harder than I could remember ever being; my balls ached and my cock twitched. I had never thought about how Corey's presence affected me. I felt more alive than I had in months. I pushed his shirt up far enough to kiss down his chest and lick his nipples, one after the other. I rubbed my face over the patch of hair on his chest and savored how it felt against my cheeks. The tip of my waiting cock brushed against his balls and a ripple of anticipation rolled through my extremities. *God, I want this!*

I kissed him hard and rocked against his groin, wanting nothing more than to tease him to the point of begging. But then logic spoke softly in my ear, jogging my memory about what my mom had said about keeping the door open. Sex needed to be fast. Maybe we could make a date for another time so I could go slowly and savor the taste of his skin.

For time's sake, I pressed in. The tightness that welcomed me sent electricity through my balls I hadn't felt in ages. It was like a power surge, and I knew without a doubt I wouldn't last long. I kissed his neck and slid my hand under his shirt so I could feel his hair again.

Too bad girls don't have chest hair. I wonder how much chest hair RC has? His arms are hairy. And his face was hairy before he shaved it. Plus, he's got all that long, black curly hair. It's freakin' gorgeous. I could probably sink my hands into those curls and pull on his hair while I pumped him full of my cum. He'd beg for it. Yeah. Yeah.

"Oh yeah," I groaned.

"Harder," Corey begged.

My eyes snapped open, and I looked down. I was fucking Corey. *Oh shit! I'm fucking Corey and thinking about RC. Not cool. Not cool.*

"Don't stop, Nicky. Please," he begged some more. Good thing his eyes were closed; I'd have hated for him to misread the apprehension in my eyes. I was freaked; I knew the expression had to be there.

I was about to pop anyway, so of course I kept going. A couple of thrusts into that sweet ass of Corey's, and I came hard. "I'm coming. Oh, yes."

"Me too," Corey gasped.

I tucked my face into his neck. "Oh, Corey. Yes." After I was done, I kissed his neck and ear before pulling out, knowing I could only spare a moment of affection.

Corey knew the drill and grabbed his things from the floor. He wiped his groin quickly with a few tissues and tossed them in the trash. We were both dressed and I was standing by my Kinect by the time I heard my mom in the hallway.

My mom entered without knocking. "I thought I told you to keep the door open," she asked with a glare.

"Sorry," Corey apologized for me. "I forgot you said that. We were going to play Just Dance 4, and I thought it might be too loud."

I love that he lied for me.

"Uh-huh," she mused. I don't think she believed him, because the way she sniffed the air and sauntered over in my direction suggested she was suspicious of something. She grabbed my chin, inspected my face, and then released me. "Just keep the door open. Your father and I are going to bed soon, so you can't play for long anyway. Twenty minutes, and your friend has to go home."

"Mom, I'm not a little kid. I can have a friend over if I want to."

"You may not be a kid, but you live in my house. If you rented your own place, you could do what you want"—she glanced at

Corey—"with whomever you wanted. Tonight, it's lights out in twenty minutes. Got it?"

"Yes, Mrs. Jones," Corey answered politely.

"Whatever," I said. "Twenty minutes is fine. Next time I'll drive to DC to visit him."

"That's fine. As long as you pay for the gas." She always threw sarcasm my way, but treated him like gold. "It was nice to see you, Corey. Be careful driving home. And thanks for the baking lesson. I had fun."

"Me too. Good night."

My mom left the door wide open. I hooked up the Just Dance game and turned the sound up loud enough to mask our conversation. "That was close," I said.

Corey walked over to me with a grin on his face.

"What?" He pointed to the mirror, and I turned to take a look. I had Corey's lip gloss on my lips and smeared up my cheek. It was colorless, but it was shiny and contained bits of glitter. "Oh no," I sighed. "How am I going to explain this? She's going to think I'm gay."

"Is that such a bad thing?" Corey rubbed my shoulders and looked at me in the mirror.

I knew what he wanted to hear. Of course being gay wasn't a bad thing—for him. But for me? What would people say? How would people react? I didn't live in DC or New York or San Francisco. I lived in Maryland. I didn't want to move. I'd lived here all my life. What would my parents say? Or my boss?

Corey watched me as he reapplied his lip gloss. "You can think about it all you want, but you can't change what you are on the inside. That mask you wear only works on those who can't see it." He walked to my door and paused. "Take it off, Nicky."

A mask? I wasn't wearing a mask. I didn't know what he was talking about. "Hey, Corey," I called after him.

He stopped on his way down the hall and turned. "Yeah?"

"Why did you come here tonight?"

He smiled and batted his eyes, much like he'd done in the kitchen earlier that night. "Sugar, a little birdie told me you needed a reminder of what it's like to fly." He gestured to me and added, "All that extra baggage you wear will only bring you down. Let it go, Nicky." He turned and walked away, wiggling his fingers at me over his shoulder and saying, "Let it go."

I DIDN'T know how to feel after Corey left. I felt stunned, I guess. I lay in bed that night thinking about what he'd said. I knew the "little bird" was M-L. She was the only one who understood me that well. Was I mad at her for meddling? No. She knew I needed Corey to help figure out my shit, but what he'd said didn't fix things, it only complicated them.

At work, all I could do was obsess over the conversation. I was glad it was a slow day and that Marcy was "illegally" texting. I was even too vexed to fuss at her.

All this time I'd thought I was straight. I was a straight guy who happened to be attracted to one hot, spiky-blond, gay guy. I was a straight guy with a boy toy on the side. Corey had never meant that much to me. At least, I'd told myself that for over a year. And all the girls I'd dated didn't mean much because I wasn't looking to get married. I wanted sex, and so did most of them, so it was a win-win situation for everyone.

Until now.

M-L was right: I was gay. Oh my God.

I'm gay. I'm not bi, I'm gay. I'm a gay guy with a girlfriend who doesn't know I'm gay.

"No, no, no. That's just stupid talking again." I shook my head and concentrated on the pizza coming out of the oven.

"What's stupid?" Marcy asked.

I turned around, hoping I hadn't had that entire conversation out loud. "Um, nothing. I was just thinking."

"Is anything wrong? You haven't been yourself lately. Is Tara turning out to be a big bummer of a girlfriend? Do you need to break up with her and you can't figure out how to do it?"

She looked way too pleased for my own good. "No, we're fine," I said.

Marcy wasn't buying it. "I can help you think of ways to do it."

"No, really, everything's good. I don't want to rewind back eight weeks and begin where you and I left off, with you trying to get into my pants. Seriously, Marcy, please let it go." I knew I was practically pleading with her, but she was relentless when she had something on her mind. I took the pizza out, cut it, and handed it to Julie on the other side of the heat lamp.

"Nick, don't worry, I'm not trying to go to bed with you. I'm dating Paul now."

That threw me. "You are?"

"Yup, two weeks and still going strong," she said, smiling like the sun. And for the first time in a long time, I saw that look in her eyes. I couldn't believe I hadn't noticed it before now. She was really happy! Marcy was happy, and I'd missed it.

"I'm sorry," I apologized. "I didn't know. I've been in my own little world lately."

She touched my arm. "It's okay. You have a lot on your mind. And you were right; you and I would have never worked out."

"I'm sorry."

"We're friends, and that's so much better." She glanced behind me, as if she'd noticed a customer at the counter. "Your friend is here."

I turned and spotted RC. Julie was taking his order. I gave him a halfhearted grin and continued working. He'd expect that. I never stopped what I was doing to greet him at the counter. Nothing would change now, no matter what thoughts were running through my mind.

FOR LUNCH, I ate a salad. I never ate salad. Truth was, I didn't feel like eating. I felt like puking.

"You look like shit," RC said. "What's going on?"

I shrugged. "I don't know." *I'm gay, and I cheated on my girlfriend with my nonboyfriend.*

"I think you do know, and you don't want to say. Fine. Keep your shit to yourself and explode all over someone else." He tapped the table and chirped, "Ooh, no, maybe you should keep it all in, go buy a gun, and ice everyone you work with like the pizza shop version of *Call of Duty*." He was teasing me. I hated that.

I growled, "Shut up. I'm not homicidal."

"Suicidal, then? You kind of have that dark-edge-around-your-eyes, slice-your-wrist appearance."

"Stop teasing me!" I liked that he wasn't acting weird after what I had said to him on Friday, but I wasn't in the mood to enjoy it.

RC snickered. "Seriously, what's up? You look bad."

"I cheated on my girlfriend," I admitted. That was only the tip of the iceberg, but I wasn't ready to confess the rest. I shoved my plate away, crossed my arms on the tabletop, and rested my chin on them.

"Hmm, a cheater, eh? Not good."

"Shut up."

"No. You're a cheater. You're a low-life sex fiend who isn't satisfied with the hot blonde you bed every weekend. They make daytime television shows about you. You should call one; maybe you could get paid to tell your story on live TV."

"I said shut up. I feel bad enough."

"Dr. Phil could help you."

"I'm not taking this shit," I said. I left my tray and stormed across the restaurant as fast as I could without attracting attention to myself. I headed down the hallway and RC yanked my arm, whirling me to face him. He shoved me against the wall and put a finger on my chest.

"Don't! You don't get to walk away. We're friends, we talk about things, isn't that what you told me? I sped off and you stalked me." He stepped closer. "Don't make me stalk you."

He glared at me, but in truth, I could see that shine in his brown eyes that said he was about to laugh. "You're making fun of me again," I said calmly.

"Maybe I am, but you deserve it… cheater."

I slapped his accusatory finger away. "Stop. All right, I cheated. I feel terrible. I do. I know I have to tell her." *But I'm not telling her it was with Corey.*

"Yes, you do. And when you're done confessing to Tara, you can tell me the rest of your problems because I can tell that's not all that's on your mind. After the way you acted in the theater, you owe me."

I hung my head. He was still dwelling on that. "I'm sorry for the way I treated you."

"You should be. Look, man, I know we don't typically talk, but I'm not blind. I know you. Something's been going on with you for a while. It's me, isn't it?" RC looked hurt when he asked that. I was scared where that question would lead. "You found out I'm gay, and now you don't act right around me. You're guarded, or something, most of the time. The theater was just a glimpse at how you really feel about me. Other homosexual friends aside, you can't handle *me* being gay."

No, I couldn't, but not for the reasons he thought. "I'm really sorry. I didn't mean to act like an ass."

"Yes, you did. Admit it, you can't handle going places with me because you think it's a date. Well, guess what? I don't date sex-crazed straight guys who cheat, so you're safe." He smacked me on the side of the head and mumbled, "Idiot."

Everybody was calling me an idiot lately.

He stared at me, and I stared back. Then we both started laughing.

"Okay, fine. I'm sorry," I said sincerely.

"Me too. I shouldn't have been so flip about the cheating. I find teasing you a little too fun sometimes. I'm sorry too." He stuck out his hand, and I shook it. It was warm and way bigger than mine. I pulled my hand back and walked away. "I gotta work."

"Okay. Bye."

I could tell he didn't know what just happened, and to tell the truth, neither did I.

I went back to work and kneaded the dough ball in front of me. I couldn't stop thinking about RC. I'd liked how my hand felt in his a little too much. Corey's hands didn't feel like his. My brain was scattered. One moment I thought I was gay, the next I wasn't so sure, and then a short while later I was back to the same dilemma. Plus, I still had a girlfriend. I pushed the gay question away often, but it kept returning like a boomerang. Denial hadn't worked; it had only prolonged the need to answer it. Gay. What did being gay mean, anyway? Maybe I was only a little gay?

I had a strong attraction to RC, and to Corey for that matter. Maybe I *was* gay?

I put the pizza I'd just made in the oven and zipped around the corner to where the ice machine sat. No one would come here unless they needed ice. I was safe for five minutes. I took out my phone and broke the rules: I got on the Internet while at work. If I didn't know what gay meant, I had to look it up.

Dictionary.com said: "of, pertaining to, or exhibiting sexual desire or behavior directed toward a person or persons of one's own sex."

I wasn't sure that helped. Did that mean I had to be attracted to all members of the same sex? I didn't find every guy appealing, only some of them. But then the opposite was also true; I didn't find every girl appealing either. Even the pretty ones. Heck, I'd *dated* girls I didn't really find appealing, but we still had sex. Dawn was probably the only girl in my history of a gazillion relationships that I found the least bit alluring. I had been sexually attracted to her. But if I was honest with myself, I wouldn't place many other girls on that list. Even Tara. Poor Tara, the revelation made me feel really bad; I knew I owed her an explanation.

But if Dawn was one of the only ones I'd been attracted to girl-wise, what about guy-wise? Until Corey, I hadn't thought about it. He was the only guy who had caught my eye, and I was very sexually attracted to him. In fact, thinking about him made my groin tingle. *Corey.*

As I thought about my sexuality and pondered the confusion that surrounded me of late, Paul walked in. Paul. He was a guy. And he wasn't bad looking. True, he was dating Marcy now, but maybe he would help a fella out. "Come here," I said. I grabbed his arm and pulled him over to the corner of the storage room where the cups and plates were stacked. No one went there.

"Dude, what's up?" he asked. His eyes were only slightly bugged out of his head, so I knew I hadn't freaked him out completely yet, pertinent word being "yet."

"You're dating Marcy, right?" I asked urgently.

"Yeah. Are you okay with that? I thought you were just friends."

"Oh, we are. I'm fine with it. I have a favor to ask." My knees were knocking, I was so terrified of what I was about to say.

"Okaay. Dude, you're weirding me out with that look in your eyes. What kind of favor is this?"

I was freaking myself out, and he had no clue. The only way to get past this was to blurt it out. "Paul, can I kiss you?"

Now his eyes popped out. He backed up a step and asked, "What?"

I held up my hand as some feeble attempt to calm him down. "Paul, please don't run. I just need to kiss you."

He shook his head and stepped closer to the door. "I don't think so."

"Just hear me out. Please?" When he didn't continue inching toward the door, I figured he was willing to listen. "I think I'm gay. I've been confused for a while, and my friend M-L kept asking about my relationship with a guy named Corey, and—"

"Corey Parrish?"

"Uh, yeah. You know Corey?" I wasn't surprised. Everyone knew Corey.

Paul smiled and relaxed. "Yes, I know Corey. He's a super great guy. And very gay."

I felt a pang of worry when he said it that way. How many times over the past year had I told myself I was "straight most of the time?" And two seconds ago, I'd been considering myself only a "little" gay. The definition I'd looked up didn't mention anything about appearance or acting flamboyantly gay; it had only cited sexual desire toward the same sex. Maybe gay had nothing to do with looks, and I had been deceiving myself as Corey suggested?

That was why I needed to find out.

"Yeah, Corey is very colorful, but this doesn't really have to do with him. It's about me." I took a deep breath, and Paul waited for me to continue like the cool guy he was. "I think I'm gay. This is really difficult for me to think about because I've been with a shit-load of women."

"I'll say you have."

I didn't need his commentary so I ignored it. "So, in order to figure it out, I thought maybe, if you'd let me, I'd kiss you and see if I felt anything."

He cocked a brow and gave me a very strange look. "I don't think that's going to help."

"Oh, come on, I have to try something. I just don't understand what's been going on in my head lately."

"What? That you might be gay?" He thought I was an idiot. I could tell.

"Yes!" I screeched.

"Shit, Nick. I don't know. I don't think this is a very good idea."

Suddenly, I had hope. "But you'll do it?"

He looked around nervously. "Yeah, all right. But no tongue."

"Anything." I stepped closer, eyes closed, and puckered up, but I stopped when I felt his hand on my chest. I opened my eyes. "What?"

"Just give me a second. I've never kissed a guy before."

"Okay." I waited.

Paul closed his eyes and shook himself. He wiggled and the motion rippled down his arms. When he was done, he stood at rest and looked at me. "I'm ready."

He closed his eyes, and I leaned in. Our lips touched. I pulled back and complained, "You have to kiss back. I can't figure out if I'm gay by kissing a mannequin."

"Okay, okay! This isn't easy, you know."

"I'm sorry." I felt bad. This was obviously *not* the same experience I'd had when Corey and I kissed at M-L's party last year. This was a big freaking deal for Paul, and I felt guilty for begging him to help me.

As soon as he looked relaxed enough to try again, I pressed my lips to his. This time he pressed back. He moved his lips and kissed me. No tongue, like we agreed. I felt his hands on my arms. He tilted his head the other way and kissed me with a surprising amount of passion.

After a minute or so, he stepped back and asked, "So? How was that?"

I took a deep breath and opened my eyes. "Don't take this the wrong way, but I didn't feel anything."

"Phew," he sighed. "Even though I'd like to think I can turn anyone on, my ego is just fine knowing you aren't one of them."

"I don't know what to do," I whined. I'm not normally a whiner, unless it is directed toward my mother and has to do with cleaning or something. "How am I supposed to know?" I looked at Paul for the answer.

"Dude, you're asking me?"

"I don't know." I seemed to say that phrase every five minutes.

Paul grabbed my shoulder. "Stop pouting and let me ask you something. What do you think of when you look at me?"

"Um, I think, 'Hey, there's Paul.'" That is honestly what I think when I see him every week.

"Do you think, perhaps, 'oh, there's one hot guy I'd like to get it on with'?"

I snorted. "No."

"There you go, then. You can't kiss someone you aren't attracted to and expect to feel something. What do you feel when you kiss Tara?"

"I feel like I'm wasting time that we could spend fucking."

"Oh, that's romantic," he said sarcastically.

"Okay, okay. I feel… anticipation. I start getting hard because I know what's gonna happen next."

"Oh my God. Is sex the only thing you think about?"

"Pretty much."

"Guys like you give us all a bad name. What a moron."

"Hey!"

"No. You asked me for a favor, and now I'm going to give you some advice. Find the person you can be with and *not* think of having sex with twenty-four seven. Sex is good; but dude, unless you want to have a string of endless nowhere relationships until you're fifty, you need to grow up. Or you're going to be alone. A kiss is like the ultimate form of nonverbal communication that tells your girl she's special. A kiss expresses what's in your heart. Sex might be the pinnacle, but you shouldn't be allowed to take the elevator to the top and enjoy the view without the journey up the mountain."

I stared at him. I seriously wasn't sure where he was going with that. "Huh?"

"Oh, Nick. I always knew your light was a little dimmer than everyone else's. What I'm getting at is that you need to learn to appreciate the person you're with. If it's Tara, great. If it's some guy that's got you questioning your sexuality, great. Go for it. But stop jumping into bed and forgetting to appreciate the one you're with. Love is about romance, friendship, and bonding in mind and soul as well as body."

"Love? I'm not in love." That word had never been in my vocabulary.

He pointed to me. "Then right there is your problem. You've been going out with Tara for like two months. You have sex with her, right?"

"Yeah."

"But you can't figure out if you love her?"

"I've never been in love with anybody."

"Nick, that's just wrong."

"What? No," I denied. "No, it's not."

"Nick, I know women. They talk to me. Most women aren't out for no-strings-attached sex relationships. And besides, if you're with Tara exclusively, then by definition that's an attached string. 'No strings' means you can come and go as you please, including fucking whomever you want whenever you want. You're on a string, buddy."

"But...." I wanted to say something, but Paul's logic made sense. Maybe I wasn't as free as I'd thought. And maybe I had women all wrong, especially if I compared the whole female population to the select group of girls I knew. *Hmm.*

"Furthermore, they want commitment," Paul said.

I had to interject. "You don't know the same girls I know. Plus, this isn't about the girls I know, it's about the guys."

"Oh, yeah, right, you think you're gay. Are you in love with Corey?"

"What? No. I don't know. I don't think so." Suddenly that question had a whole other meaning than when he had asked about me loving Tara. I didn't love Tara. I thought of her as a friend, but I didn't love her. Corey, on the other hand, meant a lot to me. We were friends, but lately I had come to realize how much I missed him when he wasn't around. I missed how I felt when I kissed him.

The revelation finally hit me: kissing Paul wasn't the answer, I needed to kiss RC.

I told him, "No, I'm not in love with Corey."

Paul smirked. "Is it that guy you have lunch with every week?"

"No!" Embarrassed, I exclaimed a little too loud.

Paul backed away a step or two. "I'm sorry I asked."

As soon as I'd said "no" I felt a pang of guilt in my stomach. I knew I didn't love RC. I couldn't, we hardly knew each other. But I felt weird dismissing the notion when RC was indeed the person I was questioning myself over. I *did* feel something, but I wasn't sure what. "Well, maybe I do," I recanted. "I don't know, Paul. I'm confused. I feel something, but I don't know what it is. I've never been in love."

"Let me tell you something. The best relationship comes when you find that person you can hang with, not kiss, and still manage to think about twenty-four seven. That's when you know it's special. Let me know how your self-discovery project works out. And for the record, you deliver one hell of a kiss." Paul winked and walked away.

I grinned and said, "Thanks."

I didn't know what to do. One thing was for sure: I had to tell Tara I'd had sex with Corey. Our anniversary was this weekend, and I didn't relish the idea of ruining it completely. She'd probably forgive me, but no matter what, I needed to grow up like Paul had suggested or my gravy-life would turn into utter shit.

Chapter 14: *Guilt*

TARA AND I celebrated our two-month anniversary with ice cream and minigolf. I had fun, but in the back of my mind, I knew I needed to tell her about Corey, and knowing that dampened my enjoyment of our date. I even turned her down for a blowjob, claiming my car was too exposed in the parking lot to chance it. She gave me a weird look, but didn't press the issue. By the end of the night, I still hadn't told her about Corey. I kissed her on the front porch and said good night.

Days dragged by.

She came into the restaurant Tuesday, and we ate lunch together. I stuck a french fry up my nose, and she giggled. Things were normal and pleasant, so why would I want to mess it up by telling her the truth? Except it was gnawing at me like termites nibbling one speck at a time until my guts were all but liquefied flesh rotting me from the inside out. Every time we made eye contact, I felt sick. I'd cheated. The worst part was that I didn't want to take it back. I didn't want to reverse sleeping with Corey; I mainly wanted to alleviate my guilt over it.

Tara could tell something was wrong. She said my color was off, whatever that meant. I told her my stomach hurt. At least that much wasn't a lie. She hugged me, and I returned to work only to end up in the bathroom several times before my shift ended.

I called in sick the next day. The burning and churning in my stomach had resulted in diarrhea. Could guilt and worry really do that? I'd never called in sick to work, but I couldn't face anyone, and I didn't want to chance working and having to dash to the toilet. The worst part about being home all day was having too much time to think.

Plus, it was Wednesday and I was disappointed I would miss my lunch with RC.

I'm living a lie. I'm a sham. I was pretending to be straight because it was easier to be with Tara than to redefine my existence.

Except… It wasn't turning out to be easy at all. The constant pull in both directions was painful and confusing and ultimately debilitating.

I stayed in bed all day and thought about my life and how much I hated myself. RC was right. I was a cheater, and the truth hurt. I had to tell Tara.

And RC… I had feelings for him. I had to, because why else would I think about him so much? He was nothing like the crowd I hung with, the people I dated, or the friends I had. He was hairy, and big, and worked in a clothing factory for gosh sakes. Terrell was a banker and had been a child model. Chrissy, although normally trashy, managed a hair salon and made pretty decent money. Dawn was a nurse. M-L worked for a law firm, and Shawna was a schoolteacher. I know it sounded bad judging RC by his job, but how much could he possibly make? And why should it matter? And if it didn't matter, then why couldn't I work up the nerve to invite him to one of my parties? Not ones I personally threw, but ones my friends put on.

Answer: because they wouldn't accept him. He wasn't pretty. And he wasn't rich.

I wasn't rich, but I was hot and they all knew it. They wanted me at those almost-orgy parties because I made the room look nice. I overheard someone say that once. The comment had never bothered me before. I liked being envied for my looks. My looks got me pretty far. But now, as I looked deeper in the mirror and realized how shallow my world was becoming, I saw my life for what it was—a shrine for self-indulgence.

That's why I couldn't tell Tara. It would ruin the perfect picture.

I think that's why I didn't have sex with her on our anniversary. I just couldn't get into her after being with Corey and obsessing over RC. It felt wrong. I worried my stomach into knots and gave myself diarrhea.

I was on my way downstairs to get more Pepto-Bismol from the kitchen when I heard my mom open the front door. "Hello. Can I help you?" she asked.

I hadn't heard the doorbell, but then again, I hadn't been thinking about anything except my guilt, Corey, RC, kissing Paul, and maybe visiting M-L again to get her to analyze my head. My next step faltered when I heard Tara's voice. "Hello. My name is Tara Jackson. I'm here to see Nick if he's feeling up to it?"

"Oh sure, come in," my mom said. "Nick is upstairs. I'll go get him for you."

I hesitated at the top of the stairs as Tara walked in. She turned toward the living room as she entered so she hadn't seen me as I crept down. I heard her say, "I don't want to be a bother, but when Nick didn't call me like he said he would, after he looked yucky at lunch yesterday, I was worried and came over. I hope that's okay."

My mom, on the other hand, *did* see me. She lifted her eyes to meet mine before she looked back at Tara and answered, "You are no bother at all. I'm glad to finally meet you. Nick is feeling much better. No need to worry. Why don't you have a seat in the living room and I'll get him for you."

My mom directed Tara where to go, and I slipped into the kitchen unnoticed. I sat at the kitchen table waiting for the interrogation that was bound to happen. My mom hated lying. I'd been punished repeatedly for lying in my youth. I knew she'd be upset to find out I'd lied this morning. Her stern glare did not disappoint. In fact, her flared nostrils sent fear racing through my veins. She was going to kill me.

She walked over and sat in the chair next to me and said, "I will not have lying in this house, Nicholas." The muscles in her jaw were tight. She was obviously reining in her anger because Tara was in the other room. Tara wouldn't hear a normal conversation, but she'd be able to hear everything if my mother started yelling. (Mom could be loud when she wanted to be.)

"I'm sorry," I said.

"No. I don't believe you are." *Damn, her voice is terrifying.* Mom only spoke sternly when she was really mad. Crap! "I think you're sorry you got caught. You go talk with Tara and then later, you and I are going to have a talk about why you told me you were scheduled off today."

I grabbed her hand. I needed to get it out and done with. "The answer's simple, Mom. I really do feel sick, and I didn't tell you because you always want to call a doctor or something. I know why I'm sick. I don't need a doctor, and I don't need an interrogation. I'm sorry I lied, but it seemed easier at the time than telling you the whole story."

I was honest. Mom always overdid stuff. She treated me like a little kid sometimes, and I was tired of it. At least for now. Being spoiled wasn't hard to take most other times.

She looked at me curiously, probably because I've never spoken up like that before. Normally I coasted along with the flow because she made most things easy. I didn't like being treated as I had been when I was seventeen, but I also never defied her decrees. I was a rule follower, remember?

"Hmm," she responded, relaxing her stance. "I'll think about that. I don't mean to be a pain, but seriously, Nick, if you lie, I can't trust you. I know you're an adult, but you also live under my roof. I only ask for honesty. I don't think that's too much to expect. You and I are having a talk soon. However, right now you need to go talk to your girlfriend, who is very pretty, by the way." She stood up and left the room.

"You're in big trouble, butthole," my sister teased. She made me jump because I hadn't noticed her in the room. She'd been standing over by the pantry, listening in while our mother scolded me. And I knew she'd remind me of it for a long time. *Great.*

"No, I'm not," I said in return.

I left the kitchen and joined Tara in the living room. She was sitting on the sofa, but leapt up as soon as I entered.

"Nick!" She rushed to my arms. "I was worried."

Her concern was sweet, but it only made the fact that I had lied to her weigh heavier on my conscience. "Thanks, Tara," I said as she hugged me. Her hair was in a ponytail and it hung close enough to my eyes for me to feel little hairs poking me. I blinked and pulled away. I didn't like hair in my eyes. "I'm fine, really. Nothing a little Pepto can't cure. I'll be at work in the morning." I tried to smile, but I only managed to lift one corner of my mouth.

"What is wrong with you? Is it flu? Or mono? Oh gosh, I hope it isn't mono."

"No, Tara, it isn't mono. I have diarrhea, like your aunt's dog."

"Eww."

"Look, can we sit down? Unless you want all the gory details."

"Eww, no!" She sat and arranged her miniskirt so her panties wouldn't show. Her expression changed from worry to deep concern. It's like she could tell I was going to say something she didn't want to hear. I faced her. I could do this. I was a man. "Tara, I lied to you."

"Oh?" she responded, crossing her hands over her knee. "So, you're not sick?"

"I am, but it's sort of self-induced because of guilt."

"Guilt about what?"

I swallowed hard. She was poised and attentive, and I was about to drop a bomb on her perfect world. "Um, guilty about cheating on you." I leaned away from her, expecting Tara to slap me across the face.

Her lips parted and her eyes opened wider. "You what?"

God, this is awful. "I cheated on you." Saying it twice was even worse.

She was fuming. I swear I could see smoke coming out of her ears. "Who with? Dawn? It better not have been Dawn," she hissed with a cat-like snarl. I could see why they called fighting between two girls a catfight. She'd almost bared her teeth as she asked.

"No. Not Dawn."

As if her intense glare could not get scarier, she asked, "Was it Chrissy? Because if you went back to that hussy after all the times I put out for you, I'll—"

"It wasn't Chrissy." There was no easy way to say it, but if I didn't tell her straight up, I thought she'd blow a gasket. "I had sex with Corey," I confessed, hoping to hell my mom and sister weren't listening in. They didn't need to know.

Something inside eased her throttle back a notch. "Corey?"

"Yeah."

"You slept with Corey Parrish." She was even more direct the second time she asked, but her expression was unperturbed.

"Yeah. I'm sorry. I've never done that before."

Then she snorted, which took me aback. She said, "Yes, you have. Everyone knows you have a thing for Corey."

I was shocked. "What? They do?" Because I'd thought only M-L had that notion.

"Yeah. Laney even bet me you'd probably cheat on me with him at some point. She said you cheated on Chrissy."

"No, I didn't. I was with Corey,"—no need to evade the subject now—"but never at the same time I was with Chrissy. Only after we'd broken up. But this was the first time I had sex with him *while* I was still going out with someone else—with you. I feel terrible."

"Did you wear a condom?"

"Of course I did. I've never had unprotected sex."

She made a shrugging motion with one shoulder. "Then we're fine." Tara was extremely casual about it, which threw me; "casual" was not in my list of expected responses.

I scrunched my face and asked, "What? That's it?" My brain was short-circuiting. What the heck was going on? I was trying to own up to cheating on her, and it appeared as though she'd expected me to screw Corey all along. "So... you're not mad."

"Nope. As long as it was with Corey. Although, if you feel the need to be with him again, I'd like a text."

"A text to tell you I'm cheating?"

"No. It's only cheating if you fuck Dawn or Chrissy or Laney. Corey is your little side-perk that keeps you going. And if hooking up with Corey every once in a while makes you a better lover, I'm all for it."

Her calm response pulled me further into my spiral of WTF. *Where the hell am I, the* Twilight Zone? "Tara, did you hear me? I cheated on you."

"Yeah, I heard."

"Why aren't you mad?" *Because I would be.*

"I'm not mad because it was with Corey, like I said. Everyone knows you're fuck buddies. It's fine. You can do whatever you gotta do as long as you use protection. But don't lie to me about it. And for goodness sakes, don't make yourself sick over it again."

I couldn't believe it. Tara really didn't look mad.

"And next time, maybe you could let me watch."

"Watch?" My pitch went up.

"Yeah. Or we could try a threesome. Two guys together are really hot. I could totally get off on watching you kiss Corey while you were inside of me."

"Um, yeah, maybe," I sputtered. I couldn't think. She was suggesting things that *maybe* I fantasized over—because threesomes did intrigue me—but in reality, it freaked me out that Tara wanted to do some of those tawdry fetishes I had only read about online. And fucking hell, Tara might even turn out to be kinkier than Dawn. Suddenly I felt woozy. This was too much.

Tara reached over and touched my knee. "Really, don't beat yourself up about it. I knew. Okay? We're fine. Just as long as we stay together, we'll be okay. I'll let you have Corey on the side, but if we're in an open relationship, I might hook up with someone too. Okay? What's fair is fair."

"Um, yeah. I guess." I wasn't sure what I was agreeing to. An open relationship? What did that mean?

Tara stood up. "I'm going home, but I'll be by sometime for lunch. I expect that you won't blow me off like you did that last time. I was really upset, but I tried to hide it. If you're going to fuck Corey, then I expect you'll spend time with me whether or not I call first. You can have what you want, and I get what I want. Agreed? And I expect you to ask before you go out with him."

She held out her hand, waiting for me to shake it. I did, my brain too fuzzy to comprehend the situation I was now putting myself in.

"One more thing. Your days off are mine. Unless we discuss it ahead of time. I'll give you a reprieve this weekend because my folks have a thing and I can't bring you, but otherwise we're together."

I walked her to the door and kissed her before she left. I couldn't think. I was stunned. I stood there motionless for a moment, feeling as though I'd just been awarded shared custody in a divorce hearing. I could see Corey whenever *I* wanted, as long as she got to see *me* whenever *she* wanted. Was I really okay with that agreement?

I numbly wandered to my room before my mom had a chance to bitch at me. Not that my mom bitched much. I needed to rest my head. I felt odd. *Is Tara taking over my life?*

My stomach churned in discontent until I puked later that evening. Something was going to have to change, or I would die from dehydration. Guilt exiting from both ends might kill me.

I CALLED in sick again Thursday, but this time I told my mom about it. I had a splitting headache from the moment Tara left, and it made me sick all over. I couldn't work like that. Besides, I only worked eleven to three. It was the easiest shift to cover.

It was Thursday night by the time my mom knocked on my door. "Honey, can I come in?"

"Yeah," I grunted.

She entered and walked over to my bed without a word about the clothes on the floor. She felt my head. "Are you okay? It's not like you to miss so many days of work. Are you sure you don't need a doctor?"

"No. It's stress."

She touched my face and smoothed my hair away from my eyes. "You don't feel hot, but you don't look so good either."

"I know," I grunted.

"Did something happen with Tara?"

"Kind of."

"I took Jenn to her room, and we made a point not to listen in on your conversation. I wanted to talk to you when Tara left, but I also considered what you said to me in the kitchen. I'm sorry if I seem overbearing. I don't wish to be."

I rolled over and worked my sluggish body into a sitting position against my headboard. I took her hand and thought about how many times over the years we had sat like this in the past and had some great conversations. She did treat me like a kid sometimes, but when had I ever voiced my desire to be treated like an adult? I allowed it because I liked being spoiled. "I know you don't mean to be overbearing, and you're not. Not really. I'm frustrated with my life and I wanted to hide it, so I lied about calling in sick. I know it was stupid. I could have just said I didn't want to go to work. I don't know why I lied."

"Maybe because you knew I'd question your level of responsibility if you called in sick because you didn't *feel like* working."

I grinned. "Maybe."

"So, tell me, what's up with you and Tara? She seems nice. And she's very pretty. I know you've been seeing her a couple of months. I didn't want to push to meet her because I thought you needed some space, but you could invite her over for dinner. Unless...." She paused and squeezed my hand.

I looked at her directly when she didn't finish her thought. "Unless what?"

Mom looked sympathetic or compassionately understanding. I couldn't read her, but it was a look that told me she knew something and didn't know how to say it. Or maybe it was because she'd always seemed intuitive in the past. She could tell something was wrong even without me hiding in my room for days. On normal occasions when I'd sleep like the dead for days at a time, she had been known to come in my room unannounced, throw open the curtains and haul my ass out of bed to do something "useful." But not this time. She had left me alone all day. It was as if she knew something. She smiled softly and said, "Unless Tara is merely a distraction because you don't know how you feel about Corey."

"Mom," I groaned, releasing her hand and slipping down into my blankets again in a futile attempt to hide my embarrassment.

"I'm not blind, sweetheart. I knew about Corey before you had his lip gloss on your mouth."

"Mom, you're killing me!" I threw the blankets back and sprang into a sitting position. Her intuition could stand some tact. "It's not about Corey." Then I had to concede because part of it was about Corey, and I knew it. "Okay, some of it is about Corey. I admit it... I like him. And yes, we were kissing and stuff the other day, but it's not about him right now. It's about me. I don't understand myself and why I do the things I do." I rubbed my face and stared at my blanket. I wasn't about to look my mom in the eye. It was bizarre enough I'd given in to her inquiry. I didn't want to share, but my mouth kept spewing the facts anyway.

Traitorous lips of mine! Always with the talking at the same time I'm thinking. My lips needed to learn when *not* to speak.

She patted my exposed knee. "I think we all go through that. And for some, figuring out who they are takes a lot more years than you've lived. I think I was in my forties before I actually liked who I was. You'll get there."

I looked up. I might have hated how easily I confessed my confusion to her, but I also needed to. I wanted to talk about it on some level, and my mom had always been there for me. "But I don't want to wait until I'm forty, Mom. I want to know now. I don't understand why I feel like this."

"Like what?"

"You wouldn't understand."

"Try me," she said.

I wrung my hands and fidgeted. *How do I say it? Where do I start?*

My moment to open the floodgates of emotion and personal turmoil abruptly ended when I heard my dad bellow up the steps, "Hey, Cathy, tell Nick there's a guy here to see him. Says his name's RC."

My worry transformed into panic. I threw the blankets back and nearly knocked my mom off the bed as I leapt over to my dresser. "RC? What's he doing here?" I glimpsed myself in the mirror. "Holy crap, I look like death." I smelled myself. "And I smell like death. Shit."

My mom came up behind me and said, "You're the king of five-minute showers, Nicky. Jump in. I'll go down and offer your friend a drink."

"He likes Dr Pepper," I blurted, and she smirked. I felt sheepish for exposing my excitement so nakedly. I certainly didn't have a poker face. I toned my next comment down, hoping my mom wouldn't read into my anxiety. "You know, if we have any, maybe you could get him one."

Mom nodded and walked out, but not before I caught the twinkle in her eyes.

Boy, am I going to have some explaining to do.

WHEN I got downstairs, RC was sitting in the living room watching baseball with my dad. He even yelled at the TV at the same time as my dad, and they high-fived. *I'm in the* Twilight Zone *again, only without Tara. Thank God.*

RC stood up as soon as he saw me. "Hey, loser." The way he punched my arm made me think he was trying to act more macho on purpose. Why? But then, RC didn't know about Corey, and he certainly didn't know about my on-again/off-again all-sex relationship with Corey. Until this point, I had been straight.

"Hey," I answered, trying to mask my unease. I looked around. My dad was watching the Orioles vs. the Astros and was oblivious to my jumpiness. He probably wouldn't pay attention if I held a conversation in the room as long as I kept it down so he could hear the announcers. He was an extreme, full-blown baseball fanatic. He watched every game he could from the time he got home from work until he went to bed. My mom allowed it because when she asked him to do something, he did it right away. They had some sort of understanding going on, and I'd never bothered figuring it out. They'd been married for twenty-eight years, and I liked the comfort of knowing they probably would be for another twenty-eight.

I snagged RC's arm and pulled him into the kitchen. My mom, standing at the counter, looked at us. I froze. "Uh, I... we...."

She held up her hand. "I'll leave."

I felt bad making her vacate the room. "No, don't. It's okay." I meant it. It wasn't like I was going to confess my personal sexual debate to RC right then and there. He had no clue what I'd been going through. I logically had to start with why he was here. I led him over to the table, and we sat down. "What are you doing here?" I asked.

"Nice. Direct. Blunt. And kind of reminiscent of when I said the same thing to you."

"Ha, ha. No really, why are you here? How'd you find me?" I wasn't bothered by it; I just wanted to know.

RC glanced at my mom, who was washing dishes or something, before he spoke. Knowing her, she was probably faking it and washing the same dish three times so she could listen in since I'd given her permission to stay.

"I stalked you," he said.

"You what?"

He smiled. "I said, I stalked you. When you weren't at work, I used my time at lunch to look up all the Joneses that live in the area. There are only thirty-six. And of them, only two families live within five minutes of your work. I drove past this house and spotted your car. Ta-da! You're not the only one with mad skills."

I laughed. "Oh, God, we are both freaks of nature. What a pair we make." I thought it was funny, but something in the look that crossed his face made me think I'd said something wrong. "So what did you do, ask Marcy for a phone book?"

"Nope, better," he said, pulling a phone out of his pocket. "Smartphone."

"Oh my God. You got a cell phone!" I grabbed it and fondled the newness. "It's the HTC with the 3-D setting. Holy shit."

"Nick," my mom warned.

"Sorry, Mom." I leaned closer to RC and whispered, "She thinks I'm going to corrupt my little sister with swearing. It's worse than at work."

"Nick," she warned again, accompanied by a glare this time.

I grinned and shrugged. "Sorry." I turned the phone on and flipped through his screens. "Wow. I can't believe you finally did it. You have a cell phone. Here, call me," I told him, handing it back. "I'll be right back. I'm getting mine."

"I don't know your number," RC yelled after me, calling through the house just like the rest of my family. Somewhere in my brain, endorphins pulsed. I liked the familiarity of his presence.

I hollered down the steps, "I already dialed it. Just hit call."

When I opened my door, my cell phone was ringing. I answered it. "Hello?"

"Hey. Get your ass back down here. Your mom's watching me."

I laughed, "Okay. On my way." I jumped down the last five steps, and my dad grumbled something about keeping it down. I entered the kitchen and plopped into the chair next to RC. "This is so cool. Now I can text you."

RC frowned. "I've never texted."

I took his phone from his grasp. "Look, it's easy."

I made quick work of getting familiar with his phone. His version was indeed better than mine. Could you say... *jealous?* I explained the icons at the bottom, and how to add pictures and video and everything. In ten minutes, RC was a texting pro.

"Okay, now take a picture and send it to me."

"Of what?"

"Anything. Take one of you."

"Um, nooo. How about one of your mom's sugar bowl?" He snapped a picture and sent it to me.

"Not exciting, but it came through. See?" I showed him the screen. "This is awesome. What made you think of getting one?"

"Duh, *you*. You said we could text and stuff. I've never wanted a cell phone, but mainly because I had no one to talk to."

"What about your mom and dad?"

"My dad died from cancer last December. I didn't eat for, I don't know, nine weeks. It's not the best way to start a diet, but after I noticed I lost thirty pounds, I decided to try and lose more. I thought my dad would be proud of me for trying."

"And your mom?" I had to ask because he looked so somber talking about his dad. I could not imagine losing mine.

"I don't want to talk about my mom."

RC's flat tone suggested he was completely serious, so I didn't want to go there. Maybe if we were alone and to that point where we told each other stuff, I'd ask him. I figured I'd give it time. "Okay. No questions about your mom. But we can definitely talk about other stuff—not parents."

"Yeah."

"So, you wanna… see my room?" I asked because I wasn't sure what else to do in the kitchen. "All my stuff is in there. My Xbox and my Kinect and my iPod, everything's upstairs. If you want to check out my stuff like I did in your apartment, then we gotta go up to my room." My mom gave me a look across the kitchen, and I pointedly ignored it. She didn't have to worry about anything. At least not yet. RC and I were just friends. We hadn't spent all that much time together outside of having lunch. Only the one night I'd gone over after work and the movie. Now he was *here,* and I couldn't believe it. Not too many people dropped by to see me out of the blue unless they wanted something. Mainly sex. I knew RC was here without pretense and that made me feel good.

"Sure, all right," he said. RC stood up and followed me upstairs.

"Keep the door open," my mom hollered after us.

I shrugged at RC. "House rules," I explained. I wasn't going to mention that Corey and I had broken that rule. After everything that had happened this week, I needed a break from thinking all together. RC was here to chat and whatever. I picked up a controller. "Play Xbox?" I suggested.

"Sure."

I rolled my chair over next to the bed and RC sat down. I plopped onto the bed and leaned against the headboard as we played Call of Duty. We played for twenty minutes, and my mom walked by my room twice. I don't think RC noticed, and if he did, he didn't say.

"What are you doing Saturday?" he asked as his soldier picked up another weapon and loaded it.

"Working," I said, opening fire on the enemy. "Die, die!"

"Oh. Okay." RC shot another target and blood sprayed the wall on the TV screen.

I glanced at him out of the corner of my eye. He looked disappointed. I wondered if the question was attached to a specific reason so I said, "I could find someone to switch with me. I work all day tomorrow. I could ask Paul."

RC looked at me, and his player got showered with gunfire. "You don't need to rearrange anything for me. I was just asking."

"No, RC, what were you planning to do? I want to know." I stopped paying attention too, and my player bit the dust just as fast as his.

"I was…. You'll think it's dumb."

I glared. "Dumb? You're talking to the king of dumb. Dumb is you not asking."

He took a breath and exhaled. I heard it. Was he nervous? And if he was, why? "I was just going to ask if you wanted to hang out. I go to reptile shows pretty often, and I thought maybe you'd like to come this weekend. It's pretty cool, especially if you've never been. You'll see more varieties of some species at a show than you would in a zoo."

"Reptiles? You mean snakes and stuff?"

"Yeah, but way more. This show is the biggest one around unless you want to take a plane or drive forever. Still, it's kind of far away, but totally worth it because they have frogs, lizards, turtles, insects, venomous reptiles, and loads of varieties of snakes. It's awesome."

This was the first time RC had spoken to me about something *he* liked. Most of the time he ragged on me about all my women or poked fun at me because I didn't know anything about what was going on in the world or on the news. I'd told him I lived under a rock, and he chuckled, but the truth was I really didn't care. I mean, I did care about starving children in Africa and stuff, but I didn't know how to help them, that was what charity organizations were for—right?

Watching RC's eyes light up when he told me about this reptile show was completely out of the ordinary for me. I had some guy friends, but we didn't hang out. I talked to Paul, but most of our conversations were about work. Which I hoped wouldn't change now that I had kissed him. With RC though, I felt different. Like, I wanted to talk about everything. And I wanted to hear him talk about everything. Snakes? Sure. Any and every topic as long as he shared what was on his mind. His voice was comforting.

"I was rambling, wasn't I? Sorry." RC flushed, and I knew he was embarrassed, but I thought it was cute.

He looked away, and I reached out and patted his knee. "No, you're fine. I'll go."

He glanced at my hand, but I had already retracted it. I might be working through some peculiar feelings I had for him, but there wasn't any reason to tell him. It wouldn't be right to lead him on especially if he didn't feel anything for me. So far, he hadn't made any kind of moves on me. It was safest to leave our relationship where it was.

He looked relieved. "Are you sure?"

"Yeah," I said. "Of course. I'll ask Paul. He won't mind."

I swear he looked overjoyed. "Great! I like to get there early. If we park before eight thirty, we'll have to stand in line for a half an hour, but it's best to get into the place before the crowds show up around eleven. Is that okay?"

"I guess. What time do we need to leave?"

"Six thirty. Unless you want to grab breakfast on the way, then we'll have to leave earlier."

"Where are we going?" The notion of getting up before the birds made me leery. I suddenly wondered if I could do it. I hardly ever got up early. I could stay up 'til four, but don't ask me to get out of bed at four.

"Hamburg, Pennsylvania."

"Isn't there a Cabela's Outdoor Store up there?"

"Yes. It's practically across the street, maybe ten minutes away."

"I thought so. My dad took us there a couple times. They have stuffed deer." I chuckled. "Okay, six thirty is fine, but I'll warn you I don't like getting out of bed in the morning, especially that early. I might be grumpy."

"Duly noted."

He grinned some more and picked up his controller again. I supposed the conversation was over as far as he was concerned. The plan was set. "You want me to meet you at your house?" I asked. "We could even take my car if you want; I bet it gets better gas mileage."

"Are you sure? That would be great. I've been putting off getting an oil change and the light's been on all week."

"No, I don't mind."

"Cool."

That said, we simultaneously started shooting enemy soldiers on the TV just as my mom walked in.

"Are you going to hide up here all night, or are you going to introduce me to your friend?" My mom smiled pleasantly, but I knew she was irked that I hadn't already introduced him while we were all down in the kitchen. Not officially anyway. She stood in the middle of my room with her hands clasped behind her back. Waiting. If I didn't do as asked, she'd probably stand there all night. I could comment about her being intrusive, but really, did I need to? I wasn't bothered.

"Sorry, Mom, this is RC. RC, this is my mom, Cathy Jones."

RC held out his hand and shook hers. "RC? Is that a nickname or your initials?" Leave it to Mom to broach the very question I had been dying to ask for a while but hadn't.

He cleared his throat. "Um, they're my initials, but also a nickname. My full name's Raffael Charles Coppola, ma'am." He looked unsettled as he told her.

"Raffael Coppola," she repeated. "What a great Italian-sounding name."

"Yes, ma'am. My father was Italian. My mother's Greek."

My mom smiled at RC and looked over at me. "I'm going to lie down and read before bed. Try not to be too loud in here." She turned and walked out.

I knew her comment contained a double meaning of some sort. We weren't loud before. She left the door open, and I was fine with it. We weren't doing anything. I turned my attention to the TV and shot someone else. After a couple of minutes, I asked that burning question, "So, why do you go by RC? Raffy's a pretty cool nickname."

"That's not what they called me in school," he replied very quietly.

I noticed RC had stopped shooting when his character stood motionless and got killed by the advancing enemy soldier, so I looked over at him to see what was wrong. He was staring at the floor, controller limply held in his grasp. "RC?"

"I was a fat kid in school," he whispered, however it was very quiet in the room after I paused the game so I could hear him well. He wasn't looking at me. He was looking down, but I highly doubted he was counting carpet fibers. He continued slowly, "Kids weren't very nice."

RC sat very still and he didn't look up. *Am I supposed to say something?* I didn't know what was appropriate to say. "Um, yeah, I know. Kids can be mean. I've done some really shitty things."

"Everyone called me Raffael until second grade. My mom liked my full name, and that's how I got introduced. Then I remember eating a ham sandwich at lunch one day and some kid had just learned that capicola was a type of ham. He started laughing and slapping the table as if he'd heard some funny joke. When another boy asked what he was laughing about, he said my named rhymed with a type of ham. The whole table started laughing, and by the end of the day everyone was calling me Capicola instead of Coppola."

"That's not so bad. I like ham." I tried sounding positive, but it didn't help.

Without reaction to my comment RC said, "They all laughed and started making pig sounds. I was already fat and ridiculed by some kids, but when those other kids started oinking whenever I walked by, it only amped up the harassment because then almost all of my class was making fun of me. It went on all year. When I returned in third grade, I hoped it would change, but it didn't. There were less random oinks in class, but I after threw up on the bus one morning the nickname changed from Capicola to Ralph."

"That's not bad. We have a neighbor named Ralph. I don't see how that's so awful when you could easily derive Ralph from Raffael."

He looked at me then, and the pain in his eyes was dreadful. "It *is* when 'Ralph' is accompanied with retching sounds. It never stopped. The noises and euphemisms for vomit continued through high school. Kids didn't oink as much, but they pretended to throw up when they passed me in the halls. I was called Vomit, Yackhead, Pukeface, and Upchuck. Kids asked questions like 'Did you lose your lunch?' or 'Can

I toss your cookies?' I made the mistake of crying in front of someone in fifth grade, and that's when it solidified into shameful taunting for the rest of my life. No one ever called me Raffy. It was always something derogatory."

RC looked away. I guess looking at me as I sat there with a stupid dumbfounded expression glued to my face was not helping alleviate his embarrassment of the personal pain he had endured in school. He'd just revealed the truth behind his nickname RC, and I gave no reaction at all. I should have, but I didn't know what to say at first. I'd been one of those guys. I was the jerk in school who pointed out the flaws in others and laughed when they puked on the bus. I was never as malicious as RC had experienced, but I also knew I was not very different from that now. How often had I judged others in my head, yet without verbal aspersions?

The main reason I hadn't called RC fat when I first saw him was because Marcy said it. Hearing her cut somebody down made me feel bad. If I'd have done it first, I don't think I would've apologized. I compared people, but I didn't look at someone and automatically think fat, ugly, poor, Asian, bad hair, needs a bath.... Okay, I did think that with RC. He'd looked scruffy and unkempt and I postulated he needed lessons in proper hygiene. It was only because I didn't know him. Once I'd found out about the job and the skin issues, it all made total sense. And now, he looked way better.

However, after hearing someone from his past would make him feel so worthless, I was angry. Raffael was his name, not Ralph or Capicola or—for fuck's sake—Vomit! And Raffy was my friend. I'd never had a friend who had been bullied like that. I had always been the one joining in the torment of others. I never instigated, but I think it was because I feared getting caught. But if someone else started the teasing, I'd had no qualms assisting... back then. I was different now.

It happened in high school. Somewhere between eighth and tenth grade, our little "gang" gelled, and it wasn't an issue excluding others. We didn't need to make fun of them or bully them for being ugly or fat. We tended to stick to our own. We were the "pretty people," as M-L had put it. Others stayed away by default. We became a gang without the hate crimes. We didn't beat others up or stuff them into lockers. We hung out and partied and drank and had loads of sex and talked about careers and college and the future. Our gang became a stagnant bubble of "senior year" even though most of us had graduated college and found the careers we'd talked about in high school.

So when RC described his past, I couldn't help but consider it could have easily been me tormenting him. It wasn't, and it wouldn't be now, but it could have been. I felt terrible thinking I had it in me to hurt him like that.

I finally worked up my nerve to whisper, "I'm sorry."

RC straightened and took a deep breath. He stood up and shrugged it off. "If that was the worst thing to ever happen to me, I think I'd be grateful. But the rest is a story for another day."

"You didn't need to say all that to me. Not if it's painful."

"Yeah, I did."

"Why?"

"Because it's like you said three weeks ago when you stalked me. I feel comfortable around you. I know lots of things about you, but we hadn't gotten around to me yet. I didn't want to dump it all on you at once, but I felt like I should start with something. After your mom asked my name, it seemed like the right time."

My heart warmed. "You feel comfortable around me?"

"Yes. It feels like you're the first friend I ever had. And if you give me shit over it, I'll pound you."

I smiled. "No. No shit."

He held out his hand. "Saturday?"

I smiled wider, shook, and confirmed, "Saturday."

Chapter 15: *Reptiles*

I DIDN'T remember a time when I'd woken up so early voluntarily. It was practically the crack of dawn. My mom looked shocked, but I told her I'd fill her in later and she didn't ask anything more about my plans. I grabbed a huge travel mug full of coffee and headed to RC's. I'd texted the night before to let him know I didn't think I could eat that early in the day, but I'd be up for a bite to eat on the way home. I arrived at six fifteen and RC came down to my car.

He got in and greeted me. "Good morning." The gleam in his eyes told me this was going to be an enjoyable day.

"Morning," I said in return.

"You sure about driving? Because we can still take my truck."

"No, it's all good. Just tell me which way to turn, unless you want to drive?"

"You'd be fine with it?"

"Sure. Why not? You've been there."

I got out, and we did a Chinese fire drill only without a red light. Once in the passenger's seat, I asked, "So where're we going?"

"Heading up to Route Thirty and then east."

"Gotcha."

RC pulled out of the parking space, and we were on our way.

Twenty minutes later, after neither one of us had said a word, RC asked, "Can you put on some music?"

"Yeah." My iPod was hooked up to the sound system, so I hit play.

When Linus and Lucy by the Vince Guaraldi Trio came on, RC said "Let me see that," and snatched the iPod from my grasp. While driving, he scrolled through my songs and then commented, "It's always great to have an iPod on a road trip that has over twelve songs on it. Not twelve bands, or twelve albums, but twelve *songs*. Dude! What the heck?"

I shrugged. "I told you I don't listen to music."

"But Nick, five of these are Christmas music. That's pathetic. Luckily I brought mine." RC set my iPod down, fished his out of his pocket and handed it to me. "Hook mine up and hit play."

"But I love the soundtrack to *A Charlie Brown Christmas.* Can we listen to the end of Linus and Lucy before I switch it?"

He grinned at me and nodded. "Sure." RC had the same whimsically amused look in his eyes he always had. I used to hate it because it meant he was about to make fun of me, but now, the idea that he was amused with my actions made me feel more connected to him all the time. It's like he was thinking about me and the knowledge of that was comforting.

When my song was over, I hooked my cable to his iPod and hit play. "Venke Knutson," RC informed me when the female (of course) voice came on over the sound system. Her pleasant soprano filled my little car, and I noticed RC's lips moving with the words. He knew the song, but he wasn't singing it for me. *Oh well.* I hadn't heard of the Norwegian singer before, but I liked her. Some small part of my brain was still amused by his obsession over female singers, and I almost wanted to turn on Aerosmith just to see his reaction. (But I didn't.)

My phone rang. "It's my friend, Paul," I explained.

"So answer it. I won't listen in."

I snickered and answered on the third ring. "Hey."

"So, tell me again why I agreed to work for you?"

"Because you love me."

"No, I don't. I hate opening."

"But you get to work with Marcy," I pointed out.

"My only perk. But now I have to work your shift and mine, which means I'm here twelve hours. No fun, man."

"Sorry."

"Where is it you're going?"

"A reptile show."

"Is it with that guy? The customer Marcy calls Scruffy Dude?"

"Yup."

Paul chuckled. "Okay. Well then, enjoy yourself and try not to think about sex or kissing or anything. Hang out with him. If it's right, you'll know. And thanks for nudging Marcy in my direction. She's really great."

"I knew you'd get along together."

"Thanks. Fill me in later."

"Okay. Bye."

"Bye."

I looked at RC. "Paul covered for me today."

"I gathered that."

A COUPLE of hours later, we arrived in Hamburg. It was a tiny town with an even tinier street. I wasn't a fan of narrow roads with parked cars on both sides, but RC handled it fine. We found a space in the parking lot next to the building, but I noticed it was filling up fast. I was glad he'd planned on getting here early.

"Now," RC explained before we got out of my car, "don't stare at people."

I gave him a look. "What? Why would I stare at people?"

"Well, you know how you like to look at my tattoos, now that you know I have them?"

"Yeah, I think they're cool. But you told me you have four, so I'm patiently waiting to see the last one."

"Which you are not," he said firmly. "You stare at my tattoos, but I know you. I'm fine with it for the most part, but the people in there may not be."

"What do you mean?"

"Nick, have you ever been around people who aren't like you?"

"How do you mean?"

"You're rather clean-cut. Nice hair, perfect skin, and not a shred of black in all the articles of clothing I've seen. What I'm saying is that you might stand out, and I don't want you gawking at everyone. These are my kind of people. Not yours."

I didn't know what he was getting at. What kind of people were *my* kind of people? I'd spoken to M-L about our group being the "pretty people," but RC hadn't been privy to that conversation. How would he know what kind of people I hung with? I shrugged off his warning. "Okay."

"Okay?"

"Yes. I'll be cool. But...."

"But what?"

"You sound... prejudiced."

"No, I don't."

"Sure you do. You just stereotyped me as 'clean-cut' and all the people in there as something other than that."

"What? No, I didn't."

"I think you did. But, whatever." I blew it off. It wasn't worth arguing over, even if his comment made me think for thirty seconds about how easy it was to unwittingly stereotype people. I probably did it more than I realized.

We got out of the car and headed to the line of people waiting to get into the building. It didn't open until 9:00 a.m., but there were already about a hundred people in front of us. As soon as we stepped behind the last person, I saw what RC had been getting at in the car. We stood behind a guy and his girlfriend or wife or something, and I had to look at the asphalt to keep from staring. I glimpsed his nose ring and that was all I could think about. It was huge. A thick, silver ring with pointed arrowheads on the ends hung through the middle of his nose. He sported a thick black mustache, which only made the nose ring easier to spot.

I glanced at the parked vehicles next to us as a way of surreptitiously inspecting his other jewelry. He had at least twenty silver hoops in each ear. Holy crap! How did a person wear so many earrings and have any cartilage left?

I felt my phone vibrate. I took it out and noticed a text from RC. I glared at him. "Really?"

He didn't comment so I opened it and read: *I told you not to stare at people.*

I texted back: *I'm not staring. I glanced at him casually. I can't help it. I've never seen so many piercings in one person's head before. He must set off metal detectors.*

Nick, I told you these were not the type of people you're used to. They're tough, tattoo sporting, pierced-n-proud, leather-clad type people. Some are hard-core enough to bring venomous animals. I don't want you making an ass of yourself staring like this is a freak show.

I'm cool. I'm not messing with anyone.

Keep it that way.

Can I comment if I see a tattoo I like?

I guess. But stop staring like you've never seen one before. It's embarrassing.

Okay. I could stare at you instead, I teased. RC tilted his head at me and glared. I smirked, knowing he didn't like that idea. But he was the one wearing a sleeveless shirt this time. I wasn't used to it. I texted again: *Your tattoos are exposed. You know I'm fascinated. I count three so far. Where is the fourth? Can I see it?*

Nick, don't make me regret bringing you.

Chill, I'm messing with you. I like the Celtic cross on your arm. I winked at him and changed the subject. *You're not kidding about the leather. Doesn't it get hot? This is summer.*

Yes, but no one cares.

"So, are you planning on buying something?" I asked out loud. Texting a person I was standing next to seemed retarded, plus I'd gotten bored.

"Maybe. I've always got my eye out for certain morphs."

"Morphs?" He'd lost me. "I thought you liked snakes?"

"A morph is a snake. They're called morphs because people have figured out how to reproduce different color and pattern variations by breeding various types together. Ball pythons normally come in brown tones. Then, variations of the browns started cropping up. Before long, breeders learned how to create new varieties by breeding certain strains together. Some are extremely rare and hard to create. I have a book about breeding morph ball pythons. I'm still learning, but I plan to do more of it as my stock increases. There's a lot of money in it if you're willing to put in the time and energy."

"Money in breeding snakes?"

"Yup. The highest I've ever seen one snake priced at a reptile show was eight thousand."

My jaw dropped. "Dollars?" I noticed a guy three people ahead of us smirk. Sure, he could listen in, but I wasn't allowed to stare. *Dumb!*

RC said, "Yup. Online you can find breeders asking ten, twenty, even thirty thousand dollars for a single snake. It sounds crazy, but people out there are willing to pay good money to find that perfectly unique snake, especially if they can create more and sell them to make an even bigger profit."

That info blew me away. It's crazy! The line began to move once nine rolled around, and we were at the door in no time. I paid, they stamped my hand with a frog that glowed under black light, and I stepped into the building with anticipation but no idea of what I'd see. What met my eyes blew my mind.

The place was packed—I mean *packed!*—with reptiles, lined up on tables in about eight different aisles. RC explained that had we gotten here later, each aisle would have already been thick with people trying to look at every specimen. As it was, the rows of tables were fairly easy to navigate and I could look at everything as we walked up each lane. I had never seen such a wide variety of snakes in my entire life. And these were not even all the kinds of snakes you could buy. RC said the ones at this show were mainly pythons and boas, but I also saw tags for rat snakes, corn snakes, and other stuff.

He explained, "We might come across rattlesnakes, some copperheads, and maybe even a snapping turtle or two. One time I saw a three-foot caiman for sale. I'm telling you, they have everything, but most vendors are selling the species the majority wants to buy."

"I saw a bunch of turtles on that table over there." I pointed, hoping we'd get to that lane soon. "But who wants to buy a rattlesnake? Because that sounds insane. Aren't they poisonous?"

"Actually, the term is venomous," he explained as we strolled. "A poison is something you ingest, whereas venom is injected into you. And yeah, I wouldn't want to buy a rattlesnake, but there are lots of people that think owning a deadly animal is exciting. One time, I walked by the guy who was selling them and overheard a customer asking to hold one. The seller said he could, but he had to pay a twenty-dollar deposit. I thought, what's the point? If he gets tagged by a rattlesnake, he's gonna be hurtin' for certain. Who cares if he paid the twenty dollars? Even if their bites are rarely fatal, it still sounded stupid to me."

I listened intently and tried not to smile as much as I was on the inside. RC was so relaxed. He wasn't normally a talker. Even when he'd come to my house to show me his cell phone, we ended up playing Call of Duty more than we spoke. That is, until my mom questioned his name, and then he spoke at length about himself. I really liked the sound of his voice when he wasn't strained or frustrated with me, or trying not to reveal too much too soon. I understood not opening up to people; I didn't tend to do that myself, but there was a difference between talking about the weather and talking about personal interests. Here, he was talking about things he knew and loved, and I could hear it in his tone. And that tone was the one I could listen to all day.

I walked past a display of snakes that were all neatly contained in individual Plexiglas boxes with locks on them, and spotted a silvery looking one with a pale yellow stripe down its back. A label on the lid said "purple passion" and the cost was set at twenty eight hundred dollars. I touched his arm. "RC, look at this one."

"Pretty."

"But it's gray, not purple."

"No. But it has lavender tones to the gray. Very unusual."

I leaned in and whispered, "Is twenty eight hundred a good price?"

"I guess. I'd have to research it if I was ever going to sell one."

I grabbed his arm again and pointed. "There's another gray one for two thousand."

He grinned at me. "Yup. A sterling. Very cool."

I was glad to have loads of distractions because that grin was starting to do things to me.

I tugged on his shirt when we came to the next table. "Look, look, this one is really yellow! Is that normal to be so yellow?" People that yellow could have jaundice. I wondered if it was sick.

RC replied, "Yes, it's a bumble bee. They are a result of a pastel and a spider."

"Spider? I thought we were talking snakes?"

He smirked at me again, most likely amused at my complete ignorance, but I wasn't offended by his pleasure in it. The way he looked at me felt nice. "A spider is a morph. Remember morphs are color and pattern variations of normal ball pythons? A spider has a stripe down its back that looks like someone dribbled chocolate syrup along its spine. Look," he said, pointing to a container that was labeled "spider." "See how the black drips down the sides of the snake ever so slightly?"

I looked. I saw it. It wasn't as dark as the ones RC told me were "normal" pythons. There were shades of brown with spots and swirls I thought were kind of pretty. But the morphs definitely outdid the "normal" ones in beauty. Some of the snakes I spotted were spectacular! And RC didn't seem bothered at all every time I pointed and tugged on his arm like a little kid going to the zoo for the first time. He was very patient and explained everything.

And snakes were not the only reptiles that fascinated me. I also saw turtles, frogs, and lizards of all kinds. There was a blue and green Australian chameleon that looked completely fake until it moved. And talk about colorful. I had never seen a more gorgeous reptile—correction, amphibian—as the poison dart frogs. Red and black, yellow and black, and blue and black; so bright and so tiny I wanted to touch them to make sure they were real. I really liked frogs. I was going to ask RC about buying a blue one when he explained the maintenance involved.

"You don't want one of those."

"Why not? They're so cute."

"Because you have to feed it flightless fruit flies and make sure the humidity is high enough. You can't be bothered to get out of bed on your day off. Are you going to put in the time required to keep it alive?"

It scared me that he knew me so well is such a short time. "Um, no. I guess not."

"Maybe in time, if we come to more of these shows and you learn about the frogs, then I'll let you get one. But for now, stick to observing. No pet should be bought without researching it first." We walked down another aisle, and he pointed to a silvery mottled snake in a huge fish tank. "Take the Burmese python for example. They're cute when they're small. They actually look similar to an axanthic ball python except they grow to lengths of nineteen feet."

"What? Holy shit. Where would you keep a snake that big?"

"Some people build custom structures for them, and some dedicate a room in their house to their snake. I find it ridiculous. In the same space, I can house fifty snakes and make money off the ones I produce. But, on the other hand, some people like huge snakes that could eventually eat you. Me, not so much. I like to hold them. I like to let them slither around sometimes. I'd be nervous if a nineteen-foot snake was moving around my house."

"You and me both."

"The worst part is that loads of people find they can't house them, and Florida has a python infestation because of it. People just let them go in the wild. Makes me angry. These snakes get big enough to eat children. People need to be responsible with the animals they own; letting them go is plain wrong."

We walked down another aisle and I took in all the displays of snakes and other reptiles and amphibians. It was cool. And believe me, I hadn't missed RC's comment that "if we go to another show" he might consider "letting me get a frog." *Ha, ha.* Like he's the boss of me. Still, I liked the implication he wanted to hang out with me. I wanted to hang around him.

We walked up to one counter (I guess you call it), and RC bumped knuckles across the display with the sales guy. "Hey, RC. How's my favorite queer?"

The guy's comment made my ears perk up, but RC wasn't flustered. He replied, "Good. This is my friend, Nick. He's new to the scene." RC tapped me on the chest and suddenly I felt like I had to give a speech on stage. I felt awkward.

"Um, hi," I said as I slowly lifted my hand. Instantly, I experienced a strange tunnel vision, or something. I wasn't in my element. Everywhere I looked there was leather, tattoos, and piercings galore. Where were the Prada bags and Gucci shoes? Dawn wore Versace. This was like the planet Mars compared to what I was used to, and it bothered me for… like… twenty seconds. Then the odd sensation of displacement vanished, and I realized I felt more accepted and comfortable on Mars than on my own planet, Earth. Was it because RC was with me? Or was it because these people seemed more genuine? I glanced around and watched people talking. No one was pointing. No one was whispering or giving anyone else a wide berth. Everyone seemed unaware they were in each other's personal space. Here, the commonality of interests crossed social boundaries. I liked it and smiled inwardly.

"What has you hanging around with this loser?" the guy asked.

I shrugged, still contemplating the enjoyment I felt in RC's world as compared to mine.

RC gave me a strange look and spoke to the man behind the snake table. "Don't mind Nick. He's not normally like this. I'm used to an arrogant bastard, not a sheepish introvert. Anyway, he's a friend. Not to change the subject, but I was looking for an albino female if you've got one."

I didn't like being referred to as if I wasn't listening, and I guarantee he knew I'd have something to say about it later. Sheepish introvert, my ass. I didn't know anyone; how was I supposed to act?

RC purchased his snake, and we walked away.

I grumbled to RC, "He seemed rude."

"Charlie? He's cool. I met him years ago. He liked my flag tattoo and told me he was surprised to find a queer guy who liked snakes. I told him I'm just a guy. We got talking, and he said I'm the first homosexual he'd ever met at a show. Now it's like a joke between us. He calls me queer, and sometimes I call him a redneck."

"Doesn't it bother you, being called queer?" I certainly didn't like the sound of it.

"No. It's what I am. The definition of queer in its purest form means 'strange or odd from a conventional viewpoint—unusually different.' That's me in a nutshell. Maybe that's why I like morphs so much. Each one is unusually different, but most are more beautiful in color and variation than the original, 'normal' ball python. So if you think about it, queers by definition are more beautiful than the 'normal' folks."

"What about that one?" I pointed to a black snake. It didn't look all that exciting. I'd seen black rat snakes before and for all I knew, it could've been one.

RC chuckled. "A pure black python is not so easy to create. You need specific genes. I haven't been able to do it yet."

What RC said got me thinking. "But, I don't know, isn't queer harsher than just being called gay?"

"Personally, I don't think so. I like the term queer, but I know others who disagree. Some think there should be an acronym or a basic term to describe anyone gay, lesbian, transgender, bisexual, asexual, androgynous, and a slew of other terms. I think it's a personal thing. I've never liked to be lumped in with all the rest. I prefer to be left alone.

"Shakespeare said, 'What's in a name? A rose by any other name would smell as sweet.' The paradox is that although names or labels shouldn't matter one way or another, they do because our emotions attach stigmas to the labels. I may be the same person on the inside no matter what you call me, but being called a faggot while I'm curled in a fetal position trying to protect my vital organs because some asshole thinks it's funny to kick the queer kid has a habit of changing a person. Me and every other kid who has gone through it. Names hurt because they yank away the threads of self-esteem that hold each person together. When someone is out of self-esteem, pride, or dignity, that person is bound to do anything just to get to the next day. Some sell themselves into prostitution or get lost in drugs. I knew someone who answered a personal ad and moved to California to live with a guy he'd never met. I haven't heard from him since. He could be happy, or he could be dead. I don't know. It might sound preposterous, but shit like that happens. People are just so caught up in their world of pain versus addiction that anything can and does happen."

RC had a point.

I had never thought about it so deeply before. I'd been avoiding the terminology because being called gay bothered me, but I wasn't sure why. I wanted to avoid the difficulties associated with being in that specific minority because I saw it as a detriment or a stigma. I hadn't wanted to get marginalized for it. I was a white male born into some level of comfort. I had a job, but I lived at home with my parents. I came and went as I pleased, and dated whomever I wanted. I feared how much that would change. If I was gay or queer, would my life on Easy Street disappear? I liked Easy Street.

I wasn't sure if I was completely gay anyway. I did like girls. I missed Dawn, and that had to count for something.

As we made our way through a thickening crowd, and I stopped to look at a display of hissing cockroaches and venomous centipedes, someone pushed past RC and must have shoved him from behind because he slammed up against my back. I felt his hands on my arms, I guess to keep him from falling farther into me, and I was pretty sure I felt his pelvis up against my butt as I caught my balance on the table in front of me. The sensation that shivered through me wiped out my doubts about me having feelings for RC. No woman had ever had that effect on me, Dawn included. Corey had come close to making me tremble to that extent when he'd pushed me up against that garage last year at M-L's and kissed me senseless, but no one else since then.

RC might not have done it on purpose, but the results were indisputable. In a span of three seconds, I conjured visions of his mouth on my neck and his arms around my bare chest. My groin woke up and my nipples got hard. He whispered my name in my ear, and I wanted him. He groaned my name, loudly, and then....

"Nick? Nick!" RC's voice broke through my foggy daydream. "Are you all right?"

"What? Yeah." I felt so nervous. I hoped he couldn't read my thoughts. "Why?"

"I said I'm sorry for bumping into you like that, and I said it at least three times before you answered. You completely spaced out on me. Are you okay? Do you get claustrophobia or something? There are really a lot of people in this building."

I shook my head. "No. I'm fine."

RC didn't exactly look convinced. He added, "Or we could head home? I'm done here, and the crowd is making it hard to look at stuff."

"Yeah, fine."

He motioned toward the exit, and I looked in that direction as I walked. I tried to stick to Paul's idea of no sexual thoughts, hang with the guy and enjoy his company, but *damn!* I swear I still felt him against my back. I was still silent when we got in the car. Grateful he drove, I sank down in the passenger side and tried to will away my feelings. I had never had to control my desires before. In the past, when I got hard, I just took care of it, with or without a girl. Now? *Fuckin' hell....*

After we were back on the highway, RC said, "Nick, I don't know what's come over you, but I hope it doesn't have to do with me bumping into you. It was an accident. I never intended—"

"Do you like me?" I blurted, losing the inner battle I was fighting. Denial was my go-to game plan, but I couldn't keep it up.

"Oh, fuck no," RC grimaced. "You did not just go there. We covered this already with the movie theater fiasco. This wasn't a date, Nick. I like reptile shows, and I hoped you might too."

He was getting angry, but I had questions I wanted to ask. "But—"

"No. We've already been down that road. Don't act like an ass again, or I'll stop the car right here on Route 78 and make you walk."

"I'm not. I'm asking if you like me because I'm thinking... maybe... I kind of like y—"

"Oh, no. Don't even say it! You don't get to be my friend and then come on to me because I'm gay and you think it's okay. No. It isn't."

"But—"

"But nothing. Last I checked you have a girlfriend. I'm not becoming an investigative experiment because you can't handle me bumping into your ass. And don't give me any bullshit about having gay friends. This isn't a survey on your diversity."

I obviously couldn't explain myself in a way he'd listen, so I didn't try. I leaned my head on the window and curled away from him.

The ride was silent all the way home.

WHEN WE pulled into a parking space on his street, RC asked, "You heading home or do you want to hang for a while?"

I was shocked he'd asked. "Are you going to yell at me again?"

"Are you going to make an ass of yourself?"

"No."

"Then you can stay if you want." He got out and closed his door.

I followed suit and walked around the back of my car. "I'm staying," I said, jumping at the chance and hoping I wouldn't do anything regrettable once we got inside. "I want to see your snake collection. You're going to let me see your snakes, right? Last time you were all secretive. I really want to see them." I hoped it didn't come across as begging, because I felt like I would be willing to beg. I was confused around him, but also anxiously hopeful.

RC gave me another weird look as we neared his apartment, but he didn't comment. Poor guy, he couldn't figure me out. Heck, I couldn't figure me out. Then my phone buzzed with a text from Tara.

She said: *Are you all right? I know I said I'd give you some space, but I had to say hi.*

Hi. I'm good.

Are you hanging with Corey?

No, I um, no. I'm with another friend. I'll text tomorrow. Okay? I want to talk, but not right now.

All right. As long as you're okay.

I'm fine.

Text me later to say goodnight.

I will. Laterz.

I put my phone in my pocket as we went inside RC's apartment, and he asked, "That your girlfriend?"

I nodded. "Yup." *Dude! It's like he can see into my head.*

Chapter 16: *Me*

INSIDE, I metaphorically twiddled my thumbs as I waited in his living room for him to return from the bathroom. The question still floated around in my head. Does he like me or not? He'd sounded offended I broached it at all, so I wasn't about to push. Maybe he didn't. Could I live with that?

"Yes, you dumbass." I heaved a sigh.

I should have been thankful he'd overlooked my flaws in the first place since I'd placed my foot in my mouth on several occasions already. As my mom would say, "Count your blessings." I could. I would. I was here. If RC wasn't attracted to me, so be it. Next step?

"Just be yourself, Nick. Be yourself."

RC returned from the bathroom and asked, "You hungry?"

"Yeah. But what about the snake tour?"

"Later. I want to eat. That's one thing about snakes: they're never in a hurry."

I grinned. "Okay."

"I have some chicken in the fridge if you want to take it out. I'm going to put the new snake in a habitat. I'll be right back."

"But I wanted to see them."

"You will."

RC left the room, and I went into the kitchen. We'd done this before, and as I set about finding the cutting board, knives, bowls, chicken, fry pan, wooden spoon, and the vegetables, I couldn't help but think about how easy it was to fall into this like a dance. I knew where everything was without asking. RC joined me and completed my steps without pause. For example... I was chopping onions, and as I reached for the bowl, he was right there with it. It happened with the chicken too. I didn't even ask. He knew to hold the pan out to me. Our synchronicity was uncanny. And, as before, we worked together without stepping on each other's toes or bumping into one another. It was as if we were two halves functioning as one. I don't function that well with people on grill whom I've worked with for months.

I wanted to ask if he felt it too, but I didn't want to muff up the moment. I'd said enough in the car on the way home. Right now, I knew it was best to remain silent. But silence... silence was a practice in patience, and I was not always patient. I had stuff I wanted to say.

We ate in silence too. I surreptitiously glanced at RC a few times, trying to ascertain whether or not he was happy about the absence of dialogue, but I couldn't tell by his expression. On the fourth glance, he grumbled, "Stop looking at me, Nick."

"Okay," I said shifting my attention back down at my lunch. Or was it supper? It was a late lunch and early dinner. Was that called supper? I didn't know, but I wasn't going to ask. I think RC liked the quiet.

After a kick-ass stir-fry meal—I'll go with meal—I asked if I could turn on some music. I knew he liked music, so I figured it was the best way to keep the enjoyable afternoon enjoyable. They say music soothes the savage beast; well maybe it staves off the beast before he becomes beastly. Sounded good to me.

He reluctantly agreed, "Um, yeah, sure. You can put on some music."

"Why do you sound so hesitant about it?"

RC replied, "Because no one's touched my CDs before. Don't.... Just don't get them out of order."

"Okay."

"Or better yet, hit shuffle and then you don't have to do anything. It's an old stereo system. It was my dad's."

"Uh-huh," I agreed.

I walked into the living room and plopped down in front of the stereo. It was indeed old—like dinosaur old—but easy to figure out how it worked. I opened the hatch-like front and the insides spun around like an old-time jukebox filled with forty-fives. I only knew what forty-fives were because my mom had some. I pulled one CD out. "*500 Days of Summer,* the motion picture soundtrack," I read out loud. "Never heard of it." I put it back and pushed play. I watched the inside turn since it was internally lit, and I heard the mechanism engage.

Because all his shit was in alphabetical order, I found the CD case and read the back. The singer on this track was Zooey Deschanel.

I stood up, listening to the plucky tones of what sounded to me like a ukulele. *Funny, I didn't know people still played those.* I closed my eyes and let myself go. If I was going to be *me* and act like that in front of RC, then he'd have to get used to the fact that I randomly danced sometimes. Only Corey knew that about me. I'd told him a long time ago I liked dancing with my little sister. It was fun spending time with Jennifer, and her friends could be really funny to watch, but I'd never told my friends because they might have thought I was less manly. Corey was the only one I trusted with the info. Now, RC was going to get an intro into Nick 202: Dancer Extraordinaire.

I recalled a song from Just Dance and tried mimicking the moves. They fit this swingy little tune quite well. I was not the best dancer in the world, if I was truly honest, but I was good at copying dance moves. That was the reason I always won that game and Jenn hated me for it. I swayed my hips and moved my arms, all the while tapping my toes. I kept my eyes shut, and I could only imagine what RC thought if he was watching. Was he watching? *I hope he's watching.* More than likely, I appeared much like a happy-go-lucky eight-year-old, spinning with my arms held gently out as if catching a breeze as I twirled.

I remembered watching my sister dance in the grass one sunny afternoon when she was six. I'd always thought she was adorable when she whirled her princess dresses around and swayed to the music. She was so beautiful as she spun, not caring what anyone thought. I tried to reproduce that innocence now, in RC's living room. He'd only seen the sex-crazed part of me. He needed to experience the goofy, carefree side as well. I could be fun. I wasn't all about the sex and women.

I heard the lyrics saying something about Su-Su-Sugar Town. The singer, Zooey Descha-something, sang, "I never had a friend or wanted one, so I'll just lay back and laugh at the sun...." I liked her voice. It tinkled like glass wind chimes.

I kept my eyes tightly shut, afraid RC *was* watching, but also afraid to find out he wasn't because then I'd be disappointed. I thought he was there because I could smell him. His soap or something had a distinct aroma I'd picked up on the first time we'd eaten lunch together. I'd liked it but was too embarrassed to ask him what it was. Now I was more nervous than embarrassed to ask because he might think I was coming on to him. I mean, it wasn't like I couldn't or didn't want to come on to him, but if I did, I was defeating the purpose of just being around him twenty-four seven like Paul suggested. If I really did like RC, I should feel something without the need to bring sexual attraction into the mix.

I thought my dancing might get a laugh out of him, but RC hadn't made a sound. Either he didn't want to hurt my feelings with snide comments or he liked watching me dance. "Liking me" was an awe-inspiring concept. Maybe I could do more quirky things in his company like I always wished I could do normally but never did for fear of ridicule. My friends didn't welcome random silliness unless alcohol was involved. If RC accepted me as I was, it would give me more reason to pursue my feelings, even if they were somewhat convoluted in my brain.

I played it cool even though the uncertainty of the moment was killing me. In my mind's eye, he was leaning against the doorframe, observing my silly behavior from a short distance away. Possibly grinning. I was having so much fun floating around, I was saddened to hear the song end and the CD player shuffle. It picked a different one.

A song I knew came on, and my heart thudded suddenly. *Oh my gosh, I can sing this one!* I was so excited. I sang way better than I danced; my chorus teacher in high school told me so. She'd said I could sing professionally but that's a hard career to get into.

I stilled momentarily, my back to where RC theoretically stood, and played the air piano I pictured in front of me. RC stifled a snicker. *Oh good, he's there.* I didn't allow his presence to draw me out of my trance, though. In that moment, I was Carly Simon. Just as the lyrics started, I pulled an imaginary microphone up to my mouth, spun around, opened my eyes, and started singing on cue.

A shadow crossed his face, and he shifted his stance. Still, I sang. Maybe he'd gotten the impression I was singing to him and he didn't like it. So far I hadn't seen any indication he liked me. That would explain the discomfort I plainly saw. He *had* gotten pissed in the car, after all. I couldn't bear the idea M-L had about him not being attracted to me at all. I was adorable, wasn't I? And if he didn't like me singing this song, what could I do? It wasn't my fault he had very little music I recognized. Plus, it had shuffled to this song. I hadn't picked it.

RC joked, "And I thought you didn't listen to music. How the heck do you know all the words to 'Nobody Does It Better'?"

"James Bond," I blurted between lyrics. "My dad loves James Bond."

RC smiled, giving me the impression he liked my singing. He also must have known this was the theme song to *The Spy Who Loved Me*. He shook his head and strolled over to the CD player, switching it off.

I protested, "Hey, I was getting good."

RC nodded. "Yeah. You should audition for *The Voice*."

I tapped my chin. "Maybe I should."

"You're so vain," RC half-joked, or at least I thought he was joking.

I pointed out, "That's *another* Carly Simon song I know." I knew it only because M-L sang it to me at one of her parties when I was doing something she found arrogant. I laughed at the time because I'd never considered my vanity a bad thing. Was it? I'd have to think on it.

He chuckled. "I bet. Is there anything you can't do?"

"Um...." I considered. "I can't rebuild a transmission. Not yet."

RC laughed out loud and marveled, "Oh my gosh. Well, I guess there's one thing I have over you. Come on, I'll show you my snakes."

THE TOUR of the reptile room, probably a spare bedroom originally, was "neato-torpedo," as Julie would say. RC had a butt-load of cages— habitats, he kept calling them habitats—and they were all lined up around the room. He had twenty-six snakes in all, eighteen of which were breeding size. I found out that Exo Terra was a brand name of reptile terrariums, among other things. He had some snakes in terrariums and others in stackable tubs he explained were good to maintain humidity and helped conserve space when most of his snakes were for breeding and weren't exactly pets. He told me he held all of them anyway so my pouty-face over the cramped, dark spaces for the snakes wasn't necessary. He informed me they were all perfectly fine. Snakes were not social animals; they were mostly territorial. And if it looked like two snakes were "snuggling" together, it was only because they were vying for the best spot in the tank. But since ball pythons were typically not aggressive, two snakes "fighting" for the same space normally appeared cozy. He took a few of the snakes out, and I even held one. A first for me. RC said it was Tuck, and it looked exactly like the snake tattoo on his arm. When it came to feeding time, I didn't relish the idea of watching them eat mice. He told me most of them ate frozen mice so I didn't have to witness the killing, but I cringed anyway. RC must have seen my discomfort and asked if I'd rather play Xbox. It was late, but not late enough for me to want to go home. We did that instead.

After a few hours of Xbox, we watched *Transformers,* and I fell asleep on the couch. Somewhere around two in the morning, I felt movement. RC lifted my feet, which I think were in his lap, and slipped off the couch. I didn't have the energy to open my eyes, nor did I say anything. He laid a blanket over me. It was a nice gesture, although a bit unnecessary given the temperature in his apartment. At 3:30 a.m.—I know because I glanced at my watch—I had to pee. I got up, took care of business, and then the stalker in me took over.

I tiptoed over to his bedroom door and peeked in. He was on his back, sheet at his waist, bare-chested. The moonlight streaming in the window gave a mysterious feel to the room, and I stepped in. One more step, then another, and before I knew it I was standing beside his bed looking down at him while he slept. For some reason, I felt like a serial killer and had a sudden urge to buy plastic wrap. Too much Dexter!

RC's chest was very hairy, as I'd surmised, and I wanted to touch it badly. Now I understood where the term "bear" came from. He was covered in curly hair and had a rounded belly, just like a bear—a big teddy bear, I thought. I wanted to nuzzle this teddy bear and feel his hair rubbing all over my face, chest, and groin. Corey was pretty, but RC's body made me instantly horny. Corey had slim, sleek muscles where RC's were bulkier. His shoulders were hard and defined. He'd told me he was fat when he was younger and always seemed self-conscious about it, but from what I saw, he didn't look fat. He had pudge, sure. His belly was a mound of hairy flesh that begged to be rubbed like Aladdin's lamp, but his pecs were tight. He'd mentioned he worked out. I did too. Maybe we could work out together sometime, and I could see how much weight he used and watch him flex.

Oh, where the thought of that was leading me. I licked my lips.

His nipples were pebbled and just visible. I pictured licking them and sucking the surrounding hair into my mouth. *Oh, God, I need to touch myself.* I reached down and rubbed my erection. I had this strong desire to jerk off over him and cover his torso with ribbons of cum. And then maybe climb on top of him and rub our sweaty naked bodies together until I was hard again so I could slip inside his ass and come again.

Shit, Paul's suggestion is never going to work. I think of sex all the fucking time!

I backed away. I had to. Jerking off was too risky. RC thought of me as a friend. Did friends sneak into other friend's rooms and jerk off watching them sleep? Um, maybe the creepy ones did. I didn't want to be creepy. I wanted to be normal. I went back to the couch and fretfully lay there until I found sleep again.

IN THE morning, I went home feeling lonely. RC shook my hand and said he'd see me later that week. RC wasn't with me right now, and I missed him. I lay in bed Sunday night staring at the ceiling trying to remember what it felt like when he looked at me. Those few brief moments when his eyes caught mine and glinted gave me such a rush. Who knew something so small could have such an effect on me? We didn't do or talk about anything sexual yet still I reacted to him. His expressions made me shiver and had me feeling warm and sappy. Come to think of it, I'd seen the same warm and sappy look on M-L's face when she looked at Shawna.

Was I in love with RC? No. I couldn't be.

I rolled over, burying my head under blankets and pillows. *Argh! I hate this. Why does my life have to be complicated?* I knew what I needed to do, but I didn't want to do it. I couldn't. Change was hard, and I liked my life the way it was.

Or so I thought.

Chapter 17: *Wednesdays*

I WAS becoming increasingly anxious about Wednesdays. Why? Because it seemed to be the only time I got to see RC during the week. I'd wanted to invite myself over a couple times, but after the *Iron Man 3* debacle, I thought I'd wait on him. He needed to make a move and invite me. Except he hadn't.

Being with him was limited to Wednesday afternoons and the occasional weekend when Tara was too busy to see me. He and I texted, but not often. I couldn't think of things to say. I couldn't very well text him about his alluring features and what I was going to do with them, like I texted to Tara. So I sent random pictures of a sub I'd made or street signs I found particularly funny, and one time it was a picture of the top of my shoe. He never told me to stop sending them, but he also didn't send goofy things back.

It was disappointing to think he had no desire to be anything more than friends. Maybe I had to broach that topic, because it was increasingly difficult to view him as just a friend when all I wanted to do was be with him and to hell with the rest of the world.

I was wiping down the counter after a slow lunch, thinking how long this day would be for me if it didn't pick up soon, when the doorbell sounded. I looked up expecting RC because it was Wednesday and spotted Corey. *Corey?* What was he doing here? I hadn't seen him in over three weeks. He smiled and walked over, so I met him by the swingy-door. I leaned against it with one arm draped along its edge.

"Hello, lover," he said seductively. Some people might take note of his tone and think it out of place in a restaurant when that sultry tone could be used better in a strip club, but it was the way he always sounded to me: sultry, seductive, and wickedly alluring. God, I hated that voice because it always made parts of me wake up when they were better remaining at rest.

"What are you doing here?" I asked, slightly nervous with a dash of happy. In the back of my mind, I knew RC would probably be here in a few minutes. If I tried, I could probably chat him into leaving. I'd already made RC's sandwich, and the boss told me I could go on break in five. Corey showing up was not going to fit into my plan. He had to go.

"I'm visiting my friend Tyler, and I wanted to see you," he pouted. "Isn't that okay?"

How could I argue with his cute face? "Sure," I said.

Corey stepped closer and placed his hand on top of mine, bringing our faces very near each other. It made me a little uncomfortable since we were in public, but he always smelled so sweet, like sugar, which made me want to lick him. Damn my overactive sex drive.

Corey reached up and made both my discomfort and attraction more difficult by tucking my hair behind my ear endearingly. But did I pull away? No. "Being with you in July," he said, "got me thinking about all the times we've been together. I've been living my dream, but I never considered your feelings in all of it. M-L said you were questioning yourself, and only now have I thought about how hard that must be. I remember when I came out." His bottom lip drew me closer. Whenever he pouted in the past, I'd wanted to suck on his lip. *Oh fuck, I can't have this now.*

He looked so adorable I almost missed what he said. "Wait, who said anything about coming out?" I leaned away, struggling not to focus on his lips.

He shrugged innocently, but the look in his eyes was anything but innocent. He was devious.

Corey continued as if I hadn't said a word. "My dad was overbearing," he said, "and suddenly had this grand idea of making me tough by having me do all the shit chores no one else wanted. He had me cleaning horse stalls and stacking hay bales. He even had the nerve to make me put ointment on one of the horses."

"Why was that a shit job? I thought you liked horses." I relaxed closer to him again, the swingy-door still between us, and Corey trailed a finger absently along my forearm.

"I do, but the injury was on the horse's penis. He'd jumped a broken part of the fence that year and the scratch under his belly got

Wade Kelly

178

infected. My brilliant father thought it would disgust me enough that I wouldn't like dick anymore. Well, he was dead wrong." He flashed a wicked grin. "It made me want to search for something comparable."

I chuckled weakly. The irony was amusing.

I knew some of Corey's story. He'd grown up on a farm, which was probably why he loved the city so much now. His father was less than receptive when he came out at the age of sixteen. Sometimes he would talk about his past when he visited my house for dinner, but we never talked long. Normally he quieted when the conversation got serious. Hearing the empathy in his offer to help me with my own internal debate was sweet, albeit somewhat disconcerting. Was I that transparent? I didn't think so. But it made me really glad to have him as a friend. I walked through the swingy-door and hoped no one would give me crap for socializing while on the clock, but talking over the door seemed too impersonal.

"I don't know what I am, Corey. There's just so much going on right now it's hard to think. Am I gay? Maybe." I hung my head and shrugged. It was hard to talk about, but he had a way of getting past my defenses. Just like M-L did. "I have a girlfriend, ya know? I've had a girlfriend as far back as I can remember. Girls flock to me like candy."

Corey stepped closer and touched my stomach with his fingers. He slid them slowly down as he whispered, "That's because your lollipop is sooo tasty." Corey nipped my chin with his teeth and giggled.

I leaned back but the door was there, preventing the action from being effective. I couldn't escape him. "Corey, not here."

Corey wasn't bothered by much so he conceded and leaned against the wall opposite me. He looked over my shoulder and his expression brightened. "Hey!"

I turned as Paul replied, "Hey, yourself. It's been ages. What have you been up to?" Paul reached out and Corey swatted his hand away, hugging him over the swingy-door. Paul smiled and rolled his eyes at me.

"Oh, nothing much. Just helping your boy figure out his shit."

Paul looked at me. "Good luck with that. I don't think Nick knows what the heck he wants."

I was slightly offended. "Hey, I'm right here. Can't you agree on my confusion behind my back like normal people?"

Paul opened the door and stepped through. I guess it was harder to have a conversation with a divider between us. He put his hand on my shoulder and squeezed. "Nick, you need all the help you can get. If you're still confused about being gay, maybe you need to stop kissing people and get to know the guy. Everybody is different. And everybody is attracted to different people for different reasons. Kissing Corey and kissing me is not going to help you figure it out."

Paul outlined my whole dilemma, and I felt an instant lump in my throat. Fuck! What would Corey say? I didn't get a chance to find out. Just as Corey opened his mouth with what I suspected was a probing question to Paul's inference to "the guy," Marcy from my left shrieked, "You kissed Paul?" I turned to address her shocked expression, but only managed to open my mouth before her hand connected with my cheek. "You asshole! He's mine."

"I'm sorry," I said, clutching my burning cheek.

"Sorry doesn't cut it," she scolded with a shake of her head that wiggled down the rest of her body. "All the times I tried to get you to kiss me, and you are kissing Paul behind my back. I don't believe it. You jerk. Well, I guess we have to make it even." She squared her shoulders and straightened her posture. "Now you have to kiss me."

"What? No," I protested.

"It's only fair. You kiss everyone else. I think it's about time you kissed me too."

"She does have a point," Corey mentioned.

I glared at him. "You're not helping."

"Go ahead," Paul offered, motioning to Marcy. "She's right. I was only trying to help you, but we should've said something to Marcy first. Kiss her and it makes us even."

"What if I don't want to?"

Marcy huffed, "So you're saying you'd rather kiss Paul? I thought you said you weren't gay, so why the hell would you kiss him in the first place?"

"Research."

She gaped. "Then do a little research on me!" Marcy's seething expression made me rethink what I'd just said. Fuck. I practically told her I'd rather kiss a *guy* than her. If I didn't kiss her what the heck would she do to me? We worked together and we were pretty good friends. If I didn't kiss her, she'd probably treat me like shit every shift we shared, or go on and on about me being gay. *How do I get myself into these situations?* "Fine," I relented. "I'll kiss you. And then this is over, okay? No more guilt and blame over my bad choices. Deal?"

"Deal," she said.

And then she jumped at me. Her mouth latched to mine quicker than a mosquito to the only warm body in the woods. And just like an insect, I could feel her sucking the life out of me straight through my mouth. Fuck "mosquito," she was a fucking leach. She pushed her tongue inside my mouth as she held my head firmly in place with her hands. She practically inhaled my body through that opening. My tongue felt like it was being sucked up by a vacuum. Good God, if that was my dick, she'd probably flay the skin right off.

I struggled for a couple minutes and finally managed to shove at her shoulders hard enough to get her to release me. She gasped for breath, as did I, and then looked at me with a wicked grin. "Wow. That was amazing."

I wasn't sure I would choose the same adjective to describe my experience, but I couldn't tell her that. She might want another try. "Yeah," I gasped.

Marcy turned to Paul and asked, "How come you don't kiss like that?"

Paul shrugged and looked at me. He was helpless, and I knew it. I gave him an empathetic look, and I think he got my meaning. Marcy was going to be a challenge, that's for sure. I knew for a fact he wasn't a bad kisser, but I couldn't speak for all his skills. The two of them walked away and left me with Corey. While my defenses were down, he rubbed my neck and fingered the back of my hair. Subconsciously I knew we were in public, but fighting against his affection was exhausting. I was simply tired of resisting all the time.

"You okay?" he asked.

"Yeah." I nodded and took one last deep breath. "I'll live, but I don't want a repeat experience anytime soon. My tongue still hurts."

Corey chuckled, and then he touched my cheek and smiled softly. He leaned forward and kissed me, but his kiss didn't threaten to rip my tongue from my mouth. And for the first time in history, I didn't resist being kissed at work. His kiss was sweet and languid, and made my muscles loosen. His was the kiss that made me want more. Not Marcy's. I pulled him into me and kissed him thoroughly before our lips parted. He smiled contentedly afterward.

"Feel better?" he whispered.

I nodded. "Much."

"Okay. I'm gonna go. I think you've had enough for today. When I'm in town again, I'll check on your progress." Corey moved his hands from my hips to my cheeks and guided my face closer so he could kiss my nose. It made me smile. "Stop being afraid to embrace who you are. And if there's a guy you're interested in, I want details." He winked and walked away.

I sighed and walked through the swingy-door to grab my lunch, but the tray was missing. I looked over at Julie. "Where's my tray?"

She pointed out into the dining room.

I turned and spotted RC in a booth by the window. He was eating, and my lunch was arranged on the other side of the table just the way I liked it. My shoulders sank, and I let my head fall back in defeat. *Shit.* There was no avoiding the subject now. What was he going to say?

I trudged out to our table and sat down. He didn't look up right away and that worried me. Was he angry? I guess he had every right to be. I gave him shit for being gay, and here I was kissing Corey right in front of him. If he yelled, I would take it like a man.

"How long have you been here?" I asked.

"Long enough."

"How much did you hear?" I figured it was a legitimate place to start.

RC glanced around the restaurant before sticking his eyebrow up. "Um, the place is empty, Nick. I heard everything."

"Oh."

"That blond kid your boyfriend?" he asked. He didn't sound angry, only inquisitive, which made me feel worse.

"Sort of. Maybe. I guess. I don't know what Corey is."

"You looked really *comfortable* with him to me. Corey? You mentioned that name before."

"Yeah." I didn't know what else to say. I picked at my sandwich and ate a french fry. I wasn't in the mood to eat. RC didn't sound angry, but for some reason that made me feel worse. He should be mad. I'd been a jerk before, and he had assumed it was because I couldn't handle him being gay. That totally wasn't it, so shouldn't he be upset I hadn't clarified myself at the movies? I expected him to.

He didn't. He ate. I picked at my food. The silence was irritating. He was finished twenty minutes later and standing up to leave.

"You're going?" I questioned.

"Yup. And you are going to walk me out to my truck."

"Oh," I said, hurriedly scooting off the edge of my seat. I dumped my trash and followed him out.

"I'm angry with you, Nick," he informed me quietly, standing by the door of his truck. He leaned against it so his posture was more relaxed than his tone, which confused me. Was he angry or not?

"Oh?" I questioned, but I didn't have any ground to stand on.

"All this time, I seriously thought you had an issue with my sexuality. All this time, I thought you were a stuck-up straight guy who pretended he had gay friends to make me feel better. You're not. You're just an asshole."

I had no response for that. I looked down, guilty as charged.

His voice was louder when he continued. "When were you planning to mention your boyfriend? Huh? *Ever?* Don't you think it would have been easier that first day to tell me you're gay too, or bi or whatever, instead of making some stupid comment about being on a date with me at the movies when all along it wasn't me being gay that was your issue? You have an issue being with *me*. I guess now I can see why. That blond kid is awfully pretty, and look at me." He gestured to himself. "I'm a sack of shit compared to that. And then you dare come on to me in the car after the reptile show? Was that part of your 'research'? You fucking asshole. Have you ever cared about anyone, really? Because from what I've seen, you *will* fuck anyone. Hell, you

kissed that girl just to make it 'even' between her and her boyfriend—
whom you also kissed! You have got to be the biggest player I've ever
met. Anyone, or anything, all at the same time. Good luck 'embracing
who you are.' I doubt you'll ever figure that out if all you do is kiss and
fuck everyone who comes along."

RC opened his truck door, and I jumped back before it clipped
me. He slammed the door and yelled at me through the open window.
"I thought we were friends, Nick. I thought you were my best friend.
How could you not tell me?"

He floored it and roared out of the parking lot, leaving me in tears.

WEDNESDAYS. EVERYTHING in my life happened on Wednesdays.
It was like those TV shows where the plot builds and everything
climactic happens right before the commercial break. I remembered
Buffy the Vampire Slayer commenting *in the show*, "Must be Tuesday."
So, this was my life: things happened and I thought, "Must be
Wednesday."

I worked eight to three. At lunch, RC didn't show. I was
depressed about it, but not surprised. He hadn't talked to me all
weekend. I hadn't seen or heard from him since he peeled out of the
parking lot. I knew where he lived, but this was not like the last time
I'd made him angry. I deserved this. I couldn't show up at his place yet.
He should be allowed space to be angry. And I had nothing to say to
him anyway. "I'm sorry" wouldn't cut it this time.

After work, I went to the one place I knew I could go, and to the
one activity which normally helped me forget everything else. I went
over to Tara's.

Her parents were home so we ended up at her friend Cindy's
house. Cindy invited us to drink shots, and soon enough we were all on
her bedroom floor passing around the vodka. A couple of hours later
Cindy passed out. It was me and Tara looking at each other and
glancing at Cindy, and back to each other again. *Hmm.* I could see the
cogs turning in Tara's mind as she slipped her shirt off.

"Are you sure?" I whispered. "She's—"

"Out cold."

Cindy was on the floor beside us. Tara pulled my shirt off and pointed to the bed. We crawled up onto the mattress, and I dove for her lips as we grabbed each other. I unzipped, and so did she. Her pink panties fell to the floor after she worked them over her ankles. I dipped my nose and rubbed my face down there, feeling her fur and enjoying the way it felt against my cheeks. Yeah, I liked the hair.

That's when my brain switched over to autopilot.

Yeah, dark hair, I sighed. *Hair like RC's. He has great hair, plus he's hairy all over. I want to touch his hairy body and rub myself up against him. Watching him sleep makes my mouth water to taste him. I miss him so much. I wonder what his pubic hair looks like. Corey and I used to rub our hard cocks together while we kissed sometimes. I want to do that with RC. Yeah, rub our cocks together. Next time I see him, I have to say something. I want him.*

My imagination conjured all kinds of things as I fucked. I could not get my mind off RC. I didn't want to be with Tara.

When she shoved me off and slapped my face, I blinked away my daydreams and wondered what I had done.

Tara glared at me. "I told you not to fuck my ass, Nick. What part of no don't you understand?"

Oh shit! "I'm sorry," I begged, reaching for her.

She batted my hand away and pulled a plush blanket over her body. "Just get out."

I looked over at her friend Cindy—she was still out cold. I felt like a heel, but at least there wasn't an eyewitness other than Tara. I got my clothes and dressed quickly. "I'll text you later."

"Don't," she said. "That really hurt."

"I know. I'm sorry."

"You know what? I'm done. This isn't worth it. Since you'd rather be with Corey, now's your chance."

"This isn't about Corey," I stressed, even though the good sense inside my head was yelling at me to thank God and run for it. I didn't exactly want her to know it was about my attraction to RC, but I also regretted everyone assuming all my personal problems had to do with Corey. Corey was innocent in this.

"It doesn't even matter anymore," she said, still looking away from me. "I hate that Dawn was right."

With the mention of Dawn's name, Tara dowsed me with cold water. I asked, "What does Dawn have to do with this?"

She finally turned her attention in my direction. "She told me we'd never last because you're gay, but I didn't want to believe her. She said you weren't the commitment type and you were only good for a fuck. That much I *could* believe."

"That isn't fair. She was the one who broke up with me. And *she* was the one who initiated sex practically every day. She's the horny hog, not me. If she thought I was gay, why'd she do that?"

She cackled. "I don't know. Ask her. Maybe she thought it was fun using you."

"But... why'd she think I was gay?"

She shrugged unsympathetically. "She said it was the way you stared at some guy back in high school. She didn't tell me his name, just that he had a blue Mohawk."

I thought about it for a minute and finally remembered him. I hadn't seen him in school before then and not after, although he could have dyed his hair a different shade and thereby disappeared from my radar. But one day he came out of the janitor's closet looking as if he'd slept there all night and it made me want to walk over and talk to him because something about his lips and his pout intrigued me. I followed him down one hall and that was when Dawn had stopped me and asked me out.

"Are we done here?" Tara demanded. "Because I'd like to get a shower and wash your stench off me."

When had she become so cruel? "Tara, I'm sorry. I didn't mean to hurt you." I did feel guilty about it and bowed my head.

"Just go. We weren't going to work out anyway. I knew that from the beginning. I was sticking it out because Dawn bet me two hundred dollars I couldn't hold onto you longer than she did."

"I was a bet?" The thought made me nauseous.

"Yeah. That's also why Chrissy kept coming back around."

"And why you said it didn't matter about Corey as long as we were still together?"

She nodded. "Yup. But I'm done now. I'm not going out with a guy who ass-rapes me when I clearly told you not to."

I stressed, "It was an accident!"

"I don't care. You've wanted out of this relationship for weeks. Admit it."

I hesitated. It sounded terrible to say it out loud. "I guess," I mumbled.

"You're out. Just go." She looked away again and curled up on her pillow. "You're free to be with Corey."

I may have been the one who penetrated her ass when I shouldn't have, but she was clearly the one who'd crossed the line sexually. She'd used me for sex and admitted it was to win a bet. How many guys did that and didn't care whom they hurt? How many times had I done the same thing? Now it had been done to me, and I felt shitty. She'd used me, and for the first time I really did feel like a slut. I was the man-whore RC had accused me of being.

I hopped into my car and stared at the steering wheel. "What do I do now?" I asked myself. Part of me wanted to drive to M-L's and tell her she'd been right about Dawn—and Tara and Chrissy and all the other girls—but I didn't want her yelling at me again. The one place I needed to go was RC's. But would he let me in or punch me? He'd probably say I'd gotten what I deserved.

I called Corey.

"Hello?"

"Hey," I sighed. "Tara broke up with me."

"Oh, yeah?" I heard muffled sounds in the background. "Why?"

I let out a deep sigh. "Because I was a bet. Dawn told her I'm gay and she didn't believe it. She used me for sex."

I heard giggling on the other end, and I sat up and tightened my grip on the steering wheel. I was about to yell at Corey when I heard more giggling, and Corey whispered, "Stop. Stop that. Nicky's on the phone. Give me a second." Then his tone changed. "Tara did that?

Wow. I'm sorry, Nicky. I thought of all of them, Tara was the nicest. But I can't believe Dawn knew you were gay. How?"

"I don't know. Tara said she's known since high school. And I think my mom knows. But whatever. I can hear you're busy. We can talk another time. I'm going to RC's."

"Is that the guy?"

"Yeah."

"Okay. Talk later. And don't let Tara and Dawn bring you down."

"Too late." I hung up. I ended up crying all the way over to RC's house. He'd have to let me in. He had to. If he didn't, I didn't know what I'd do. I felt so empty.

Chapter 18: *Forgiveness*

IT WAS late, but RC still answered the door. No greeting, he merely started speaking as I walked into his apartment. "Wow, you look worse than I feel. I didn't think that was possible."

"I had a crappy night," I said. "Can I crash here?"

He hesitated, but nodded. I guess my pathetic appearance overruled his good sense. I still held to my assumption that he was mad at me, but RC was probably more mature than I was so he didn't feel the need to get all shitty with me, as I would likely have been with him were the roles reversed. RC was a good guy. Was I? M-L would probably think so, but Tara would probably spit in my face the next time I saw her. No, I wasn't such a great guy.

I was an asshole.

RC walked over to the coffee table and then offered me a tissue. "Here, you have half-dried yellow snot smeared across your cheek."

I freaked. "What?" I dashed to the bathroom and inspected myself. "Oh my God," I cried, mortified at the sight. The night could not get any worse. I had yellow snot *and* lumpy boogers smeared across my face. My humiliation was now complete. I wanted to crawl behind the toilet bowl and die.

RC spoke through the closed door. "Take a shower. You'll feel better. There's a clean towel on the rack."

"But...." I started to protest.

"Just do it, or I'll come in there and throw you under the faucet myself."

I stripped out of my shirt and turned on the water. I was pathetic enough. I didn't need to add more shame to my grief by provoking RC to crash in here and force me to bathe.

The hot water washed away my tension, at least for a little bit. I stepped out and dried off. I caught a whiff of myself and lifted my forearm to my nose. "RC," I whispered. *Oh fuck. Now I smell like him.* This wasn't going to help me at all. My sense of smell was my third favorite of the senses. I sniffed my arm again and my dick twitched. I looked down and complained, "Not now. Shit. I can't have you waking up like this. He doesn't like me like that." I cupped myself and squeezed gently. I didn't want to get hard. I couldn't get hard. RC had already gotten angry with me for suggesting stepping outside friendship. Or at least I started to and he'd yelled at me. He'd called me a slut and a man-whore and had been right all along. I couldn't tell him now that I liked him. I couldn't tell him now that he'd been right about me. I couldn't.

"It's humiliating," I explained to my reflection in the mirror. A little voice in my head reminded me of the snot on my face. "Yeah, smeared snot is bad, but not as bad as if I'd had puke on my face. It could have been worse."

I made sure the towel around my waist was secure before I opened the door and went looking for RC. I found him in the kitchen reading and sipping tea. "Hey, can I borrow something to sleep in?" I asked.

He glanced at me, but immediately went back to reading his book. He took another sip and said, "Sure." He left the room without looking at me again.

Could I really be that repulsive?

There was no way he was attracted to me. He hadn't looked twice. I glanced down. My six-pack abs glistened with remnants of water droplets. The little bit of hair I had below my navel disappeared where the towel started. My nipples were standing erect. I could get a hard-on looking at myself, so if RC bolted the first opportunity he got chances were ninety-nine to one he wasn't interested.

"Here," he said, handing me some clothes.

I turned, shoulders slouching from disillusionment, and took what he offered. I returned to the bathroom and got dressed. When I was done, RC handed me a blanket and pillow and gestured to the couch. "You need anything else?" he asked.

I shook my head. I didn't feel like talking. I tossed the pillow at one end and flopped across the cushions.

RC hesitated at his bedroom door and said, "See you in the a.m."

I grunted, and he left me alone with my guilt and shame.

I COULDN'T sleep, so I was up before him. I made the coffee and started an omelet. I remembered how he liked it, and I enjoyed making breakfast for him. The apartment wasn't very big, so I heard the water running through the pipes in the wall and knew he was in the shower. In any other circumstance I'd have been tempted to sneak in. Maybe join him and lather up his hairy chest and groin, but not today. I felt lousy.

I sat at his tiny table in my normal seat. RC liked having his back to the wall so he could look around the room, and I didn't mind heeding to his preference. It was his house. He walked in behind me, and I heard him take in a deep breath.

"Mmm, smells good in here."

"I made food." I glanced at him, but he was inspecting my creation on the stove.

"And coffee. Thanks," he said.

I picked at the bits of omelet on my plate. "You made me breakfast a couple times, it's the least I can do."

"I thought you only knew how to make ramen noodles?"

I smiled. I liked how he was acting normal again. "Well, I guess I can make other stuff too. I can cook hot dogs, grilled cheese, and eggs. And probably, if I put my mind to it, I bet I could make a cheesesteak sub without a recipe."

RC chuckled. Coffee mugs clinked as he removed one from the cabinet, and the spoon tapped against the porcelain sugar bowl. I'd seen him repeat these actions several times, and in my mind's eye it was as if I stood next to him. I knew what he was doing without watching. I smiled inwardly even though my mouth remained a frown.

He sat his mug on the table. "You want to talk about last night?" he asked, walking over and taking a plate out of the other cabinet.

"No." And I seriously meant "no." I didn't know what to say. I was in denial about my denial over being gay, and telling him what I'd done to Tara would make last night way too real. Denial was good. Because telling him I'd been used like a whore was not happening today.

"Okay."

I ate in silence as he prepared his plate and sat at the table with me. I didn't look up. Why should I? He would see something in my eyes, I knew he would. I got the feeling he was an emotional guy. I bet he'd see straight into my heart and know what I thought about myself—what everyone else thought about me. After I finished, I shoved the plate back and set my elbows on the table, covering my face with my hands. I tried not to cry. I did. But I couldn't help it. Being here, not being probed for answers, RC sitting quietly and supportively by my side, made me weak. I was normally great at holding my feelings in. No one saw me cry, except maybe my mom once or twice, but no one else.

Yet there was something about being in his presence that broke me down. I felt like I needed to be vulnerable with him, that I could be vulnerable and it would be all right.

Then he did the worst thing imaginable. He apologized. "I'm sorry about the other day. I was angry, and I yelled. I shouldn't have. You probably had your reasons for not saying something, and maybe I should have given you the chance to explain without blowing up. So... I'm sorry."

I crossed my arms and laid my head down and let it out. I shook with my sobs, and I felt his hand on my shoulder. He squeezed it. He was comforting me, and that made me cry harder.

After some time, he offered, "If you want to stay here, you can. However long, I don't mind. But my clothes won't fit you so you have to go home and get some things. And if you don't want to talk, we don't have to talk."

I nodded, my head still resting on my arms. I would have looked up, but I had a feeling that snot was dripping down my face and all over my shirtsleeves. I didn't want to make him sick right after he'd eaten. Come to think of it, I needed to blow my nose ASAP. I pushed back from the table and departed quickly. He didn't need to see me. No one did.

I found tissues in the bathroom next to a bottle of contact lens solution. I wiped the rivers of mucus from my nose, lips, and chin, and turned the water on in the sink. I rinsed my face and dried it on a towel. *Oh God.* I looked at my reflection. I looked horrid. My eyes were bloodshot. My nose was red. And mucus was still leaking down over my lip. *Eww.* I didn't want him making fun of me. I stalled leaving the bathroom. If I waited a couple minutes, maybe my nose would stop running. Maybe my eyes would lose the redness. Maybe rinsing them with contact lens solution would help.

I grabbed the bottle and held it up. It was a ten-ounce bottle and not specifically made to drip in the eyes. When I held it up, a stream came out and practically bathed my face and neck. "Shit," I exclaimed, righting the bottle and blinking repeatedly. "I can say I successfully rinsed my eye," I commented sarcastically into the mirror. "And my face, and my shirt. Idiot." I was already soaked so doing the other eye wasn't a big deal. I only made sure to do it faster. Then I recapped the bottle and set it back where I'd found it. I wiped my face and replaced the towel on the bar.

"Contacts," I mused. I remembered seeing RC wear glasses once, on the first day, but not since. I checked his glasses case, and it was empty. I smiled at my reflection. "He's wearing glasses today, cool."

I like men in glasses.

I lifted an eyebrow at myself, wondering where that thought had come from. I glanced over to the door and then back at the mirror. "Have I always liked guys wearing glasses, or is it the prospect of RC wearing glasses that excites me?" Yes, I was talking to myself but did that really matter? I'd come to terms with being a dumbass. I was okay with it. I checked my face one last time. I looked bad, but I thought he'd understand. I was composed. And now I was sort of excited to see my friend in his glasses. "My friend?" I questioned, but ended up shaking my head in protest.

I was in denial about a lot of things, but liking RC wasn't one of them. I thought about him way too much, and in all the nonfriend types of ways. He made me feel good all the time, and I never felt pressured into doing anything. I got hot and horny thinking about his hairy body and the prospect of him kissing my neck. I was way into him.

My problems resided with RC. I wished I had a chance with him. Just because he was gay didn't mean I was his type, even if most people had always been attracted to me. M-L said people were attracted to different things. I liked dark curly hair and green eyes. If I could find a guy who liked my stylish brown hair, my blue eyes, and my ripped abs, then we'd be made for one another. Somewhere, there was a guy like that. Until I found him, I was fine with RC. He was almost perfect. And if eye color was the only thing on my "negative" list, then there was no reason to put this off any longer.

I liked him and he needed to know.

I took a deep breath and headed back out into the apartment, but RC was gone.

I found a sticky note on the microwave.

SORRY, NICK. I had to leave for work. I just figured I'd see you later so I left you to your troubles. Here's a key. Feel free to leave and return whenever you want.

~RC

I PICKED up the key and pocketed it. I couldn't blame him for leaving. I'd taken forever in the bathroom. I heaved a sigh and surveyed the scene: typical living room, entryway to the kitchen, front door, door to snake room, and—I suddenly felt mischievous—the door to his bedroom. It was normal to snoop on people, wasn't it? My conscience didn't warn me not to—I think it was broken—so I went ahead and entered.

I turned on the light. His chest of drawers was dust free with only one framed picture sitting on top. His dad, I presumed. I opened a drawer and found his shirts neatly folded. Another drawer had socks and underwear. Hmm, RC had a few colored Andrew Christian underwear. I liked them. He also wore boxers. I liked boxers, but girls didn't so I hardly wore mine. Tara used to tell me they weren't sexy.

I closed my eyes and pictured RC in boxers. Boxers are typically loose. I bet I could slide my hand up his thigh and inside the leg hole so I could fondle his balls. Corey had really big balls for such a skinny guy. I wondered what RC's looked like. *And did he shave his balls like Corey, or were they hairy like the rest of him? Mmm, hairy balls.* I licked my lips.

"Stop it, Nick." I shook off my daydreaming.

I closed the drawer and kept inspecting. He had a weight bench in his room. It barely fit between the wall and the foot of the bed, but it was perpendicular to the window to allow for chest presses. I sat at the end of the bench, picked up his free weights, and did a couple of curls. *Not bad.* He at least used a decent weight. It would be nice to work out together.

I set the dumbbell back on the floor and moved over to his bed. I could smell him. It had to be the soap he used, because after I used it, I smelled the same. The scent drove me crazy and made me think of him. I touched the pillow. The sudden realization I shouldn't be in here gripped me, so I fled his room. I paced in the middle of the apartment and rubbed my face.

"What am I doing?" I asked.

I knew I needed to leave. Snooping was not cool. I was invading his privacy and breaking his trust. I left, locked the door, and passed some shady looking people on the way to my car. *This neighborhood sucks. I better not find spray paint on my doors.* I didn't, so I left in a hurry.

AT HOME, my mom practically met me in the front yard. She opened the door for me and glared. "Where've you been?" she asked sternly.

I pushed past her into the house, and she closed the door. We held our conversation in the entryway. "I was at RC's."

"Oh." The slight intonation of her tone suggested my response was not what she'd expected.

I explained, "You probably thought I was at Tara's, but I wasn't. I left after our date. We have… *issues.*" That was putting it mildly. "Truth is, we broke up."

"Oh."

Boy, Mom was full of witty comebacks today—not. "Mom, I need some time. I know you want to know what's going on with me, but I still don't know."

"Okay. But I'm still waiting to have that conversation. You know? The one where you explain why you lied and told me you had off instead of the truth. Little white lies or big fat ugly lies, each are still lies."

"I know. I forgot."

"How could you forget?"

I could tell she was hurt. "I'm sorry, Mom. I just…." I breathed in deeply and exhaled. "I don't know. Do we have to have this conversation here? I don't want Jenn listening."

"Do you want to talk in your room?"

"Okay, but can I have ten minutes? I've had a rough night. Strike that. I've had a rough couple of months."

"Have you?" My mom stuck her eyebrow in the air. I didn't think she believed me.

She left me alone for a little bit, but wound up at my bedroom door ten minutes later. "Are you ready? I don't want to pry, but I always thought you and I had talked easily in the past. What's so difficult this time?" she asked politely, sitting on my bed and rubbing my outstretched leg like she'd done a hundred times before. My mom was very affectionate, and I had never minded her comforting touch. Only now her compassion was going to break me, and I didn't want to cry again.

"I don't know where to start," I huffed.

"Start anywhere. How about the beginning?"

"That's too long," I whined.

"Then start at the end and work in the details when appropriate."

Why does she always have to be so understanding? If she were mean, it would make my job as a rebellious son easier. But she wasn't. My mom's wonderful. She's always been there for me. I rolled over and buried my head under my pillow. I cried, "I don't understand why I have to label myself, Mom. I'm just me. Can't I live from one moment to the next without having to answer to other people's opinions on how I should live?"

The sentence probably didn't make sense out of context, but my mind had been a pinball machine of late. And if I couldn't think straight, then she wasn't getting any straight-up answers.

She squeezed my shoulder. "Oh, Nicky, life isn't that simple." She tried lifting my Invisibility Pillow—which was kind of like Harry Potter's cloak—but I yanked the corner back down. I needed the safety it provided.

Through the feathers and cotton fibers, I heard her say, "But if it helps, I'm comfortable with whatever label you choose."

I knew what she meant. I also knew she'd known long before me. I heaved a sigh. "Mom," I groaned, still under my pillow. "Does Dad know?"

She chortled. "Your father is unaware of most things. But I also think he'll accept you no matter what."

I rolled over. My head was uncovered and resting on my protection device. I was exposed and vulnerable. My mom sat there looking at me with the most understanding expression I'd ever seen. "Mom… I'm gay."

"Uh-huh."

I huffed and rolled back over, covering my head again. I complained to her, but yelled into the mattress, "Why do you have to say it like you've known forever?"

When she didn't answer, I peeked out from under the pillow. She was smirking. I tossed the pillow back and glared as I sat up. "Mom! Stop laughing. It isn't funny!" I fussed.

"I'm not laughing at the situation. I'm laughing at *you*."

"That's worse!"

She laughed even more. "I can't help it. I think I had the same conversation with your sister about a boy she likes. So I'm laughing because you remind me of a sixteen-year-old girl. She huffed and buried her head under the pillow too."

The mental picture was sobering, and my huffing and puffing ceased instantly. "Really? Jenn acted like me?"

"Exactly like you."

"Oh, shit," I lamented. I dragged my ass off the bed and over to the mirror to straighten out my hair. I couldn't act like Jennifer. I had to be more mature than that. Once I was presentable, I turned around. I took a deep breath and said, "Okay. I can do this. I'm not acting like a girl. I can talk to you like an adult."

"Can you?"

I gaped. "Uh-ah! Yes. I certainly can." She smirked. I complained, "Stop laughing!"

My mom crossed the room and cupped my face in both hands. "I'm sorry, sweetie. I don't mean to laugh. I'm tickled pink you still talk to me after all these years. I had hoped it wouldn't change when you became an adult."

"It's hard, ya know? I don't know what I feel. Yet, I feel like I've been denying it all my life."

"And Tara?" she asked, letting go of me.

"We broke up. She thinks it's because of Corey, but it's not."

"No?"

I shook my head. I looked down and notice a hole in RC's sock; I'd worn his clothes home. "I think Corey played a role in some things. He helped me to realize I've been in denial for a long time. But he's not the one I want to be with."

"Who, then?"

I had to tell her. Even if he didn't feel the same, my heart was set on RC. I looked at his sock on my foot and replied, "RC. I'm going to stay at his place a couple days. I need time to think about everything." I moved toward the bed, and she stopped me.

"Is RC.... Do you...?" She let the question hang, but I knew what she meant.

I nodded. It was embarrassing to talk about, but she knew more about me than most. I owed her for being so fair with me all these years. "Yeah, I think so. I'm still working through it."

"And Corey?"

I smiled. I knew she really liked him. "Corey's a really good friend. He'll be around."

She nodded and let go of my arm. She understood. Mom always seemed to understand me. She caressed my cheek and then kissed it. "Thank you for being honest."

I smiled. "Mom? How long have you known?" I sat down on the bed and lifted one foot across my knee.

"Um, well, maybe... four years."

I was shocked. "What? How?" I pulled his sock off one foot and waited for her answer.

"I don't know. Some things mothers just know. I think it was in the way you looked at people."

I took off the other sock. "What do you mean?" Because I didn't think I looked at people funny.

"I'm not sure I can explain it. But there were a few times over the years when I caught you looking at people if we were in a large crowd like at a baseball game or something, and something in your eyes told me you were gay."

"So it wasn't the way I acted or how I dressed or talked or anything?"

Again, she laughed. "Oh, goodness no! Corey, yes. His flamboyance gave it away from day one, but you? No. Very subtle. Like I said, it's the way you looked at people. When I saw the expression on your face when Raffael visited that night—oh, wow. Pure panic. I knew you liked him way more than as a friend. There was a tenderness in your eyes I can't say I've seen in you before."

I slumped forward, elbows on my knees. "I'm not sure he feels the same way."

"Did you ask?"

"No."

"You should. There's nothing worse than unrequited love. And if you don't ask, you may never know."

"I know. I will. It's complicated because of Tara and Corey. I think RC's mad at me. I want him to cool down before I hit him with 'Hey, I like you. Do you like me?' I don't want the tension between us to get worse."

"Tension? Really? From what I saw when he was here, you couldn't have been more comfortable with one another."

I grinned. I liked hearing her say that. "You think?"

"Yup. I think."

She walked over to the door and said, "Text me sometimes. Okay? I'd like to know you're still alive."

"I will."

After she left, I packed a couple things to take to RC's, and in the middle of stuffing a backpack, I got a text from Tara.

I'm sorry things between us got so messed up. I hope you and Corey are happy together. Really. I do.

I didn't want to correct her, especially when I wasn't sure I should mention RC if we weren't a couple. All I replied was: *Thanks. I hope we can still be friends.*

Sure, she sent back.

I pocketed my phone and finished packing. I also grabbed a few work shirts for the rest of this week and my toiletries from the bathroom. When I was done, I paused and looked around my room.

"I'm going to stay with RC. Wow," I marveled. I didn't know what that meant to him, but it was a huge step for me. It meant I was letting another person into my world. No one ever got close, and physically close, I'd learned, didn't count. I'd always had my space, which was sort of why I rarely spent the night with a girl. I wanted my safe haven. I liked my room, my stuff, my family, my territory, and my Invisibility Pillow. If RC entered it, I had to share. Could I? And what if he wanted to change things and rearrange my habits and rituals? What if he hated my SpongeBob shirt?

"Oh fuck, I need to chill," I mumbled. I took a deep breath and decided to grab some coffee before I left. I wasn't living with him; I was staying with him for a couple of days. It wasn't the same. I'd be fine. I turned out the light and closed the door.

Downstairs, Mom had already filled a travel mug with coffee. *God, she knows me so well.* I sipped it. Perfect. "Thanks, Mom."

"I love you, dear."

"I love you too. And it's not like I'm leaving for good, I'm just taking a break."

"Okay."

"Tell Dad I'll call him later."

"Okay."

"And tell Jennifer, when she gets home from school, I said bye."

We exchanged hugs, and I headed back to RC's.

I HAD a later shift, four to eight, so it enabled me to unpack my stuff and play Xbox for an hour. Work was boring, but at least no one visited unexpectedly. Sometimes I liked the same old, same old. Marcy griped about having to mop. Paul threw pepperonis on the floor after she swept. And I talked to everyone on my shift in a variety of silly voices. Things were good. My world was happy again. It was the same world as before, only now the shade was greener—kelly green.

By the time I returned to RC's, he was home.

"Hey. I see you brought your stuff," he said, pointing to the picture on the end table and my games on the coffee table.

"Yeah, is that okay?" I hoped it was. I followed him into the kitchen and sat at the table.

RC was cooking something, and it smelled good. "How long are you planning on staying?" he asked. I couldn't tell what answer he was looking for. His tone was even, and he wasn't looking at me. He was stirring something. I smelled garlic. *God, I love his cooking.*

I replied, "Um, I don't know. I haven't thought about it. I work tomorrow eleven to eight. And Saturday, eight to three. I'm off Sunday. I think I work eight to five three days next week, but I can't remember which ones. I won't be around too much. My regularly scheduled Saturday off is next week, the twenty-fourth. Paul worked for me when you and I went to Hamburg, but he didn't switch, he just filled in."

"That was nice."

"Yeah. Paul's a really great guy."

"So I figured. And is he a good kisser?" he asked randomly.

"What?" I questioned, thinking I could not have heard him correctly.

He turned around. "I asked if he was a good kisser. Because I heard you, when you were all talking. I know you kissed him. And then you kissed that girl Marcy, who thinks I'm fat. And the boy toy with the spiky hair."

I dropped my gaze to the linoleum floor. "Corey. His name is Corey." And I'd thought my week could not get worse. I was wrong.

RC mused, "Corey. Right. And this type of behavior is normal for you and your friends? Is there anyone you know you haven't slept with or kissed in public?"

I wished I could say I detected a hint of sarcasm and anger in his tone, but there was nothing veiled in the way he spoke. He was still pissed. "I thought you said you should have given me a chance to explain. And you were sorry you yelled at me."

RC turned, spatula held in the air like a magic scepter. "I...." he started to retort. He placed the spatula on the counter and continued in a more controlled voice. "I'm sorry, Nick. I'm really trying to be sorry about yelling at you but it's difficult. I'm still angry you lied to me. I'm upset you hid your sexuality from me, especially when you knew I was sensitive about it."

"It's not easy to talk about."

"And I get that. I do. I didn't come out to anyone until I was in college, but I still got beat up for it when I was younger. I didn't come out to my mom until my dad died last year. I know it's hard, but you're the only guy I've ever trusted in my house, with my stuff, or concerning my life. You're my best friend, Nick. So yes, I'm angry you didn't trust me."

His eyes bored into my soul and I teared up. I'd already cried. I wasn't going to do it again. I held my breath and willed the emotion away. "I'm sorry. It's not easy to talk about. I can try, I guess."

"You promise to try?"

I nodded.

"Okay. How about we talk about something else tonight?" he asked, turning around to cook.

Good. He wasn't pressing for answers right this second. I have time. "Okay. Like what?"

"We're both off next weekend. You want to do something?"

My gray cloud brightened. "What do you have in mind?"

RC took some plates out of the cabinet and scooped food onto them. He brought them over and set them onto the table, one in front of me, one where he normally sits. And then he went to a different cabinet and took out glasses. "I think I'll keep that a secret."

I didn't think I'd heard him correctly. I furrowed my brow. "A secret?"

He filled the glasses with water and brought them over. "Yeah. A secret." His eyes glinted. "You like surprises, don't you?" RC looked too chuffed with himself for me to question his intent.

"I guess." I gave him a weak half smile, but didn't question him further. I had to trust him. Instead I looked at my food and picked up my fork. It was an Italian stir-fry of chicken, basil, artichokes, garlic, asparagus, tomato chunks, and penne pasta. "Wow, this looks great."

"I wanted to make something special. You looked ragged last night." RC stabbed a piece of chicken and lifted it to his mouth. "This is my mother's recipe."

"It's delicious," I commented while chewing. I swallowed and took a sip of my water.

"I know I'm harsh sometimes, but I do forgive you for not sharing personal information. I haven't exactly been forthcoming with my shit. I always get screwed when I trust people. I can't fault you for the same caution."

"I understand. And thanks. Maybe we can talk about some stuff when we get to wherever you have in mind?"

"Yup. That's the plan. Get away from all this. Away from familiar places and familiar hang-ups and try to be ourselves—no fences or walls."

"You're ready to do that?" I asked.

"Maybe. Are you?"

"Um, yeah. I think so." I ate a few more bites. RC was quietly eating when it hit me he was wearing his contact lenses. "Not to change the subject, but what happened to your glasses? I thought you were wearing them today?"

RC paused between bites. "Why do you ask?"

"No reason. I've never seen you wearing glasses. I remember you having them on once at the restaurant, and I noticed the case in the bathroom. Do you always wear contacts?"

"Yeah," he said, terser than I expected.

"Why?" I questioned. "There's nothing wrong with glasses." I almost let it slip that I thought glasses were hot on guys, but I was only now getting used to myself thinking about guys that way. No need to push the gay thing too fast. Corey said I had to accept who I was and that needed to be one day at a time.

"Sometimes people are the issue. I don't wear them much, only when my eyes feel dry."

"But—"

"Drop it, Nick," he said. The anger in his tone scared me.

"Okay." I went back to eating. The dish was really tasty. RC was a terrific chef. I wondered why he worked in a clothing factory and didn't take up cooking professionally. I glanced at him a few times during the rest of the meal, but he was either deep in thought or trying hard not to engage me in any way. He never once looked up while he ate.

Next weekend would prove interesting if we started talking about our secrets and personal information. What was he hiding? First the fear of showing his tattoos, and now he didn't want to talk about his glasses. RC was an odd one all right.

Chapter 19: *Miscommunication*

RC TOOK me to a freakin' amusement park. How fucking cool was that? I thought staying at his place all week was the greatest, and then this. Holy cow. When we pulled into the parking lot, I about jumped out of my skin.

When he'd said "surprise," I thought maybe another reptile thing or concert since he's into music, but he fucking drove me two and a half hours north to an amusement park in the middle of nowhere Pennsylvania. I'd never heard of Elysburg before and now I knew why. It's too freaking far away! But he took me to Knoebels Amusement Park. He explained it was America's largest free-admission park. Free admission? How hadn't I heard of it before? Way cool. The park rides opened at 11:00 a.m., so we got there about fifteen minutes before that.

"You are amazing," I gushed as we walked toward the entrance. I patted his shoulder and caught his smirk before he turned his face away.

We opted for the all-day passes to ride whatever we wanted. It was easier. But the park also had an option to buy a ticket for each ride individually, which I thought would work great if my mom and dad came here sometime. She didn't like to ride every ride and at places like Hershey, her money was wasted on standing around waiting for whomever to get done. Here, she wouldn't have to pay to mill about.

The park was also different from other parks because it was predominantly what I call "boardwalk rides" or carnival rides. Family rides like the Swinger and the Tea Cup ride I remembered from family vacations to Ocean City. Or when we went to the Reese fire hall carnival. I'd loved The Scrambler as a kid. They had bumper cars and a giant carousel, the Tilt-A-Whirl, and something called the "Whipper." It was like being transported back into my childhood. And I swear the rides looked older than me too. I don't think I ever laughed as hard as I did that day. RC completely outdid any surprise from any holiday or birthday. He took me to an amusement park. *Shit!* And we weren't even dating. He proved how much my friendship meant to him. He'd called me his best friend, and then he brought me here. Hot diggity dog. I was floating on air—no, make that ice cream. I was floating on a sea of coffee ice cream smothered in chocolate syrup and whipped cream with crumbled Oreo cookies on the top. I was in heaven.

"ARE YOU sure we have to go?" I asked, pouting and clasping my hands together in front of him.

RC laughed. "Stop begging, Nick. We're coming back tomorrow."

"Tomorrow?" I perked up.

"Yes. I told you in the car when you were playing with my iPod."

"Oh. I wasn't listening."

"I gathered that. I said I knew there would be too many rides and not enough time, so we are staying in a hotel down the street tonight and coming back in the morning. This way, we can get a good night's sleep and eat a good meal instead of hamburgers."

"I like hamburgers," I protested.

"I do too. But I'm still trying to maintain the diet I'm on. I'd rather go someplace I can eat a salad."

"You never eat salad when you're with me."

"No. The pizza shop is typically my one meal a week to splurge."

"What about the pasta? Carbs aren't good for losing weight."

"No. But sometimes pasta is all I can afford. And if I ate tuna out of the can in front of you, I thought I'd look pathetic."

"Nah. I don't care. I just like being with you."

RC looked away.

He was quiet when we got into the car, and it made me wonder if I'd said something wrong again. I was always saying something wrong. I already knew he had lots of tuna at his apartment; why should it matter? I didn't know what made him quiet this time, so I chose to ignore it. We drove down some winding streets and ended up at a Best Western about twenty minutes away. He'd told me we were spending the night somewhere, but then he pulls into the parking lot of a Best Western hotel.

A hotel? Suddenly an invisible knife jabbed me in the gut. I knew what went on in hotels. Was he bringing me here expecting something? We'd played and laughed and waited in a zillion lines, but he'd never given me any indication it meant anything sexual. We were hanging as friends.

My heart was racing and my hands were sweaty, but not because it was hot out.

He parked, and I grabbed my bag without looking at him. He wasn't talking. I wasn't talking. Suddenly this was awkward and confusing. I didn't know what to do, how to act, or what he expected, so I followed his lead. He walked in, and I waited next to him while he signed in, took the key card, and headed toward the elevators.

I was silent on the way up. The door dinged. I swallowed hard.

I dumped my crap on the bed and fled to the security of the bathroom. I wasn't prepared for a hotel stay. I hadn't brought condoms. Had he? He hadn't so much as touched me suggestively, so why would he think this was acceptable? I showered, dressed, and walked over to the bed, pretending to root through my stuff. While I was poking around, I heard the bathroom door close again.

I slipped under the covers of the bed closest to the window. It was habit for me to pick that one. If my family went anywhere over the years, my mom always wanted the bed closest to the bathroom. So automatically, I claimed this bed. RC's stuff was on the dresser. He hadn't turned down the covers on the other bed yet. It was hotel squared.

I lay there listening to the water running in the bathroom for a long time. He seemed to be taking an extra-long shower. Why? *Is he in there waiting for me?* Fuck, I didn't know. He'd called me a slut before. He'd commented on how easy I was. What if RC was testing his theory by waiting in the shower until I couldn't take it any longer and joined him? Would he really expect me to do that? Did he think of me as a nymphomaniac or something?

I reached under the blankets and touched myself. *God, I'm hard.* All the worry over whether or not we were going to have sex had made me, of course, think of sex, and now I was rock hard and ready for action. *Damn my overactive penis.* Why couldn't I go someplace and *not* think of sex? Was that too much to ask? I'd done well all week.

I was scared when we pulled up to the place, but now all the waiting made me want sex even more. I didn't like the idea that RC thought about me like Tara did, but I'd been daydreaming about touching him so maybe I would have my chance tonight? It was at least something. I pinched the base of my cock, trying to will away my desire to stroke it. I didn't want to come in the bed alone. If I was honest, I wanted RC to be the one getting me off.

What the hell is he doing in there?

Just when I thought about throwing the blankets off and storming into the bathroom, the door opened and he entered the room fully dressed in a T-shirt and sweats. His hair was still wet, and I could tell he'd combed it since it wasn't tangled as it hung loose around his neck and shoulders. It wasn't the first time I'd seen his hair down, and it was as gorgeous as I remembered. Dark, looping curls that begged my hands to slip in and never return. I wanted to touch him so badly right then.

RC, on the other hand, seemed oblivious.

He walked around between the beds, slipped under the covers of the other bed, reached up, and turned off the light.

Surely he wasn't going to remain over there? I mean, what the heck was he thinking? We were in a hotel. *I'm easy, right?* He had to have brought me here to have sex. I admit I was a little apprehensive before, but now… now I was getting pissed contemplating the possibility he expected me to do all the work. *What the fuck? That was not fair.*

I lay there waiting, and waiting, and waiting—forever. RC wasn't moving. Maybe he *did* expect me to make the first move, but I didn't understand how he'd come to that conclusion. He was the one who'd brought me to a hotel. He was the one who'd made all the decisions as to where we went and what we did together the entire day. Why all of a sudden would he expect me to get out of bed and go to him? *Unless he really did see me as an easy slut, desperate and assertive enough to take sex whenever it's available.*

That whole idea made me sick. No, RC couldn't think that. He wouldn't. *Would he?* There had to be another explanation. My groin pulsed, reminding me that although I was agitated—and having an internal debate over it—I was also still horny for the man who was apparently sleeping in the other bed. I'd had enough. I threw the blankets back and reached for the lamp.

I switched it on and exclaimed, "Are you fucking kidding me?"

RC turned his face my way and squinted against the harsh intrusion of light. "What? What's wrong?"

"You! You're what's wrong. Are you seriously going to sleep?" I was angry and I wasn't holding back. I was normally a very nonconfrontational person, but this time I couldn't contain myself. "We're in a fucking hotel!"

"Yeah," he mumbled. "The park is a couple hours from home and they have two-day passes." RC moved to lean on one elbow and look at me. "I told you that in the car on the way here when you didn't pay attention the first time. Did you forget again?"

"No. I heard you. But you brought me to a hotel. I can't believe you're going to sleep."

"What else am I supposed to be doing?"

"Having sex," I complained. "That's what normal people do in hotels."

"Nick... I didn't mean to...." RC hesitated, looking quite baffled.

"Do you expect me to believe you have no intentions whatsoever of sleeping with me?"

He paused, but eventually shook his head. "No, Nick."

Not what I wanted to hear. "Seriously?" My voice went up an octave, and *yes,* I was getting repetitive. But I couldn't believe what I was hearing. "You're going to sleep, while I, on the other hand, am lying here hard as hell for you." To prove my point, I got out of bed and pointed to my tented crotch. "Look at this! My dick's a fucking flagpole, and it's all your fault."

He didn't look up. "I'm sorry I gave you the wrong impression."

"You didn't even look." I stepped closer and pulled my waistband down over my rigid cock. "Look at this! How am I supposed to sleep?" My hard length bobbed in front of me as I held my pants out of the way. It really was a grand looking cock, if I said so myself. *Maybe I am porn star material?* I could always give it a chance. Maybe thousands of women would ask to see it one day, or touch it? Yeah... or maybe thousands of *men?*

A little niggle nudged my brain. *Men?* Did I want thousands of men ogling me? No, not really. All I wanted was one man to look at me. I wanted RC to look at me and give attention to me and my pulsing cock. This hard-on was for him, not thousands of faceless guys all over the world.

When RC finally did look up, I did not get the reaction I was hoping for. Instead of lustful, he looked annoyed. "Jeez, Nick. Could you put that thing away?"

Annoyed? Why would anyone be annoyed at the sight of my cock? I put it away as asked, although I did so incredulously. "What is your problem?" I snapped.

"You!" RC countered, asserting himself for the first time. He sat up and leaned against the headboard. He looked angry and something inside me was worried this conversation was not going to be a good one. He continued, but with less threat. "Look, I'm sorry. Okay? I didn't intend on misleading you. But we're not having sex, so you can take your *flagpole* and go back to bed."

I threw my hands in the air. "I just don't get you. We had the best day at the park and you're going to spoil it by *sleeping*? What the fuck? I can't believe you're not attracted to me. Most people would be jumping at the chance to end their day with a good, hard fuck. But nooo, not you." I admit I was a bit dramatic with the hand waving and accentuation of the word "no," but whatever.

"Nick. Fuck!" RC yelled. He was hot, and I noticed a vein standing out on his neck. He was practically seething. I'd thought about him as a sort of bear, but maybe I hadn't considered that some bears are grizzlies. Did I just stir up a sleeping grizzly? Maybe I shouldn't have pushed, but I just didn't get why he didn't want me.

"Do you ever listen to yourself?" he asked with the same amount of disbelief in his tone I had had a second ago. "You are the most arrogant, vain, self-centered person I've ever met." With that, he pushed aside the covers and stood up in front of me. "For one thing," RC asserted, poking his finger in my chest, "the last time I checked, you had a girlfriend. And second, being the total fucktard that you are, you also have a boy toy on the side. So even if I was interested, I wouldn't compromise the best friendship I've ever had for a one-night stand with a *player* like you. As much as the concept may be foreign to you, sex isn't so trivial to me. I want commitment, Nick, and—big shocker—that ain't you."

I swallowed hard. His words, and his loud delivery of them, stabbed my heart like razorblades through latex balloons. Fuck!

He was breathing hard, and he gazed at me, his face mirroring shock over what he'd just said. And me? I was stunned equally speechless. He'd called me out on all my shit. Double fuck! I was a complete asshole. RC was right. Tara told me I wasn't a commitment type of guy. She'd said it was all about sex. RC saw it too.

I should have ended the confrontation by admitting my guilt and asking forgiveness, only my brain seriously enjoyed denying the harsh realities of life and only latched onto the positives. My culpability could wait. Something in what he said left a tiny shaft of light in my dark chasm of shame. I swallowed again and asked in a weak voice, "I'm your best friend?"

His roiling expression reddened his cheeks as he growled, "Fucking hell, Nick. Don't you ever pay attention? I've said it three times already. Yes, you are my best friend. And if you keep questioning it, I'm going to have a best friend with a broken nose. You've gotta be the biggest idiot I've ever met." He ran his hand over his face, presumably to calm his nerves. Quietly, he answered, "Yes, Nick, you're my best friend." He took another deep breath. "Maybe I never learn. Maybe I'm a glutton for punishment. But I have never had anyone stalk me because they couldn't stand the thought of never seeing me again. It was probably the nicest thing anyone's ever done, so yeah, I keep hanging on when you do and say stupid things because I think you're a great guy underneath it all."

I smiled. "I don't think anyone thinks of me as highly as that." RC always made me feel really good, even when he yelled at me. I wanted to hug him so much.

RC sighed. "Can we just go to sleep and talk about this tomorrow?" He lifted his covers and crawled back into bed.

"Together? Sure," I chirped, hopping onto the bed beside him as he pulled the covers up.

"What the fuck? Nick! Don't you ever stop?" He growled and shoved me away.

I sat back on my folded legs. "What?" I didn't think there was a problem. I held my hands out to the side and said, "You said sleep. You put 'we'"—I shifted both hands over to the one side—"and 'sleep'"—I moved my hands to the other side of the imaginary line in front of me—"in the same sentence, and I'm fine with that. But I don't want to sleep over there." I lifted my chin toward the empty bed.

"Well, you're not sleeping here."

I huffed, letting my hands fall onto my thighs. "Let me just ask you one question. If Tara and Corey weren't in the picture, would you consider it?"

He narrowed his eyes as if suspicious of my intentions. "Letting you sleep next to me or having sex?"

"Both. Either. No… both." It was a hard call. I wanted both.

RC sat up, wriggling his way to lean against the headboard, but he didn't seem enthused about it. "Nick," he explained. "I really don't want to have this conversation. I want to sleep. Alone."

"Are you sure?" I grinned, trying to lighten his mood.

He wasn't smiling. "Nick, look, you're a great guy. I like you. And as I said, you're the closest friend I've ever had, and I don't want to screw that up for anything."

I felt that lingering exception and asked, "But?"

"But…. You're a slut."

Jeez, we're back to that again. I suddenly felt nauseated about my promiscuity for the first time. "Oh," I replied.

"I'm sorry. There's still a lot you don't know about me, but one thing you need to know is how serious I think of sex. And until I think you're going to view sex the same way and commit to something real, I can't go down that road with you. From what I've seen, you don't put any thought into who you sleep with. All those girls… how many have there been? And that blond sweet tart who drools on the floor over you…. It's disgusting."

"Corey doesn't drool," I corrected.

"The fuck he doesn't. Everyone drools after you. You can have anyone. You don't need me. And if we sleep together, it won't be long before you take your dick elsewhere, and I'm left with a mound of regret and self-loathing for allowing it to happen."

Damn. Why does he always have to sound right? "But," I had to ask, "if they weren't in the picture, would you want me? Because Tara and I broke up last Wednesday. That's kind of why I was upset. And Corey was never my boyfriend. I'll text him right now and tell him we're done."

"Why didn't you say something about Tara? You've been at my apartment all week."

"I know. I've been having a great time. It's been the best week of my life actually. So I didn't tell you about Tara because… because she said some things that were humiliating, and I didn't want to admit them. Call it a pride issue. She said…." I had to pause since this was the closest I'd ever been to being an open book. I hated people seeing my faults and failures. "Tara said she used me. It was all about the sex. She knew I'd never commit, and she even had a bet going she could keep me longer than Dawn." I hung my head and waited for his response. I only hoped he wouldn't laugh.

I felt his hand on my knee. "I'm sorry, Nick. I know what that feels like to be used."

I looked up. He was there, staring at me, eyes dripping with sympathy. Couldn't this develop into something? "So, I have to ask." *Because my mom told me I should.* "Do you like me? More than friends. Even if it's just a little, I gotta know. I have to know if I have a chance with you now that you know I'm not seeing anyone."

I think it hurt to answer my question. He actually paled as he considered it. But eventually he nodded. Slightly. And then he quietly added, "Yes, I like you. And yes, I want you."

Oh my God! He'd just given me the green light. *He wants me. And I want him.* I only needed to prove I wasn't the complete asshole everyone thought I was and commit. I could do that. Maybe. I sagged as I considered it. This was huge. Could I commit to one person without having had sex with him first? And RC was a guy. If I said yes to him, then I'd be admitting I was gay, like, to the world. I'd have to come out as a gay guy to more people than merely my mom. And what if things didn't work out with RC? Could I revert back to sleeping with women?

Too many simultaneous thoughts made acid burn in my throat.

I bolted for the bathroom and chucked in the toilet. I retched one more time, and then I felt a cold towel next to my face. RC stood there holding it out for me. "Thanks," I said, taking it and wiping my face off.

"I'm sorry I was so blunt. I didn't mean to make you puke."

He looked sad, and I felt bad he'd assumed it was about what he'd said. It wasn't him I was sick about, it was me. He held out a hand and I took it. "It wasn't you," I said, turning to the sink so I could get the sour taste off my tongue. RC watched me brush my teeth. He leaned on the doorframe and I observed him in the mirror. He looked torn.

I spit and rinsed my mouth and turned to him. We looked at each other with a weird uncertainty hanging in the air around us. I didn't know about RC, but my heart accelerated as the seconds passed. I may be a total dick, and it was completely true that I'd never put much thought into whom I'd slept with in the past, but as I took note of all those features about him that turned me on, I couldn't help but get hard again. His brown eyes were so caring. His lips were full and made my mouth water when I considered kissing him. And that hair! Oh fuck, I wanted to sink my hands in those curls and tug as he sucked me off. Not to mention the fact that he was covered in the same thick, black hair that grew on his arms. I was dying to run my hands all over him. RC was right in that I'd always been a fucktard, but he was wrong if he thought I couldn't change and commit. Darn tootin' I could commit. I would commit to *him*. I stepped forward and reached for his hips, but RC stepped back.

"What are you doing?" he asked, alarmed. Or guarded, it was hard to tell.

"Well, I was going to kiss you. But I'll settle for a hug."

He stepped back again and held up his hand. "Um, I don't think so."

I had to convince him, if possible. "RC, you're right. Pretty much everything you said is true. But!" I asserted my conjunction. "I can change."

"Why?"

"Because, you make me feel comfortable, and I don't feel comfortable around many people. When I'm with you, I feel good. I'm happy. You look at me, and my balls tingle."

He chuckled. "Wow, romantic."

I laughed too. "I admit I'm not good with romance. I don't know much about anything but fucking."

"Honesty is a good start. So what are you saying?"

I inhaled and exhaled. This was it. "I want to give us a try. More than a try, I want to prove to you I'm not only out to get you in my bed. I want you. All of you. And if I have to go without sex until you believe me, I'm willing to do it."

He paused momentarily and lifted his eyebrow. "Are you sure? What's the longest you've gone without sex before?"

"Um, about twelve days. I think."

"You'll never last."

"I will! It's been ten already since I broke up with Tara."

RC shifted his gaze to my tented sweats.

"I swear it has a mind of its own." I pushed against it, trying to reposition myself so it wouldn't stick out so much, but nothing worked. I exhaled loudly.

RC chuckled.

"I can't fix my dick. Okay? I told you I'm hard for you."

He grinned. "I suppose I should be flattered." He paused, and then said, "Okay. Let's say we go for it. How do I know I can trust you? Because my track record for trusting people has always fucked me over."

I shrugged. "I don't know."

"I also have to tell you I'm not into cheaters. I joked about you cheating on Tara because joking was easier than busting your ass over it when I was still sort of worried you'd decide our friendship wasn't worth the hassle. But now? I take those things seriously, Nick. I'm a one-man guy."

"I hate how right you are all the time." I pushed past him and walked over to the bed. That guilt I was trying to deny reared its terrible head and made me nauseous all over again. I sat, and he joined me sitting on the opposite bed. "I felt bad about cheating, I did. Tara didn't care because it was with Corey."

"Corey?"

"Yeah." His sudden silence made me answer him eye to eye. "What? Why do you look angry?"

"Because I've never felt jealous before."

"Of Corey? You knew I slept with him."

"Yeah, but it was easier thinking you cheated on your girlfriend with another girl. I don't like knowing it was with him. He's so… pretty."

"Yeah, he is, but he's not you."

"Obviously!"

"No, what I mean is, I'm into big hairy guys. I'm not into Corey like that. He was my first boyfriend, but we were never officially dating. He helped me see myself differently. He'll always be my friend, but he's not what I'm looking for in a boyfriend. You are."

RC touched my knee. And I kind of wished his fingers traveled up my thigh, but whatever. "I'll give us a try, Nick, but I'm not having sex with you anytime soon. You need to prove yourself trustworthy first. You have a terrible reputation."

My guilt-induced nausea turned all butter-fluttery. "I will. I promise. I know I have a bad rep, and I am determined to change." I beamed. Those words were the best words I'd ever heard.

"And if you want to sleep next to me tonight you can, but don't expect anything because I'm not kissing you, nor am I getting you off in any way, shape, or form."

I jumped up. "Deal!" And then I realized my tent pole was practically in his face since he was still sitting. "Oops, sorry," I said as I stepped to the side. "Let me just go take care of this." I dashed to the toilet one more time and relieved myself in short order. When I got back to the bed, RC was lying on one side, lights out, and I crawled across to the opposite pillow. I felt shaky as I slipped under the sheet and got comfortable on my side so I could look at him. I was really, truly in bed with RC. I was probably going to get hard again.

"I hope you aren't going to stare at me all night," he mumbled. RC was lying on his back. I couldn't tell if his eyes were open or not. Too dark.

"I might."

I thought he would ignore me, but to my delight he rolled to face me. *Damn, I wish there was more light in the room.* I saw enough of a glint in his eyes to know they were open. And as my eyes adjusted to the dark, I could make out the features of his face. I couldn't help myself, and lifted my hand slowly to touch him. He closed his eyes. I fingered the hair on his jaw and over his lips. I seriously wanted to kiss him, but that would have been pushing my luck. One step at a time.

RC murmured, "You're evil, Nick."

I snickered and withdrew my hand. Sleep was good. After all, we were going to spend another day at the park together in the morning.

Chapter 20: *Trust*

"NICK," I heard my name, but I wasn't sure where it was coming from. "Nick," I heard it repeated more urgently.

No one in my dream had been yelling my name. I was lying on a beach, nude, watching RC as he sipped a strawberry daiquiri and read his Kindle. I was relaxed and happy. I stretched and yawned.

"Nick, get off me," RC grumbled. I looked at him and he was gone. His drink sat there half-empty, but no RC.

I felt good. I was draped over something warm and my lips tasted skin. Salty skin, sweaty and rough. I sent my tongue out for a lick and that's when I was jolted awake by RC's powerful shove. "I said get off me!" he growled.

I was slightly perturbed, but it was RC. I was getting used to him yelling at me for stuff. "What?" I asked innocently.

He glared. "I think you know."

"No. I don't. I was sleeping. I was dreaming about you. We were on a beach and you—"

"I don't care. I don't want you grinding your erection into me, okay? And what made you think licking my neck was acceptable? I said sleep together. Sleep. I didn't agree to a wake-up woody and Dracula sucking on my neck."

I glanced at his neck and gasped. "Oh, no. I gave you a hickey."

"What?" he cried as he shot out of bed.

I laughed as he clambered for the bathroom mirror. "I was joking," I called after him.

He came back in and scowled. "You're evil."

I laughed some more. "Good morning to you too, sunshine. Did you sleep good? I think that was the best I've slept for ages."

"It was fine."

"Fine? Only fine?"

"Yeah. It was fine until you decided to hump me in your sleep and draw little circles on my chest with your fingers. It's too fast, Nick."

"I'm sorry. I've never slept in someone's arms before." I duck-crawled across the bed on my knees until I was in front of him. "I liked it, a lot. Didn't you?" I took his hand in mine and rubbed his fingers.

"Yeah. I did. But it made me want to do things."

"Good things?" I asked, raising my eyebrows and flashing my sexy smile.

"Yes, good things, but not *now* things. Look, we need to get dressed and eat breakfast before check-out."

"Okay."

RC went back into the bathroom, and I followed. I heard him peeing, but I opened the door so we could talk. "Is the plan the same as yesterday?" I asked.

RC shook the droplets off his penis and turned around. He looked upset. "Why do you think it's okay to walk in on me?"

I took a step back. "Oh, sorry. I didn't think about it." I started to shut the door and RC stopped it.

"It's okay. Just, next time, let me take a piss by myself."

"Okay." I shrugged and asked again, "So, the plan's the same?"

Evidently, RC could not remain irritated because he chuckled instead. "Oh, Nick. Yeah, same plan." RC picked up his toothbrush, and I nodded and walked out.

When RC returned from the bathroom, I had already changed my clothes and tucked my things into my knapsack. RC looked worried as I approached him. "So, when we're at the park, can I touch you?" I asked.

"Um, how do you mean?" RC asked dubiously, shifting his expression to DEFCON 3.

I gestured. "Like yesterday, we were just hangin', standing in line, glancing at the signs, talking smack about fuck all, but we were just friends."

"We're still friends, Nick."

"Yeah, but now we're friends with *potential*. And I might want to touch you." I stepped closer and alarms flashed in RC's eyes. DEFCON 2. He might have been poised and ready to mobilize the troops, but I touched his bicep anyway. "Like this." His arm was strong and solid, and I massaged the muscles as I slid my fingers up to his shoulder and over to his neck.

RC didn't answer, but I heard him swallow. I think he enjoyed my caressing, but at the same time he feared it. I saw the torment on his face. He wrestled between shoving me away, like he'd done to get me out of bed, and allowing me to have my way.

I took it a step further. "Or this," I said, moving my attention down RC's chest. I didn't linger over his nipples even though I could feel them through his shirt; instead I took hold of his hand and lifted it in mine. "Can I hold your hand?" I asked, innocently caressing the back of it while I seductively grinned at him. I knew I had the most wicked expression. No one could resist it easily.

He shivered. RC closed his eyes as if relishing my touch. And I noted his chest rising and falling faster. Then suddenly he pulled away. "No."

"Why? Is it the sex thing? I swear I won't push for sex. Not on the rides anyway."

RC replied, "It's *no* because you make me nervous."

"About...?"

"About trusting you. About trusting my feelings. About letting you in." RC walked around to the other side of the bed after taking a fresh shirt out of his bag. He removed his current shirt and reached for the clean one.

I leaped into action and bounced onto the bed, perching in front of RC on my knees, lusting over his bare chest. I snatched his clean shirt and held it behind my back. I teased, "Nope. Can't have it until you agree to let me hold your hand in the park."

"Nick, come on." He tried swiping his shirt from me, but I switched hands.

"Nope. And if I had it my way, you'd go shirtless all day."

"What?" RC grabbed for the shirt. I weaved and bobbed and evaded RC's clumsy attempts to recover his shirt. If RC wanted to, he could have taken it easily by pinning me to the bed. I enjoyed the playful exchange, and I think he did too. He said a second time, "Give me my shirt."

"Nope." More dodging and dancing on my knees.

RC stopped trying and placed his hands on his hips. "Nick. Give it."

My eyes turned wicked. "Nope."

We stared at one another. Me, holding the shirt behind my back, and RC, shirtless, yet smirking. That is, until I touched him. He had two Chinese symbols on his left pec, which I traced with my fingers. RC took in a sharp breath, but didn't swat my hand away until I circled his nipple and lightly pinched it. (Something I enjoyed.)

"Nick! Fuck! Why do you have to make this so difficult?" He grabbed the shirt when I wasn't paying attention and slipped it on.

"I'm sorry. I guess I don't know how to restrain myself. I look at you and feel really—"

"Shit!" RC exclaimed, his hand going to his eyes. I don't think he was listening to me as he stumbled to the bathroom and fumbled for his contact solution.

"What's wrong?" I asked from the doorway.

"I think I got a hair in my eye. It's sticking to my lenses. I knew I should've taken them out last night."

"Why didn't you?"

RC dripped some solution in his eye as I watched. He wasn't looking in my direction when he said, "You know how I said I don't like people staring at me?"

"Yeah."

"Well, I don't." His eyes were closed, and he was leaning on the sink with both hands.

"Okay. But I have a hard time not staring when I think you're sexy."

RC snorted. "Yeah right."

I pressed the issue. "No, it's true. For months now, I haven't been able to get you out of my head. I'm really attracted to you. I like your smile and your thin beard. I like your strong shoulders and your hairy chest. And I seriously have a thing for your hair. You're the perfect combination of everything that makes me horny." I know it wasn't an elegant speech, but it was what I felt.

RC sighed. He leaned on the sink, still blinking the excess solution from his eyes, because I could see it dripping onto the back of his hand. "I wish I could believe you, Nick. I feel as though I've been walking around in a dream ever since we met. I often think nobody could be as straightforward as you. But I've also spent way too many years pushing everyone away. It's been so draining."

"Well, I hope you believe me," I told him. "My mom hates lying, so I've tried to always tell the truth. Corey was the one who made me see I've been in denial. But you're the one I want. *Really* want. I even told my mom about my crush on you."

"You did?" He turned, but winced and went back to messing with his eyes. Looking at me was not working out.

"Yeah," I said. "I told her I'm gay, and she told me she knew right away I liked you."

"I wish you had said something."

"I know. I'm sorry. Ever since I can remember, I've felt this disconnect. I didn't know why boys fascinated me, but then Dawn came along, and I got swept up in a constant wave of sexual gratification and before I knew it years went by. I can't tell you how many girls I've slept with. But I also can't tell you which ones I actually enjoyed being with. Maybe Dawn. I don't know. I often wonder if I really did like her, or if I'm attached to her memory for sentimental reasons because it was my first time. She is pretty, but she's also the most manipulative person I've ever met." I heaved a sigh. "So, there you have it. I've been confused a long time and you walked right into the middle of my personal struggle. When I learned you were gay, it only added more chaos to my confusion."

"Sorry."

"You're gay, I'm gay—we can be gay together."

RC chuckled. "Weirdo."

I joined in and laughed a little at myself. My comments were pretty stupid sometimes. "So, back to the subject at hand, what does any of this have to do with your contact lenses? I thought people were supposed to take those things out at night."

RC's laughter died, and he hung his head. "There's a lot you don't know about me, Nick."

I shifted my stance. I hated standing still in one spot for so long. I would have rather had this conversation on the bed. Or while playing Xbox. "Yeah, so?" I asked when he sounded agitated. "I know that. But I don't get why—"

"My eyes aren't brown, Nick," RC blurted. "Oh, I feel sick." RC rubbed his stomach and paused again. This was taking way too long in my opinion. "Nick, I haven't shown anyone my eyes since Bobby Carter in the tenth grade."

"What?" I questioned. "What are you talking about?"

"You don't know what I've been through."

"No, but I'll listen if you tell me." I tried to sound compassionate. He didn't get to see this side of me much.

"Can you go back in the other room? Please?"

"But I want—"

"I'll tell you, only give me a minute."

I closed the bathroom door and glanced at my watch. We had five minutes until checkout. I grabbed the key card off the dresser and bolted out the door, making sure to flip the security latch around to keep the door ajar. In the elevator, I texted RC: *I'm in the lobby returning the key card. I noticed it was almost 11 and I didn't want to get in trouble for checking out late. I'll be right back.*

He didn't need to panic and think I'd left. It was bad enough I'd joked about the hickey.

It didn't take me long, so I was back in a few minutes to find RC packed and ready to go. "Cool. Are you ready?" I asked in the cheeriest voice I could muster.

"Not yet."

"Are you going to look at me?" I asked. RC was looking at the floor, and I purposely stepped into his field of vision. All RC had to do was look up and tell me what was going on. I hoped he would.

"I wear colored contacts, Nick. My eyes aren't brown."

"You said that before. Why?"

"Because I don't like people staring at me."

"Well, what color are they? Are they red or orange or something bizarre like that? Because that would be cool, like something out of *Doctor Who*. I've heard albinos have red eyes. Are you an albino?"

RC snickered and shook his head. "No, Nick. I'd have white hair and very light skin."

"You could dye your hair."

"I'm not albino."

"Then why change your eye color? How bad could they be? Violet? That would be awesome!" I reached out and touched his head. If he wouldn't look at me, maybe I could take advantage and stroke his hair. It was like chinchilla fur between my fingers, his hair was that soft.

"No, not violet. They're green."

"Green?" I asked, feeling my heart jump inside my chest. "Green's my favorite color."

"They aren't a normal green, Nick."

I could not believe my ears. *Green?* "So? Whatever shade they are, I'm sure they're beautiful. As I said, green's my favorite color. I mean *seriously* my favorite eye color. Back when I met Marcy, I was attracted to her dark brown hair and her lovely green eyes, and I thought she was my vision of perfection, except I work with her and I don't date coworkers. And then there's the fact she's a girl, and I finally realized I didn't want to be with girls, so that made all her great features a little less wonderful."

My rambling did it. RC looked up. I gasped as our eyes met. We remained motionless for a few moments. His eyes were stunning, and I felt drunk on his beauty. I stepped forward into the space between RC's parted knees, into his personal space, and caressed the side of his face. I removed his glasses and smoothed the wisps of hair away from his forehead as I continued to study the depths of his eyes.

RC was silent as I touched him, but the emotion swirling in his eyes was like the eye of a hurricane. I bent forward and kissed each of

RC's eyes, one after the other, and then straightened again so I could memorize their loveliness.

RC hesitated, his expression faltered, and then he busted out laughing. I stepped back, chuckling as well, although I wasn't sure why. "Nick," RC said between loud guffaws. "That had to be the cheesiest move you've ever made."

I smiled. "Yeah, probably."

RC continued snickering for a few minutes, but eventually the laughter we shared died down.

I inched closer and caressed the side of his face and said, "I wanted to kiss you, but you said you weren't ready. You have good reasons. I know I'm not virtuous or monogamous and all those other words that M-L uses, which I have to look up in the dictionary when I get home. But I also know I can change—for you. So if I have to keep at a distance until you trust me, I can do that. I won't push. And whatever made you hide these amazingly beautiful eyes behind fake contacts—the explanation can wait. It had to have been bad for you to hide like that."

RC took a deep breath. His hands gripped my thighs. Not in a sexy way, but as if he was holding on for dear life. Then he explained, "They used to make fun of me, the kids in school. You know, for being fat. And then some girl was listening to the sound track from *Wicked* and "One Short Day" came on at lunch. All it took was for *one* girl to say my eyes looked like the Emerald City, and then another to say it was a waste on a guy as disgusting as me. They laughed. Then more girls laughed. All I remember was everyone laughing and pointing at my expense, and those girls took away the last ounce of dignity I had left. I was a fat, green-eyed waste of breath. And I was gay. No one wanted me. I figured no one would *ever* want me."

RC leaned his face against my abdomen, but I lifted his chin and forced him to look up. "I wasn't lying when I said I thought you're sexy. But now.... Raffy...," I whispered his real name, "you're truly beautiful to me. I can't change what they did, but knowing what you went through makes me so proud of you for surviving. And if it takes me years to convince you of that...." My voice hitched, and I had tears in my eyes. I collapsed into RC's arms, sitting in his lap and hugging him tight. "I'm sorry," I sobbed. My emotions were too great to contain.

"You didn't do it."

"No. But back in high school, I was the guy who laughed as someone else did. I'm sorry. Not only for you, but also for all those I didn't step in to defend. I'm just as guilty for letting it happen."

RC hugged me back. He had tears in his own eyes. I was in his arms. RC. I couldn't believe it. He held me tight for a few minutes and then moved us both farther back on the bed. He rolled to the side and I slipped off his lap and onto my back. RC looked down into my eyes, positioned very close, and laid a hand on my chest. *Oh God. And I'm supposed to exercise self-control now?*

"I feel like I'm dreaming," RC whispered. I pinched his back, and he yelped. "Ouch."

I grinned. "See, not dreaming."

I lay there beneath him, all but pleading with my eyes. He had to know I wanted to kiss. But should we? Sex was a huge step. And if he kissed me, I was 99 percent sure sex was where it would lead. RC wasn't ready, but he also looked hungry.

RC's deliberation was determined for us as the hotel room door opened and a woman gasped. The housekeeper stood wide-eyed with her hand over her mouth. Then she started speaking Spanish and pointed at us, and RC smiled awkwardly.

I got off the bed and spoke to her in Spanish, and she started giggling.

RC asked, "What did you say?"

"I told her we were just trying out the bed."

"No, you didn't."

I grinned. "No, I didn't." I picked up my bag and RC did the same. I said good-bye to the housekeeper, and the two of us headed toward the elevator. I explained, "I told her we got distracted after checkout and I was glad she came in when she did because in another five minutes we would've been naked."

"Oh my God. That's worse!"

"Relax. She said her cousin's gay. We startled her because she wasn't expecting anyone to be in the room, and she's never seen two men in bed together. It was shocking, yet funny."

"She said that?"

"Yeah."

"And you speak Spanish?"

"Yeah."

"Handy skill."

"There's a large number of Spanish speaking people in Carroll County. I think it helps with communication."

We walked side by side to the car outside. I felt really good for the first time in my life. Being with RC made me see things more optimistically. I got in the front seat and checked my phone: Mom and Corey. I texted back.

"Who ya texting?" I noted a twinge of jealousy in his voice, and it made me smile.

"Corey. He asked how my weekend was going." I looked over at RC and touched his arm. "No need to be jealous. He asked if I had feelings for you."

"Your boyfriend knows about me?" RC's emotions were so easy to read. I can't believe I hadn't seen it so plainly before. He was really jealous of Corey.

"Yes and no," I said. "He knew I had a crush on a guy named RC. And now he knows, because of my mom, that I'm spending the weekend with you. So when I texted back 'I'm embracing who I am,' he asked if he could meet you."

"He did?"

"Yeah. And by the way, he's not my boyfriend. Remember? I told him I'm no longer available for 'extracurricular activities.'"

"Is that why you laughed just now?"

"Yeah. And because he said he's happy I 'lost the mask.'"

"Mask?"

I nodded. "Uh-huh. That's what he's called it for, like, a year. It's a metaphor for an invisible barrier I've been clinging to, pretending I'm straight when I knew deep down I wasn't. Ever since I met Corey, I knew I was denying what I am. I'm gay."

"You sound surprised."

"No. Not surprised. Relieved. Happy. I want to be myself *all* the time, and not only when I'm with Corey, M-L, or you. So right now, I'm feeling pretty good."

RC replied, "Me too." He reached over and touched the side of my face. I loved the feeling of his big hand on me. It was warm and rough, and I could feel the strength in his fingertips. Nothing like a girl. He was very manly, and I liked it more than I thought possible.

Chapter 21: *A New Me*

OH. MY. GOD. You talk about the perfect day? The second day at the park was bliss on a stick, like those chocolate-covered ice cream desserts only without melting down your hand. I was walking on air. No… I was skipping. Literally. RC thought I'd gone bonkers because I could not stop smiling, and I skipped down the pavement between attractions.

Why would I not?

RC liked me. He liked me! He let me hold his hand and everything. I realized that made me sound like a girl, maybe like Tara or Dawn or even my little sister Jennifer, but it wasn't as if I could put my hands on his dick. RC had made those instructions very clear. And I was okay with it. Sort of.

There was a time, not long ago, if a girl had told me she wouldn't put out, I'd have dumped her and moved on. I mean, why bother hanging with someone if I wasn't getting laid? Sex had been my number one priority for years. What M-L had said made sense now. I was looking for something deeper, and maybe I *was* growing up. My feelings for RC sure felt stronger than anything I'd experienced before. I used to think there wasn't anything better than an orgasm, but the breathlessness of ejaculation never lasted long. It was fleeting.

Hanging at the park all day kept me in a constant state of semierect anticipation, but oddly, I wasn't bothered when he didn't grope me in the lines or pull me behind any of the buildings to get me off. Being with RC made me want sex, but it also taught me I could be excited all day and still want to stick around for more torture-inducing conversative foreplay. (Wait, that's probably not a word.)

RC got me hard with a look. He made me shiver with excitement. I didn't know who the fuck told him that his eyes were a waste on a guy like him, but if I found out, I'd be tempted to beat the shit out of the person. He's fucking hot. Of course, this was the new me talking, and I was basing my opinion on the new RC as well. He told me he'd lost a lot of weight. And I was a douche in high school. Perhaps I would have treated him the same way those bullies did years ago? I hated considering I could have been one of those assholes who destroyed his self-image, but dwelling on it wouldn't change the fact that it had happened. People were shit. I knew that.

Today, though, I was a new person. I let go of my fear about being gay, and I gave in to some of my impulses. I touched his hand, his arm, and fingered his hair. I used to do these things with the girls I'd dated because I knew they liked the attention. With RC, I wasn't as confident. I worried he might smack me or tell me to stop. I think he allowed me to do as I wished because I kept it clean.

Best part? For the first time since I'd met him, RC didn't tell me to stop staring. When a person stands in line at a ride for any amount of time, there is practically nothing else to do besides look at stuff. So I looked around for about three milliseconds, but my wandering eyes kept coming back to him. RC. I wanted to look at him. He promised me he'd never wear his contacts again, at least not in my presence, and those gorgeous eyes made my insides all rubbery and my cock stand at half-staff. I stared, and I know I blushed when he occasionally smirked and made eye contact with me, because my groin was very awake all day. He had to have known I was thinking about sex most of the time, but he never told me to stop staring. I was so happy.

I was not the kind of person who normally sat around overanalyzing shit, but thinking and staring while standing in line gave me something to do since making out was not an option.

RC would have had me with the hair. I loved his hair. But now that I saw the most beautifully intense green eyes of my life, there was no going back. As I thought about it, I was actually glad I hadn't known about the eyes at first. If I had, I would have worried about my feelings being based on lust. Knowing I was horny before I knew made everything we did now more real. I'd also put two and two together and figured out I'd been attracted to him before his skin cleared up and before he shaved his squirrel-nest beard. I'd liked RC when we first ate lunch together because he treated me like a person, not an object. And when I'd figured out he was gay, my urges became more sexual but not based on his eyes. I wanted that hairy body. I was attracted to his size and his masculine characteristics.

"What are you thinking?" RC asked.

I glanced up. "What?"

"You've been staring at my groin for five minutes," he said, leaning in presumably so the couple behind us couldn't hear him.

I felt guilty. "Sorry. I was thinking about your hair."

RC did not look convinced. "Really? Are you sure?"

"Yes. Yes and no. I was thinking about lots of things." I stepped closer and touched his chest. I licked my lips. "I was thinking about you in general. I think this is the happiest I've felt in a really long time. I feel free." I took a deep breath. "And despite my natural fuck-everything instincts, to be with you, I'll wait forever if I have to. I will."

"You say that now."

"No, I mean it. I've been thinking about it all day. Every line we stand in, I look at you and touch you, and I think how much I've liked you even when I didn't realize it." I reached up and stroked his jaw. I loved his gangster beard. "You're so different than anyone I've met before. And I don't simply mean your looks. It's everything. My friends are shallow and superficial. Maybe that was why I never felt relaxed around them. Hanging with that crowd feels like an ongoing popularity contest. And I think I was afraid that one day I'd fail. Now, I don't care." I looked into his eyes, I mean deeply into his eyes. "I want to do whatever makes *you* happy. I want to be yours. Only yours."

"I'm not rushing into bed with you, Nick, no matter how charming you are. You need to give me time."

"I know. I get that." I was standing very close, but somehow I managed to step closer. My stomach was touching his, and I was still cupping his jaw and rubbing his beard with my thumb. I licked my lips again. "I can wait," I whispered as I leaned forward and rested my weight against him. I slipped my arm around his hip and put my head on his shoulder. Part of me expected him to tense up or push me away, but I was glad to be wrong and feel his hand in my hair. He pulled me more tightly to him, and I sighed. Maybe the people behind us said something, I didn't know. I didn't care. I was in his arms—a millisecond of heaven—and I was remaining there until we got on the ride.

We were next for the haunted house ride and when the attendant opened the gate, we got in the car. I held RC's hand as ride jolted forward, moving on the metal rail. It was the oldest ride I think I'd ever seen. The special effects were cheesy and I laughed more than anything. It was supposed to be scary, but it could have only been scary to little kids, five-year-olds and under. There were fake vampires and mummies, and a big plastic spider hanging from the ceiling. The car tilted left and right every so often as it curved around the track. I thought the fake screams were hilarious.

It never occurred to me RC had been silent the whole ride until we stopped at the end and exited. He wasn't looking at me, but at least he still held my hand. I could have walked to the next ride in silence, but something inside told me he needed to talk now. I found a line of bushes outside the haunted house ride and led him into privacy.

"Are you okay?" I asked, trying to look into his eyes, which was difficult because he was doing everything he could *not* to look at me.

"No." His voice was strangled. That was when I noticed his cheeks were wet.

I reached up and removed his glasses, even though he tried to pull away. "Raffy, look at me." He did, and his eyes were red from crying. "What happened?"

"It's stupid."

"What is?"

"Me. Crying. It's stupid."

"Obviously something upset you. What was it?" I tried to wipe away his tears, but he wouldn't let me, and stepped back and hastily did it himself.

"Stop. I'm not a baby."

"You're crying like one," I quipped. Not very nice, but it was a gut response.

He scowled. "Gee, thanks."

I shrugged. "I'm an ass, what can I say?"

He looked at me and then grinned. "You are. But I'd rather have your company than anyone else's."

I tried again. "So, why were you crying?"

"That ride. That stupid, cheesy, haunted house ride. I didn't remember it until we went through the doors and into the dark. They had the exact same haunted house ride on the Boardwalk in Ocean City when I was a kid. My dad used to take me on it every year. I remember thinking it was the scariest ride ever, and how my dad always kept his arm around me. I remember covering my eyes and peeking through the cracks to glimpse the fake zombies and corpses. I remember that same huge spider suspended at the end of the ride that made me jump when it swung down at the car. I remember all of it." He started sobbing. "I remember getting on that ride every year with my dad. I miss him so much."

RC collapsed into my arms, crying on my shoulder, and I held him tightly. After several minutes, when his heaving sobs subsided, he leaned back from my embrace. "Thanks Nick."

He allowed me to wipe the tears away. "Any time," I said. I knew he wouldn't let me kiss him, and if I tried it would only look as though I was taking advantage of his weakened state, adding more to my reputation of being an ass. I didn't need help redefining "ass." Instead, I leaned in and kissed his cheek. Tenderness was more appropriate anyway. I wasn't always a cad.

RC caressed my cheek, and tears welled in his eyes again. "You know that day… back when you were singing?" His breathing hitched and I could tell he was trying hard not to sob again.

I nodded.

"I turned it off because I knew I'd cry… if I listened to you sing the rest of that song."

"The one by Carly Simon?"

He confirmed, "Uh-huh. My mom used to sing it to my dad." He shook as the sobbing overtook him. "It was like their song. My dad loved James Bond movies. He would have liked you, Nick."

Now I was crying too. If anyone walked by I could only imagine how pathetic we looked clinging to one another in a secluded spot next to the building. I felt awful for him. And I had unwittingly compounded his sadness. I held him tightly as I cried, "I'm sorry. I won't sing it again. I didn't know."

RC pulled back, suddenly serious. "No, Nick. Don't say that. My dad would have loved it." He didn't remain composed, however; the tears erupted again. "I think he would have sung along with you. You have to sing it again to me. Please?"

"Okay. But if you cry, I'll cry, and I won't sound very good."

"Then I guess your chance at winning *The Voice* will be shot all to hell."

I started laughing through my tears. "I guess so."

"Oh fuck. I think I'm done for the day." RC released his hold on me and wiped his face.

I pulled the hem of my shirt up and wiped my nose. Only clear liquid, FYI. "Really? Can we ride the Scrambler one more time? And I thought you wanted to get on the Pirate Ship?"

"I did. I guess we can. The Haunted House ride took a lot out of me."

I took his hand again and smiled. If he wasn't up for making decisions, surely I could make them for the two of us. "Just follow me. We'll hit a few rides, and then I'll drive us home. Okay?"

RC nodded. If I could guess the look in his eyes, I'd say it was *longing*. He appeared to be looking at my lips. Maybe he wanted a kiss? I could only hope. I handed his glasses back and tugged him in the direction of the giant Pirate Ship. I knew we couldn't leave the park on a bad note.

"Nick?"

"Yeah?" I glanced his way as we walked.

"I like hearing you call me Raffy."

I grinned. "I like it too. Raffy's a great name."

"I still want to be RC to the general public. Okay? I've been called too many bad names over the years, and I don't want to chance the indignity again."

We stopped at the back of the line. "I get it. I'll keep Raffy to myself." I felt warm inside, but I didn't think I blushed. Blushing was for thinking about sex in the wrong contexts. No, I felt giddy because I had a special name for him that was just mine. Then I thought about my mom and told him, "My mom's gonna want to call you Raffael. She likes the name."

"That's fine. My mom calls me Raffael too."

"So, can I ask? Is your mom still living?"

He looked at the ground. "Yes. She's a nurse."

"Oh. And do you still talk to her?"

He shook his head. "Not since I came out. She won't return my calls."

I felt bad for him and at the same time, I ached for my mom. I'd come out and it was as if she'd known all along. "And your dad died last year?"

He nodded. "December first."

Summer was almost over, and December was coming up fast. I didn't know what to say about that. It sounded so trite, but I still said, "I'm sorry."

RC didn't say anything, but he reached across my shoulders and side-hugged me. I looped my arm around his back and we remained in that position for the remainder of the time we were at the park. I almost didn't want to get in the car.

BACK AT RC's, I didn't know what the next step should be. I had planned on staying a couple more days, but now? I didn't know. I followed him into his apartment and waited for him to suggest something.

RC threw his keys on the coffee table and asked, "So, um, are you staying? Or going home?"

He looked as unsure as I felt. "I don't know. If I stay, then I'm just gonna want to touch you and do stuff."

He nodded. "Yeah. I thought the same thing."

I stepped closer and trailed my fingers down his arm. "I guess I should go." But I didn't want to. "Do you want your key back?"

"No. Use it whenever you want."

"Okay. I guess I'll see ya later."

"Yeah." I love how he sounded strained and disappointed as he agreed with me.

I looked him in the eyes. "Can I hug you?"

He nodded.

I circled his neck and pulled him close. I felt his arms around my back and his face pressed against my ear. I felt his breath. Seconds later he was nipping my skin. Tingling sparks radiated outward from the spot where he kissed me. I had fantasized about RC kissing me there and the real experience exceeded my expectations. I felt shivers down my spine, down my arms, through my chest and into my groin. My breathing sped up, and I pressed into him as I quietly groaned. "Oh yeah. So good."

I was losing myself in the moment and the feel of his lips on me. I wanted more. So much more. Yet it also occurred to me this was not part of our deal. As much as it pained me to do so, I jumped back. "Hey! You just kissed my neck."

He blushed and hung his head. "I know. You should really go."

"Don't be sorry. That's probably the one of the most sensitive spots on my body. I liked it." I grinned wickedly and touched his arm. "You *do* want me."

He tilted his head back and sighed. "Yes, I want you. That's never been the issue." His gaze returned to mine, and he added, "Please just go."

"Okay. But feel free to kiss my neck anytime."

He grinned weakly. I could tell it was hard from him to pull back. Reluctantly, I did as asked and walked over to the door. "When will I see you?"

"Wednesday."

I pouted. "Really? Not sooner?"

"Tomorrow night?"

"I work."

"Tuesday night?"

I whined, "Paul's coming over to watch baseball. It's the only night this week I had free when we made plans." I suddenly had a great idea. "Hey, why don't you come over and join us? Just us guys. Baseball, beer, Doritos. It'll be great! And you can meet my dad."

"I've met your dad, Nick."

"Oh. Yeah. I forgot."

"You forget a lot of things. Yeah, sure, I'll come over."

I WASN'T sure how things would go with RC and Paul and my dad in the same room, but it was fun. RC was reserved, but he came out of his shell by the end of the night. Best of all, I think my dad liked him. And Paul was cool. He greeted RC warmly—very Paul-like. I think RC was thrown by his friendliness. They had never spoken before, even though RC was in the shop every week, so Paul's gentle smile and touchy tendencies made RC smirk several times.

We stood out by the car for ten minutes after the game was over and Paul had said good night. I was surprised my mom didn't come looking for me. "It was a great game," I said.

RC nodded. "Yup. You've said that twice now." He was leaning on his truck door, and I was awkwardly standing in front of him. "I like your friend Paul."

I grinned at him. "You've said that twice now."

RC smiled widened. "I know. I'm messing with you."

RC's "no kissing" rule was killing me. I felt knotted up inside. I didn't know what to say. I wasn't used to spending time talking to say good night. I always kissed the girl thoroughly at her front door, and then waved as I drove away. RC wasn't kissing me. RC was standing there patiently, waiting for me to say something intelligent. I had nothing. All I wanted was a kiss. A kiss and maybe a little friction up against his groin. And maybe his hand on my ass. And groaning into my mouth. And—

"Nick? If all you're going to do is stare at my shoes, I'm heading out."

I looked up sharply. "What? I guess I'm not good at this." I didn't know how to be enthused so I let the blah reality seep into my reply. Then I sighed heavily. RC snickered, so I questioned him, "Why are you laughing at me?" And he was smirking. I hated that. Why was he always laughing at my expense?

"I'm amused because you look pathetic."

"Sorry," I replied, sounding anything but.

He snickered some more. "No. I like it. You're out of your comfort zone, and you're doing it for me."

"What does that mean?" I didn't like the sound of him enjoying my suffering.

"It means you're used to everything being about sex."

"I am. I don't know what to do right now. I feel like no matter what I say I'll sound stupid." I rubbed the tip of my shoe on the driveway. If I looked up, it would only make my frustration worse. I wanted to kiss him. And looking into his eyes made me burn for even more than that.

"Close your eyes," he instructed.

I snapped to attention. "What? Why?" Something inside me jumped, and I noticed how soft his features looked. I hoped he had decided to give in. It had only been a few days since we decided to take this slow, but oh God, it was like watching two snails race uphill.

"Just close your eyes."

I did. I stood stock-still, waiting, hoping. I felt his hand on my cheek. My lips parted as I sucked in a quick breath. His hand was large and warm and he slid his thumb over my lips. My heart was racing as his hand slid slowly down my cheek, onto my neck, around the back of my neck so I felt his fingers in my hair. When he released me, a small sound escaped my throat, and I felt the urge to lunge forward. But I refrained, hoping my restraint pleased him. Seconds passed, and he didn't touch me again. I was breathing hard by the time he finally spoke.

"You can open your eyes, Nick."

I snapped them open.

RC looked drained. Perhaps he was struggling with his own desires. But if he was, I really wanted him to be over them already. "You really are beautiful," he said.

I should have had a response, but I didn't. I felt weak under his gaze. I was breathing so hard, and all I could think about were his lips. I wanted to feel his facial hair against my mouth, pricking the corners of my lips. I wanted to taste his breath.

"Go inside, Nick. I'll see you at lunch tomorrow, but then we'll probably have to wait until Saturday. I work days and you work night shifts this week."

Yeah, I vaguely remembered telling him.

RC touched my cheek again. "I wish this was easier, but you don't know what I've been through."

I found my voice. "Then tell me. Tell me why you don't trust me. Tell me what happened to you. Tell me how long I have to fight against myself. Please?" I rasped, "I want to kiss you Raffy, so bad."

"I know," he said, opening his truck door. "I'll think about it." He got in and shut the door. Through the open window, he added, "I know this is hard for you, but it's comforting to see you exert such effort for me."

He gave me a weak smile and drove off. Being his "boyfriend" was officially the hardest thing I'd ever done. I trudged back inside and took a cold shower. The sheets felt just as cold wrapped around me when I later went to bed. I had the feeling the one night I'd slept in his arms had ruined me because it was hard to think of anything else, and yearn for anything less.

Chapter 22: *Waiting*

"YOU'RE IN a rotten mood," Paul said.

I looked up. "What?" I hadn't heard him approach. I was cooking a steak. "I guess I'm trying to get this order done so I can get my lunch ready."

"This order?" he asked, pointing to the ticket hanging on the metal strip.

"Duh."

He walked around behind me to my left, took two burger patties out and tossed them on the hot surface. "Then you'll probably need these."

I gave him a look, glanced at the burgers, and then checked the ticket. Yup, sure enough, I'd read cheese steak and the ticket read cheeseburger. "Shit!" I huffed. "I guess I'm having a cheese steak for lunch."

"Don't sweat it. I'll eat it on my break. I know you prefer chicken salad."

"You don't have to do that," I replied. Paul was being nice. Come to think of it, he'd always been nice to me, ever since I started here as a matter of fact. I leaned on the wrapping station behind me and folded my arms across my chest, watching the burgers sizzle.

"I know I don't have to, I want to. But tell me, does your moping have to do with RC? I noticed you lingering by his truck as I pulled away last night. Things not going well?"

"Kind of." I stepped forward, picked up the spatula, and flipped the burgers. I thought about what he'd asked. Should I tell him my troubles? How much did guys share before it crossed a line?

"You don't want to spill? Okay. Whatever. I thought we were friends, but if this is too much for you...."

He started walking away, and I dropped the grill spatula fast enough to snag his arm. "Wait. I do. I just... I don't want to sound like a girl whining to my BFF."

Paul grinned. "You're funny. Just spill."

"He wouldn't kiss me," I complained.

"Hmm. Interesting. Reasons?"

I let out a breath, flipped the burgers, placed a slice of cheese on each one, and then said, "Private. And what I mean by that is I don't even know. He's had a rough past or something."

Paul shrugged. "So, you give him time."

"I'm trying. But every time I'm with him, I want to kiss him so bad. I've had a permanent hard-on for weeks, and he wouldn't even kiss me good night. I can't sleep. Ever since the hotel room, I don't want to be anywhere but in his arms. And to top it all off, I don't know what to say anymore. I've never had to think of things to talk about. Tara and Chrissy and those girls, they talked enough for six people. It's just me and RC, and he's kinda quiet. Ya know?"

"Yeah, I noticed that. But you've known he's quiet for a long time. You guys have eaten lunch together in silence every week for three months. So it isn't his taciturn personality that's vexing. What is it?"

I moaned quietly as I replied, "I don't know how to stop thinking about his body."

Paul chuckled.

"Stop laughing! I'm attracted to him, okay? I happen to like big, hairy guys."

"No, by all means, like away. But I'm laughing because I told you so."

I narrowed my eyes. "Told me what?"

"I told you people are attracted to different things. I told you that kissing me wasn't going to help you decide if you're gay. And that knowing if you really like a person comes when you can be around them, not kiss them, and still have a hard time thinking of anything else. And you've got it bad."

I remembered. "You're not kidding," I whined. "I've never had to do this before. With girls it was easier. I take them out, we fuck, I work all week until we go out again. I've never had to think about it. I don't know what to do now. And what if I screw this up? Coming out, even if it wasn't hard with my mom, pretty much destroys the safety net. I'm not going to be one of those guys who swings both ways for convenience. Been there, done that. I'm gay. I know because this much torture over a guy would never happen if I was only in it to get laid. He's the one, Paul. I don't want anyone else, and I'm scared shitless."

Paul took the spatula from my grasp and removed the burgers from the grill, placing them on the prepared roll. After the order was assembled, he called the number and motioned for me to follow him into the back. When we were alone by the ice machine, he said, "First, comparing what you have with RC to all the girls you dated is only going to give you a headache. It is *nothing* like that. This is real. You fucking around for years was a waste of time. All it did was cloud your brain. Second, sex in a vacuum is empty. RC is your chance at a relationship. Start by getting to know him. Sure, sometimes you start with sex and that works out, but it sounds like sex isn't an option. So, before you blow what could be a really good thing, take the choice behind door number two."

"Which is?"

"Getting to know him. You've never looked this ragged out before last weekend, so what happened? You said something about a hotel. Did you have sex and he freaked, or what? Because I noticed all the flirting going on between you when we watched the game."

"You did?"

"Dude, you're like an open book. And the way he kept blushing?" Paul snorted. "Sickening. So what happened?"

"We slept together. I mean really slept. No sex. RC took me to this amusement park over the weekend and it was too far away to do the whole park in a day, so we got a hotel and rode the rides two days in a row."

"Wow. That sounds amazing. Why'd he take you there?"

I shrugged. "I don't know. I guess he thought I'd like it."

"And did you?"

"Duh."

"Then it sounds like he's got you pegged."

"I guess. I don't know."

"Then what's the problem? Tell me what happened in the hotel."

"I told you. We slept together. And now I can't get him out of my mind."

"I'm not sure I'm following you. Why were you in bed together in the first place?"

"Because I'm a pushy bastard."

"And?"

"We hashed everything out after I assumed he took me there for sex. I told him I broke up with Tara—"

"I was wondering about that."

"And he finally admitted he liked me. I said I wasn't sleeping in the other bed all alone, and he reluctantly let me sleep next to him." I smiled. I couldn't help smiling. "I woke up in his arms, Paul. It was the most amazing feeling I've ever felt. Well, until he yelled at me and told me to get off of him. Apparently I was humping his leg."

"Yeah, sounds like you." Paul laughed. "So wait, why are you so blah today? You like him, he likes you; sounds good to me."

"Yeah, but…. RC wants to take things slow, given my reputation. And that sounded easy when I agreed to it, but… oh God, I want to kiss him so baaaad." I whined again, hopping slightly where I stood, allowing my head to fall back as I pouted over it.

"Nick, jeez, you're pathetic. What happened to Corey?"

"We were never really together. We're still friends."

"Oh," he grunted.

"Oh, there's another thing. Tara told me Dawn bet her she couldn't keep me longer."

"Longer than what?"

"Longer than she and I dated. That's the reason she didn't care I cheated with Corey. She wanted to beat Dawn. Bitch."

"You cheated on Tara with Corey?" Paul asked, perplexed.

"Yeah."

"When?"

"A while ago."

"But haven't you had a thing for RC that long?"

"Kind of."

Then he whistled. "I'm sorry. I can't keep up with this. Your life is like a soap opera. No wonder you're frustrated RC isn't kissing you. You're not used to waiting for anything, are you?"

"No. So what do I do in the meantime?"

Paul laughed, but I didn't bother huffing about it this time. "Think back to before you knew he liked you. What did you do then?"

"I watched. I paid attention to the things he likes. The music he likes, the food he likes, and how he is hyperaware of all the eyes in the room. I noticed how he watches people to make sure they aren't watching him. He's really self-conscious like that."

Paul's eyes finally lost their glee. They softened as he looked at me, and he touched my shoulder, giving it a light squeeze. "Then go back to doing that. Watch him. Listen to him. Don't think about kissing him. Think about all the little things he does that make you want to know more."

"But what about—"

"No buts. You're coming off a history of sexual conquests. It ends here. Let yourself enjoy him without any of the other stuff. If it's meant to happen, it will. Naturally. I watched you last night during the game. I watched you watching him. I've never seen you so happy."

"Really?"

"Really. So don't screw it up."

"Thanks. Nothing like a little pressure."

"Just be yourself. All the vanity aside, you really are a great guy, albeit a little dense."

I opened my mouth to protest, but he was dead on. I wasn't the smartest nut in the box. "Thanks, Paul."

"No problem. What are friends for? Besides, if RC took you to an amusement park on a date, then he sounds like a keeper to me."

"Who said it was a date?"

Paul cocked his head and replied, "Oh, yeah, because all my buddies take each other on surprise, overnight stays to amusement parks all the time. I think he was flirting with you; like courting but without the flowers."

"Huh." The idea that Paul might be right suddenly made me warm all over. "Flirting." I smiled and walked back to the grill. RC would be here soon. I couldn't wait.

WHEN RC walked in, I felt a fiery rush ripple through me. Paul had said not to think about sex, but it was going to be difficult. RC grinned at me, and I grinned back with a lift of my chin. I had our food prepared already, so all I had to do was punch out.

We sat in silence and RC seemed like himself. He ate and read the newspaper. I guess I'm the one who had the problem. I ate a fry.

"You okay? You seem off?"

I hate that he knows me so well. "I'm fine."

"Are you pissed at me for something?"

"No," I said. "I'm just pissed at myself. I'll live."

He folded the paper and laid it on the table. "When's the last time you had sex?"

I scoffed, "Uh! It has nothing to do with—"

"When?" he insisted.

"Two weeks."

"Then that's why you're edgy. Since I've known you, I don't think you've gone longer than five days. Add to that last weekend's… frustrations, you have to be wound up tight."

I huffed out a lungful of air and laid my head down on the table. "Why'd you have to point it out?" I moaned.

RC chuckled. "Sorry. But it should get easier one day at a time." I felt him touch my hair. I groaned quietly, and he snickered, but he didn't remove his hand. Thank God. His fingers felt wonderful caressing the back of my skull.

I heard the front doorbell tinkle and then a familiar voice exclaimed, "Oh, how marvelous! I see my Nicky's finally embraced himself. You must be RC."

I sat up, hating that RC removed his affectionate fingers. Corey was extending his hand to RC, and RC was just about to shake it. "Um, hi," RC said cautiously.

"My name's Corey Parrish, but you may call me Mr. Fabulous," he joked as he plopped down in the booth next to me.

"Okay." RC didn't sound thrilled Corey was here.

"I'm kidding," Corey assured, patting the back of RC's hand. RC tensed up from the attention.

"What brings you here, Corey?" I asked, hoping to rein in the conversation before it strayed. "I think I've seen you more since you moved to DC than when you lived in Westminster."

"I know, right? Well, as it turns out, this guy I'm seeing is originally from Ellicott City, but his parents moved to Westminster a year ago."

"A guy you're seeing? As in exclusively?" I asked, shocked to hear the words pass through my lips.

"Yes, can you believe it?"

"I thought you didn't do boyfriends?"

"Well, I didn't. But for him, I'm thinking I just might make the exception. We're going out tonight on our *fourth* date. He said he'd like me to meet his parents sometime soon, maybe this weekend, so I'm staying with Laney a couple of days. The commute to DC is so long. And have I mentioned how expensive it is living down there? It's awful."

I chuckled. "Duh. Yeah. But Laney? I thought you were done with our old gang. That's what Mary-Louise told me."

"I am. But Laney's cool. I think she's on the cusp of separation as well. The pack is too exclusive these days. It's getting tighter, and she's sick of Dawn's shit. She said Dawn thinks she's the queen bee, more like a European hornet, and everyone else has to follow her lead. Ha! Are you going to her party on Saturday?"

"What party? I wasn't invited."

"You're always invited, Nicky. They can't throw a party without you."

"Maybe." I settled my eyes on RC.

"What are you looking at?" he asked, brow arched.

"You want to go with me?" I asked. "We're both off Saturday night."

He shook his head. "Um, no. I don't think so."

"But they're my friends. They should meet you."

Corey piped in, "Ooh, honey, I'm not sure that's a good idea."

I was offended and glared at him. "Corey! Seriously? Why would you say that in front of my boyfriend?"

The corner of Corey's mouth did this little thing, and I knew he was amused by my reference to RC as my boyfriend. *I think it's the first time I've done that.* "Because it's the truth," Corey answered. He patted RC's hand. I was surprised RC didn't pull it away. He didn't like people touching him, and this was the second time Corey had. Bold. Corey had to have felt the tension in his hand. It was emanating from him. As Corey continued talking, I reached across the table and took RC's other hand. RC contained a grin, but he could not stop the glow on his cheeks. *So, fucking cute.* RC squeezed my fingers.

Corey said, "Sorry, big guy, but that crowd is not very accepting of newbies. And a big hairy bear is going to stick out like a used condom in the middle of the kitchen floor. Not a good idea."

"Can you be more disgusting?" I pointed out.

"No, Nick. I like his honesty," RC said.

"Sugarbear, I don't mince words. I've been dicked around all my life—in more ways than one—and I'm done pretending. I've been done for seven years. I was out on the street at sixteen, and I never looked back. I lived under a bridge for three months and slept wherever I could find a roof to cover my head. Friends' cars, closets, offices, the gym locker room; you name it. I finished high school with a three point nine GPA and went to the community college on financial aid. I wore the same pants every day for three months. I've been at the bottom. Dodging the facts doesn't make you stronger, it makes you fearful."

I was surprised by his assertiveness. "Corey, wow, I've never heard you speak so confidently."

"I know," he grinned. "It's because of Tyler. He's... inspiring. I think I'm on the verge of something great."

"I'm glad."

"And I'm thinking of moving back here."

"Really? I thought you said you'd never do that."

"Well, I moved to DC because I wanted to be a part of the gay community. What I found was that *some* parts of the culture are embracing, and others are highly competitive and vicious. I think I need to be in an area that won't kiss me on one cheek and claw my face to shreds on the other. Ya know? Plus, DC is so expensive. I can't afford it. My lease is up in three weeks so I'm looking around Westminster, Frederick, and Leesburg. And I'm contemplating going back to college. I never finished."

"What are you thinking of studying?" RC asked. I was glad he felt he could join in the conversation. I wanted him to like my friends, and Corey was one of my closest.

Corey answered, "Tyler says I'd make a great beautician. What do you think?"

I grinned and agreed, "Yeah, I could see that." I casually touched Corey's hair, smoothing it over his ears as I had affectionately done many times before. "Your hair and makeup are always perfect." The blue glitter above his eyes reminded me of the green he'd worn the first time I kissed him. Come to think of it, Corey was always "glittery" in some form or fashion. I caressed his jaw briefly and said, "I think that would be a great career path." I winked.

"Thanks, Nicky."

RC cleared his throat and let go of my hand. "I think I'm going to head back to work."

He stood up, and I felt the sudden separation. I'd have to wait several days to see him again and I hated it. "Really?" I whined. I had to stop doing that because it wasn't very manly to whine every time I didn't get my way. "Corey, can you scootch?" I slid over and Corey got the hint. He stood up, and I followed.

"I'm ordering lunch. We'll chat before I leave," Corey said. "It was great to meet you. And honey, if you need some tips on hair products to control the frizz you got going on with those curls, just give me a shout. I think I know just the thing to keep them silky."

"Yeah, um… thanks." RC nodded uncomfortably and turned toward the door.

"Laterz, Corey. Hey, RC, let me walk you out," I insisted, following him through the door and over to his truck.

"I'm sorry you had to see that. I wasn't thinking about how I normally touch him. Corey's very affectionate, and so is my mom; I guess I need to stop. I didn't mean to make you jealous."

He paused, thinking about what to say I guess. "I'm only a little jealous."

"Liar."

He relented. "I'm a lot jealous, okay? You say he's just a friend, but he's an extremely attractive friend who's obviously very close to you. Plus, you have a history."

His hands were in his pockets, so I stroked his forearm. "We do. But Corey is always going to be my friend."

"I know." He continued to stare at me with a longing in his eyes I can only imagine spoke of how much he wanted to kiss me. Then he turned and opened the truck door. "I'm gonna go. I'll see you Saturday."

"And the party?"

He cocked his eyebrow. "Are you sure you want to take me? I've seen a few of your friends. Besides Paul, I don't think I fit in with your crowd."

"Please? I'll introduce you. I've known most of them since middle school. We hang out all the time. If you're my guy, I want them to know."

He smirked. "Am I?"

"What?"

"Your guy, you dumbass."

"Oh, right. Yeah. Of course you are. You're my guy. My official boyfriend." I grinned at him and folded my arms in the open window on the truck door. "I thought we decided that already."

RC smiled. "We did. But I like hearing you say it. Okay. I don't think it's a good idea, but I'll consider it for you."

I beamed. "Thank you."

RC rolled his eyes. "Good-bye, Nick."

RC GAVE in. We went to the party at Dawn's house that weekend.

On the way up the driveway, RC stopped short. "I forgot my phone. I need to go back to the car."

"What? No. You don't need it. I'm the only one you talk to."

"True, but what if I want to gossip about the people in the room? Wouldn't you rather have me text you than to voice my opinion openly?"

"Um, good point."

"You go ahead. I'll snag it and meet you inside."

"Are you sure?"

"Yeah. Don't worry, I won't leave you here."

I walked up to the house. It reminded me of my days in college. Every light in every room was lit so you could see everything from the outside. The music was blaring so loud, I didn't need to go in to hear it clearly. I could see maybe fifty people though the windows from the front porch alone. Hanging on each other, drinking, making out, these twentysomethings didn't look all that mature to me. The activity appeared to be the same from when we were all in high school pretending we were college students holding frat parties, which melded into college students having actual frat parties. "I can't believe any of these people have jobs," I mumbled as I pushed the doorbell.

Elaine answered the door. *Oh God, Elaine.* Poor RC was about to enter a house full of my ex-girlfriends. Terrific. "Hey, sexy. I didn't know you were coming," she said, reaching for my hand and tugging me inside. Before I could say anything she pushed me up against the wall and latched her mouth on my neck like a remora. When her roving hands hit my crotch, I pushed her away.

"What are you doing?" I asked hotly.

"Sorry, lover boy, I forgot you switched to the pink side. Is Corey with you? Dawn told me you left Tara for him."

"Dawn?" What did Dawn have to do with anything?

"Yeah. She said it was bound to happen, but it won't last."

"What?" I questioned almost as loud as the music. Dawn's assumption was offensive. "Why would she say that? There's nothing wrong with Corey."

"It's you," she yelled back so I could hear her. "Dawn said you don't have staying power. She said you're flighty."

"That's ridiculous!" I shrieked. I was offended before, now I was downright angry. "Where's Dawn?" I demanded. She pointed, and I stormed off.

I found her in the living room lying on top of Chrissy with her hand up her skirt and her mouth on her neck. *Disgusting. They should find a room for this sort of thing.* "Dawn!" I shouted. When she didn't respond, I tried again. "Dawn!"

Chrissy opened her eyes when Dawn pulled her mouth away. Chrissy wasn't speaking. The look in her eyes, plus her body language, told me she was seconds from coming. Dawn's hand was still moving under her skirt. Yup, I called it. Chrissy threw her head back and started moaning. I looked away.

"So, Nick, what brings you here?" Dawn asked, nonplused.

I turned my attention back to her and found her sucking on her fingers. My stomach turned. True, I had tasted Chrissy myself many times, but something in me had changed. The thought of it now made me queasy. I tried not to think about her fingers in her mouth as I demanded, "Why did you spread rumors about me and Corey? And what makes you think I can't commit? Just because Tara lost your little bet doesn't mean it was my fault."

Her eyes widened. "Oh, so she told you. Oh well. I'm not spreading rumors, Nick. You haven't been with any girl for more than five months. And Chrissy doesn't count because you started and stopped too many times."

I glanced at Chrissy. "Is she your girlfriend now?" I had to ask because she appeared way too satisfied for this to be a first time occurrence.

"Sort of. She's with Terrell, but we like to mix things up."

"Oh." I didn't care, but I thought it was one more reason leaving my high school gang was more than a good thing; it was survival. M-L was right, I was growing up and moving on, and these people were going to sleep around long enough to share STDs or worse.

"Where's Corey?" she asked. "I haven't seen him in ages."

I blinked and refocused. I was drifting off in the memories of my past and realizing how thankful I was for the changes within me. "Um, Corey's not here. We aren't a couple."

Dawn laughed. "See? I called it!"

Chrissy started laughing too.

"No, you don't understand. Corey's not my boyfriend because I have a different one."

She didn't appear to believe me as she looked around the room. "Well, where is he?"

"He's...." I looked around. "I don't know. He went back to the car for his phone. He should be here."

"It doesn't matter. It won't last. I'm actually surprised you're with a guy, though."

"Really? Tara said you knew I was gay back in high school."

"Oh, I did. But I thought you'd remain in denial for at least another two years. Too bad. I was set on getting you into bed one last time. You were so fun to play with. So easy to manipulate because you think with your dick." She licked her lips and gave me an evil stare as she reached up Chrissy's dress again. Chrissy moaned again, and I backed away before I puked.

Dawn's degree of using people—using me—felt like acid on my skin. How could she be so insensitive? She'd been my very first girlfriend. I'd lost my virginity to her, and it was all a part of some elaborate game. I'd never realized how she used everyone.

I took my phone out of my pocket and saw three unread texts from RC. First one: *The girl at the door won't let me in.* Second: *Nick, I'm not going in there. That girl was rude and mean. Come out. I want to leave.* And third: *Nick, I'm giving you two minutes. If you aren't out here, I'm leaving without you. They might be your friends, but they are NOT mine.*

Oh shit! I left Dawn, Chrissy, and the party immediately, but I could hear their laughter chasing me out the door. They didn't matter. Nothing mattered. I bolted out the door and caught up with RC as he was pulling away from the curb. He stopped long enough for me to hop in.

He didn't look at me, and the low rumble from his throat spoke volumes. "I don't want to talk about it. But don't ever ask me to do that again."

I felt horrible. I didn't know what Elaine said, if it was indeed her who answered the door, but I could only imagine how bad she'd treated him when they were all using me. RC didn't fit the "pretty people" crowd. And come to think of it, neither did I.

IT TOOK a little while, but RC got over the degradation I put him through. He knew it had been unintentional, but the biting comments "that girl" made were reminiscent of his past. He wasn't going to step into a situation like that again by choice. I got that. And I didn't plan on going back again. As far as I was concerned, that chapter of my life was closed. I didn't need to be a popular kid anymore to feel good about myself. I had friends now, real ones, like Paul and Corey and M-L, and I had a boyfriend.

BY TUESDAY, we were at my house again watching the game with my dad and Paul. We had fun, even though the O's lost to the Yankees five to seven, and I liked the idea this was becoming a usual thing. RC said good-bye at the door and headed out. I was disappointed, but what could I do.

When I closed the front door and turned around, I noticed his cell phone sitting on the coffee table. I snagged it and sprinted out the door. "Wait," I hollered, trying to catch him before he drove away. Luckily, he hadn't left. In fact, he was just getting into the seat. He shut the door to the truck and turned the engine over just as I rounded the bumper. I spoke between gasps. "You… forgot your phone."

I handed it to him through his open window, and he smirked at me. "Thanks, Nick."

RC paused longer than I expected with this mischievous gleam in his eyes. *He's laughing at me again.*

"Why are you looking at me like that?" I asked. I'd never seen such an expression on him. He seemed amused, playful even, with a hint of wickedness that excited and scared me at the same time. I'd never known RC to be "wicked"… ever. I was wicked, he was the cautious one.

He turned the engine off and got out of his truck.

I was confused. "What are you doing?"

He slipped the phone into his pocket and explained, "I left my cell in there on purpose." RC smirked again. *What the heck's going on behind those eyes?*

"Why would you do that?" I asked. "I can't text you if you leave your phone here. You know I like to send messages every morning and every night. And like twenty times in between."

"I know." RC stepped closer. "But don't tell me you've never done that before. It's the oldest trick in the book."

"Done what? I still don't understand…." I stopped talking when he cupped the side of my neck.

"A ruse so I get to do this," he said, closing his eyes and leaning in.

His lips touched mine. And for a second, I seriously thought I was having one of those dreams like I do about Corey. I got hot and cold and sweaty. I didn't move because I was sure that if I did, I'd wake up licking my pillow or something stupid like that. But as he kissed me, and after I realized I was kissing him back, my brain switched back on and I reached out. I slid my hands onto his hips and squeezed his sides, and his hand circled me until it stopped on my lower back. His lips were soft and hard, commanding yet hesitant. This kiss was every emotion I could think of all at once. I think it was because we'd been avoiding it for so long, and now that it was happening, I thought I was dreaming. As soon as my entire body was aware of how much of a dream it wasn't, he pulled away.

I whimpered and stepped toward him.

"That's enough for now, Nick," he said, halting me with the palm of his hand.

"But...."

RC grinned. "No matter how nice it is to see how much you want to kiss me, I still think too much too soon is a bad idea. One step at a time, okay? Step one: I kissed you. If we move to step two in your parents' driveway, I might lose control and have you naked in the cab of my truck. How would that go over if your mom came out to find you? Worse yet—your sister?"

"Eww. Good point." He made sense even if I didn't want to follow good reasoning. I wanted to be irrational and reckless. I *wanted* to end up naked in his truck. I stepped closer, hoping he wouldn't back away. "What if I want to be naked? Would you take me home with you?" I asked, knowing full well I used the most seductive tone I had. I touched his stomach and moved my fingers in little circles, hoping to let him know how much I wanted through that slight touch.

"Nick.... Don't look at me like that."

"Like what?" I grinned licentiously. I knew exactly what he was talking about.

He swallowed visibly. "You're evil."

"I know." I licked my lips and leaned forward. I kissed his neck and I felt his hands on my hips again. His fingertips curled inward as he squeezed me there. I swirled my tongue over his skin and nipped him with my teeth. I kissed my way up to his jaw and chin as I wrapped my arms around his shoulders and sank my hand in his beautiful hair.

Our kiss wasn't controlled and sweet this time. This kiss was heated and as aggressive as a steam engine roaring down a mountainside. He wrapped his arms tightly around my back while pressing his hips into mine. He lowered one hand and cupped my ass, holding it firmly, an action which spurred on our kissing intensity. I lifted my leg and curled it around his thigh, rocking slightly.

Then my mom called from the porch, "Nick? Are you still out there?"

RC uncoupled our bodies, leapt back, and stuffed his hands into his pockets as if my mom were a Catholic nun and we'd been caught tasting that forbidden fruit. He looked downright ashamed as he studied the ground at his feet.

"Yeah, Mom. I'll be right in," I called. I was glad she hadn't ventured off the porch. I wasn't ready to have the conversation where she chastised me for making out in the driveway with my boyfriend. Jennifer had rules, and I knew they applied to me too, even if I was technically an adult. Mom always said decorum was best no matter what my age.

I glanced at RC. He still looked out of sorts. "You okay?" I had to ask because he didn't look okay at all.

"Remind me to bring your mom flowers or something. I owe her one."

I wasn't sure how to take that. Was it that horrible to get caught kissing? "Are you embarrassed to be seen with me?"

RC looked me dead in the eyes and huffed. He shook his head and replied, "Are you seriously making this about you? Nick, this is about me. I told you I needed time. You have no clue how hard this is for me. I haven't had sex in a long time. A *long* time. I want you, I do, but I'll be damned if I'm going to repeat all the same stupid mistakes I made in the past. I can't this time, Nick. Not with you."

Why did he sound so desperate when he said that?

I stepped closer and surprisingly, he didn't shrink away. I cupped his cheek and said, "I'm sorry. I got carried away. You feel so good, ya know?"

He smiled weakly and leaned into my touch, closing his eyes briefly. "I do know. I want you, Nick. So badly. But you don't know all the shit I've been through. None of this is easy for me."

"I didn't mean to push you, but I liked having your hand on my ass."

He chuckled. "It's okay. You've got a great ass."

That made me smile.

We gazed into each other's eyes a few quiet moments before he kissed me again. I felt his breath on my face as he sweetly teased me with his lips. His nose rubbed over mine as he pulled away. "I'll see you later."

I sighed and watched him climb into his truck and drive away.

Chapter 23: *Camping*

IT WAS a Saturday and the pizza business was really slow for some reason. Who knew why. Maybe folks were out picnicking or something. It was a nice day, if a bit cooler than normal. I wouldn't have minded a picnic. Picnics had food. Picnics had Frisbees and potato salad and lying in the sun on a blanket. Picnics did not include scrubbing the grease off the grill hood and sweating my ass off. I would have loved a good picnic. Or maybe a day hike to Cunningham Falls? RC might like that.

As if I had been speaking my thoughts out loud, Paul called over to me, "Hey, I got an idea. We should go camping."

"Camping?" I craned my neck so I could see him and shot my best you-must-be-joking look his way.

"What?" Paul asked. "You don't think it would be fun?"

"I think it would be fun!" Julie said. She walked over and started rubbing my calf as if trying to coax me into agreeing. I was on a ladder so I could get up inside the hood vent. It was stinky and sticky and sweltering. I hated this job. It would have been nicer if she could have reached my neck and massaged the kinks out of it. "Fun in the sun, hun. We've all worked together for ages and haven't once done something fun."

I opened my mouth, about to remind her of the time we played volleyball over the pizza oven with a balloon left over from a little kid's birthday party, and that was when she held up her finger and said, "And playing volleyball that time doesn't count."

"Why not? I enjoyed it."

Julie went on to explain, "*Fun* is when all that happens is hitting the inflated object over the pretend net. Not-so-fun is when the 'ball' lands on the 'net' and melts, causing a huge mess and lots of work."

I relented. "I see your point. But camping? How are we all going to get off on the same day? Besides, I like my creature comforts. Air-conditioning, Chinese takeout, Netflix streaming. All good things to have when on vacation, and forests don't include them."

"Oh, come on Nick. You aren't a wimp, are you?" Marcy said, entering into the conversation after she finished with the only customer we'd had in two hours.

"You're going too?" I asked, climbing down the ladder.

"I don't know. I guess." Marcy looked over at Paul. "You want me to come too, right? This isn't a guy thing. You want your girlfriend to go camping with you. You didn't bring it up at work just to leave me out, did you?" She looked worried. I've never seen Marcy look worried before. She was always sassy and brash and sure of herself. Since she'd started dating Paul, she had turned into this insecure nervous Nelly. It was as if she was scared she'd do something wrong and he'd break up with her. It was kind of cute, but then again, if I were Paul, I'd have been annoyed by now. She needed to get a clue.

Paul walked over to her and touched the side of her cheek. "Marcy, of course I'd want to include you." Then he looked at me again. "And Nick. All of us. Although the place I have in mind has a six-camper limit unless we book more than one campsite. Which we can, but I think six is a good number."

"Sounds good and understood," Julie said, standing tall and proud, saluting Paul as the grand pooh-bah of our little squad. "But can I bring Laney? She's my best friend. You have Marcy and Nick has...." She paused and furrowed her brow. "Are you bringing RC?"

"Yeah, I guess so. If he's up to it. The last time I took him to a party with my friends, it was a disaster."

Paul pointed out, "That's because those aren't your real friends. We are."

"I'll say we are!" Julie said proudly.

Oddly, that phrase made me think of "The Chipmunk Song," and I found myself shouting, "Okay!" Everyone looked at me funny, and I had to apologize. "Sorry. Overzealous."

"Wait," Marcy interjected. "What happened to Tara?"

"Um, we split up." I thought Tara would have shared the news of our breakup with someone, and I'd never have to admit to anyone that I'd broken up with her. Somehow it seemed easier if they all found out from someone who wasn't me.

"Why didn't you tell me?" She looked mad. Why was she mad? She had a boyfriend. Or had she forgotten?

"Was I obligated to?"

"Yes," she demanded. "We practically spend every single day of the week together, Nick. The least you can do is share personal details like when you decide to drop a skank so we can celebrate together. I would have bought you a beer for that one."

"Marcy, you're twenty. You can't buy me a beer." Something in her eyes told me she was thinking thoughts that needed to disappear. She was conniving. Planning. Marcy was one opportunity away from reverting back to the Marcy who'd tried to get me into bed every single day we worked together. The old Marcy needed to stay away. I liked the new Marcy. I liked the Paul's-my-boyfriend Marcy.

Paul, gotta love that guy, read my mind. He pushed the hair at Marcy's temple over her ear, as he was often prone to do, and smiled. "That's a great idea, sweetie. How about I buy Nick the beer and you have a Coke." He winked, and Marcy grinned. She closed her eyes and leaned into his touch. I mouthed to him, "Thank you," and he winked.

"So, RC it is," Julie said. "Next time he's in, I'll talk to him. He'll go."

"So, you're dating RC? When did this happen?"

"A couple weeks ago."

"You're gay? Oh my God! You're gay!" Marcy pointed at me like this was headline-worthy and she was Lois Lane.

And Paul, being in tune with my brain, turned her away from me and walked her toward the back of the restaurant. "Let's leave Nick alone to finish cleaning the hood vent, and I'll fill you in on all the details, okay?"

"Then it's settled," Julie announced while I was half-thinking to myself about my idiot friends and half-listening to the elevator version of "Payphone" coming through the overhead speakers.

"What did we agree to?" I asked. I'm so fucking absentminded sometimes, I sincerely felt as though I'd missed something important.

"Camping," Paul said. He had reemerged in time to take a pizza off the end of the conveyer belt. "I'm bringing Marcy. Julie and Laney are sharing a tent. And that leaves you and RC in a tent." Then he smirked, "Can you handle that?"

"Shut up."

Paul snickered.

I addressed Julie next. "By Laney, did you mean Laney Peterson?"

"Yup. Do you know her?"

Did I know her? I laughed internally at the irony. "Yeah. We dated for three weeks."

Paul laughed harder. "Wow, this trip should be interesting. I'll look at the schedule and see when most of us are off at the same time and ask the boss to switch some people around for the ones who work. Sound good?" Paul was a natural-born leader. I liked how secure he made me feel. If he had been a Civil War general, I would have followed him anywhere.

"Yeah. Sounds good."

The phone rang and Marcy went over to answer it. Paul came up to me and whispered, "I didn't tell Marcy originally because I was trying to give you space. Are things working out with you and RC?"

"Yeah. Real good. Although sex would be nice, but I'm learning to live without it. Twenty-four days and counting. It's not so bad."

Paul looked at me unblinking. He looked in one eye, and then to my other. Then he placed his palm against my forehead and asked, "Are you feeling all right?"

I shoved his hand away. "Shut up."

Julie hung a ticket in the pizza area and looked our way. "Sausage to go, Pinocchio."

Paul held his hands out to the side. "Jules, Pinocchio was a wooden boy who lied all the time. I never lie."

"So?" She shrugged, unaffected. "It was the first rhyme I could think to chime." And off she went with a tra-la-la in her step. If I could bottle that energy, I would put Monster and 5-Hour Energy drinks out of business.

Paul looked at me and shook his head. "I'm not sure I'll ever understand women. But Julie? She's got to be the strangest of them all."

"True. But she's cute. Like a little puppy."

Paul laughed and left me at the grill so he could work for five minutes.

If today dragged on any slower, I might end up having to clean the drain under the sink in the back. All the grease that got clogged from washing dishes had to be scraped out every so often. The smell could make a person puke. I mean seriously. Dis-gus-ting.

I WENT straight over to RC's. I'd gotten off late; leave it to some Boy Scout troop to decide to get pizza and ice cream right before closing. Argh. I was irritated. I was supposed to go home, but I missed RC. I wanted to ask him to go camping. I wanted to take him someplace good and replace the bad memory of Dawn's party.

RC opened the door with a smile. "Hey. I didn't expect to see you." He welcomed me in with a sweep of his hand.

I felt a warm rush inside me. I felt that same rush practically every time I was with him. In his presence, I felt good. I walked in and turned around. "I know," I said. "But I had something to ask you, and I didn't want to wait."

"I have a phone."

"Yeah, but it's not the same as seeing you face-to-face."

"Okay. Ask away. Do you want me to sit down, or is this standing-conversation material?" He smirked.

"Shut up. I'm trying to be serious. I want you to come camping with me. There's a really nice state park in Western Maryland that is only a couple of hours away."

His eyebrow shot up. "Camping? Intriguing. Seems very unlike you. There's no Wi-Fi in the woods."

I huffed. "I know. That's what I told them."

Whatever interest building in his expression died. "Them?"

"My friends... at work. They want to go camping, and I want to bring you."

RC's scowl wasn't hard to miss. I could have read it even if I were blind because he growled at the same time, pushing past me and leaving me alone in the living room. He was not thrilled, and I couldn't blame him. I took a deep breath and followed him into the kitchen. "RC, it's not going to be like before. I promise."

His back was to me as he leaned on the counter, yet his tension was visible in his stiff stance. Without turning around he said, "Nick, I know you mean well, but I don't want to go."

"Please," I asked as sincerely as I could. "These friends are different. I work with them. You know them, sort of. Paul's going. And Marcy."

RC turned a glare my way. "Oh, nice. You mean the girl who called me fat."

Idiot! I am a total fucking idiot. "Yes," I admitted. "But I swear she's different. She's gotten over me, and she's dating Paul. She's nicer now. She'll behave." *Or I will fucking kill her.*

"I don't know."

I reached up and lightly touched his shoulder with one hand and covered his right hand with my other. I whispered, "Please, Raffy, for me?"

RC turned his head and looked me in the eye. Even with the dull yellow light over the sink barely illuminating the room, my breath hitched in my throat. I could never seem to get used to how incredibly rich his green eyes were. Like emeralds against black velvet, they sparkled. Especially when he was this close to me, inches from my face, the vibrancy of his gaze made me shiver. I touched his jaw, ghosting my fingertips over the path his trimmed beard made along the bone. RC closed his eyes.

After a few seconds, he opened them again and sighed. His expression was no longer tense, but aching. I knew what he wanted even before he leaned forward and kissed me. He turned his body during the kiss and his hands were on either side of my face, holding me there. His kiss was slow and deliberate, sweeping inside my mouth and caressing my tongue with his. Not out of desperation, RC kissed me with a certain gentleness and completeness I would not have expected.

We had rarely kissed after that first night in the driveway. It was all a part of his "getting to know one another" plan. He specifically outlined the omission of any activities I'd normally engaged in with past relationships: kissing, stroking, blowing, sucking, frottage, rimming. Basically, everything fun. I knew I'd live. This was my first real relationship. We spent time together, but not every second. Tara had been overwhelming in the amount of demands she made on my time. RC wasn't like that. He worked and I worked. We had lunch together at least once a week, but we didn't go out every weekend. And the kissing parts of our dating became an elusive mystery to me as to when and where they might occur. But I'd gone with it. I knew RC would tell me eventually what had happened in his past that made him so hesitant. Plus, I liked not calling the shots.

He kissed me to the point of making my legs weak before he pulled back. "Okay," he said. "I'll go. But you gotta be careful, Nick. I swear if you asked me to jump off a bridge or slit my throat, I'd probably do it."

Silly man. I smiled. "I won't. I promise. I won't hurt you."

RC ran his palm over my cheek and feathered his fingers through my hair before touching my ear, trailing his fingers down to my neck. I watched him watch the path his fingers made. He was studying my face and hair and neck. I suddenly felt self-conscious. In the past, I could not have named a time when I'd felt embarrassed to be so examined. I knew I had no imperfections to speak of. My skin was flawless. My hair was perfect. And my ears were normal, correctly proportioned ears. I'd studied myself in the mirror many times and marveled over my physique. I knew how amazing I looked.

What worried me now was what RC would think. What if there was something he didn't like about me? I knew it wouldn't be as extreme as to say I was ugly, but what if he didn't like blue eyes? What if he preferred brown? What if he liked guys who were shorter than him, or taller? We were almost the same height. What if RC wanted to be with someone smart? I knew I didn't have a lot to offer. I could be his arm candy or possibly his sex slave, but I couldn't think of any other attributes I had worth mentioning.

In order to avoid the possibility of RC pointing out some unseen flaw, I leaned into him and hugged him. I rested my head on his shoulder and tucked my nose next to his neck. I could feel where the hairs were growing back.

RC's embrace was strong and firm. His hands moved over my back, and one slid upward and into my hair at the back of my head. RC sighed again.

"Oh, Nick," he breathed in a barely audible voice. He squeezed me tight, and I pressed as close to him as I possibly could.

"Can I spend the night?" I spoke into the collar of his shirt.

"That's not a good idea. I'm not ready."

"But we slept together in the hotel that time. Nothing happened then. Just because I want to spend the night tonight doesn't mean I'm gonna push for sex. I know you want to wait. We can. I just want to be with you." I know I sounded like I was whining. I had to. I was feeling extra pathetic tonight. It was because of that kiss. He'd annihilated me with it. That had to be the reason. RC totally destroyed my macho air by kissing me more tenderly than I ever thought possible. *Shit!* Corey never kissed like that. He was urgent. RC was... loving. Tears welled in my eyes. *Don't make me leave you tonight. Please Raffy.*

"Are you shaking?"

"No," I lied. I was shaking because being in his arms felt warm and wonderful, and he was going to tell me to go home any second. I didn't want to leave.

"You are." He rubbed my back. "Fine. You can stay. But if I wake up with your mouth on my dick, I'm going to kill you after I come."

I laughed and leaned away. "Yeah, way to keep that notion out of my head."

He smiled and kissed me again. "I was attempting humor. I know I'm always serious. I trust you."

"Really?"

"Nick, you might act like an ass, and you certainly are vain and arrogant, but you have the most compassionate heart I've ever seen. I know you'll wait until I'm ready, because I know you don't want to hurt me."

"I don't. Ever."

"I know. It's taking me a while to believe it, but that's only because of my past. I don't have a history of good calls and wise decisions. I fall for straight guys. I fall for assholes. And I fall for people who don't care about anything but a fuck."

I looked away and whispered, "You just described *me*."

He lifted my chin and shook his head. "Maybe. But that's not the man I've come to know. You've got a good heart. My only hesitation has to do with me and my shit, not you. I want it all out between us before we do anything. I'll tell you soon. I promise."

I THOUGHT I'd feel weird camping with my ex-girlfriend, but I didn't. Corey was right. Laney had changed. She didn't bring up the past at all, and she was extremely polite to RC. And Marcy? She was just as nice. I even caught her chatting with him while I stuffed the sleeping bags into our tent. I don't know what she said, because I was too far away, but RC smiled before she walked away.

After all the tents were up, and Laney and Julie had dinner going, and Paul was messing with the fire, RC and I took a walk. It was early evening when we walked around the back of the camping area through the ferns and found a path to follow. I picked up a rock and threw it, hitting a tree thirty feet away. I had good aim. I'd pitched in high school, but baseball didn't interest me enough to pursue it in college.

We picked our way through the underbrush with nothing but nature for company. It seemed so remote even though I knew other campsites were only a few minutes' walk in any direction. It felt peaceful here. Serene. After a short drive, I'd been transported someplace beautiful. We came to a clearing that had a gigantic swing set on a hill along the woods line. "I guess civilization can't be dodged for long," I mused aloud.

"I guess not."

I walked up to it and sat on the nearest seat. "I haven't done this for ages, not since my sister was little." I began to swing. Legs under—back. Legs out—forward. Legs under—back. Legs out—forward. "Come on," I urged RC. "Get on. It's like being a kid again."

He didn't say anything, but he did sit on the seat next to me and start swaying a bit.

"When I was little," I explained, "I could flip off these things and do a summersault in the air before I landed. I'd probably land on my head if I tried that now, though." RC swung silently. "Did you swing when you were a kid? Or did you like the monkey bars?"

I forced myself to go higher as I thrust my legs forward and back. Higher and higher. Faster and faster. It felt like flying. *I wonder how many people on drugs get hurt on these things if it feels like flying and they're too high to know it's not. What if they let go at the top of the arc? Shit, that would hurt.* I looked down at the ground, which looked impossibly far below.

In my minidiscussion with myself, I hadn't noticed RC stop swinging. He was still sitting on the rubber seat, yet not moving. He was silent and toeing the dirt at his feet. I slowed—casually of course—until I joined him. I rotated the seat, chains twisting, until I faced him. "You didn't like the swings when you were little, did you? Sorry. We don't have to sit here."

He studied the ground with somber intensity. Something was going on that I had no clue about. Mary-Louise would know what to say. She was good with deep conversations. Me? I felt dumb asking, so I sat quietly and twisted my seat back and forth until I was practically spinning in a full circle when I lifted my feet.

"I never liked being a kid, Nick," RC finally whispered.

I halted my rotation, knowing it was rude to twist and swing if he was ready to talk. "I'm sorry." I didn't know what else to say.

"I was too fat for the monkey bars; I couldn't hold on. And the other kids teased me that the swings would break, so I never even tried. I never even glanced at the seesaw."

He wasn't looking at me. He kept his eyes fixated on the ground. I couldn't blame him for not facing me. Painful memories seemed less exposing when you didn't look the other person in the eyes. I kept quiet, something I'd learned from Mary-Louise, hoping he would continue.

"Other kids teased me about everything," he went on. "I never had any friends. I didn't talk to anyone but my dad." He paused again. I knew talking about his father had to be hard. "Then, when I was eight, my uncle came to live with us. His wife left him and my dad felt sorry for him, I guess. He liked playing games. He walked me to school and told me not to listen to the other kids. He said I was special."

"That's nice," I commented. I was trying to remain positive when RC sounded so depressed. I was worried, though, where the conversation would go. Why did he sound so down?

"When I was twelve, he caught me looking at some magazines."

What kind, I wondered? "Playboy?"

RC shook his head. "Play*girl*. I was scared he'd tell my dad. He said he wouldn't. He said it would be our secret. A few months later, when my parents were at a dinner for my dad's work, he came into my bedroom. I thought it was to say good night."

A chill raced through me. RC was *not* implying what I thought he was. No!

"He went over to my secret stash and found other magazines. He stood there flipping through the pictures of naked men and then told me he could help me understand my sexuality. He said I had to embrace it. At first, I thought he meant he'd be supportive if I came out to my parents, but then he set the magazine down and unzipped his pants."

"Don't say it." I reached out, trying to touch his hand, but he yanked it away.

"He fucked me," he hissed as he glared at me.

I felt cold, but I couldn't look away from the deadness in his eyes.

"A twelve-year-old kid, and he forced me to do whatever he wanted. It went on for a year before my dad walked in on us. My dad beat the hell out of him, and he ended up in the hospital. My dad would have faced assault charges except my uncle, his brother, pleaded guilty to rape. He's in jail. I don't know how long."

"Oh my God." I was close to puking when he continued his horrific tale.

"I thought it ended when my uncle went to jail, but it didn't. My dad was distant for a long time, as if he blamed himself. He became very religious and took me to church. He wanted me to know God loved me, but I didn't understand how God could allow something like that to happen and love me at the same time. In high school, I came real close to coming out to my dad. I liked a boy named Roy, and I wanted my dad to know. But the day I decided to come out, I found his Bible open on the kitchen table and some literature about homosexuality sitting next to it. I was afraid he wouldn't accept me, so I didn't say anything.

"Years went by, and I stayed silent. My dad supported me when I dropped out of tech school. He encouraged me to take classes at college, but he didn't ridicule me when I dropped out. And then I had the chance to tell my dad again, when I met a guy named Ronald. I thought, if I had a boyfriend, surely it would be easier to say I'm gay. Ronald could be my support. I thought he really liked me."

"Didn't he?" I couldn't stop myself from asking. Part of me didn't want to know what came next.

He shook his head. "He wanted to use me, but I didn't know that. We met at work. No one had ever given me a second glance, so when Ronald did, I was too caught up in the thrill to question it. He asked me out. I said yes. We went to the movies once, and he took me to Subway. He said he liked chunky guys." He snorted a bizarrely strangled laugh. "I was so stupid."

I reached out again and touched his arm. This time, he didn't pull it away.

"He took me to a gay bar. We had a few drinks. We went back to my place and surprisingly my mom wasn't home. My dad worked nights that month, so we had the house to ourselves. Initially I was glad because I hadn't told either of them. As far as my parents knew, I was an overweight straight guy who couldn't find a date. Anyway, we sat on the couch and started messing around. He groped me, and I did the same to him. Before I knew it, we both had our pants off and he was flipping me over on the couch. I said I didn't want to fuck. I hadn't trusted Ronald enough to tell him about my uncle, so when he pinned me to the couch, I started panicking. I thought we'd mess around a bit and that fucking wasn't on the agenda for weeks since we'd sort of just met. I was dead wrong.

"He shoved my legs apart and pushed his fingers inside me. I begged him to stop. I said I'd suck him off or eat his ass, anything, only I didn't want penetrative sex. He didn't care. He laughed. He said I'd led him on the whole night, and I was getting what was coming to me. He said he was going to fuck me good and hard. I screamed as he forced his way inside me. When he left, I felt dead inside. Everything my uncle had done to me...." RC choked back a sob. "My uncle made me feel ashamed, but all that seemed so innocent compared to Ronald. He.... God... he used me like a whore. I showered and cried like a baby against the tile wall. That was five years ago."

His story made me sick. How could that guy do such a thing? I might be a slut, but I'd never had nonconsensual sex. Tara was the only one I'd ass-fucked without consent and it had happened by accident. I would have never consciously done that. I think that was why I felt so bad about it. I squeezed his hand. "I'm sorry," I whispered. It was the only thing I could think to say because nothing else seemed right or appropriate. I couldn't make any of that go away.

"That's why I've waited so long and why I wanted to wait with you."

"You didn't want me to repeat history." It was a terrible truth to voice.

"Exactly. I didn't know what would happen if we... I haven't been close to anyone. I haven't even thought about a relationship since Ronald." He lifted his gaze to meet mine. "If we... mess around... and I ask you to stop—"

"Then I stop!" I replied instantly. "I'm not gonna hurt you." I reached up and stroked his jaw. "I'm not in this for sex. I'm in this for you."

He smiled weakly. "I guess it's still hard for me to believe."

"Then would you believe I'm in it for me? I'm in this relationship selfishly soaking up your attention and affection because I can't get enough of how it makes me feel to be with you. I've never felt so cherished, and I don't think I could live another second if I lost you. So I'm in this purely out of an egocentric motivation of survival."

RC erupted in laughter. "I'm not sure that entirely made sense, but it does sound like something you'd say. I believe you, Nick. That's why I trust you."

I walked my swing closer, keeping my butt wedged in the rubber seat, and gazed into his amazing eyes. Eyes I loved even more because they still retained a shiny brilliance even after everything he'd been through. Our knees knocked. I felt his hand on my thigh. I wanted tell him I'd never hurt him like that, but in those seconds where we stared into each other's eyes, I knew he knew. Words were unnecessary. Instead I kissed him. Sweetly. Tenderly. Lovingly. He didn't need another guy to overpower him. RC needed warmth and compassion. I might be stupid most of the time, but if I'd learned anything, it's that sex didn't solve much. RC needed to call the shots, and now I knew exactly why.

When our lips parted, he touched my face and whispered, "I love you, Nick." I opened my mouth, but he stopped me from responding with a finger. I wanted to respond. I'd never had anyone say that to me. Not even Tara. Or Corey. I pleaded with my eyes, and he shook his head. "Don't," he said. "If you say those words now, I won't know if they're out of pity. Don't say anything. Please?"

He took his finger away. "Okay," I said. I kissed him again. I was better with my lips than words anyway.

We must have made out for over an hour. I wasn't watching the time. All I know is that when we finally broke apart to catch our breath, it was dark. I could only see by the moonlight. The park was creepily silent, except for cricket calls.

Chapter 24: *Finally*

JULIE SAVED us some food, so we ate by the fire. Although, after hearing his story, I didn't feel like eating. Marcy and Paul said good night about fifteen minutes before we finished our dinner, and Julie and Laney said they were going to the bathhouse. After we cleaned up our dishes and made sure the fire was safe to leave unattended, we crawled into our tent and got situated. I was questioning my choice of leaving my inflatable mattress at home, but what the heck, it wasn't like sleeping on the ground was going to kill me. I'd done it plenty of times at parties and stuff. Some random floor or the ground outside—eh, I could handle it. Although, I figured I'd wake up with an aching back.

RC reached for the flashlight I'd hung from the top of the tent and stopped. He cocked his head as if he heard something. Then I heard it too. Marcy and Paul were going at it, and the sound traveled. RC leaned on his elbow and looked at me. "Is that going to bother you?"

"What? Listening to them fuck? I don't care. Do you?" Because there was a strain in his expression. What was he worried about? He knew I didn't like Marcy that way, and I wasn't into Paul. So why was he staring down at me with a look that… was almost… lecherous? RC wouldn't be contemplating doing what I thought he was contemplating. That would be too good to be true, not to mention way too soon considering our conversation earlier. Besides being very cliché: go on a camping trip, get laid, and then get thrown out by the park ranger in the morning. Or worse, get hacked to bits by a psychopath. Ha, ha. No, that wouldn't really happen.

But right when I thought I was just "hopeful thinking," RC leaned down and kissed me. Thoroughly. His lips were soft, like the kiss we'd shared on the swing and in his kitchen. He swept his tongue into my mouth and kissed me so tenderly I thought I'd melt for how liquid my bones felt. He was such a good kisser!

Not that he was the best kisser in the world. I think Corey was really amazing. Only when RC kissed me I felt like I was floating. That had never happened before.

Then he pulled back and whispered, "Remove your shirt."

"Are you sure? Isn't this a little sudden considering—"

"Remove your shirt," he insisted, turning off the flashlight.

At first, the darkness was complete. Then, after a few seconds, I could make out RC's shape from the faint glow the dying fire cast over our tent, ours being the closest to the fire. I quivered with anticipation as I did as he asked. I wanted him so badly. I yanked so hard I nearly clocked him in the face with my elbow as my shirt came over my head. "Sorry," I whispered guiltily.

He put his finger to his lips and shushed me.

RC eased me back down onto my sleeping pad and rubbed my chest. He moved his hand over my nipple and he circled it with his thumb before descending and lapping at me with his tongue. I gasped and grabbed the back of his head with my hand. His hair was soft and long, and I massaged the base of his skull as he licked and kissed my chest. I can't remember ever being this turned on. My previous girlfriends had kissed me like this—Corey had kissed me like this—but in all that time, years and years of dating girls (and Corey), nothing had ever made me tremble with anticipation to the degree that RC did with a few seconds of attention from his mouth, lips, and tongue.

He made me breathless and I wasn't even undressed yet. His warm hand slid down my side as he kissed his way south. When he got to my jeans, he stopped. RC lifted his gaze and looked at me as he palmed my erection through the fabric. His eyes blazed with lust, as much as I could tell in the faint light, and told me everything I needed to know. Without a word, I lifted my butt, allowing him room to slip off my pants.

RC gave me another sign to keep quiet, and then he took me into his mouth.

"Raffy…," I rasped, throwing my head back and tilting my hips.

I bit my fist to keep me from screaming, but I know I was louder than he would have liked. I couldn't help it. The guy I'd been fantasizing about for weeks was finally going down on me. *Holy shit!* The hot warm flesh of his mouth felt incredible. He didn't have the experience I had, yet it didn't seem to matter. RC wasn't a virgin, but he also hadn't had Corey either. Corey had taught me all kinds of things about pleasing a man, even though most of it I could figure out myself. But RC? His experience was shitty to say the least, so I was surprised how adept he was at this.

He rubbed my thigh and moved his hand over my hip and pelvic area. He caressed me as his head bobbed and his mouth sucked. RC trailed his fingers all over me, and suddenly the words "making love" had meaning. RC was making love to me, and this wasn't just another excursion into the woods to fuck in a tent like Paul and Marcy. It wasn't carnal release from pent-up sexual tension. As he touched me, the lust in my groin transformed into a burning need to give myself over to him in whatever way he wanted. It was no longer an act about *me* and *my* need to come. I wanted this to be about *us*. I felt through RC's touch the deepest connection I've ever felt to another person. In that moment, I knew I was his.

And I wanted him inside me.

"Raffy," I whispered my warning as I drew near release. I tightened my grip on his hair and lifted my hips, reveling in the feel of his friction. "Raffy," I whispered desperately. "I'm gonna… I'm gonna…." And I came. My abdomen tightened as I pulsed within his mouth. RC didn't let up until he knew I was done.

He moved off me, yet continued touching my legs, stomach, and chest. My eyes remained closed, but I felt him settle next to me, his large warm hand resting over my heart. I looked over and found him watching me.

"You okay?" he whispered.

I nodded. Why the heck would I not be? I was spent. I couldn't move. It took all the energy I had to simply breathe. What the hell would happen when we had *sex* sex? Good Lord, he'd probably kill me. I closed my eyes again. *Breathe, just breathe,* I told myself.

He must have known I was wiped from his attention because he didn't question my stillness. Nor did he ask for reciprocation. He scooted closer, and I felt his breath on my neck. He kissed my jaw below my ear and slid his hand up to cup the side of my neck. I felt his thumb caressing my jaw.

"You are so beautiful," he said softly.

I had to look at him. It didn't matter if my muscles wouldn't budge. I wanted to see his face. I rolled my head sideways and opened my eyes. The adoration I saw would have taken my breath away if I hadn't already been bereft of air. I couldn't say anything. I knew it was better if I remained quiet. Something in my stupid little head got it, and I just *knew* that silence beat stupid remarks or ill-constructed attempts to say something nice. Instead of talking, I mustered all my strength and pushed him onto his back. I nestled my face against his neck and collapsed against his side.

Lucky for me, he still had enough loose blanket next to him to fling over my naked body so I didn't freeze overnight.

THE NEXT morning produced a pleasant change in my attitude. Maybe it was the woods, maybe it was camping with my friends, or maybe it was the realization that RC was my boyfriend and I really enjoyed the way he touched me, kissed me, and looked at me. I felt giddy.

"Would you stop smiling?" RC growled under his breath.

I looked up from the other side of the campfire. "I can't."

"Well, I *was* going to suggest remaining discreet, but I can see that won't work. Good thing I'm not robbing a bank; you'd give it away." He might have sounded irritated to others if they were nearby, but I could tell he wasn't. Not really. I think he wanted to be discreet because he's the kind of person who doesn't like others in his business. But something in his eyes told me he was proud to make me that fucking transparent.

"Good morning," chirped Marcy, the moaner from last night.

"Morning," I said, still keeping my eyes on the green-eyed sex machine standing opposite me. He had no idea what switch he flicked on last night, but holy fucking hell was I going to have a tough time containing my one-eyed serpent now. *RC, you are in for one hell of a—*

"Oh, my God. Nick!"

Well shit. Marcy can't let me daydream for five minutes? She has to interrupt my internal dialogue for.... "What?" I asked.

"You. Look at you," she said.

"Look at what?" I had no clue, and she was emphatically gesturing at me. I looked myself over, but noted nothing extraordinary. "Am I wearing the wrong shirt?"

"Yes, but that's not my point."

I looked down again and saw I was wearing RC's shirt. That did explain why it was draftier. "Oh. RC, I'm sorry. I didn't realize."

Paul chuckled next to me. "That's not what she meant," he explained.

Laney gasped. I followed her eyes, which were pointed at my crotch. I glanced down and there it was as plain as the early morning sunrise. My penis was sticking out from under the hem of my—RC's—shirt.

I gasped this time and turned around, attempting to put it back in. That was when I discovered my pants weren't actually closed. My zipper was all the way down and my belt was unbuckled. *Shit, how did I...?* The questioned lingered a moment, and then I remembered I couldn't find my underwear when I pulled my pants on because everything in the tent was a hazy dream. RC had not only blown me the night before, but he'd woken me up with a morning hitchhike to heaven, further advancing my apoplectic state. My plan was to stumble to the car hoping I'd left my bag in there, but I stopped at the fire to…. *Fuck, I don't remember.*

I felt hands on my shoulders and I looked up into Paul's eyes. "Dude, look at me." When I did my best, he continued. "Marcy has a way with words, but it wasn't just the angle on your dangle that had her flustered. It was the salacious hunger in your stare. Nick, I saw it too. It could be that I've had way too much sex lately, or that I've watched too much *Teen Wolf* with Marcy, but I swear if you were a wolf or a mountain lion, you would have leapt over the fire and eaten RC. What's up with you, man? I can practically see the heat radiating off you."

I swallowed, and that was when I noticed how hard I was breathing. "Oops," I said.

"Pull yourself together," Paul stressed, looking deeply into my eyes. His proximity was kind of creepy. "I'm glad you like him so much, but you can't walk around in public with that look on your face or your Happy Gilmore hanging out. You got it?"

I nodded. I felt spaced, as if on drugs, but I got it.

"Come on." Paul prompted me to follow him over to RC's truck. "Have a seat. I think you need a moment to cool down. The two of you obviously got all hot and heavy, and although I'm happy for you, I'd rather not see you ripping your clothes off or forgetting to put them back on. Learn some tact."

"Tact. Got it." He left me, and I flopped my head back on the seat. I took several deep breaths and opened my eyes to find RC standing next to me.

"You okay?"

"Apparently not. Paul thinks I'm one Hannibal Lecter away from eating you alive."

"Yeah, well, I'm okay with that." He reached out and squeezed my hand.

"How are you? I mean, all that in the tent was very unexpected considering…."

"I know. It sounds more painful to you because you're hearing it for the first time. And although I never want to live through it again, it's been a long time for me. I've had years to sift through my emotions and talk to therapists. I'm okay. I think that after I told you, and you looked so hurt—like you really felt my pain—it only made me want you more. I've wanted to suck your dick for months."

My belly quivered. "Oh, man, don't say that again." I swallowed hard. "If you do, I'm liable to allow Happy Gilmore all the public attention he wants."

"Happy Gilmore?" RC asked, confused.

"That's what Paul called it."

"Please don't. 'Dick' sounds just fine. Dick, penis, cock, even prick, but not Happy Gilmore. I'll think of Adam Sandler every time I go down on you. Do you want that?"

"Oh, hell no."

He let go of my hand and touched my thigh instead, rubbing it and trailing his attention higher and higher until he nudged my ball sac.

I turned in the truck seat and straddled him in the doorway, my knees on either side of his hips. I kissed him while his wide hands gripped me. I tugged him closer with my legs as I wrapped them around his body. I think we were seconds from crawling fully into the cab when I heard Paul complain.

"Ah, excuse me? I thought I asked for tact."

I peered guiltily past RC's shoulder. "I can't help it."

He glared. He huffed. Then he smirked and shook his head. "I guess I can't blame you. You've had the hots for him for months. It's about time you hooked up. I made pancakes if you want some. And Marcy cut up fruit. Julie brought muffins. We don't have to check out until twelve, but we should break everything down after breakfast to make it easier. Come eat… or not. But if you're going to have sex, please do it in the tent."

Paul walked back over to the fire.

"You want to eat? Or have sex?" I asked, knowing what I wanted.

"Food sounds good. I want a bed the next time I have you."

I quivered again. I don't know what made me so easy to stir up. Whatever it was, RC had it in spades. He turned me into putty with a look and a touch. "Okay," I whimpered.

RC smirked. "Are you okay?"

"Yeah." I whimpered again.

"You don't look very good. And you're breathing very rapidly. You're not having a heart attack, are you?"

I shook my head. I knew what it was. *Desire.* I was quaking with desire. I wanted him. I needed him. "I want you to fuck me," I uttered, pawing at his chest with my hand. "I want you inside me so bad."

"Nick, are you sure? You've never—"

"I want you. Please," I begged, twisting my hand in his shirt. "Right now. Can we find a hotel? I need to feel you inside me."

I could see him working through it. His eyes studied me as if weighing my plea against his sense of restraint. "All right."

I released his shirt and pulled my legs in and turned in my seat. *I guess I won.* RC hurried around the side of the truck and hopped in. "We'll be back soon," I called out the window to Paul as we drove off.

FOUR VERY long miles down the road on Highway 68, we found a Comfort Inn. RC paid for a room, and I followed him in after he moved the truck in front of the last room of the building. *I guess he was attempting to be discreet.* Once in the room—door closed, curtains drawn—I ripped my shirt off and reached for his.

"Stop. We don't need to rush. We have a couple hours before Paul will wonder what happened."

I could hardly breathe for need of him. "Raffy," I rasped as I reached again for his shirt.

"Slow down, Nick. Breathe. It will happen. There's no need to rush."

He was being logical, and I was throwing my engine on full throttle. Logic was stupid. I fucking needed to be fucked. Fuck logic. I yanked him into a kiss and let him know with my tongue that slow wasn't an option. I was writhing against him. I know he felt my erection. If I rubbed against the carpet, people in China would have been able to feel it. I grabbed his ass and rocked my hips.

I didn't even know we had been walking backward until he shoved me onto the bed. "You don't take no for an answer, do you?"

I shook my head, breathing hard, gasping for breath, and watching him. RC wasn't angry. And he wasn't afraid. He stood over me exuding power and dominance, and I shivered. He reached for the hem of his shirt and slowly pulled it over his head. Then he took his ponytail holder out and fingered thorough his hair. It was long and wild. Next, he undid his belt and pushed his pants down his hairy legs. There he was before me, a great bear of a man, with a penis larger than any I'd ever seen. Not that I'd seen many. I'd seen one. Corey was not so endowed. RC strutted forward and the great bobbing mass sticking out from him like a javelin made me reconsider my previous fervor. That thing was going to skewer me!

RC chuckled.

I looked up. "What's so funny?"

"You. You look as though I'm about to saw you in half."

I pointed at his full salute. "You might. That thing's huge!"

He chuckled. "No, it's not." He crawled onto the bed and slid up next to me, rubbing my stomach and smiling into my eyes. "I think that's just your subconscious rethinking your virginity."

"I'm not a virgin," I refuted hastily. Yet after he shot me a look, I backpedaled. "Well, I guess I am. I'm an ass virgin."

"I figured. Corey looked like a bottom to me. And you *are* very dominant in every other aspect of life. Are you sure you want to do this? It's not like anal sex is our only option. We can do other things. We could take a shower and jack each other off. Suck each other off. I'm not in a hurry."

"You don't want to?"

"Oh, I want to. But I don't want you to think we *have* to. We can do that another time."

Yes, I was scared, probably my first time ever, but I'm not the guy *Diary of a Wimpy Kid* was written about. I was only freaking because I thought he was gigantic. Now, after a few minutes of taking in his hairy body and tattooed skin, my mind was shaking off fear and switching back to sex mode. No—I wanted him.

I pushed him back and kissed that hairy chest, licking his nipples and rubbing my hand all over his inked skin.

RC chuckled. "I take it that's a no."

I bit his nipple, and he sucked in a breath. "I want you inside me, Raffy. Today. Now. I'm not waiting until we get home. You started something last night when you blew me. You weren't afraid. After everything you've been through, you weren't afraid of sex. So I'm not giving into fear either. I want this. I want *you*." I looked into his eyes. So beautiful. So green and glowing like the forest we'd walked through yesterday.

He rolled me onto my back. "Okay. But I need to get you set first, loosen you up." He crawled off of me and grabbed his pants. From the pocket he produced a travel bottle of lube and a condom.

"Where did you get those?" I wondered.

"The check-in desk had a table with soaps and lotions, toothpaste, and condoms. I guess they get a lot of people asking for them. I don't know. I snagged them and the lady didn't bat an eye."

RC lubed his fingers and went to work. I had done this to Corey plenty of times, but Corey had never done it to me. Let me tell you, it's not a pleasant experience. "Stop clenching," RC urged.

"It's not very fun. I feel like this is a body cavity search at the airport."

"Really?" RC gave me a look, one that said he took my complaint as a dare. "How about now?" he asked devilishly.

I was about to ask what he was referring to when his finger nudged my prostate. At that point, I wasn't talking.

"That's it. Relax." He continued probing, touching me, twisting his fingers inside. By the time he rolled me onto my stomach I was practically a sack of mashed potatoes. He kneaded my ass and positioned his body, but it wasn't until I felt him slop more lube on my asshole that I spoke up.

"Wait."

"What's wrong? Second thoughts?"

I turned over, careful not to kick him in the nads as I brought my foot around. I held my knees and pulled my legs back. "I'm fine. I want to look at you."

RC smiled softly, emotion pouring from his eyes. He leaned forward and kissed me, caressing my chest and mashing his groin against mine.

I kissed him back, loving the way we felt, naked together. Maybe if we lived together, I'd institute a no clothes rule on Thursday nights, or something?

A minute later, the world slipped into slow motion as I felt him sink into me. My ass tightened around him, almost refusing him entry. I felt uncomfortably full and the pain as he stretched me made me pause to consider my earlier eagerness. But then his eyes caught mine. I fell into those large green pools and everything around us blurred like the edges of a charcoal sketch rubbed by the artist. His eyes kept me focused, and I relaxed, welcoming him in.

He kissed me everywhere he could reach. My neck, my chest, my chin, my lips—nothing was left wanting of his touch or attention. He thrust into me, undulating rhythmically, yet all the while declaring through kisses that I was his most cherished possession. Just as in the tent, I knew exactly what I was: his. I slipped my hand into his hair and moaned as he rocked.

"Oh, God. Raffy…. Yes…. More…. Oh fuck…."

RC on the other hand, said nothing. He fucked me steadily yet silently as he moved his hands all over me, touching and rubbing, loving me so tenderly, which was in utter contrast to what the other parts of him were doing. His dick felt like a vibrating chainsaw. Or maybe a jackhammer or a wrecking ball? I could hardly feel my lower extremities. He pounded me. Yet for all the pain I sort of felt, there was also an overabundance of "holy shit" and "hummina, hummina, hummina" going on down there. Every muscle of my body was quaking. He was ripping me apart, yet I was a willing victim of his lambastic assault. I pulled one leg wider and howled as he rammed yet another part of me inside which had sat undiscovered moments before.

"Ahhh!" I screamed in ecstasy. And then I came, spewing wave after wave of fluid from my body. White flashes exploded behind my closed eyes as shards of me flew asunder, annihilated by an act that had never produced such results in all the years I thought I knew what fucking meant. This was different. This was me coming undone because of him.

RC collapsed over me, heaving and sweating. His kissed my arm. "You… okay?" he asked between struggling breaths. "I can't explain… what came over me." He took a deep, calming breath and exhaled. "I shouldn't have fucked you that hard. I lost myself in how good it felt." He touched my hair. "I didn't mean to lose control."

"Yeah. No worries," I answered, also struggling to gain composure. "I'm good." I was so wasted, I couldn't even lift my arm to touch him.

We lay there panting for several minutes. I couldn't open my eyes to check the time. Eons later, I looked at him. He was still breathing. Good. A heart attack during our first time would have sucked. "Hey, Raffy. We probably have to leave soon." My breathing was far from normal, but I could at least talk. Logically, I knew we had to go before we fell asleep and woke up at dinnertime. I didn't want to piss off Paul. He was my bud.

RC's draping arm slid from my stomach to my chest. He gently caressed me with his fingers, an action that, for some reason, stirred more emotions in me. I knew, just knew, I had to say it. Now was right. "I love you," I whispered. He opened his eyes. "And I'm not saying it as a form of pity, nor am I delusional. I think I'm high on endorphins, but I know what I feel. I love you. I've known it for a while now."

RC lifted himself enough to lean on one arm and kiss me. "I believe you. I can see it in the way you look at me."

I grinned, and he kissed me some more.

WE RETURNED to camp with forty minutes to spare. Plenty of time to break down our tent and scarf down some cold pancakes. I didn't care about anything. The whole forest could have been on fire, and I don't think I would have noticed. I was in love.

AS SOON as we got to RC's and closed the door, I was on him like white on rice. Legs, arms, mouth, groin, all the parts I had pressed up against him desperately trying to crawl inside his body. But RC grabbed my arms and yanked me off.

"Chill. Nick. We just got home. Let's get a shower and think about sex afterwards. I still have your dried cum on my stomach from earlier. Okay? Besides, aren't you still sore? I gave it to you pretty good."

I denied it. "Fuck sore. I want you in me again." I rubbed my hands up and down his chest. "I want your huge cock filling me." I was breathing hard. I've never felt so desperate. "Don't tell me you don't want it too. I can feel that you do." I palmed his erection.

"Yeah. I do. I guess I worry maybe we're going too fast."

"No," I said, stepping back and whipping off my shirt. "Not too fast. Just hard and fast enough. I want you. I need you. I waited so long for this, and now that you started it, I'm not letting it end. Not after what you did to me in the hotel room. It felt like a hand grenade went off in my balls. I've never come so hard in my life. If that's what you do to me? Then bring it on!"

I dropped my jeans on his floor, stepped out of them, and jumped again into his embrace. I kissed him hard and tangled my fists in his luxurious hair. RC did not disappoint me this time. He picked me up and walked us into the bathroom. I had to let go in order for him to disrobe, but in a few minutes, we were in the shower lathering each other up. I'd never taken a shower with another person. And believe me, the wait was worth it.

After kissing under the spray of water for a few minutes, my need to have sex lessened. I think it was because I saw this look in his eyes, deep and caring, which made me think about the fact that he hadn't had a relationship like this either. We were discovering everything together. I was no longer desperate, but inquisitive. I wanted to map his body with my hands like a blind man reads Braille. I needed to know every inch of him. I slid my soapy hands over his pecs and rubbed his hard nipples. RC groaned.

"You like?"

He closed his eyes and nodded. When I dipped my head and started licking and sucking on his nipple, he moaned appreciatively. "Oh, Nick. Mmm." He rubbed the back of my head as I continued sucking. I nipped him gently between my teeth and swirled my tongue around. "You know... how... you said your neck was your spot?"

"Mm-hmm."

"Oh God, Nick. You found mine."

I switched my attention to his other nipple and glided my hand down to lather his balls simultaneously. He groaned louder, and I loved it. I would have sucked on his nipples a lot longer if it hadn't been for the head of his dick poking into mine. The shivery sensation that touch produced reminded me that there were other things I wanted to do, so I gave his nipple one last, hard tug and leaned back.

His penis was bobbing in front of him, as mine was standing straight out in front of me. I got this silly notion to thwack it, so I did. I rotated my hips left and then jerked them back, causing my swollen cock to swing against him. I giggled.

"What are you doing?" RC asked, giving me a bemused look.

"Having a sword fight. Come on, give me your best shot."

"Um, no. Let's get finished here and head to the bedroom. You got me all stirred up inside."

"No, come on, just once. Swing at me." I flicked my hips and my penis bounced into his.

He chuckled and conceded, "Fine, you goofball." He swung his hips, but too slowly to produce the desired effect, and missed me entirely.

"Not like that. Like this," I instructed, overly exaggerating my move and swinging my bobbing cock in his direction. I hit the mark and slid my shaft across his entire length. The slippery feel was stimulating and tickled and made my balls shift. *Oh, fuck yeah.*

RC moaned and closed his eyes again.

"Stop. You're gonna come if you concentrate too heavily on the ecstasy of it. Don't. Just think of hitting me with your penis."

He chuckled again and flipped his stick my way. I countered with a block and knocked his bouncing buddy back the other way. I tilted my hips and did it again. Soon we both were into it, knocking each other around, sliding skin-on-skin, like snakes in a mud pit, only with bubbles. And RC was laughing. Totally not what I expected in a first showering-together experience, but it was awesome.

Our dance of the heated hip hustle lasted a few minutes before the laughter died and panting ensued. My cock was gliding over his, his over mine, and before we knew it, we were pressing into one another, grinding and shooting. I held to RC and he clung to me as our parts pulsed together.

"Wow," he breathed heavily. "I never thought I'd do that."

"Come in the shower without using your hand or mine?"

"Yeah. Especially after that swatting thing you started."

"Oooh, but skin and suds feels so good."

He grinned. "Yeah, it does."

We laughed and lathered each other up and down and up again, but it was more about touching and feeling and exploring than coming again. We only got out because the water went cold.

"Shit, I still have soap in my hair!" I yelped.

"Sucks to be you." RC laughed as he bolted from the tub and grabbed a towel.

I had to rinse in cold water, which sucked. Plus, I didn't like the effect cold water had on my body. It was hard on my ego to look down at that shriveled little thing. Especially when I thought RC was bigger than me. Not much, but some. My initial shock was how large it seemed knowing where it was going to end up. Now, though, I wasn't too bothered.

I entered his bedroom to find him sprawled on the bed. I dropped my towel and crawled onto the bed like a hunting cat, but rethought my objective and headed to the foot of the bed instead of the head.

"Nick?" RC questioned.

"You don't get to have all the explorative fun. You trust me, right?"

"Yes."

"Then close your eyes and chill. I got this covered." I winked and then took his Italian sausage into my mouth. It stretched my lips, but I worked it like a pro. I'd learned quickly what Corey liked, which was pretty much the same things I liked. RC couldn't be that hard to please. The key was in a good combination of sucking action, rhythmic bobbing of the head, and assisted stroking of my fist when very little of that bad boy was going to actually make it into my mouth. He was too long and wide.

I fondled his balls and rubbed the skin underneath, but as my finger touched his anus, RC jerked hard. "No. Please, Nick."

I stopped sucking and looked at him. He was terrified. I crawled up next to him and kissed his jaw tenderly. "I'm sorry. I didn't mean to scare you or overdo anything."

"It's okay. I'm just not... I can't...."

I kissed him deeply, and he relaxed under my touch. He rolled me over onto my back and jacked me slowly. Several minutes later, he had me begging to get fucked. I don't know if that makes me a huge bottom or what, but having his dick inside me was more empowering than I imagined. The look in his eyes as he came was all because of me. The moaning and panting that came from his throat was all because of me. I did that. And when he collapsed over me, I felt more connected to him than to any other human being on the planet. He was mine. And I was in love with him.

He kissed my neck after ditching the condom and pulled the blankets over us. "I guess you're going to spend the night."

"Duh. You're going to have to use a crowbar to get me out of this bed."

He grinned. It wasn't an amused look like usual, but a comfortable look. A look that said he was glad I stayed. He whispered, "I love you," and that was when my heart exploded. RC loved me. He loved me. No one had ever used those words before, and fuck me, I started crying. I buried my face in his neck hoping the tears would stop before he noticed. It didn't work.

"Nick?"

I sniffled. "Yeah. You're the only one who's ever said that to me and suddenly I got all emotional about it. I can't help it." I sniffed again. "I think it's being in your bed and in your apartment. We're really a couple."

"Yeah, we are. I feel it too."

I rolled back and wiped my eyes. "Really?"

"Yeah. I've never told anyone I loved them."

"Me neither. You're the first."

RC caressed my cheek. "I liked you from the first moment I saw you. I only hesitated because I couldn't believe a guy like you would even consider a guy like me. You're perfect and I'm...."

"Perfect for me." I finished his thought before he had the chance to fill in the blank. "You are perfect for me," I reiterated. "And I love you."

RC pulled me close after he turned out the light. And I fell asleep listening to the steady beat of his heart.

Chapter 25: *Mothers*

SLEEP DIDN'T last. My phone rang loudly in the middle of the night and jolted us both awake.

"What?" I asked frantically, searching in the dark on the covers.

RC groaned and rolled over. "Nick, turn that thing off."

I got out of bed and found my pants on the floor by stumbling over them when my feet got tangled in the legs. "I Kissed A Boy" by Slipstream was playing. "It's Corey's." I fumbled in the dark to retrieve if from my pocket.

He grunted. "Corey has his own ringtone?"

Hmm. RC already mentioned being jealous, maybe I needed to change the song? "Hello?" I answered.

"Nicky? Help me," he implored.

The skin on the back of my neck ran cold. "Corey? Where are you? What's going on?"

"Nick?" RC asked very seriously. I saw his dark shape sit up in bed and then he turned on the light.

"I don't know," Corey sobbed. "I woke up here. Everything hurts. Help me."

"Where's here? Corey, where are you?" I looked at RC. Corey was hurt, and I needed to fix it. I had to help him. "Tell me where you are."

RC read me like a book. He got out of bed and tossed me the shirt he found on the floor before pulling on his pants.

Corey's voice quivered. "I don't know. A parking lot." He was sobbing so hard, I found it difficult to understand him. "I hurt, Nicky. I'm scared."

"I know. It'll be okay. RC and I are coming to help you, but you have to tell me where you are. Can you see anything?" I knew the best thing to do for him was to talk smoothly and evenly and not give away the fact I was about to fall apart with worry. I had never heard him like this. Corey was confident and fun and able to take care of himself in the most dire conditions. He had proved that through years of living on his own. But this wasn't the same Corey who spoke now. His voice was tiny like a mouse and hard to understand between sobbing cries.

"There's a sign for PetSmart."

"Good. Anything else?" *Calm, I need to be calm.* I struggled to yank on my pants and RC set my shoes on the floor in front of me.

"Um, Advance Auto Parts." His answer was more controlled. Perhaps asking questions was helping him to focus.

"PetSmart and Advance Auto Parts. Good. Stay on the phone with me, okay?" I looked over at RC. "There's a shopping center at the corner of 97 South with those stores. Maybe he's there?"

RC said, "I hope so. But it's less than ten minutes away. If he's not, we can easily search every shopping center until we find him." It felt good knowing RC was in this.

I remained on the phone as we flew out the door and over to where RC had parked his truck. He held my hand as I talked to Corey; RC was my rock just as I was Corey's.

It was the longest nine minutes of my life. I wanted to tell RC to drive through the red light as we sat there, but as I opened my mouth, it turned green. Corey was sniffling on the other end, but I think talking to me was helping ground him.

"You have incredible luck," RC commented, pulling his truck up next to Corey, who was lying in the middle of the asphalt curled into a ball twenty feet from the entrance of PetSmart. Thank God for the bright lights and huge signs.

I shoved my phone into my pocket as I jumped out and ran to him. "Corey?" I said, gently touching his face. I knew he was alive because I had been listening to him breathe the entire way. He still held the phone to his ear. "Corey, I'm here," I said. He rolled to the side, and I could finally see his face in the light of the streetlamp. I gasped, "Oh my God!" Part of his face was purple, his nose was bloody and crooked, and his lips were split in a few places. "What the hell happened?"

"Nicky?"

"Corey, we need to get you to a hospital." I looked him over, wondering if I should move him or call for an ambulance. "Can you tell me what happened?"

"I don't remember," he sobbed.

I smoothed the hair away from his eyes. "I need to get you into the car. Can I pick you up? Are you hurt anywhere else?"

"My ribs."

I lifted the hem of his shirt. "I see a nasty bruise. You might have broken ribs."

"You should probably call an ambulance," RC said.

I looked up at RC standing across from me and disagreed. "The hospital is only ten minutes away. We can get him there faster." To Corey I explained, "Let's go slowly, okay?"

Corey tried to move and gain his footing, but he was too weak. I slipped my arms under his knees and around his back and picked him up. It was a strain, but he was light enough. RC pushed the seat back as far as it went and helped me get Corey in his truck. It was a tight fit, but we managed.

Corey was on my lap so I couldn't get to my phone. Something told me to call my mom. I needed her support and know-how. "Can I use your phone to call my mom?" I asked. RC handed it over and I dialed. It was two thirty in the morning.

"Hello," she answered groggily.

"Mom, I'm okay, but we're heading to the hospital, and I need you."

Instantly awake and on the urge of panic, she asked, "What happened? Frank, wake up. We're going to the hospital."

"I know Dad works at five. It's okay if he stays home."

"No, Nicky, tell me what happened." I heard rustling on her end. I could tell she was up and getting dressed.

I explained, holding him close to me. "It's Corey. It looks like he got beat up. I don't know. RC and I are taking him to the hospital. I know it's a lot to ask, but he has no one. Can you please help us? I just know they're going to ask all sorts of things I don't know how to answer. Please?"

"Of course. I'm already dressed. I'll grab my purse and meet you there. Make sure you go into the emergency room entrance."

"I will, Mom. Thanks."

Once we entered the emergency room, the triage nurse had too many questions to wrap my brain around. What happened? Did he have insurance? Was it assault? Who could we call? It all came at me like an avalanche and poor Corey looked frightened out of his mind. I was on the verge of stuttering, and possible hyperventilation, when my mom touched my shoulder and said to the nurse, "I'm here to help. Let me fill out the forms for Corey Parrish, and I'll be able to answer whatever you need." The nurse sat there stunned momentarily, but handed her the clipboard and instructed us to have a seat. Apparently a broken nose wasn't a huge priority.

I wheeled Corey over to the waiting area—RC had grabbed a wheelchair for him upon entering—and peered at the forms my mom was filling out. Name, address, phone number, insurance carrier, employer, and the like. I didn't think she put the correct answers for some of them, but I wasn't going to question her.

I looked at Corey. Even though we were the same age, he appeared so much younger as he cried and squeezed my hand like a vise. He had been hurt so much in his young life, and I'd taken for granted how easy mine had always been. My mom told me a couple of times I'd lived *The Life of Riley* and I didn't know what that meant until I googled it. It was some '50s TV show and the saying was associated with a contented or "kept" life of ease or certain comfort. I had lived like that.

My parents loved me. I still lived at home and worked a terrific job. I had friends. I had a fucking fantastic boyfriend. My mom didn't even freak about me being gay; she was cool with it. What did Corey have? His parents had kicked him out. He had a job, but I didn't know how great it was. He'd said he had a boyfriend, but where was Tyler now? Corey was, most likely, alone.

Correction: he had me. I was going to see to it he was never alone. I leaned over and kissed his temple. "It'll be okay, Corey. I'm not leaving you. You got that? I'm here."

My mom walked over and stooped down in front of him. "Corey. I know this is hard, but I need to ask you some questions. Will you talk to me?" Her voice was soft like a kitten curled up in the sunshine. It made me proud she would take such good care of my friends.

Corey nodded.

"Okay. First, have you tried calling your parents?" I didn't like that she asked, but I knew she had his best interests in mind. She added, "They may want to know where you are."

"No," he said very quietly. "They don't. When Tyler didn't answer, I called them. When I asked for help because I didn't know where I was, my mom told me never to call her again or she'd change her number. Then I dialed Nicky."

I touched the back of his head. "Oh, Corey. I'm sorry."

My mother lamented, "Okay. No parents. I already put myself down as your emergency contact. I put our address and Nick's dad as the party responsible for payment. Unless you have health insurance at work."

"No. I lost my job two weeks ago. They were cutting back, and I was the last hired."

My mom patted his knee and kissed his forehead. "We'll take care of you, Corey. I don't want you to worry about anything."

"Tyler didn't answer? Weren't you with him tonight?"

Corey started crying again. "I... don't know. I... I don't... remember anything. I hurt so much."

I leaned closer and tried comforting him. "Shh. I'm here. We just need to get you admitted."

Just when I thought waiting and the worry would give me an aneurysm, RC returned to my side. I knew he hadn't left, but he was acting odd and had been pacing the waiting room most of the time my mom was attending to Corey. "This is ridiculous," he said. "Look at him. He needs a doctor, and they said they have more urgent emergencies to handle first. Stupid!"

Corey curled into a ball as much as the wheelchair and his aching ribs would allow. RC leaned over and kissed my temple and then whispered in my ear, "I'll be right back. I'm going to take care of this for you." Something in his eyes gave me hope. "I'll be right back, Mrs. Jones. Corey, Nick's got you."

His voice was full of strength. I knew he would take care of me, of Corey. I nodded and he walked over to a nurse at a desk. He said something, and she picked up the phone. She said something and handed him the phone. He talked. He hung up and walked over to a double door that read "hospital personnel only."

He was staring at his feet, tapping his toe and nervously rocking. I had no clue what was going on. Then the door opened and a nurse with dark curly hair stepped through. She stared at RC momentarily and then clasped his arm. They talked. I couldn't hear anything, but I saw lips moving. RC pinched his eyes. Was he crying? Then the woman put her arms around him, and he put his face on her shoulder. His shoulders bobbed, and she rubbed his back.

Not long after, RC pulled back and wiped his eyes. He nodded, and she kissed his cheek. Intuition told me it was his mom or an aunt. She looked very much like him. He walked her over to us and said, "Nick, this is my mom, Annia Coppola. She's the head nurse in the Cardiology Department. She's gonna help Corey."

"Can you? Please? This is so much. I don't understand everything."

My mom held out her hand. "Hello. I'm Cathy Jones, Nick's mom."

Corey explained, "She's my parent."

"And Corey's mom." My mom grinned.

Of course no one questioned anything. Corey was an adult. Mainly, the paperwork was so the hospital got paid and they covered their legal ass in case of being sued or something. We weren't suing, we just wanted Corey fixed up.

My mom was like super woman, but RC's mom was an angel. She descended on Corey and miracles happened. RC said it was because she knew everyone in the hospital and asked for favors. I didn't know, nor did I care how things got expedited. She got him x-rayed by one department and got him pain meds and everything. She walked me through calling in the police to take a statement because of his broken bones. The sheriff's department told me a similar case had been called in and their deputy would be with us shortly. He was already in the hospital.

After a couple hours, Corey was looking better. His cheeks had color again, and not just purple. He also said his brain was less fuzzy.

He would need his nose reset, but everything in a hospital took forever, so we were still waiting. At least he had a bed to rest in. The door opened, and instead of a nurse or doctor, it was my dad.

"Honey, I told you you didn't need to come down here," my mom said, hugging him.

"I know. But I couldn't sleep. And then my alarm went off followed by Jennifer crawling into our bed crying because she couldn't sleep worrying about Corey, so we're both here."

"Jennifer's here?" I asked.

"She had to pee," Dad said.

Jennifer came into the room seconds later and rushed over to Corey, hugging him gingerly. "Oh, Corey. I'm so sorry."

Corey didn't have a comment, but I could tell having my entire family here made him feel better.

RC's mom came back in and looked around the crowded room. "Um, I think there's a two-person limit."

"Oh. Oops," my mom shrugged, guilty but not sorry in the slightest.

RC's mom added, "And there is a police officer who wants to talk to you, Corey."

"Okay. Will you stay with me, Nick?"

I squeezed his hand. "Of course."

Everyone left and an officer from the sheriff's department took a statement. Corey held my hand tightly the entire time, but he didn't cry until the guy left.

Now that he was calm, Corey remembered some of the details. As it turned out, Corey had been at a party with his boyfriend, Tyler, and things went terribly wrong. The reason the police were at the hospital was because Tyler was in another room, but in much worse shape. The officer could not release the details until further investigation, but he said Tyler was alive. Corey wanted to see him, but the nurse had said it wasn't possible. Thankfully, RC's mother assured Corey she would check on Tyler and report back.

Corey told the officer everything he could remember, but he said his memory was very spotty. After the officer left, he reiterated a few things to my mom and dad and RC.

"I remember seeing some guys doing coke," Corey explained, "and I told Tyler I didn't want to stay. You know how I hate drugs."

My sister nodded. "Yeah. Because your sister did heroin and used to hit you when you were little." He'd shared that at dinner once, but it surprised me how much my family paid attention to the details.

"Exactly. Tyler said he didn't care about my insecurities. He said they were his friends and I would just have to deal until he was ready to go. So I sat on the arm of the couch and waited for him to bring me a drink. He did. That's the last thing I remember."

Annia stood at the foot of the bed, his chart in hand. "Which makes sense. You had the date-rape drug in your system. You should feel better soon. You're lucky all they did was break some ribs and your nose. They could have raped or killed you."

Corey looked down at his hands, clasped together in his lap holding mine between them. "I know. I should have left."

I glanced at RC, who was watching his mom. She put the chart down and walked out of the room. RC followed. I squeezed Corey's hand. "I'll be right back, Corey. I promise," I said before dashing out the door after them. My family was there; Corey would be fine.

"Mom, please don't shut me out again," RC pleaded as I stepped up next to them.

She flicked her eyes at me and then again to RC. Her lips pursed and brow furrowed, she seemed to be thinking over her response. She took a deep breath. "It's hard not to think that that could be you in there."

"Mom," RC begged. "He didn't get beat up for being gay. He was at a party with the wrong guy at the wrong time."

"Do you think it would have turned out that way if he'd been out with a girl? If your friend had brought a girl as his date, they wouldn't have turned up at that type of party, would they?"

"He might've if he dated some of the girls I know," I slipped in, talking out loud without thinking.

She glared at me. "He could have avoided this if he'd been straight."

RC protested, "You don't know that. Sexuality has nothing to do with statistics on date-rape drugs and assholes looking to pound somebody senseless. Corey shouldn't have been there, but he's not in the hospital for being gay. He's here for being stupid."

"Hey!" I cried.

RC glanced at me. "Sorry. Look, Mom, you have to let this go. I'm gay. Uncle Charles didn't do this to me. I've known I was gay since I was ten. I like boys. I like *this* boy." RC touched my arm. "Nick is my boyfriend. I love him. We're going to live together and make a life together, and I want you to be a part of that. Please, Mom. Dad's gone, and you're all the family I have left. I need you."

I wanted to protest and say I'd be there for him, but I knew enough to hold my tongue. His meaning was clear to me. So I listened, and he said something else, but my brain looped "we're going to live together" over and over like a broken record skipping the same lyrics repeatedly. *He wants me to live with him?* I felt all warm and fuzzy. Like when I'd gotten a rabbit for the first time in fourth grade. I was happy and sappy and emotional. *RC loves me.* I laced my fingers through his and squeezed his hand.

"I just...." RC's mom was crying when my brain finally caught up to where the conversation now sat. I'd daydreamed and missed some of it, but for the most part I could figure it out. She had issues with him being gay. His uncle had raped him when he was young—he'd told me that part. People did tend to have a problem accepting the reality of sexuality and always wanted to explain it away by some horrific trauma. Some of us never experienced trauma. Some of us were gay and remained gay without logical explanation outside of simply being born that way. I was gay. I'd denied it for a long time, but it was only because I'd thought it was easier to exist within the "normal" boundaries of society. Being gay seemed harder to deal with. And maybe it was, but I had also come to understand I couldn't live happily if I was in denial. There was always a struggle for one over the other. I'd gone for years feeling empty.

I was in a different place now. I was in love. And if I was in love with a man, so be it.

"Raffael," she sniffled. "I worry that this life isn't going to be easy for you."

RC touched her shoulder. "My life has never been easy. If obesity had been my only obstacle, life still would have been hard. Kids treated me awful, Mom. And then the name calling, because apparently I'm a euphemism for vomit, compounded my shame. I've been picked on for one thing or another my entire life. Even my eye color."

She looked shocked. "Why? You have beautiful eyes."

He snorted. "Because kids in school are mean and some girl decided eyes like mine were a waste on a fat, ugly sack of shit like me."

"What? No. That isn't true."

"Yes. It is."

"Is that why you wore brown contact lenses for years?"

"Yeah."

"And I thought you did it for variety. As something fun."

He shook his head slowly. "No, Mom."

"But you're wearing your glasses now?"

"Because Nick yelled at me for hiding. He likes my eyes."

I held up a hand in defense. "I didn't yell at him."

"Hiding? Why didn't you tell me?"

RC sighed, "Because what Uncle Charles did was worse. Because Dad nearly ended up in jail over it. Because I knew the name-calling wouldn't hurt me like losing you and Dad. I needed to know you loved me. I didn't want you to blame me for anything."

"So you hid your eyes, and hid your name behind initials, and hid your sexuality because you didn't want to hurt us?"

RC nodded. "I wanted to tell Dad, especially when he was near the end. I wanted to, but I was afraid." Now RC was crying.

She pulled RC into a strong hug. He hugged her back while I watched the people milling by who glanced their way. People were strange. They wanted to know what was going on, you could tell, but at the same time, this was a hospital and people were always crying.

A few minutes later, they separated. She caressed his face and looked like she needed a few more minutes of hugging, but she held back. "I have to go. I'll check in on your friend, but I have other patients." She shifted her attention to me. "It was nice meeting you. I'm glad my son found someone special." She glanced back at RC and added, "And really cute."

"Mom." RC ducked his head. He was embarrassed, but in a good way. He smiled at her and I could tell he was happy. "Can I call you?"

She nodded.

"Will you come over to my place for dinner sometime?"

She nodded again. "And tell your mother, Nick, it was nice to meet her." She kissed RC's cheek and walked away.

Before he said anything, I read his mind. "So, you moved out after your dad passed because your mom freaked over the gay thing."

"Pretty much."

"But it looks like your mom's coming around."

"Looks like it." He beamed. "You carry Lady Luck in your pocket, Nick, and things always work out for you. I guess I was hoping some of that good fortune would drift my way."

I lifted his hand and kissed it. "Welcome to Planet Nick. We have cookies."

"Dork." RC chuckled.

"Thanks." I grinned. I took it as a huge compliment. "Although I think you're closer to whale size than me."

"Nick, it's an urban legend."

I was confused. "What is?"

"That the word 'dork' means 'a whale's penis.' Look it up. That definition is not in the dictionary."

I exhaled heavily. "Well that sucks," I complained.

"Sorry to deflate your sails. But if it makes you feel better, I do think you're hung quite nicely." He winked.

I blushed. "Thanks." That *did* make me feel better.

WE VISITED Corey one more time before we left. He was fine. My mom told me he'd be staying in my room once he was released from the hospital. I was going to protest, but that was so immature. I knew he needed my room and my family.

As RC and I drove back to his place, I remembered Corey telling the police officer he'd seen Terrell at the party. The officer had asked if he remembered any of the guest's faces.

Terrell. That was where we needed to go next, but first I had to work all day on zero sleep. My body was going to protest big time.

Chapter 26: *Terrell*

I RANG the doorbell at nine thirty Monday night. I had only ever been to Terrell's once. It was nice. Very posh. He tended to keep his place off limits because sometimes people puked. His furniture was too fine for puke. I couldn't blame him. I was just about to leave when a girl opened the door.

She was naked.

"Nick. Wow, I didn't realize Terrell invited you. I'm glad. Come on in." She stepped back and waved at me to enter. RC tried to follow, and she stuck out her hand. "Um, were you invited? This is an exclusive party. Unless there's a plumbing issue I'm unaware of, you'll have to wait outside."

I took his hand and insisted, "Nancy, he's my boyfriend, not a plumber. And we're only here to speak to Terrell. I'm not staying."

She frowned. "Too bad. I've always wanted to suck your cock."

RC's hand tightened around mine. Her comment had shocked him and me both. True, I often got treated like a sexual god, but no girl except Dawn had ever come out and said something so blatant.

After I walked through the foyer, it made more sense. Her nakedness, the overtly sexual stare, everything. This was not a normal party. RC and I entered the living room and found naked people everywhere. Porn played on the television, but it was superfluous. This was live porn. People I knew were having sex all over the place. My jaw dropped. I thought things like this only happened in cities like Los Angeles.

I guess I was clueless. Behind closed doors, anything was possible.

My eyes swept over the table covered in condoms to see Terrell sitting on a chair by the fireplace. Beth was in his lap using her legs to support her as she bounced rapidly on his dick. I would recognize her cries anywhere, as well as the heart-shaped tattoo on her ass. I took a deep breath and walked over to them.

When Terrell looked at me, I asked, "Do you know anything about Corey getting hurt last night?"

"Corey?" he asked. "No."

"Hi, Nick," Beth greeted me, still bouncing on her pogo sick, moaning and panting as she spoke. "Why are you still dressed? Take… your clothes off… I'll do you next."

Her offer was not unheard of given the group I knew and used to hang with, but hearing it this time made me feel sick. I was grateful that I'd come to understand the need for change way before I ended up in a room like this. "Um, no. I'll pass. Terrell, Corey? He got beat up. He said he saw you there."

"Keep going, keep going," he urged, cupping her ass and assisting Beth through a few more lap hops. Then he moaned and growled as he came. "Okay, baby, give me a second." She climbed off, and Terrell removed his condom. At least he'd used one. After tossing it in the trash, he spoke to me like a porn star in between takes. "Look, I don't know anything. I went there to pick up some money John owed me. That's all. I didn't know Corey got hurt. I'm sorry, but I can't help you. Now if you don't mind, you need to leave. I didn't invite you, and I certainly didn't invite him."

The way Terrell looked at RC made me angry. I felt hot all of a sudden. RC must have sensed it because he pulled on my hand and led me to the door. "It's not worth it, Nick. Let's go."

Out by the car, I puked. RC handed me a napkin. I closed my eyes and tilted my head back on the seat as he drove my car, but after we parked at his house, I was still unable to move. "What the hell was that back there?" I said, eyes closed, willing away my nausea.

"I don't know."

I opened my eyes and looked at him, the streetlights illuminating the car enough to see by. "That could have been me," I said. Hearing the words made everything so real, so ugly, so sickening.

"You gonna puke again?"

I shook my head. "I'm sorry."

"For what?"

"For being so vapid and caught up in the coming that I didn't care where I was going. For being vain and self-obsessed and blind to being used. For being a part of a group that...." I couldn't finish because I shoved the door open and leaned out as I hurled bile onto the curb.

RC rubbed my back. When I was done, he pulled me into a hug. "Don't dwell on it, Nick. Be glad you got out before you got AIDS or some other STD. Or before you died of a drug overdose."

"I've never done drugs," I whispered against his chest.

"You would've. I noticed some needles in a dish. They're not a safe crowd to be with."

I squeezed him around the middle. I loved being in his arms. I couldn't imagine a better, safer place to be. "Were you serious about me moving in?"

"What? Um, yeah. I guess I should've asked first. I got caught up in the moment. I haven't talked to my mom for nine months."

I moved so I could see his face, but not enough to pull out of the security of his embrace. "I'm glad you finally did. That has to be hard. I'm really close to my mom, I couldn't handle not talking to her."

"I know. It's been bad." Then he smiled. "But meeting you made everything better."

I reached up and touched his chin. I seriously loved his beard. I could touch his face all day. I caressed his lower lip and dropped my eyes to follow my finger.

"Don't kiss me."

I snapped my gaze back up. "Why?"

"You smell bad."

"Gee, thanks." I eased out of his arms, reached for the door handle, and stopped. "Wait. Can you drive us to my house? I want to talk to my mom. Plus, I can grab some more of my stuff if I'm gonna be living here."

"I didn't say it had to be now. Are you sure?"

I rehooked my seatbelt and nodded. "Yup. There's no place else I'd rather be."

TUESDAY, AFTER work, I greeted RC with a kiss in *our* kitchen. "I got a text from Terrell on my way home. He wants to meet me. Alone."

"Fuck no," he said strongly, shaking his head. "You are not going to meet him alone. I saw that guy. I don't care how strong you are, you wouldn't stand a chance against him. And what if *he's* not alone?"

"Come with me?"

"All right. And don't think I didn't notice your reference to coming home." RC winked and smiled at me.

I kissed him again and texted back: *I'll meet you, but I'm bringing my boyfriend.*

RC pointed to the fridge door. "Where'd you find this?" It was the piece of paper that read "turkey" I'd spied on the fridge that first day I visited him.

I grinned. "In your drawer. I shoved your socks over to make room for mine and found it." I sauntered closer to him. "I think it's sweet. You save mementoes."

RC lifted his eyebrow. "I think it's astounding you know what the word 'memento' means."

"Ah!" I swatted at him playfully, but I could never be mad. He was fucking adorable. I kissed him instead and felt my phone buzz.

Terrell had responded: *Fine. No one else. I don't need this to get out.*

I texted back: *When? Where?*

7:30. At that park in Taneytown.

K.

I glanced at my watch. "We have about an hour before we have to leave."

RC's eyes flashed wickedly. He knew exactly what I was suggesting. "Beat you to the bedroom," he declared, taking off in that direction.

I laughed heartily and followed him.

I tore my shirt off as I entered the room. RC was standing by the bed, but he wasn't stripping. "What's wrong?"

He shrugged. "Sometimes… sometimes I wonder what would happen if I gained it all back."

"Gained what? The weight?"

"Yeah. I'm fat enough now. I worry that you'd—"

"Stop," I stressed. I tugged on his shirt, and he allowed me to remove it. I rubbed my hands over his Buddha belly and then kissed him. "I love you just the way you are."

"But—"

"But nothing." I ran my hands over his torso, up to his strong shoulders, down his arms, and around his hips. "Would I be happy if you lost more weight? Sure. Because I know it would make *you* happy. But if you gained it back I'd still want to be with you. I love you. I can't think of any other words than those."

RC smiled and kissed me. He moved his mouth to my neck and his hands down to squeeze my ass. He sucked hard and I groaned. I had wanted that for so long, I started writhing in his arms and thrusting against him. RC pulled back, chuckling. "You're so easy."

I locked eyes with him and growled, making quick work of removing his pants and shoving him onto the bed. "I told you that's my spot. It felt like an ignition switch when you sucked that hard." I crawled on top of him and rubbed our naked bodies together. "I am so gonna make you scream, and with all the exercise I have planned, you won't have time to gain weight."

I winked before latching my mouth on his throat, marking him as he had done to me. I kissed my way down until I got to his throbbing erection and took him into my mouth. RC gasped and moaned and then gripped the sheets in both hands.

I sucked his shaft, enjoying the smooth texture on my tongue. I could feel him pulsing in my mouth every time I slowed my pace. "Nick," he rasped.

The sound of my name voiced in rapture as he shivered from my attention made me smile so wide, I wanted to give him more to howl about. "Hand me a pillow," I said. When he did, I instructed him to lift his hips.

"What are you doing?" he asked suspiciously.

"You trust me, right?"

"Yeah."

"Then lift your hips and pull your knees to your chest."

"Nick, I—"

"Do it. I'm not going to hurt you." We stared at one another for a very long minute before he closed his eyes and did what I asked. Once he was propped up and easier to access, I licked his ball sac and sucked on his testicles. I had an arm curved under one side of his ass so I could touch his chest and rub his right nipple. I massaged his inner thigh with my other hand as I licked as much skin around his balls as I could before moving my tongue lower.

I knew this area scared him. He had told me not to touch him there once before, but I knew his fear was from previous abuse. At some point, he'd learn I wasn't like those other guys. If I kept trying, one flick of my tongue at a time, eventually he'd trust me to fuck him. I didn't bank on today being the day, but I was hoping he'd let me get a little farther along than last time.

His pucker was tight as I darted my tongue over it.

"Nick," he rasped.

I massaged his thigh and his groin, and then moved my hand to his penis. I stroked it slowly. "Relax."

He was breathing heavily, but he wasn't trying to stop me.

I licked his hole again. When he didn't protest, I licked it a third time, but this time I fully engaged my lips and flattened my tongue over as much skin as I could, lapping at him and feeling his anus relax as I did so.

"Oh God, Nick," he moaned loudly. I coated my finger with saliva and tickled his entrance. "Nick," he warned, lifting his head off the pillow.

"Shh. Relax. Let me do this. Please?" I had no intention of fucking him, but he didn't know that. This was more of a test to see if he would trust me with what scared him the most. When he threw his head back, breathing harder but not pushing me away, I grinned.

Again I sucked on his ass, swirling my tongue over his tender parts until I heard him moaning louder, "Oh fuck! Nick…. Oh God."

He was thumping his fist on the bed, and I felt triumphant.

I grabbed the lube we had on the nightstand before he had a chance to reconsider my actions. I coated my fingers and took fellatio one step further by teasing his entrance again with my finger, making circles around it and then pressing it inside. He flinched and fell silent. I watched his facial expressions as I slowly removed my finger and then slid it back in. I did it again and watched him. RC looked as if he was holding his breath. His expression appeared strained. Perhaps he was fighting personal demons, but I was going to continue until he told me to stop. I inserted a second finger.

I repositioned so I could get my mouth on his dick as I pumped his ass with my fingers.

"Nick," he gasped again. "Oh, Nick," he moaned louder.

I bobbed my head, sucking and licking rapidly in time with my plunging hand. I twisted my fingers around, nudging his prostate and caressing his inner walls so this experience would stick with him in a good way. He moaned again, and I snickered silently.

His palm slapped the mattress, and he tilted his hips toward my face. That was when I felt his fluid filling my mouth. I swallowed and kept sucking. He jerked several times before he grabbed my hair and cried, "Oh shit, Nick, stop, stop, stop!"

I did. I grinned into his sated eyes right before I nudged his prostate with my fingers.

He cried out, and I removed my fingers, chuckling sadistically.

I crawled up next to him, and he glared at me. "You're evil, Nick."

I smiled wickedly. "Yeah, but ya love me."

He growled, turned sharply, and pinned me to the bed. I was so hard by the time he touched me, I exploded in three strokes, spurting white ropes all over the place.

I sighed contentedly, but RC grumbled. "The headboard, really? You managed to hit the wall, the lamp, and my eye with that one."

I sighed again. "What can I say? I'm thorough."

"And your ass is helping clean that shit off."

I opened my eyes and grinned. I knew he wasn't really angry. My cum was still dripping down his cheek, and it made me laugh. "You are so sexy when you're mad."

He chuckled. "What am I going to do with you?"

"I don't know. Handcuff me to the bed and tease me with a feather boa?"

He laughed and kissed me, not caring that I still tasted like his cum, but savoring the flavor of what it meant to be together.

I DIDN'T want to leave our bed, but we had other business to attend. Namely, Terrell.

I stepped carefully across the ground, mindful not to trip. It was freaky enough Terrell wanted to meet me. I didn't need to fall and appear weak or clumsy. I didn't know what he'd do. Even though I'd known him for years, I didn't *know* him at all. I squeezed RC's hand tightly as we approached him. He was leaning on the sliding board, in its shadow, surveying the rest of the playground as if waiting for someone to jump out from the tree line. I could tell that meeting me here made him as nervous as it made me.

"Well," I addressed him directly when we approached, "what do you have to say?"

Terrell glanced at me, glanced at RC, and then looked around. "I lied last night. I do know some stuff about Corey."

I jumped at him, but RC's arm crossed my chest like a restraining bar on a roller coaster. He didn't allow me to move an inch, so I eased back and took a deep breath. I restrained my anger, but my voice was not so veiled. "What do you know?" I hissed, gritting my teeth.

Terrell glanced around again and then answered, "I was there, at the party. I took care of a transaction, and as I crossed the apartment to leave, I noticed Corey."

"What was he doing?"

"He was...." He hesitated. "Corey was all but passed out. He was groggy and incoherent. And his nose was bleeding. One guy slapped his face to see if he'd react. He tried to, but he couldn't lift his arm. They tossed him on the carpet and kicked him a few times. Then one idiot rolled him over and grabbed for his belt." Terrell swallowed hard, but continued. "That's when I stepped in. I said I knew Corey, and he owed me money. I asked for first dibs at his ass."

I was seething, sick and horrified that I'd once called him "friend", yet he would do something so terrible to another friend. "I can't believe you would—"

"I didn't, Nick, I swear! I didn't do anything to him. I picked him up and headed to the bedroom. Once the door was locked, I took him out the sliding glass doors and around the back. I had him in my car and down the street in minutes. Then I dumped him in the parking lot by PetSmart."

"What?" I exclaimed. "Why didn't you take him to a hospital? He had broken ribs and a broken nose, and had been drugged. Why would you—"

"Because I couldn't afford to get caught, Nick. I had drugs in my trunk. Okay? Not all drug dealers are shady-looking characters. Some of us dress well and play the part of law-abiding citizens. I wasn't going to get caught on camera by the emergency room, dumping Corey off on the sidewalk. I made sure his phone was charged and he had your number."

"But...." I paused for thought, breathing heavily while trying to contain the rage I felt. "How could you leave him? Anything could have happened."

"I didn't leave! I drove away and circled back and watched him until you got there. I felt bad." He hung his head.

"You should! He was so scared."

"I know. I'm sorry, Nick." Terrell reached into his pocket and handed me a piece of paper. "Of all the guys Dawn fucks over, I never understood her obsession with Corey. I've always liked him."

Again, ice water down my back. "Dawn? What does she have to do with this?"

"Nothing directly. But she's always had it out for Corey. I think it has to do with that time you saw him coming out of the janitor's closet."

My brain wasn't so good at switching gears. But after following Marcy's sporadic conversations for so long, I must have gotten better at it. "Huh? I don't remember Corey. I remember some homeless-looking dude with blue hair."

Terrell grinned. "That was Corey. He looked way different with a Mohawk, malnourished and skinny as a rail. But I saw you watching him right before Dawn stepped in front of you."

"How? Why?"

"I was after her. She was after you."

Everything came together at once like a movie flash sequence. I remembered Corey, and Dawn, our first kiss, Dawn introducing me to Shawna and Laney. I remembered meeting Terrell and Steve, and seeing Chrissy for the first time. Dawn knew I was attracted to Corey back in high school, but she'd decided to use me instead. She'd basically orchestrated the whole thing like a puppeteer, and I'd been oblivious.

I think RC understood it too, because he slipped his arm around me.

Terrell handed me a paper. "This is a list of names of all the people I remember from that night."

I unfolded it. I recognized a couple names, but for the most part they were unknown to me. "What about a guy named Tyler? Do you remember him?"

He shook his head. "No."

"Corey said he went to the party with Tyler. He said he'd called him a couple of times, but got no answer. Then, at the hospital, I found out Tyler was admitted with head trauma and broken bones." Some of this I exaggerated, but he didn't need to know that. "Tyler's in a coma, Terrell."

"Look, I already said, I don't know any Tyler. I didn't see him. I don't know what happened. I saw Corey, and I got him out of there because I couldn't let something happen to a sweet guy like that. But I gotta go, man. Do what you have to, but try to keep me out of it."

"I won't mention your name, but Corey already said he remembered seeing you. And you know I have to take this list to the police."

"Shit. Okay. Yeah, I know. I gotta go cover my tracks. Again, I'm sorry about Corey. He's a great guy."

"Yeah, he is."

Terrell stepped away from the safety of the sliding board's shadow and reached out to RC. "It was nice to meet you."

RC shook his hand and replied. "Yeah, and I hope I never see you again."

Terrell nodded and walked off. What could he say when there was nothing *to* say?

LATER THAT night, after RC fucked me so hard I saw stars, he held me close and whispered, "You love him."

I knew he meant Corey. "Yeah. I do. I guess I never thought about how close we are. I mean, I never thought we talked long, but I guess we did because I know everything about him. Until tonight I never realized how special he was to me, or how strongly I've been drawn to him ever since I was sixteen. He feels like the brother I never had."

"And your mom feels the same way. I saw it in her face when she walked into his room. She was worried about him like a mom. Too bad his own mother doesn't care about him that way."

"I know. It hurts him deeply that his family doesn't want him, but I also know how much he loves *my* family."

"I think your family is great. Very normal."

I chuckled. "Yeah, I guess. I never thought they would be. I guess I figured they'd treat me like Corey's family did." I adjusted my head so it rested more comfortably on RC's shoulder, and he hugged me tighter to his side.

"I heard your mom talking to your dad the other night. She said it didn't matter how old Corey was. He could have been three, thirteen, twenty-three, or thirty, she still felt like he deserved the support of a parent. She said everyone deserved support as they grew and matured into adulthood. And then your dad said something like, "Well, Cathy, the boy's got us now." RC choked on his words. "I really like your parents, Nick."

I lifted my head and looked down at him. He was crying. I was crying. So I had to chuckle. "Me too."

I kissed him and he rolled me over. As his lips traveled down my back and over the curve of my ass, I started humming softly. I didn't know why this particular song came to mind, but all of a sudden the words to "Nobody Does It Better" made sense. His presence in my life happened when I wasn't looking for it. RC wasn't a secret agent, but he was strong and the love in his eyes stopped me from running away and denying who I was. I recited the lyrics in my head as I hummed, but the need to sing to him as he made love to me was overwhelming.

"The way that you hold me...," I sang as he caressed my chest and ribs. "There's some kind of magic inside you."

RC entered my body as if I were a second skin. His rhythmic passion even and steady as he rasped, "Oh fuck, Nick. I love you so damn much."

I sang the next line of lyrics and he roughly grabbed my cheek and brought my mouth to his, sucking on my tongue as his thrust harder. Perhaps comparing him to his dad while in bed was a tad freaky, but I got the impression he took my reference as the compliment I intended because his zeal increased. His dad had been his hero and best friend. I think he knew I saw him in the same light.

As we climaxed together, I held him as we panted. RC rolled off and removed the condom while I wiped myself off with the T-shirt I'd worn earlier that day. Once comfortably situated in our bed I rested my head on his chest and ran my fingers over his furry pecs.

"What do the Chinese symbols mean?" I'd been dying to know.

"Hope. I've been holding onto the notion that one day I'd find a reason for living, especially after all I'd gone through in my past."

I didn't want to come off self-obsessed so I remained silent. I wanted to be his reason, but I didn't want to assume.

And then he said, "I found my hope in you."

I buried my face in his neck and held him tightly all through the night.

Chapter 27: *Loose Ends*

"OH MY God, Oh my God, Oh my God." Marcy was screaming in a whisper. She rushed up to me and shoved a ticket into my hand. "That guy at the counter is talking on his cell phone to someone who knows someone who just arrested your friend, Terrell Burke."

"What?" I asked. "How do you know that?" I tossed two burger patties onto the grill. "And besides, Terrell and I aren't exactly friends."

"I know that, silly. Anyway, I overheard him talking while I was ringing up another order. He said something like," Marcy mimicked what I suspected was the customer's husky voice, "'I told Greenburg it was a bad idea bringing him in. Terrell Burke is a small-time dealer. I want his supplier. Yes, I know....'" She then reverted back to her own voice and finished her explanation, "And then he said something else. I thought you'd like to know."

"It doesn't prove anything. There could be several guys named Terrell Burke." The phone in my pocket buzzed. I hated taking it out because what if the boss came waltzing around the corner? It could have been RC, but it was only Chrissy.

She texted: *Thanks for being an asswipe, Nick. Terrell was arrested today because of you.*

I didn't know why they blamed everything on me. Corey was the one who gave the police his name, not me. And Terrell was the stupid one who told me he was a drug dealer and had drugs in the trunk of his car. The police probably came around to question him and they found syringes on his coffee table. It sounded feasible to me. I typed back: *I don't know what you're talking about. I didn't tell the police anything.*

It had to be you. You know everything and everyone. And you fucked enough people I wouldn't put it past you to sleep with a cop and give away our group's secrets. I always knew you couldn't be trusted.

I didn't sleep with any cops.

Oh, that's right, you've got that gross "boyfriend." Good luck with that. I give you two months tops.

I can tell you're screwing Dawn; you're beginning to sound like her.

Fuck you!

Hahahahhaha. Whatever. I'm changing my number tomorrow. Good-bye Chrissy. Have a nice waste of a life.

I turned my phone off. If RC texted, I hoped he would understand I'd turned mine off to avoid further harassment. "Hey, Marcy," I called. She looked up from filling the ketchup bottles. "You were right. I just got a text from Chrissy. She's pissed."

"I knew it!"

Paul took a pizza out of the oven and slipped it into a box. "Haven't you figured out how intuitive she is? Dude! She totally called you and RC months ago."

"She did?" I was surprised. "When?"

"When you went out to apologize. She said you had a look on your face when you came back. She bet me five bucks you'd end up with him."

"No way. She hated him. Plus, I wasn't gay back then."

Marcy laughed. "Oh, yes you were. I could see it in your eyes, but you were so adamant about dating Tara I let you think I didn't know. My cousin's gay. He told me he went through the same thing—dating women as a way of denying his feelings. He said it didn't work very long. He told me you'd crack eventually, but he said it was easier if you figured it out now before some girl got pregnant."

"But you kept hitting on me."

"Sure, why not? You're hot as hell, Nick. What girl wouldn't want a piece of that action if it's going off the market soon? I tried. You shot me down. And now you've got that starry-eyed, over the moon look in your eyes all the time. You were bound to fall in love and embrace the gay. I'm glad you did both with the same person."

"Me too. So, you're all right with everything. You were sort of pissed in the beginning. And you were rude to RC."

"I know. I apologized when we were on the camping trip."

"When?"

"When you were taking a shower before we made the campfire. RC looked lonely and awkward, so I tried to cheer him up. You know, help him feel included."

I remembered. I hadn't wanted to sleep in a tent with him and stink, so I'd taken a quick shower after we hiked around the lake but before we sat on the swings. I didn't want to leave him, but he assured me he'd be fine. And when I got back, he was talking to Marcy. I swear, any normal person would guarantee I did drugs with the way my brain shuts down. But yeah, I remembered. I said, "Thanks, Marcy."

"So, Nick," Paul said, cutting another pizza. "Are we on for Sunday? The Ravens play in Miami. I'd like to see the game, and watching it with your dad is a hoot."

I grinned. Paul thinking my dad was a hoot was a hoot in itself. "Ha, yeah. Sure. RC's in, and Corey's excited to see a football game."

"I want to come," Marcy cried, hopping up and down. "Please?"

"All right," I relented. This was my group, my buddies, my family; I had to include Marcy.

When the door tinkled, I looked up. In walked RC. *Must be Wednesday....* Wait. My thoughts ground to a halt. Today was Tuesday. "Hey, what are you doing here?"

I met RC by the swingy-door and gave him a kiss. I heard Marcy behind me gushing. "Aww. So cute."

"I brought you these," RC said, handing me a bundle of carnations. "We've been *together* together for one month."

I'd never gotten flowers before. It felt weird. I didn't know what to say. "Thanks."

"And I got you this," RC said, handing me a chocolate bar.

My smile widened. "Awesome!" I took it and opened it immediately. "Now I know why girls like gifts so much." I kissed him again. And again.

"Wow, I never got that kind of treatment. It must be love."

I turned toward Corey and smiled. "You never brought me chocolate at work."

"Hey, Sugarbear, how goes things?" Corey smiled, hugging RC. He handed him a paper bag. "Here."

"Good. What's this?" RC asked, pulling out a plastic spray bottle.

"I went to a hair show with my new friend Stacy. I picked this up for you. It's a leave-in conditioner that should help keep the frizz down. Your curls are way too pretty to let them fuzz up like that."

"Thanks. How're your ribs?" RC asked.

"Painful, but manageable."

"And Tyler?" I asked.

"Better. He should be released from the hospital soon."

"Your steak's burning," Paul pointed out.

I rushed back to the grill and flipped it in time. In three weeks, I was going to get my one-year evaluation. No need to screw up that puppy. I finished the order and told RC I'd meet him in a booth shortly. Corey followed him, and they sat talking while I worked. I liked that RC was giving him a chance and not allowing our past relationship to become a wedge.

"That's it!" Julie declared to the befuddlement of all those around her. She was standing near the heat lamp, head cocked to the side, pointing up.

"What's it?" Paul asked, thinking for the rest of us.

"This song, ding-dong. 'Crazy For You.'"

Marcy asked, "What about it? Isn't it really old?"

Paul giggled. "Yeah, I guess. It's from 1997. *NSYNC."

"Exactly!" Julie proclaimed excitedly. "That's who RC looks like! Joey Fatone. It's been bothering me for months."

"Oh my God," I groaned, my head falling backward.

And Paul started laughing so hard he tripped over his own feet and landed on the floor. Clenching his sides and laughing to beat the band.

"What's happened to him?" Marcy asked.

"I told Nick… the same thing…." Paul kept laughing; however, I did not.

I didn't know who this guy was, but I figured I would be googling him as soon as I went on break. *Joey Fatone. Oh my gosh.*

Dawn came storming in, and my joy died. I hadn't seen her in the restaurant in a long time. Come to think of it, I hadn't seen her dressed and sober in a long time. I wrapped the cheese steak and wiped my hands, but before I could walk out into the dining room, everyone else converged on her path. Paul, Marcy, Julie, even RC and Corey, stopped what they were doing to confront Dawn.

"Get out of my way," she demanded.

"No," Marcy growled.

"I don't think you're welcome in here," Paul said.

RC was at the back of the pack when I joined it on the dining room side of the counter. He put his arms around me. "No," I said, pulling away. I weaved through my friends and stepped up to the queen bitch herself.

"Dawn, go home. No one wants you here."

"You're one to talk. No one wants you either."

I pulled my shoulders back. "Sure they do. I'm hot." I gestured to my person. "Everybody wants a piece of this, whether or not you direct their actions. I know I'm sexy and nothing you can say will change that." I feathered my fingers through my hair. "I'm that damn good-looking and you're jealous because I don't swing on your tree." I licked my lips suggestively and held up my hand. RC took it, I knew he would, and I brought his arm across my chest and held it there. "I'm his. Now and always. And I don't care what you say or who you say it to. My reputation is sound."

"Ha! That's a joke," she sneered.

"It's the truth. I may have had a bad rep for fucking loads of women, but that was mostly your doing. No one will dispute, though, the fact that I don't lie, I trust my friends, and I'm done caring what the world thinks of me. I'm queer." I used RC's preferred term because I really liked the definition of it. "I'm in love with Raffael Coppola, and if you're going to judge me for loving another man, then that testifies against your own character, not mine. My real friends love me for who I am, and you, Dawn Treger, can go fuck yourself."

I thought she'd slap me. I thought she'd yell. I thought Dawn would have something to say to defend her position. But she didn't. She gaped at me. She looked at all my friends standing behind me and slowly backed away. I guess the truth was a little too hard to refute.

And when that door closed, all of us cheered in unison and the customers in the store clapped.

"Who wants ice cream?" I asked.

Corey replied, "I do!"

"Looks like I missed something," Mary-Louise said, walking up to our huddle. "Dawn almost ran me over squealing wheels out of the parking lot."

I stepped between Paul and Marcy and hugged her. "Hey. What are you doing here?"

"We met my dad for coffee," she said, looking around at everyone. "So what happened here?"

"Nick told Dawn off, and she ran away with her tail between her legs," Corey said, hugging M-L and kissing Shawna's cheek. "Hey, darlin'."

"Damn, and I thought coffee with my dad was interesting."

"Oh yeah? What happened?"

"Nothing. He was quiet and nice and this was the first time he didn't bring his Bible with him."

Shawna added, "I think he's wearing down because he likes me."

I smiled, happy to hear it. "That's great. M-L, I want you to meet someone. This is RC. RC, this is Mary-Louise. She's one of my bestest friends."

RC held out his hand, and she shook it fondly. "It's wonderful to finally meet you. I can honestly say I've never seen Nick happier, and I've known him many years."

"Thanks." RC blushed.

I don't think I could have planned a better afternoon if I'd tried.

Epilogue: *Tomorrow*

IT'S WEIRD to think about where life can take you. A couple of years ago, I would have never, *ever,* banked on falling in love like this. But I did.

I glanced around my living room and marveled at the amount of change, but I also marveled at the things that hadn't changed. My dad was still watching sports, although now he had moved onto Ravens games instead of the O's. Corey was still baking devilishly delicious chocolate desserts with my mom, except he had enlisted Laney and Marcy to assist. And Paul still occasionally gave me the feeling he was flirting with me. These things were the same.

"Do you want another beer?" RC asked during the commercial break. He leaned in and pecked my lips as he was prone to do at every available opportunity.

"No, I'm good," I replied, snagging his arm in order to prolong his departure and beckon another kiss with my pleading eyes.

He grinned. His lips caressed mine with the gentle embrace of butterfly wings. *Did I just use that analogy? Oh no, I'm not changing in good ways.*

"Oh my God, get a room," Marcy fussed, entering from the kitchen with a spoonful of something.

I laughed and released my hold on RC's arm. He grinned at Marcy, gave me one more kiss, and then continued on his way into the kitchen for another drink.

"Taste this," she said, offering me a bite of something that looked like pudding.

"What is it?" I asked, eyeballing the glop in the spoon and sniffing it suspiciously.

"It's custard or something."

"Does it have almond extract? I don't really like—"

"No, darlin'," Corey shouted from the other room. "I would never taint something with almonds if I knew you were going to eat it."

Marcy added, "I suggested almond extract, and Corey insisted it be vanilla because you don't like almonds. He remembers everything about you from your dislike of almonds to your bizarre aversion to maraschino cherries."

"They are seriously nasty," I asserted as I crinkled my nose.

RC returned with his water. Water, because although he loved Dr Pepper, it was not helping his diet drinking one every week. He sat on the sofa next to me and commented, "Yeah, I think I need to ask Corey about all the little things I don't know about you. Him knowing all this crap about disliking almond extract does not help my jealousy over how close you two are. I want to know details that *no one* knows."

I tasted the pudding custard stuff. "Mmm, it's good. But it tastes like Crème Brûleé."

"Fantastic!" Corey complimented, entering the living room in a flourish with flour on his cheek and a batter-covered spoon in his hand. "I'm impressed you called it on the first guess." Corey took Marcy's hand. "Come on, honey, you don't get to skip out on the egg whites."

Before he had a chance to leave, I asked, "Why would it surprise you? You made me Crème Brûleé last year for my birthday, remember? Chrissy dumped me the week before so she wouldn't have to buy a gift, and you made it for me at midnight. It was the first time you spent the night at my house because Jennifer was at a friend's house."

He stopped and stared at me. "You remember that?" he questioned softly, bringing his spoon-filled hand up to his heart.

"Of course. It meant a lot to me. Just like you mean a lot to me." I smiled at Corey, but I felt RC shift in his seat on the couch. I knew he was uncomfortable about our relationship, but Corey was like a little brother to me. I hoped one day RC got that.

Corey tapped me on the nose with his messy spoon and replied, "Well, don't that just tug at the ticker." He winked and pulled Marcy back into the kitchen. I chuckled internally. He might not spend much time with Julie, but I had the feeling they'd get on well together. Maybe at the next football party.

I turned to RC, whom I knew was feeling left out. "Hey," I said softly, reaching over to stroke his jaw. "I heard what you said. Corey's got nothing on you, Raffy. You're the only one in this world who can ignite my soul with a glance and melt my heart with a kiss." His eyes softened, and his lips slowly lifted at the edges. Almost shyly, RC leaned forward and kissed me.

My dad sighed and commented, "Well, I guess I should stop pulling for Paul."

I kissed RC again, and looked over at my dad. "What are you talking about?"

"Of all the boys you brought home, I liked Paul the best. But I can see it's not Paul you chose, so... I'll have to get used to RC if he's the one you love."

My brain wasn't adding up the information my dad was supplying. I sputtered, "W-what? Paul? Why would you think...?"

"Son, you've had all number of people in this house. I lost count of the girls you brought home or mentioned you were dating. Although, I never understood why you went out with them when you've been gay for years." *Fuck me! My dad's known all this time too.* "But I figured you had to sort out your own life. When you brought Paul home, I thought 'now here's a son-in-law I can relate to.'"

Paul gushed, hand on cheek. "Aww, thanks Mr. J. That's sweet."

Paul may not be gay, but he could surely "out-gay" a number of homosexuals Corey knew, and that knowledge made me laugh. "Dad, I was never dating Paul. We work together."

"Oh, I know," Dad said. "But I hope you don't break up during football season. His knowledge of the game is astonishing. These weekly game-night parties have been outstanding!" In the middle of talking to me, Dad turned to the TV and yelled, "Go, go, go!" Ironically, it was the same time Paul hollered the same exact thing.

Two peas in a pod, both wearing matching Flacco jerseys. *How cute.*

My mom was right. My dad is oblivious to most things. It was clear to me, if not to anyone else, Dad liked Paul because they were very much the same. I repositioned myself so I was sitting across RC's lap instead of next to him. It was cozier, and I could lay my head on his shoulder. While Paul and my dad high-fived after a touchdown, I kissed

RC's jaw and ear, and then whispered, "I hope you know my dad likes you too. He's just super fond of Paul."

RC squeezed me around the waist and kissed my nose. "Yeah. It's fine. In their own ways, both your mother and father have accepted me into their lives. Your dad's a sports nut and so is Paul. I get it. And I know your mom is super keen on Corey, but just wait until I show her how to make my mom's spaghetti sauce. I'll have them both eating out of my hand." He winked.

I snuggled closer. "Mmm. I can't wait. Is that the sauce we made that one time in August?"

"Yup."

"Oh my God! My mom will never let you leave. You know she wants to take cooking classes."

RC smirked. "Well, I can teach her how to cook. My mom's incredible. My dad's mother came from Sicily and brought all these old Italian recipes with her. She taught me when I was a kid. Mainly because I had no friends, and I never left the house."

I felt bad for him hearing that, but I also knew he was not dwelling on his hardships now. He was a new man, just like I was becoming.

New. I liked hearing that word.

RC and I resumed our kissing, noses rubbing, breath mingling, unhurried, tranquil and carefree, as the rest of our little gang cheered at the television or baked things in the kitchen. He interlaced his fingers with mine, and I sighed contentedly. This was the man I loved.

Snuggling against RC's neck, I closed my eyes and thought about my life and how far I'd come in the last five months. This group was so different than the one I'd started with this year, and it got me thinking thoughts about my future. Tomorrow held so much promise. I could do anything, be anything, become anything because I had family and friends who would be with me, stand with me, care about me, and love me… tomorrow. And all the tomorrows to follow.

Life could not possibly get better than that.

WADE KELLY lives and writes in conservative, small-town America on the east coast where it is not easy to live free and open in one's beliefs. She writes passionately about the controversial issues witnessed in real life and strives to make a difference by making people think. Wade does not have a background in writing or philosophy, but still draws from personal experience to ponder contentious subjects on paper. When not writing, she is thinking about writing, and more than likely scribbling ideas on sticky notes in the car while playing "taxi driver" for her three children. She likes snakes and has a tegu (lizard) living in her bathroom.

Visit Wade Kelly at http://www.writerwadekelly.com, http://writerwadekelly.blogspot.com/, or https://twitter.com/WriterWadeKelly. Contact Wade at writerwadekelly@gmail.com.

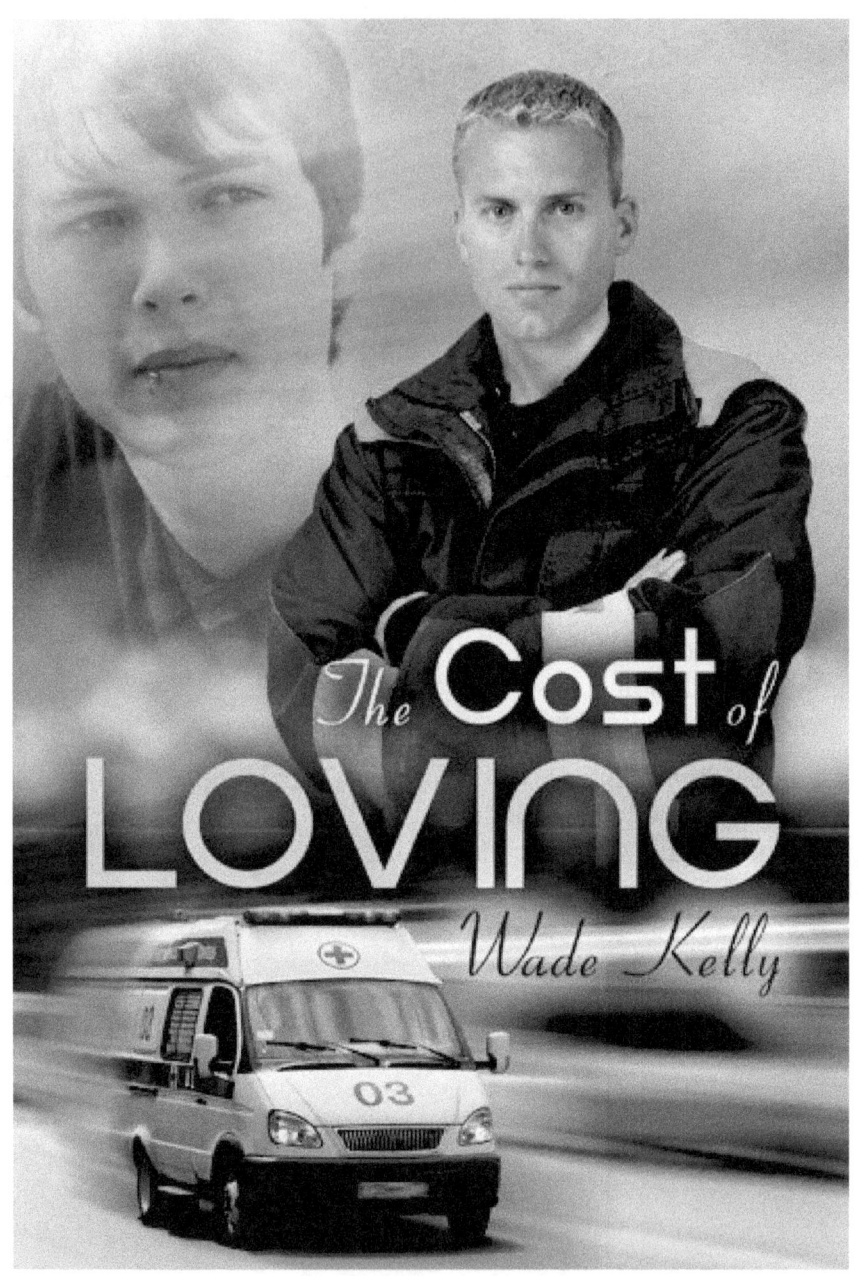

The Cost of Loving

Wade Kelly

http://www.dreamspinnerpress.com

When
Love
is not
Enough

Wade Kelly

http://www.dreamspinnerpress.com

MY ROOMMATE'S A JOCK?

Well, Crap!

Wade Kelly

http://www.dreamspinnerpress.com

The Art of Breathing

of

TJ Klune

http://www.dreamspinnerpress.com

TEMPESTE O'RILEY

Desires' Guardian

DESIRES ENTWINED SERIES

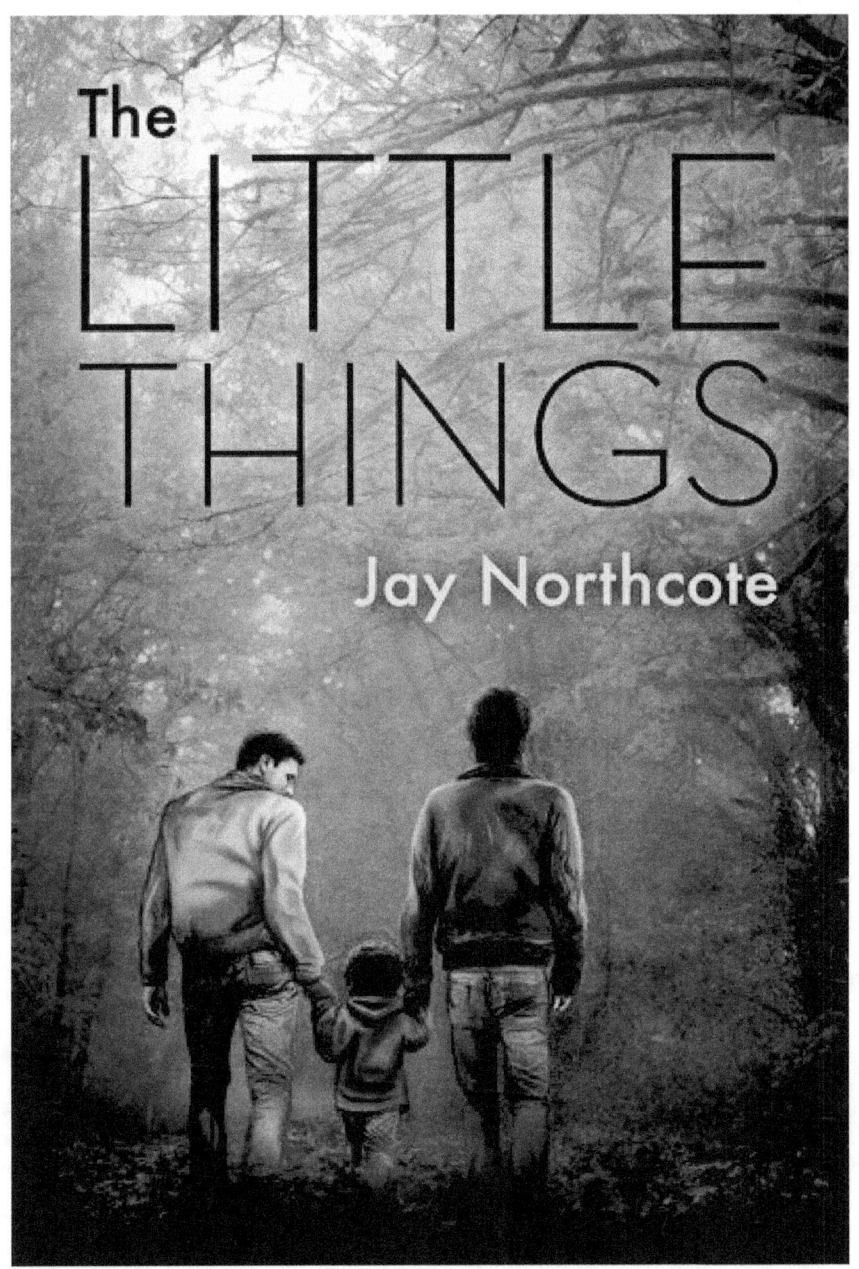

The
LITTLE
THINGS

Jay Northcote

http://www.dreamspinnerpress.com

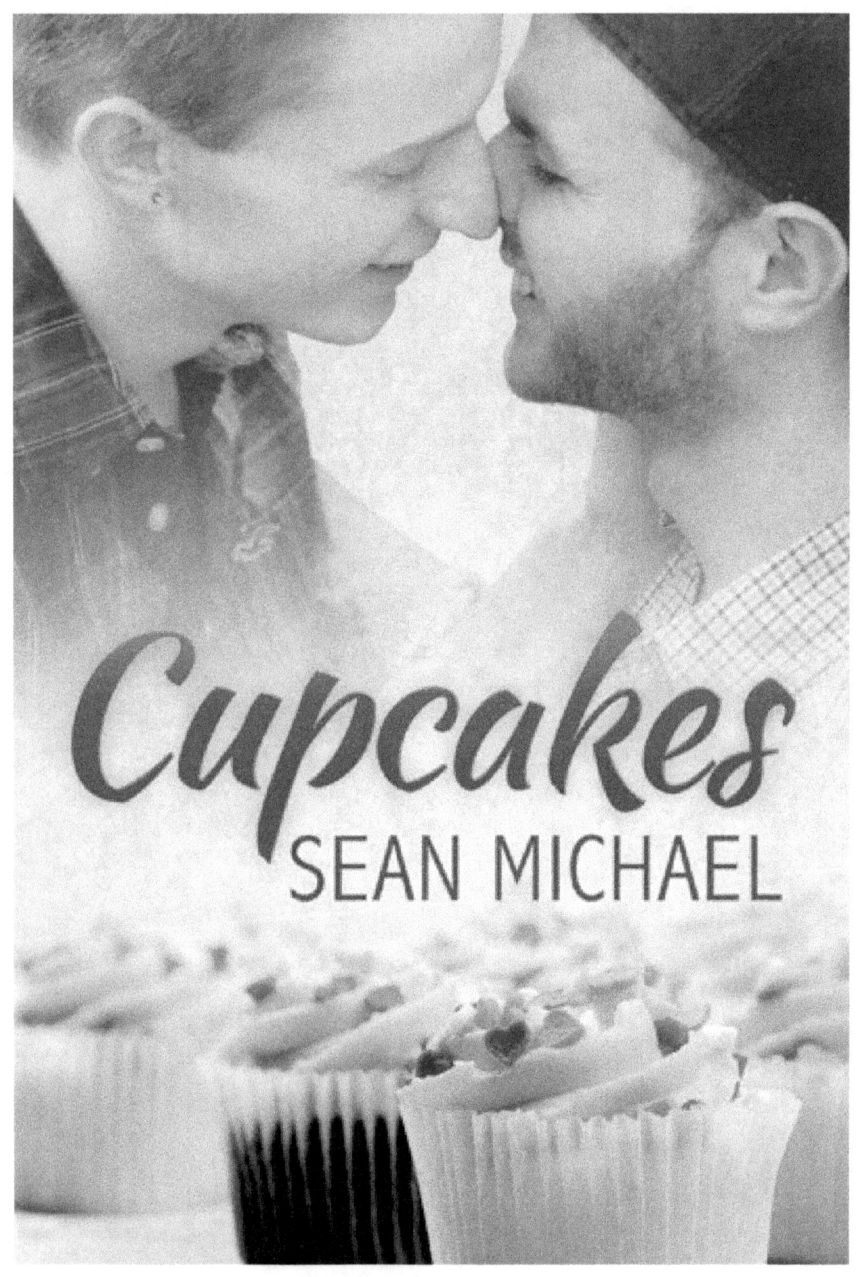

Cupcakes

SEAN MICHAEL

THE RETURN

BRAD BONEY

http://www.dreamspinnerpress.com

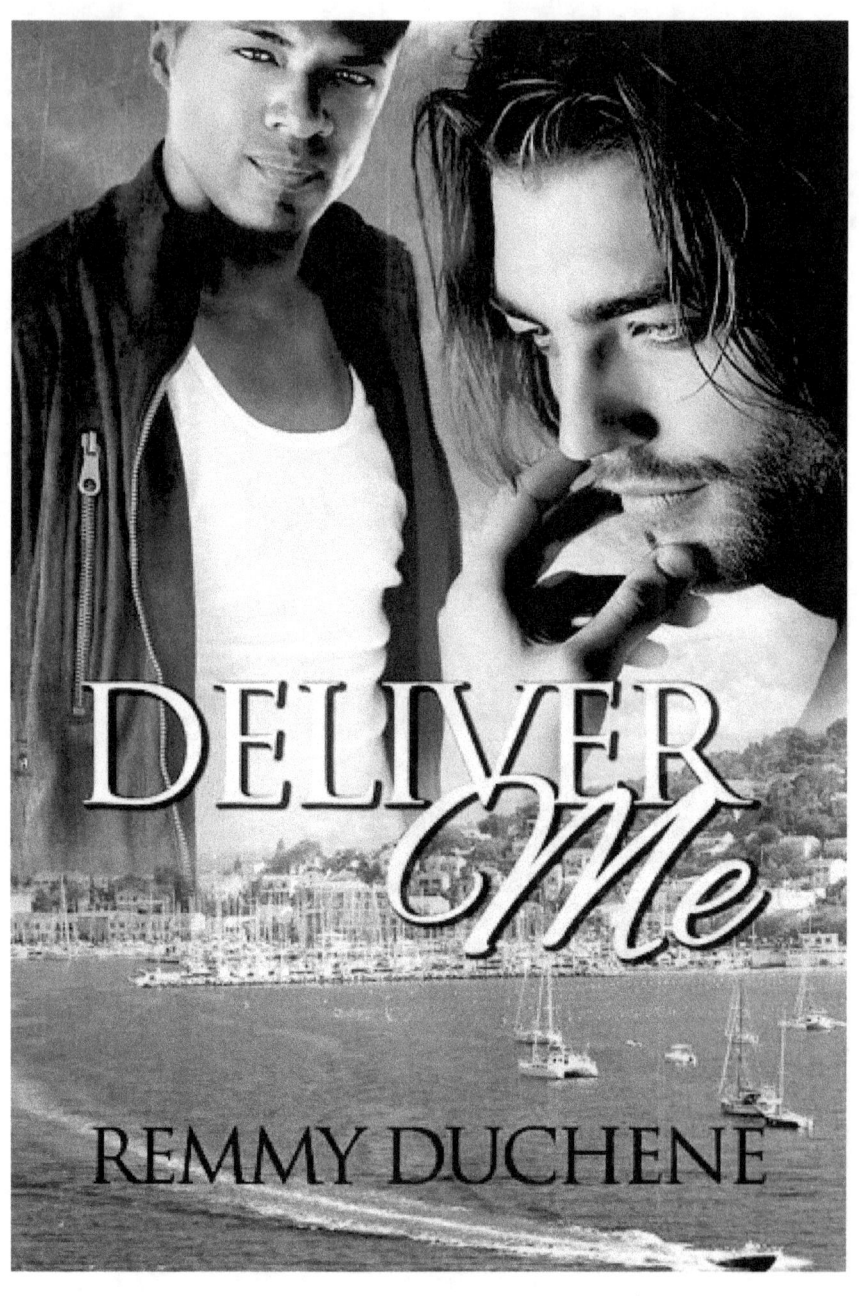

DELIVER
Me

REMMY DUCHENE

http://www.dreamspinnerpress.com

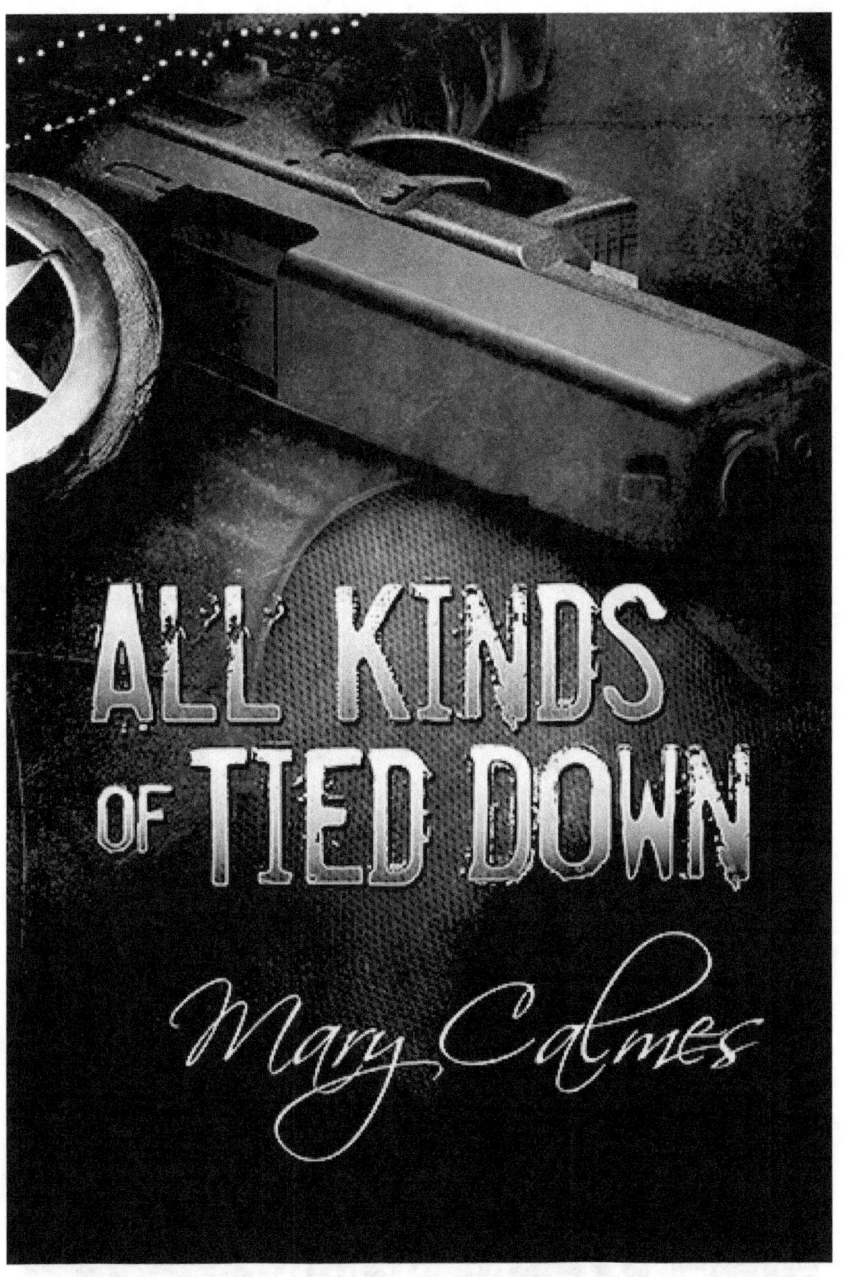

ALL KINDS
OF TIED DOWN
Mary Calmes